# EARTHFIRE

Mike,

Thank you for the
fire ceremony. May your
inner fire burn
brightly and long!

Robert Simmons

Also by Robert Simmons

With Kathy Helen Warner

*Moldavite: Starborn Stone of Transformation*

# EARTHFIRE

## A Tale of Transformation

## Robert Simmons

**Heaven & Earth Publishing**

**Marshfield, Vermont**

ISBN: 0-9621910-2-7
Library of Congress Cataloging-in-Publication Data
is available from the publisher.

Cover Painting:
Holy Fire (Panel 3). 1986 © Alex Grey. www.alexgrey.com

Poem: "Last Night" © Antonio Machado
Translation copyright © 1983 by Robert Bly
from Times Alone  Wesleyan University Press
used by permission of Robert Bly

Cover Design by Kathy Helen Warner

Printed in Canada

**Visit the *Earthfire* website at
http://www.earthfire.net**

To Kathy

# Acknowledgments

My wife, Kathy Helen Warner, has been a multi-faceted ally throughout my creative process, assisting with plotting, editing, character development and book design, as well as giving immeasurable amounts of moral support, friendship and love. My friend Pamela Barclay has served as midwife to the story's birth, in many long hours of labor. Will Maney's intuitive readings and friendship have helped me see a little farther. Norma Ream's astrological consultations showed me the patterns of connection. Other friends who gave freely of their time and energy in the editing process include Naisha Ahsian, Paul Saint-Amand, Barbara Krieger, Be Hussander, Ted Warner and Greg Warner, and I am grateful to them all. Additional thanks go to Mary Klinker, Judith Sult, Patrice Alexander, Sean Willey, Moebius Simmons, Joyce Morningstar, Joan Sheldon, Shelley Colvin, Pat Howard, Leonard Gibson, Elizabeth Gibson and all those who read the manuscript and gave me feedback.

I wish also to express my deep appreciation to the authors named throughout the text whose work has informed my writing and enriched my life.

Some day, after mastering the winds, the waves, the tides, and gravity, we will harness for God the energies of love. And then, for the second time in the history of the world, humankind will have discovered fire.

—Pierre Teilhard de Chardin

# —— Prologue——

A fire is burning on this earth. It is erupting spontaneously in a million places, and we watch in fascination as it moves to engulf the planet. Whether it will finally manifest as the physical fire of mass destruction, or as the holy fire of spiritual rebirth, no one knows. Some say it will be both. I believe we can still choose, and that each choice makes a difference.

My name is Will Lerner. I used to work as a shopkeeper with my wife, Helen. My life then was mostly defined by the rhythms of openings and closings, of customers, bills and taxes. But all that has been left behind. Now I am a traveler, without an occupation. Or perhaps I've become a chronicler of the change. Helen says I'm a spiritual pyromaniac, but that's her idea of a joke.

We seem to be living in times of breakdown—family breakdowns, cultural breakdowns, nervous breakdowns, collapses in the web of life itself. But a new light is also dawning on the horizon of the soul, promising the possibility of break*through*. I have glimpsed that dawn inside myself and in others around me, and it has set a spark within my heart. This is the story of how I, my wife and a few friends discovered the Earthfire, and of how it changed our lives.

I have read that our world is held together by the tension between opposites—good and bad, happiness and sorrow, growth and decay—but the question arises whether there is something greater than these things. And if that greater thing exists, can we attain it? Can we allow it to open us, to flood through us and water the wasteland we have made? If such a flood began, how many of us would welcome it and how many would fear it? How many would plant seeds in the new earth, joyfully surrendering to transformation, and how many would retreat to an interior desert, preferring to endure emptiness? These answers are not yet known, but I believe that the issue of *how many* people turn in each direction will decide whether our planet is renewed or destroyed. And we won't have to wait a long time to see how this turns out. We are in the middle of it now.

Sebastian once said to me, "By the time you begin to comprehend the game, you're a player. Then it's too late to opt out." That is how it feels to know the Earthfire. Once you have experienced it, you are filled with the harrowing hope that *everything* can be healed—the wounded environment, the plague of greed, the insanity of war, the strange inner emptiness that leaves us numb at the brink of self-destruction. I say the hope is *harrowing* because if you see this healing vision and believe it, the feeling comes that you ought to do something about it, and the implications of that can be overwhelming. You begin to understand that the potential for renewal does not necessarily lead to its fulfillment, and that apparently not all people wish for it. In fact, many will fight fiercely against any change, hanging on to whatever power they have. So what do you do? You can't go back to sleep and pretend to be unaware of what is happening. You can't assume that someone else will take care of it. You've become a player, and you have to decide what you are willing to risk.

In writing this tale, it was difficult to know where to begin. I wondered, should it start with the first breakthrough, when a voice from another world spoke of death and rebirth? Or would it be better to begin with the prophecies we found, foretelling the crises of the modern world? I was tempted to put everything else aside and commence with the Earthfire itself, the mysterious experience that electrifies the body and illuminates the mind and heart. For it is that which insists on being announced, shared and perhaps spread throughout the world. When I asked Helen about it, she answered in her practical way, "Start where it began for you." So I searched my memory. In one sense, the origin of my transformation dates back to the afternoon when I met her. But its acceleration began on a certain fateful day in our little shop, when Sebastian's letter arrived.

# —— *Shadow* ——

From the top of the red rock pinnacle, the three climbing men looked like insects ascending an upturned terra cotta bowl. The golden disc of the sun hung low on the horizon, making their creeping shadows long and ominous. They moved carefully, picking their way among boulders and jagged crevices. Two of them wore black, while the third was clothed in khaki hiker's pants and a white shirt. The more thickset man in black was perspiring heavily, and he cursed under his breath when he caught his foot on a protruding ledge. His companion was silent. It was the man in the white shirt who spoke.

"Mr. Almey, I've been up here dozens of times and I've never seen a UFO. How can you be so sure we'll see one this evening?"

"A man who knows where and how to look can find whatever he wants." the heavy man answered. "That's why I asked you to meet me here."

The three trudged onward, making their way slowly up and around to the back side of the small mountain, which was invisible from the highway below. The incline increased as they drew nearer the top, and all of them were forced to use their hands for climbing the steepest rock faces. At last, they reached the platform of a sheer cliff, a ledge carved in the rock wall that looked down on the desert floor below and gave an unencumbered view of the surrounding stone mounds and mesas. The sun was setting and the clouds on the edges of the western sky had turned a deep red.

The man in the white shirt stood on the cliff's edge and gazed at the horizon. "What a beautiful sunset."

"It looks like blood," the younger man in black muttered.

"You're a poet, Stevens," chuckled his heavy companion.

The three men sat on the stony precipice while the sun went down and the twilight surrounded them. The man in the white shirt scanned the landscape repeatedly while they waited, but the other two men's eyes followed him. As the darkness deepened, he turned to them and asked, "Did you bring flashlights? The moon won't be up for awhile."

"We brought two," said the thickset man. "We didn't think you'd need one."

The man hesitated, "Yes ... I have my own, of course."

After a silence, the heavy man asked, "My old friend the general gave you quite a lot of information, didn't he?"

"Yes, I suppose he did. I haven't had time to read it all thoroughly. And then last night someone broke into my office and stole my computer, which makes everything more difficult."

"The general's information wasn't on your computer," Stevens said.

The man in the white shirt stiffened. In the darkness, his hand moved imperceptibly to cover the outline of the computer disc that protruded slightly from one of the front pockets of his khaki pants. His heart began to pound, and he had to will himself to breathe slowly and speak calmly. "No, it wasn't. I have it on a disc ... back in my car. I can show you if you want to see it, after we get down from here. But ... how did you know the data was not in the computer?"

The heavy man uttered a nasty laugh, "Let's just say Stevens is on very close terms with the thief. Now, Doctor, if you'll hand over your car keys, we won't trouble you to climb all the way back down."

The three figures battled briefly at the cliff's edge, the sounds of blows and shouting voices quickly dissolving into the empty desert night. The man in the white shirt fought desperately, struggling to fling his keys over the ledge, but they clattered to the ground. The heavy man groped for them on his hands and knees, while Stevens held the the other man against the rock wall.

"Ah, here they are. Now Doctor, what was the use of all that foolishness? Of course, one might say that about your whole career. Stevens, take care of him."

There were more shouts, and then a scream, and silence. A moment later, two small white lights were visible, jiggling unevenly along the mountain trail, as a pair of dark figures made their descent. But the disc they sought lay behind them, shattered on the bloodstained rocks, beneath the body of the dead man.

# — 1 —

The store was quiet after I stilled the beeping of the alarm box. Enough sunshine came in through the front window that I didn't need to switch on the lights. I took a breath and looked around. The display tables were covered with minerals and crystals, the shelves were loaded with books, and the jewelry cases were empty, as they would be until I filled them from the safe. I lit a small bundle of sage and walked through the room waving it over and around everything—from the hanging plants in the sunlit front windows to the chairs in the reading area beside the bookshelves. It was a ritual I enjoyed, and Helen said it purified and cleansed the space for the coming day. When I finished my circuit, I remembered to open the front door a bit so the smoke could get out. Then I went to the back room and sat down at my desk.

The sweet smell of the sage hung in the air and the morning silence made me feel calm and thoughtful. I looked around at the familiar furnishings and at the mementos on the walls. Here was the store's first dollar, pinned to the bulletin board with "Best of luck!" scrawled on it by a friendly customer. Next to it was the yellowed article the local newspaper wrote about our opening. Just to the right, in an antique frame, was the picture of Helen and me in front of the shop in our wedding clothes. That was one day before the store opened, and two hours before we got married.

The Missing Link was one of the many metaphysical stores that had sprung up across America. We chose the name to describe it as a place for finding tools for the rediscovery of what is missing in one's life, and to point out that evolution isn't over yet. The shop itself grew out of a romantic merger.

Before I encountered Helen, I had owned a small jewelry store, but it was lost in a divorce. At forty, I had started over, designing and selling a jewelry line for the tourist stores along the New England coast. I knew enough about the trade and the local market that it was fairly easy to make a living, but I wasn't quite satisfied. I went about my work without enthusiasm. I wondered if I had reached my life's destination, or if I should be searching for something more. My friend Robert, who taught high school psychology and moonlighted as an actor, diagnosed my problem as a mid-life crisis. He told me it was normal at my age.

That annoyed me. As I groped to find the cause of my emptiness and the purpose of my existence, I didn't appreciate hearing, "Don't worry, everybody feels that way." I didn't want to believe that my malaise was simply a consequence of age. Actually, when I thought about it, I realized I had always carried the same discontent, a yearning to connect with a source of meaning in a way that gave significance to my life. But I didn't know what to do with those feelings, so I just kept on working, my disappointment emerging as a rather sarcastic cynicism about the world.

Robert's wife Jane, a local actress and piano teacher, had insisted that I go along with them to a party one Sunday afternoon in April. I felt uncomfortable attending a birthday celebration for someone I didn't know, but Jane said there would be interesting people there. Since my divorce, she and Robert had been trying to help me get out and make new acquaintances. Even though my emotional wounds were still raw, and though the thought of a room full of strangers made me nervous, I agreed to go. After a drink, I started enjoying it.

I was standing near the middle of the room—the whole place was one enormous open space, the inside of a converted church—debating with an older bearded gentleman, Mr. Graves. Our subject was the best hypothetical means to deal with robbers and burglars. He was of the pacifist persuasion, and he spoke with sincerity, though for my part I was arguing mainly for sport.

"So what would you do if you heard them breaking in downstairs?" I asked. "Would you use a gun if you had one, or just call the police and hide in your bed? Or what if the phone line was cut and you couldn't call the police?"

"Why, I would simply go downstairs and speak with them. There is no one with whom one cannot communicate, with sufficient patience and understanding—even you, sir," he smiled. "I would explain to the unfortunate malcontents the societal pressures that had forced them into their desperation, pointing out the futility and self-destructiveness of the actions they had chosen. Then I would attempt to help them financially by means more productive than stealing my wife's silverware. I would offer them loans, or perhaps even employment."

"What if they still preferred the silverware?"

"Why I would give it to them, of course. But I would not expect that to happen if I communicated effectively."

"But what would you do if you thought they were going to kill you, or your wife?" I said. "What if they had guns and you had a gun? I mean, as long as we're discussing this, let's get to the essence of it."

Mr. Graves looked upset. He stared at my gin and tonic and then at me, as though to decide whether to blame me or the alcohol for my rude questions. He took a deep breath, "There is no stimulus sufficient to lead an enlightened person into violent action. That situation is unlikely to happen to me because I am embodying the proper peaceful attitude. But if it did ... I would not attack."

"Well sir," I said, touching the top of my head with one hand. "My hat is off to you. I disagree with what you say, but I will defend till your death your right to say it." We both laughed, although I thought his chuckle was uneasy. We stood there gazing around the room, and I noticed Jane moving in my direction with the other woman beside her.

"Samuel," the slender, dark-haired woman spoke to Mr. Graves. "It's good to see you. How's Caroline? Is she here with you?"

Mr. Graves smiled and turned, giving the newcomer his full attention, "Good evening, Helen. Yes, she's here somewhere. I lost track of her while discussing life and death issues here with Mr., umm, ah ..., Mr. ..."

"Lerner," Jane interjected. "William Lerner. Helen, this is my friend Will. Will, this is Helen Waters."

"Nice to meet you," I mumbled.

Jane went on, "Helen is the woman who did the readings at the Tarot party I told you about, Will. And she has just started a business selling crystals."

"I understand you're a jewelry designer?" Helen asked. Her eyes were a deep, dark brown and her gaze was penetrating. After a few seconds, I looked away, feeling unexpectedly embarrassed.

"Not exactly. I mean, I'm not really a designer. I make some jewelry and I contract some to be made for me, and I sell it. I'm in the jewelry business, but I'm no artist. I'm more of an entrepreneur, I guess."

"He's a good salesman," put in Mr. Graves. "He practically had me talked into buying a shotgun." He chuckled and said, "There's Caroline.

Helen, please be sure and say hello to her. I know she wants to ask you over to do a reading for her." He pressed her hand and walked away.

Both women looked at me curiously. "A shotgun?" Jane asked.

"Just an imaginary one. We were comparing philosophies. Mr. Graves seems to believe that the innocent have nothing to fear and no need to defend themselves. I was just playing devil's advocate."

"I think the devil has enough advocates already," Helen said. "Samuel is a sweet man."

"Yes, but he's living in his own world."

"And who isn't?"

"Me," I said. "I'm making a determined effort to live in the real world."

"Which one is that?"

"The one on the evening news. The one where burglars can't be sweet-talked out of robbing you."

"Well, how are things in the real world?"

"Mostly they stink."

"They do?"

"Absolutely. Think about it. The earth is overpopulated to begin with, and the governments and corporations are run by people who are either too greedy or too ignorant to protect the environment. There are wars everywhere, with people killing each other over ethnic and religious differences we can't even understand. And how about the threats of nuclear, chemical and biological terrorism or war? A disaster of monumental magnitude could happen any day. All over the planet, people are so miserable they're addicted to every kind of drug they can get their hands on." I took a sip of my gin and tonic. "And on top of that, the religions are collapsing because their leaders are hypocritical and corrupt, and they don't have the answers people are looking for. Everybody's afraid of dying, but they spend half their lives watching television, where they get so desensitized to violence that teenagers are running around shooting each other for fun. So yes, since you asked, the real world is a mess." Again I looked away from Helen. I had said more than I intended to, and I felt self-conscious.

"Well," she replied, taking a small step toward me, "What do you think about changing it?"

"Changing crime and greed and corruption and war? Sure, I'm ready. Just point me in the right direction." I took another sip of my drink.

She touched the center of my chest with her index finger. "In there. That's the right direction. If you change that, everything else has to follow." She smiled at me. "It's good that you care about these problems, Will, but maybe you shouldn't view things so negatively. I believe we attract into our lives whatever we hold in our thoughts. The evening news tempts us into perpetual anxiety, and if that's all we think about, how can we bring any beauty into the world?" She glanced over my shoulder. "I see Jane is beckoning me. Nice to have met you, Will."

I fingered the spot on my chest where she had touched me, as I watched her walk away. For the rest of that party, I kept noticing Helen. Wherever I went in that big barn of a church, I would look up and find my eyes on her. Sometimes I noticed her looking back at me, and that penetrating gaze made me nervous. It was as though she were seeing into me. Yet, in spite of my discomfort, I was drawn to her. And that, too, was strange, because it wasn't the same type of attraction I had known with other women. By the time I left the party with Jane and Robert, I was asking them about Helen Waters. I wanted to know where she lived, whether she was with anyone, and how I could arrange to see her again.

As it turned out, I didn't have to arrange it.

Two days after the party, Robert and Jane were coming to my house for dinner. We had planned it the week before, and Robert arrived early to help me with the cooking. While we were chopping vegetables and comparing notes on the day, the phone rang. It was Jane.

"Will, I'm sorry, but I don't think I can make it to dinner."

"What's the matter?"

"Nothing really. But I was just leaving for your place when my friend Helen Waters arrived. You met her at the birthday party. I had asked her to dinner here tonight, and I forgot about it when you invited Robert and me. I can stay here with her, and you and Robert can spend the evening together."

"Why don't you just bring her with you and come over? There's plenty of food." I felt oddly nervous, and eager at the same time.

"Are you sure it's all right?"

"Of course. I enjoyed meeting Helen at the party. Bring her." I tried to sound casual. "Maybe she can read my Tarot cards or something."

Jane covered the phone receiver and had a short conversation with Helen. Then she said, "Okay. That'll be great. We'll be there in a few minutes."

At dinner, I sat next to Helen, across the candlelit table from Robert and Jane. On impulse, I had made the stir fry with tofu instead of chicken, and when Helen said she was vegetarian I sighed with audible relief.

"What is it, Will?" she asked. When I explained, she simply said, "Very intuitive of you."

"More like dumb luck, I'd say. I bought the tofu because I liked some I had in a Chinese restaurant, but I've never actually cooked any before. And speaking of dumb luck, I think this dish tastes pretty good. How about you?"

She smiled, "It's delicious, and I don't believe in dumb luck. I prefer to call such things synchronicities."

"Synchro-what?"

"Synchronicities—harmonious coincidences—events that are linked by meaning, but not by cause and effect. My grandmother used to say that synchronicities—she called them 'serendipities'—occur to remind us that the universe is alive and magic is everywhere."

"And is that what you believe?"

"Yes, actually, I do."

As the evening went on, I started looking at Helen more often, and anticipating the gaze of those dark eyes rather than avoiding it. Though Jane had told me that Helen did Tarot readings, I hadn't been sure I wanted one. An hour or so after dinner, I finally felt intrigued and courageous enough to ask.

"Helen, Jane tells me you're a psychic."

"I wouldn't say that exactly."

"But you give readings, right? You did that Tarot party for Jane's friends."

"Yes, I did."

"Well, I'm not sure I believe in that stuff, but I was wondering, if you have your cards with you, what would you think about doing a reading for me?"

"If you're asking for a reading, yes."

"What do you mean?"

"I only do it when people ask. It's an important part of the process that one *request* the guidance a reading offers. In asking, you involve your energy, and that pulls the pattern of the cards together. It also allows my guides to tap into you and give me information." Her seriousness surprised me. I was still skirting the edges of this idea, not sure if I wanted to open up to it, or to Helen.

"Could you find things out about me even if I didn't make a request?"

"Maybe, but I wouldn't. And if I told you things you didn't ask to hear, you probably wouldn't listen." As she spoke she looked into my eyes. Again I felt oddly uncomfortable. It wasn't that she was staring at me or trying to intrude, it was that her eyes were completely open. There was no protective veil, and that made my own shields painfully obvious. I turned to her again.

"All right, then. I'm asking. Would you read the cards for me?"

She smiled. "Right now?"

"Yes, now."

"I'll get my deck."

Robert and Jane went to the couch on the other side of the living room (to give me privacy for my reading, they said), while Helen and I sat cross-legged on the floor. Helen asked me to touch the card deck and hold in my mind the question, "What do I most need to know now?" After that she shuffled the thick, oversized cards and asked me to cut them into three piles. She put the piles together and began turning cards face up in a pattern. I saw images of people and symbols—swords, cups, long wooden rods, gold discs with inscribed stars, a skeleton horseman in black armor.

"Hey, that's the Death card. Can't we yank that one out and put something else there?" In spite of my skepticism, I felt a twinge of anxiety.

"Don't worry," she said. "Give me a minute." She scanned the pattern of cards, sometimes closing her eyes and touching one. After a few moments, she began to speak.

"I can see you are moving out of a period of difficulty and confusion into a time of greater happiness and more light in your life. This card at the foundation, the Three of Swords, shows that you are carrying painful wounds from the past, but the central card is the Four of Wands. It pictures people who are joyous, coming out from their walled city to celebrate in the open air under a canopy of flowers. I think this is saying that now is an important time for you to let go of any self-protection that keeps you confined. You can open up and trust the universe and realize that the wounds are in the past."

I glanced over at Robert and Jane, but they were involved in their own conversation. "I guess I should mention now that I've just been through a rather painful divorce. I suppose there isn't any other kind."

"Yes, I knew about the divorce. Jane told me. But see what the cards are saying. Though there is this grief at the foundation, the Seven of Cups is moving into the past. This card shows someone confused by illusions—and in this case I would say that the illusions may be the emotional expectations you had about that relationship. Cups are related to emotions and spirit." She looked up, seeming to focus her eyes on some point behind me, remaining silent for several moments. Then she looked at me again and spoke, "Your guides are telling me you should remember that there is a deeper reality behind the illusions, and that your hopes for true love were not completely wrong, only misplaced."

"My guides? What guides?"

"Your spirit guides. There are several around you. I saw one of them when you were touching the deck a few minutes ago. He looks quite old but he has a very joyous, mirthful energy."

My skepticism rose again, but there was also a sense of fascination. "You *see* spirit guides? Around me?"

"I did for a moment. But let's go on with the reading."

"Oh, okay, right." I focused on the cards and listened.

"Supporting the Four of Wands in the center is the Ace of Cups. This is a wonderful card. It shows the hand of the divine offering a sacred chalice. In this position it tells us that if you come out from behind those inner walls you'll receive a gift of grace and emotional upliftment. Sometimes this card symbolizes the Holy Grail, the vessel that gives each one who drinks from it that which he most desires." Her voice became more forceful. "The desires fulfilled by the Grail are not those of the everyday self, but those of the soul. In its deepest sense, this card says that in emerging from your protective shell, you allow a flood of grace to enter and transform your life. And look, crossing the center card is the Fool card. This is usually viewed as what stands in your way. In that context, I see that you are reluctant to make yourself vulnerable by trusting too readily. You may fear making a fool of yourself. But the Fool has divine protection because of his innocent trust and belief. Even as he walks obliviously off the edge of a cliff, he is uninjured because of the purity of his trust. So I see this card as saying that your fear of being a fool stands in the way of your liberation, but the card's message also encourages you to follow the example of the Fool and trust. You'll be protected, and it is important that you take this opportunity. These moments don't last forever." She glanced up. "Are you with me?"

"Yes, but nervously. I don't relish the thought of falling off cliffs." It was true that I did feel anxiety, but I wasn't certain whether my fear was of the Fool's fall or of leaving the security of my cynicism. Maybe that *was* the Fool's fall. Sometimes, I thought, it's more comfortable to fantasize about your dreams than to realize them. I glanced down again—Helen was pointing to another card.

"Don't worry. Look, here in the sky position is the Sun card. This position gives us a 'weather report' on your spiritual life. The Sun tells us that your emergence from behind the inner walls is blessed with great light and warmth. See the happy child with his arms wide open? That's how you can feel. That's what you're being offered."

"Why don't I feel that way now?"

"That's what the next card shows us. In the near future position, we have the Hanged Man."

"Terrific. I'm hanged in the near future. This is what happens when I trust? And why am I hanging upside down?"

"The Hanged Man isn't about punishment. It's about the enlightenment that comes from taking a different perspective, looking from a new frame of reference. See the light around his head? I think this means that you will benefit from trying on points of view that are unfamiliar to you, and embracing what gives you the new vision that inspires you."

"Such as Tarot readings?"

Helen smiled. "Yes, if they inspire you. And remember, the cards operate on many levels at once. The Hanged Man's awakening can be as simple as solving a personal problem by trying a new viewpoint, or as profound as achieving spiritual enlightenment through a complete inner surrender."

"Up to now, I haven't been big on surrender."

"You should try it sometime. It can be the door to freedom, and it's certainly what your cards so far seem to suggest. Now let's go on. In the self position you have the Two of Cups ..." She hesitated, took a deep breath and spoke again. "This card shows a man and woman exchanging two cups, which symbolizes the giving and receiving of emotion. Above them floats a winged lion and the caduceus, which is an ancient symbol of healing. That tells us that their exchange is a blessed and healing thing."

"Sounds like true love," I said, without thinking. Helen looked startled. She glanced at me and then averted her gaze. A moment later she went on.

"It can mean a romance. It often does. But it can also indicate the coming together of the male and female components of your being, the unification of self. And that is quite a healing experience. It can be the result of the new point of view which the Hanged Man indicates you will discover in the near future. Now, let's look at the next card. The High Priestess is in the environment position. This card shows a female figure seated between two pillars. She wears a crown shaped like three phases of the moon, an ancient symbol of the Goddess. A crescent moon at her feet also indicates her stature as representative of the Goddess. The pillars are a gateway to initiation into higher knowledge, and the curtain between them shows that the knowledge is now veiled. I see this as an indication that your initiation into a more spiritual life is around you now, waiting for the moment of your change in perspective which will allow the veil to drop."

I felt a mixture of eager excitement and nervous anxiety, overlaid with my old pessimistic skepticism. Nonetheless, I was drawn into the story unfolding in the pattern of the cards, into the promise of new life, into the sound of Helen's voice. After a moment, I spoke. "I see that the priestess is sitting in front of the curtain, holding a scroll. Is she someone who already knows what's behind the veil? I mean, this is in my environment, right? Could that card be you sitting here giving me this reading?"

Helen hesitated for a moment. "It could be on one level, yes. But I think it is deeper than just this Tarot reading. A person can sit in the place of an energy, like the Goddess energy pictured here, and be a temporary conduit for it, and it's true that I feel a personal connection to that card. But an archetype like the High Priestess isn't contained in any one individual. I feel this is saying that your environment is filled with a great deal of potential spiritual growth, and that the form of what will come of it is still hidden. Let's go on to the next card."

"Couldn't we skip that one? It looks so fatal."

"I told you not to worry." She smiled, and I felt my shiver of fear dissolve. "The Death card in a reading rarely signifies physical death. It usually indicates the end of a part of one's life, like a relationship, a habit pattern, or a self-image. In this case, Death shows up in the position called 'hopes and fears'. This may simply mean that you have anxiety about physical death, or about the ending of some aspect of your life. At the same time, notice the sun rising between the two pillars on the horizon. Death is inseparable from rebirth. Looked at from this perspective, the card may tell us that you are hoping for a new beginning even as you fear letting go of the old way."

I felt as if she had read my mind, not just the cards. "That actually makes some sense to me," I said. "When I was going through the divorce, mostly feeling miserable and lonely, I occasionally noticed a little part of myself that was quite joyful. It was as if on some level I knew I was on my way to something good."

"Well, it looks that way here too. Your outcome cards are the Eight of Pentacles and the Lovers. The Eight of Pentacles shows an apprentice or craftsman who is totally engrossed in his work. He is making pentacles, which symbolize the things of earthly life. The message of this card is that you will be called to do a lot of work that is new to you, and that you should simply do it. Outer appearances don't matter. They will eventually take care of themselves if you try to embody the dedication of this single-minded artisan."

"Is this inner work or physical labor?"

"I think it will be both."

"And where does it take me?"

Again Helen hesitated. She closed her eyes and touched the last card.

She seemed to be listening. When she finally spoke, her voice was a bit unsteady, "The final outcome is ... the Lovers. This card, like all of them, can have multiple levels of meaning. My sense is that you can look forward to a unification of all the parts of yourself, and that this can bring you great happiness and a much more active spiritual life. The Lovers card shows the figures of a man and woman, plus an angel overhead who blesses them. Notice that the man looks to the woman and the woman looks to the angel. I've read that this tells us that the feminine aspect can see Spirit directly, and the masculine aspect sees the divine through relationship with the feminine. You can understand this if you think of how the logical masculine side of oneself can appreciate the divine only through experience of the intuitive feminine side."

"That sounds great, but it's kind of abstract. What about the mundane level? Is this saying I'm heading for a new relationship?"

She glanced up at me again with that open, vulnerable gaze. She looked quickly back to the cards. "Yes, it could be saying that. There are numerous levels of meaning, and the cards often work on more than one at a time. I guess my advice is to do the work that needs doing, and all aspects of what the Lovers card is offering to you will show themselves." She quickly mixed the cards together and slid them back into the deck. "Any questions?"

"Yes. How about you going everywhere with me so you can do readings to help me make all my decisions?"

She smiled, and I caught a spark of mischief in her eyes, "It's tempting, but probably not very practical. Perhaps you should learn to read the Tarot yourself."

"It looks complicated, and doesn't sound like as much fun. But maybe I'll try it sometime. I do have another question. How do you see and hear my 'spirit guides'? And why don't I know about them?"

"Are you certain you don't? I'm sure you must know the voice of your own intuition. Anyway, I'm afraid this is the start of a long conversation, and it's getting late. I have to work tomorrow."

"Well, I hope we'll get the chance to have that conversation. Thanks for the reading. I feel like I have a lot to think about."

"Me too," she said softly. "You're welcome."

We stood up and went over to Robert and Jane. Helen said her goodbyes to them and to me, and in a few minutes she was gone.

I stayed up talking with Jane and Robert. I asked them about Helen, if she was attached to anyone, whether they thought she liked me, what my chances were if I asked her to see me again. I felt strangely elated, as though destiny had touched me. Although she had said nothing to indicate it, I guessed and hoped that the Lovers card at the end of my reading might refer to us. To my own bemusement, I believed the reading and I viewed the future with a mixture of enthusiasm and apprehension. The more I thought about it, the more I wanted to see Helen again.

"Why don't you call her?" Robert asked.

"But it's after midnight," I said. "Don't you think it's too late?"

"She's probably just gotten home. Weren't you saying you hoped she made it safely? I don't think she'd mind your checking on that."

Jane gave me the number and I called Helen's apartment.

"Hello?"

"Helen, this is Will Lerner. I'm still sitting here with Jane and Robert, and I, uh, wanted to check to see that you made it home all right."

"Well, that's very nice of you. I'm fine. I just came in." Her tone was friendly, and I thought she seemed happy that I had called.

"Thanks again for the reading," I said. "It's really making me think."

"Me too ... Yes, the cards are interesting, aren't they?"

"They really are ... Helen, there's one other thing I wanted to ask—would you like to get together sometime? Maybe for dinner or a picnic or something?"

"Yes, Will," she answered softly, "I'd like to see you again." Then, in a more conversational tone she added, "How about the beach?"

"Great!" I answered, unable to conceal my eagerness. "When?"

"I could come over Saturday about one. Will that work?"

"That's wonderful. I'll be waiting."

From the night of that reading onwards, we became increasingly inseparable. As I got to know her better, I came to see Helen as a woman of multiple dimensions. On the spiritual level, she was my teacher, introducing me to meditation, hands-on healing, divination, the "channeling" of inner guidance, and the uses of affirmations, rituals and visualizations. When we worked together, she was disciplined, focused and disturbingly tireless. But when work was over, she knew how to put other things aside and have fun. She loved dancing, but was shy about singing. She loved to cook, and to eat, her delicious repertoire of natural foods. As we spent more time together, I found myself letting go of coffee, alcohol, meat and sugar. (I told her I had always thought those were the four food groups.)

A year after we met, Helen and I were married, and we opened our store, the Missing Link, the next day. The place was a true collaboration, bringing together her knowledge of spiritual and metaphysical matters and my experience with jewelry and gemstones. Although our money was initially very limited, within a year the place was filled with crystals, gems, minerals, jewelry and metaphysical books. It became more than a store—it was a center for people who were opening up to newfound inner spirituality. I did a lot of that sort of opening myself as well. With Helen as my guide, I learned to meditate, to read the Tarot and consult the I Ching, and to sometimes feel what she said were the energies of stones and crystals. I never saw my spirit guides, as Helen called them, but she often got messages from hers, and I had to admit the advice was remarkably good. Our life became more and more comfortable and happy, and the days were punctuated with magical moments and great conversations with the fascinating variety of people who visited the shop. Many were just beginning, pursuing the thread of new yearnings and visions. Some were veterans of esoteric occultism. A few were ill, seeking new modes of healing. My new life didn't make me forget the "real world" of the evening news, but it did help me to see how alienated that world was from people's natural goodness and humanity, and the individuals I met gave me fresh hope that everything could change.

Once a big eighteen-wheeler pulled up right in front of the store entrance, and the driver lumbered in. He was a huge man with powerfully muscled shoulders and a tattoo of a dragon on his right forearm. I was sure he must have stopped for directions. "What can I do for you?" I asked him.

"What kind of a store is this? My spirit guides made me turn off the highway and drive here. What do you sell? There's something here I'm supposed to get."

A bit flabbergasted, I conducted him through the store, showing him crystal spheres and amethyst geodes, channeled books and dowsing pendulums. Finally he picked up a piece of translucent green stone. It was Moldavite, a meteoric gemstone which was very popular for its powerful energies.

"This is it!" he cried. "I've been seeing this stuff in my mind every time I meditate. I'll take this one."

"You've seen this in meditation? Did you know what it was?"

"Nope. I just knew how it was supposed to feel."

"What will you use it for?"

"Meditating, increasing my psychic ability, and fishing."

"Fishing?"

"Sure. I'll hold this stone and call the fish to my bait. It works great with a quartz crystal. I'll bet this will be even better." With that, he made his purchase, climbed into his truck and drove off. A few months later, he visited again and told us the stone was working well ... in all three areas.

Except for the fact that he didn't look the part, our truck driver was a typical customer. Every day people came in and discovered what they were seeking. Some of them spent hours, looking and touching, basking in what they called the "energy" of the store. The Missing Link became a destination, a place where people could share and pursue their awakenings without fear of ridicule. Standing daily in the middle of this phenomenon, I wondered at what I saw and heard, and I puzzled over what it all might mean.

## — 2 —

I came out of my reverie, still sitting at my desk in the store's back room. There was a lot to do before opening. I started by going through my basket of mail, separating the junk from the bills, and picking out the few pieces that appeared to be actual letters. Among them, I noticed the return address on a thick envelope. It was hotel stationery from somewhere in Arizona, but the name of the hotel had been crossed out, and across the top were the handwritten words "Your Raving Correspondent." Sebastian! After two months! I regarded the envelope, turning it over in my hands. On the back, there was a drawing of a multi-pointed star radiating rays of light. I was eager to open it, but thought I ought to wait for Helen to arrive. She would be as anxious as I was to find out what had happened on the quest Sebastian had begun. I looked up towards the ceiling, remembering that our first meeting with him had occurred in the room right above my head.

On occasional nights at The Missing Link, we sponsored talks by authors, teachers, healers, psychics and others whose work was of interest to us and our customers. It was at one of those talks that we encountered Sebastian.

That particular evening, a woman was doing a lecture on crystals and a channeling of information from what she called her Angelic Teachers. Helen and I sat near the back of the meeting room, which was the living room of an apartment upstairs from the store. We rented it for extra office and storage space, and for the talks. About twenty people, including a burly red-haired man with a short beard, were seated on chairs we had arranged around the floor. Though most of the attendees were regular customers and friends, the redhead was a newcomer. I noticed him fidgeting and looking exasperated as the speaker detailed the spiritual applications of several stones. During the channeling, in which her Teachers spoke through her in a strange, almost Irish accent, he looked even more agitated. When the question and answer period after the channeling began, he raised his hand.

"How do you know the crystals have the effects you were talking about?"

"My Angelic Teachers give me the information when I meditate."

"Well, I mean no disrespect, but how do you know this information is not just coming from your own subconscious? How can someone be sure that you're not, perhaps unconsciously, making this all up?"

The speaker looked annoyed. She was not used to skepticism at her lectures. "Obviously you don't meditate or you would know how it feels. It is *not* my subconscious, and if you have the sensitivity you can *feel* what the stones are good for."

"But that doesn't leave much room for scientific investigation."

"*Science!* Science can't even deal with what I do!"

"I'm a scientist, and I'm here because I'm trying to understand what you do." The man's tone was calm but firm, and his questions were familiar ones to me. I had asked them myself. I wondered what the lecturer would say.

"I can't explain anything in those terms. Maybe Will could talk to you about this later." She pointed me out in the back of the room and then asked, "Any other questions?"

After the program was over, as people were retrieving jackets and folding their blankets, he came over to me. "Can you make heads or tails of this stuff?" he asked.

"I think so. That's what I try to do all day. I've been working on it ever since I met my wife." I put out my hand. "I'm Will Lerner and this is Helen Waters."

"I'm Sebastian," he said, grasping my hand in his thick paw and smiling at Helen. "Sebastian Smith. Are you the owners of this place?"

"We own everything here except the building. Did I hear you say you're a scientist?"

"Well, most of my work has been in engineering, what you might call the practical side of science. My inspiration was Miss Dee, my high school physics teacher. She told us that science was the pure search for truth, and that its application would eventually solve all the world's problems. I set out to be one of the problem-solvers, not completely successfully I must admit. But since I became an accidental mystic, I've gotten out of that line of work almost entirely."

"An accidental mystic?" I inquired.

"Yes," Sebastian replied. "Some things have been happening to me lately. At first I thought I was having a nervous breakdown, but now I think it may have been a spiritual awakening of some kind."

"That sounds like a story I'd like to hear."

"And I want to ask you about crystals, and those angels with the funny accents. Can we talk now?"

I glanced around the room. Almost all the people had left. I waved to the last of them and turned back to Sebastian. Something about him interested me, and I wanted to find out what he had to say. "I can stay awhile. Helen, what do you want to do?"

"I think I'll take the car and go home, if Mr. Smith can give you a ride."

"No problem at all," said Sebastian.

When Helen had left, Sebastian walked to a table with some crystals and stones on it. He picked up an amorphous green stone, a Moldavite about two inches long, and held it out to me. "Do you believe this stuff really works?"

"It depends on what you mean by 'works.' That's a piece of Moldavite, and it's one of the stones that I'm sure has energy."

"How do you know it has 'energy'?"

"I've felt it, and I've observed hundreds of other people feeling and reacting to it. It's known as one of the strongest stones in the realm of spiritual energies."

"And who decides that?"

"It's just my observation that people who are using stones for meditation and are exploring their spiritual uses talk about Moldavite as a very powerful stone. It's known scientifically as a tektite, which is a mysterious class of glassy objects associated with meteorite strikes. Legends connect Moldavite with the Stone of the Holy Grail, and it's been found in amulets at least 25,000 years old. I've read that stones of this type have long been revered in Asia and Tibet as well, and that their Sanskrit name is *agni mani*, which means 'fire pearl.'"

"So why do they call it that?"

"I have a theory, but why don't you just close your eyes and hold this piece for a minute, and we'll see if you feel anything." Sebastian took the stone and held it pressed between his two palms. He sat on the floor and closed his eyes. "Now, just breathe slowly and deeply," I said. "Relax and don't try to feel anything in particular. You can let your mind wander."

I waited and watched him. After about a minute, he spoke. "I'm getting a pulsing in my palms. And this stone is getting warm. It's getting very hot." He opened his eyes and looked down. "My palms have turned bright pink.

That's very interesting. How do you explain it?"

"I'm not sure I can, but my theory is that it works through a kind of resonance, a state in which one's own subtle energies connect and harmonize with those being emanated by the crystal or stone. It might be similar to the way your state of mind can be affected by the energy levels or moods of the people around you. Anyway, quite a few customers have told me that getting Moldavite seemed to accelerate their spiritual growth."

"It's a big stretch from red palms to spiritual growth," he protested.

"I once met a woman who read palms, and it *was* for spiritual growth."

Sebastian grinned, "Somebody stop him before he puns again! Now don't dodge the question. Even if your energy resonance idea is right, why would that have anything to do with something spiritual?"

"I don't know. That's the mystery. But I can tell you what convinced me that there is a real spiritual connection—if you want to listen to a story."

"Sure, tell me a story, and then I'll tell you one." He went over to the old brown couch and sprawled across it, propping his head up with his hand. He was quite a large man, barrel-chested and big-boned, with muscular arms and a belly that spoke of hearty appetites. His close-cut red hair and beard made me think he would have looked at home in a toga—like some aristocratic hedonist of ancient Rome. His blue eyes twinkled with humor and intelligence. "Ready when you are," he declared.

I sat down on the rug in front of him. "Helen and I have been together a little over three years. We opened the store the day after we got married."

"No honeymoon?"

"I usually say that the store *is* our honeymoon. Anyway, I was not much of a believer in crystal energies or any of the rest of this mysticism when we started. Helen had shown me that she could get good information in meditation and through her card readings, and she claimed to feel the energies of the stones. She said meditating had increased her sensitivity. I was curious, so I started sitting with her in her morning meditations. I usually held a Moldavite stone in one hand, just in case it would help. I guess it was five or six weeks later when I sat down one morning to meditate alone. I turned on the stereo and put on a piece of flute music, *Mooncircles* I think it was called."

"Was that something new for you?"

"No, we often used that piece. But on this day, I thought I would try to visualize something. The music has a quality to it like the flight of a bird, so I decided to imagine myself flying. At first, I pictured myself lifting up out of the chair, but with my body still sitting there, lifting up and drifting right through the ceiling and the roof, hovering in the air over the building. That wasn't too hard to do, so I let the music sort of narrate a flight over the countryside. It was a sunny spring day outside, and I visualized flying around over the town. It was pleasant, though I was under no illusions that I was really going anywhere. I knew I was still sitting in the easy chair. But the next thing that happened surprised me.

"Without my trying or intending to alter what I was visualizing, the scene changed. I saw and felt my imaginary self flying much higher, being drawn up and up until I could no longer see the town. I was going into space, and after a few minutes I could see the whole earth behind me. I could still hear the music, and as it changed, my vision changed again. I was flying further away, towards the sun. Its beautiful gold-white light entranced me and filled me with yearning."

"Were you still aware of your body at this point?"

"Yes, on one level, and of the music as well. But in the experience it felt as though the music and the images I was seeing were in total harmony with each other, and that they were in some real way showing something to me."

"What happened next?"

"Well, as I got nearer and nearer to the golden sun, another emotion came over me. I felt as though I wanted to merge with its radiance. As I got closer I noticed a filament of light, like a very thin cord, extending in a long curve from the center of the star to me. It connected to the center of my chest, and as I looked down I noticed there was a little replica of the sun inside my chest. It was about as big as a softball, and that's where the cord of light from the real sun connected to me. I had a rush of wonder as I saw this, and then I heard a voice."

"A voice? Whose voice."

"I don't know. Helen thinks it was a spirit guide. Anyway, it said to me, 'The Light you seek without is identical to the Light within you.' And at that moment a huge flood of joy washed over me. Back in the room, I opened my eyes and looked down at my hand with the Moldavite, and as I did that a rush of almost electrical energy flowed into my hand, up my arm and into my body. My whole spine felt charged, and I noticed that seven spots along the center line of my body were even more electrified, like little stars inside me. I thought 'Oh, so those are the chakras,' I just sat there, completely blissed out, listening to the last notes of that lovely music. A moment later, Helen came down to see what was going on. The first thing she said was, 'Will, there's light all around you.' While she was getting dressed upstairs, she had felt something happening with me and was drawn to investigate. As I related my experience to her, the intensity of it gradually withdrew, and I was left in a mood of awed peace."

"You sound that way now," Sebastian said. "Why is that?"

"Every time I repeat the story, some of the feeling comes back. But we started this because we were discussing stone energies. I had never sensed anything from stones and I had my doubts about what other people claimed. But when I went to work the day of that meditation, I could feel tingles and vibrations from *every single stone* in the store. I was practically useless for getting anything done, because I kept sitting down on the floor with boxes of crystals, holding them and experimenting with these new sensations."

"Can you still do that? I'd like to test you."

I shook my head. "Not like that time. Sometimes I have a day or an hour when I'm tuned in, but I don't know when it's going to happen. Still, now I have a better understanding of what crystal healers are talking about, and I'm not so skeptical. If I could always be in the expanded awareness I experienced that day, I'd probably be sensitive to all sorts of things."

Sebastian didn't answer right away. He was looking past me, stroking his red beard. Finally he said, "If we could bottle that, we could save the world ..." Then he chuckled, "And get rich, too! Now let me ask you, how much of that experience do you attribute to your Moldavite?"

"It's hard to say. But my story is far from the only one." I briefly told Sebastian about the truck driver. Afterwards, I continued, "My idea now is that these stones can be catalysts to opening one's consciousness, when the situation is just right, or when the person is ready. I think they can oil the hinges of a door that is ready to open, but they can't usually blast through a locked vault."

He sighed, "And there are a lot of locked vaults out there, don't you think?"

"Yes, I guess there are. I spend my days selling oil for people's inner hinges, and I feel good about it. But if one could really start handing out the combinations to those locks, I think people would gladly open up, don't you?"

"I'd like to believe it, Will. Some would, I'm sure. But others might be too addicted to the feeling of control. Or too afraid of losing it. I nearly was." He closed his eyes and took a deep breath that was almost a shudder. "Maybe I still am."

"What do you mean by that?" I asked. Looking at the stocky figure of Sebastian sprawled on the couch, I wondered who he really was. I had only met him an hour before, and already I had told him one of my most person-

al stories. Yet I felt an immediate connection, a kind of kinship, and I trusted him.

He sat up and grinned at me. "I promised you a tale for a tale, so now I'll
tell you why I came here tonight." He looked around the room. "Have you
got a beer anywhere?"

"Sorry, no. I quit drinking alcohol not long after I met Helen. She does-
n't drink, and it wasn't doing me any good anyway."

"Ah, well," he sighed. "Maybe it's better this way. How about a cup of
water?"

"Right away, sir." I went to the cooler and brought back two glasses of
spring water. Sebastian took his and sat up on the old sofa. I settled myself
on the floor in front of him.

"I told you I was an engineer," he began. "Actually, I worked on weapons
research for Pantheon Inc., the defense contractor. Most of what I did
involved computer programming. I worked on technology for the Strategic
Defense Initiative. You know, 'Star Wars.'" I nodded. "I can't discuss most of
what I did, because it's classified, but I can tell you that I was good at it, and
I believed that my life was headed in the right direction. I was earning good
money, and I got to play with lasers and a lot of other nifty toys. I even
thought that I was making the world a safer place by providing our country
with a missile-defense shield. On top of that, I was engaged to the boss's
daughter. What better gig could a red-blooded, red-headed American boy
hope to find?"

"But it didn't work out?"

Sebastian grinned wryly, "You could put it that way."

"What happened?"

"My father-in-law-to-be had me lined up for a promotion, a supervisory
position in the company, to begin shortly after the honeymoon. He called
me in to his office several times to discuss the job, to fill me in on what I
would need to know, and he gave me company documents to read. The more
I learned, the more nervous I got. I found out that we were working on projects that went way beyond self-defense for America. There were massive
offensive weapons, particle beams for destroying satellites and even cities,
and individual ones for killing people without leaving a visible wound.
There were projects for weather control through atmospheric manipulation,
and plans for technology to trigger earthquakes. The CIA was involved, too,
supervising research and buying our products. Some of our systems didn't
even work, and Pantheon knew they would never work, but the programs
were kept going to haul in money from the Pentagon."

"So did this cause a crisis of conscience that forced you to quit?"

"Not exactly. My boss explained things in a way that kept referring to patriotic duty and the national interest, and my own economic well being. I was uneasy, but not ready to crash my own applecart. I just kept working, and telling myself that this was the way of the world. But I also started reading things besides the company documents—books about what you might call the dark side of the Establishment."

"You mean conspiracy theories?"

"In a word, yes."

"What do you think of them?"

"Well, that's another conversation, but I'll just say that what I read ran the gamut from ridiculous and unsubstantiated to well-documented and bone-chilling. And don't forget, I *knew* that some of that stuff was real. Within a few weeks, as the wedding day approached, I started having trouble sleeping, and when I saw my fiancée we usually ended up arguing. That's when the dreams started and the real crisis began."

"When was this?" I asked.

"A year ago last April, just two months before the wedding was supposed to happen."

"What did you dream?"

"At first it was voices calling to me, telling me things I had to do, but I couldn't understand the words. They came for several nights in a row, and I began to grasp that they were telling me I had to change my life—that I needed more light. I thought maybe I should sleep with the lights on, so I tried it, but there was no change in the dreams. Then I started getting a feeling like pins and needles in my head while I was dreaming, and the voices I heard were singing. A couple of times, my mind was blasted by the most intense light I've ever seen. Usually it woke me, and sometimes the light in my head stayed on for a few minutes afterwards. When I woke up like this I had the feeling that I knew a lot of information about significant things."

"What things?"

"It's maddening, but I can't remember much of it now. Part of it seemed spiritual, and some was scientific. Actually, some of the insights came as answers to programming problems I was working on at home—not the military stuff. Those I wrote down."

"But not the spiritual information?"

"That was harder to express—it came more as feelings. It scared me, because I didn't understand why I was thinking these things. And then the past lives started."

"What do you mean?"

"I started dreaming these vivid technicolor movies, and I had a different identity in every one of them. It was very intense and very weird—two or three of these movies every night, and every movie ended with my death. Sometimes I was a man, sometimes a woman or a child. Sometimes I died violently, or of some illness, once or twice from old age. But they just kept coming, and I didn't know if they would ever stop, or why I was seeing them. Hell, I didn't even believe in reincarnation."

"I remember reading something once," I said. "I think it was Voltaire, about a man who complained to his friend that he found the idea of reincarnation incredible, and his friend asked him if he didn't find it just as incredible that he had even *one* incarnation."

Sebastian looked down into his water glass. He sighed, "Well, that's true enough. But those past life memories, or whatever they were, were almost too much for me. That was when I went to a psychiatrist. He wanted to give me anti-psychotic drugs, but I decided I'd rather tolerate the dreams."

"Are they still going on?"

"No, the whole process lasted for just over three weeks. The dreams tapered off a few days after I saw the shrink. Maybe my subconscious was scared by the idea of those drugs. I know my conscious self was. I was relieved when the experiences stopped happening, but in a curious way I also missed them. And I wanted to find out what they meant—what they really were. I decided to take a few months off, live on my savings, and investigate."

"What about your fiancée?"

Sebastian grimaced. "Our relationship was a casualty of my experiences. She wanted me to take the drugs and go ahead with the wedding and the new job. She was totally against the idea of my spending time and energy exploring what to her seemed like a frightful episode. She accused me of wanting to wallow in my 'craziness.' Maybe she was right, but I couldn't do what she asked. So she broke off the engagement, and I decided that, under the circumstances, it would be better if I quit my job too. Since then, I've been teaching programming workshops to make a living while I spend my free time contemplating big questions and harassing the owners of metaphysical bookstores."

I studied the face before me. We couldn't have been more different on the surface. His thick body, red hair and beard contrasted sharply with my average build and thinning brown hair. He had worked on technology for the military, while I had always been a self-employed member of the counterculture, selling my wares through craft shows and in boutiques. Yet here we were, drawn together by a common denominator of mysterious inner experiences. But our connection went deeper than that. There was a sense of likeness, a rapport that made me feel a kind of kinship, as though I had found a long-lost brother. "So, has your investigation come up with any conclusions?" I asked,

"Not yet. But I'm studying the mystic paths, as many as I can find. That's partly why I'm here. I want to understand what happened to me, and whether it's a disease, a healing or an awakening. And I want to know whether I can learn to call these things up at will."

"Would you do that if you could?"

"Yes, I'd have to. After all, I'm a scientist." He straightened, grinned and gave a mock salute. "I'm committed to the search for truth, and I'll search till I'm committed." He chuckled and added, "I hope *that's* not true."

The two of us talked on for hours, Sebastian's keen intellect leaping from one subject to another, always searching, it seemed, for the insight which would be the key to understanding his experiences. It was after midnight when he dropped me off at the house where Helen and I lived.

# — 3 —

I heard the bells jingle on the front door of the shop. I shoved Sebastian's unopened letter into my desk drawer. "Helen? Is that you?" I called out.

"Hi Honey. Why haven't you put the jewelry in the cases yet? It's almost nine."

"Oh. I had no idea what time it was. There was a letter from Sebastian in the mail. He's in Sedona, Arizona."

"Sedona? Is he finished with his seminars? What does his letter say?"

"I haven't looked yet. I was waiting for you, and daydreaming a little."

"My beloved woolgathering husband," she sighed. "Let's open the store and then we'll both read the letter, okay?"

"Your plan is my command."

We turned on the lights and opened the safe, moving behind the counters and filling the glass cases with gold and silver jewelry, set with crystals and multicolored gemstones. Before we finished, the store was already starting to fill up with browsers. The seaside town where we lived was at the height of its summer season, and our normal crowd of metaphysical customers was swelled by ranks of sunburned tourists. Helen and I were immediately busy answering questions, showing jewelry and explaining the energies of the stones.

I spent about twenty minutes with a woman who was looking at rings. She appeared to be around sixty years old, although her makeup and outfit made it hard to be certain. She wore a multicolored flowered blouse over a black swimsuit, with a straw hat, sunglasses and beach thongs. Her fingernails and lips were painted bright crimson. She carried a canvas bag with towels, a purse and a camera in it. She seemed a classic tourist. The woman kept picking up two rings, first one and then the other, and trying them on, holding them up to her flowered shirt. "Now, which one looks better, the purple or the green stone?" she asked.

"Well, the green Moldavite goes with the leaves and purple amethyst goes with the flowers," I said.

She looked at me over the tops of her sunglasses with a glint of mischief in her eyes, "And which one will raise my Kundalini, lower my blood pressure, purify my aura and hook me up with a tall, dark and handsome spirit guide?"

I chuckled to cover my surprise. "That would probably take both of them."

"Yes, it probably would," she mused. "And that would definitely require a discount. What can you do?"

"For both? Let me see ..." I took the rings and scrutinized them while making mental calculations. "How about twenty percent off?"

"Make it twenty-five and it's a deal."

"Done." We exchanged smiles and nods. I started writing a receipt. "Would you like to sign up for our mailing list?"

"Here's my card. I'm a trance channel—a medium. My name is Rhoda Entwhistle, but my spiritual name is Radha ... after Krishna's lusty consort, you know. I drove up here to go to the beach, and I decided to check out your shop. A friend of mine recommended it."

"Nice to meet you, Rhoda ... or Radha." I copied the address and telephone number onto her receipt. "What kind of channeling do you do?"

"Stiffs and stones, mostly," she chuckled. "I help people contact their dead relatives, and I write about crystal energies. Sometimes I even get messages from higher up ... You were right, you know. I do need both of those rings."

"Well, I'm glad of that—"

"Say, if you need any work done, give me a call. I'll give you a free session in exchange for the discount."

"Well, thank you. I—"

"Here's my check. I've got to get to the beach." She turned towards the door, and then looked back at me. "You know, I didn't always work for myself. I used to be a psychic's assistant. And do you know what the best part of that was?"

"Don't make me guess."

"Well, when I wanted to quit, I didn't need to give notice. Ha ha. Blessed be! And don't forget to call me for that session." She turned and left.

It was early afternoon before Helen and I had a break. We stood together in the back room eating the pasta she had ordered from our favorite Italian restaurant for lunch. Taking a bite, I thought of Sebastian's letter.

"Do you remember the time we went to this restaurant with Sebastian?" I asked.

"The night he told us about his dream?"

"If it *was* a dream." I said. We both were silent, our thoughts moving back to the spring afternoon two months earlier, when Sebastian arrived at The Missing Link looking for our help.

Throughout that winter, Sebastian had come to the shop dozens of times. Often Helen and I joined him for dinner at the local restaurants or went upstairs to the workshop space to share a pizza and talk. Sebastian was a relentless pursuer of explanations. He always wanted to know *why*—whether the issue was science, history, politics, the paranormal or the spiritual. One late afternoon in May he came into The Missing Link looking overheated and a bit jumpy. As soon as he was alone in the store with Helen and me, he started talking rapidly.

"Remember the dreams I told you about, Will? They're back, but I'm not seeing past lives anymore. Now it's extraterrestrials, for God's sake! As soon as I drift off to sleep, I'm seeing little gray men and big blue ones. They blue ones are overwhelming and the gray ones are disgusting, and they both scare the hell out of me. I don't like this. I'm turning into an article in the *National Enquirer*. Helen, have you got any rocks in here for inducing amnesia? I don't think I want any more mystical memories."

Helen walked up to Sebastian and hugged him. Then she stood back and said, "Sebastian, you seem distressed."

He chuckled through clenched teeth, "That's a mild way of putting it."

"We're closing in about half an hour. Would you like to lie down upstairs in the workshop space until Will and I can come up and talk?"

"Lie down? No. I'm not in the mood for a nap. Wait for you? Okay. I can do that. Is there any beer up there?"

"Sorry, no. But we have herbal teas in the kitchen cupboard."

"Anything really powerful for calming? How about Thorazine Mint, or Valium Orange Spice?"

Helen smiled, "Why don't you try chamomile?"

Sebastian let out a long sigh. "Okay. Thanks, both of you. Now, just point me at the stairs." I gave him the key and he walked into the back room and up the stairs to the apartment.

At six, we closed the shop and went upstairs to see Sebastian. We found him sitting in an old, frayed easy chair by the window. We crossed the room and sat down together on the couch that was next to him.

I spoke first. "So, what's going on?"

"I don't really know. It's like I told you. I've started dreaming again, and feeling the vibrations as I'm going to sleep. But I'm not remembering past lives, or whatever I was seeing before. Now it feels like I'm me in this life, and I'm seeing ETs."

"What's happening in the dreams?" Helen asked.

"It's pretty disjointed, but it feels like some kind of memory from childhood, or a dream from back then. For the first couple of nights, I just saw faces—you know, the ones people call the Grays, with their bulbous heads and those enormous black eyes. But this week the dreams started becoming more detailed."

"Can you remember what happened in those?" I asked.

"Well, they've all been following the same pattern. The first thing I recall is that I can see bright lights on the walls of my bedroom, the bedroom I had in my parents house. I hear a low buzzing sound that kind of vibrates my body. Then I hear a soft scurrying in the hall and I get scared. 'They're coming,' I tell myself. I see shapes in the dark, like children. But they aren't children. It's the little gray ones. Next, one of them is standing over my bed, looking down at me. I try to yell but no sound comes out. I try to jump out of the bed, but I can't move. Usually that's when I've been waking up, but last night there was more. After the gray guy looked at me, I started to *float* up out of the bed, on my back, and I floated right through the closed window! Then the scene changed again and I was in a round white room on a table. There were more of the gray ones, and one of them stuck a needle up into my nose. It hurt, a lot, but I still couldn't make any sound."

I interrupted, "The pain didn't wake you up?"

"No, and I wondered about that later for another reason. But let me tell you the rest. After the gray guys finished poking and prodding me, I blacked out for a minute and then found myself standing in a corridor outside a doorway. Next the door sort of melted or dematerialized, and I could see inside the room in front of me. There was a chair or bench across the room, and sitting on it was another ET. But this guy was tall, and he was *blue!* And he was sort of glowing. I heard his voice in my mind telling me to come inside, and my feet just walked me in there. I was amazed, because I thought I wanted to take off in the other direction. Anyway, the next thing I noticed was a beam of blue-white light that must have been turned on from the ceiling. I was standing in it, and as soon as it hit me I was in total bliss. It was overwhelming, but it was weird, because part of my mind was watching this and saying, 'What's going on here? How is he doing this to me?' Most of me couldn't have cared less, as long as it didn't stop. I tried to speak to the blue guy, but all that would come out of my mouth was 'Ahhhh ...' That observer part of my mind tried to make me walk out of the blue-white beam, but my body was feeling so much pleasure that it just didn't want to move." Sebastian paused and looked down at his hands. He shook his head slowly, then lifted his mug of tea and took a drink.

Helen asked, "What happened then? Did you wake up?"

He shook his head again. "No, not just then. After a minute or so, the blue guy turned to look at me. His eyes seemed to have the same effect on me as the beam I was standing in. While he was looking at me, I felt like I would do anything for him. Then he opened those amazing eyes wider and *smiled* at me. I felt an even bigger wave of energy, and I must have blacked out, or whited out. It seemed as though I had disappeared and was just floating in an endless space. Then I felt like I wanted to rub my nose. It was itching and it hurt. And I remember thinking, 'How can my nose be itching? I don't even have a body.' The next thing I knew, I was in bed, holding my nose with my right hand. I looked at the clock and it was 4:23 AM. I turned on the light, and do you know what I saw?"

"Blood," Helen said.

"Yes. It was all over the pillowcase. I'd had one hell of a bloody nose. How did you know?"

"Your dream wouldn't have made you as nervous without that, would it?"

"No. It wouldn't have. But the blood makes me wonder if I was even dreaming, or if something happened." Sebastian held the mug in both hands and looked out the window. "I don't understand this. Personally, I think this ET stuff is for lunatics. Then again, maybe that's my problem. Maybe I should have taken the medication after all. At least I wouldn't be having these dreams, and I *would* have a fiancée." He sighed. "I've never told you how my mother died, have I?"

"I don't think so," I said. "It was quite a long time ago wasn't it?"

"It happened when I was seventeen. She killed herself in an asylum. My father had her committed because she had started hallucinating that she was getting messages from outer space. She told everyone that flying saucer people were here to save the earth and that they wanted her to help them. People thought she was crazy, of course, but she refused to stop talking about it. When my father put her in the asylum, she got paranoid. She kept saying that the FBI and the CIA were monitoring her, and that they were helping the people who wanted the planet to die."

"The poor woman," said Helen. "Did you visit her?"

"I did, on the weekends. And whenever I came, even in cold weather, she insisted we walk outside. Then she would tell me about the doctors being part of the conspiracy, and she kept saying that I knew that she was right, because I'd been *with* her in the saucer. I couldn't remember or believe anything like that, but whenever I came to see her she would calm down and sound almost rational. I guess I got used to it, because I started to feel like the situation was kind of weirdly normal. Then one weekend I went with my father to visit a college I was thinking of applying to, and that's when she did it."

"She committed suicide while you were away?" I asked.

"I guess I've always been afraid it was partly *because* I was away. I was the one person she still trusted. She never spoke to my father again after he had her committed. At the time, I was quite confused, and I was angry with him myself. I felt bad for her, being confined that way. But I was also upset with her for acting so crazy. I have to say, though, that she seemed to be getting better in her last weeks. One of the hospital nurses had a lawyer friend who she introduced to my mother, and he was starting to work on having her commitment overturned. She told me she was planning to write a book when she got out. Anyway, the weekend I went away, my mother apparently managed to get a bottle of some sedative, and she took the whole thing." Sebastian sighed, exhaling with a shudder that was almost a sob. "After that, I blamed my father even more than I blamed myself for her suicide, and I felt desperate to get away. I didn't want to have anything to do with him, so I abandoned my plans for college and joined the army as soon as I was eighteen. After I got out, I used government money and loans to put myself through college, but I never tried to contact my father. Since that all happened, I've been completely negative about the entire subject of UFOs and ETs. Maybe that's why these dreams are making me feel so crazy."

There was a silence. Finally Helen said, "Will, we have to share our story with Sebastian."

"What story?" I was puzzled for a moment before remembering. "Oh, that story, from Sedona ... Are you sure we should? I mean, it wasn't a dream."

"*What* wasn't a dream?" Sebastian inquired. "You're going to have to tell me now, whether you think you should or not." He shifted in the armchair and smiled wearily, "If it'll take my mind off my delusions, I'm ready for it."

"I don't think this will make you forget about your dreams, but it may still be of some help," said Helen. "This happened the winter before last, on a trip we took to Arizona. Will should tell you the first part of it."

"Okay," I said. "That winter, Helen and I decided to make a buying trip to the gem and mineral show in Tucson, Arizona. Our crystals and jewelry had been selling well in the store, and we wanted to find new suppliers. We finished our buying in three days, and our return plane tickets weren't scheduled for three more days, so we decided to do some vacationing. People we had met at the show told us Sedona was the place to go—that there was beautiful scenery and great energy. At the time, I was still skeptical about the 'energies' of places, but we decided to visit anyway. We drove north about five hours from Tucson, and we checked into a hotel. The next day, we asked some people about the energy 'vortexes' our friends had mentioned, and they suggested we go to Bell Rock. We drove there, through some stunning red-rock landscapes, and then we parked the car and started hiking up the rock, which is hundreds of feet high." Sebastian was listening intently, and some of the stress seemed to have gone out of his face. I felt encouraged as I continued.

"We climbed up about a third of the way. Helen was looking for a good spot to sit down and meditate, and she found what she wanted next to a big flat square rock. We set up a grid of Moldavite and crystals on the rock and sat beside it. Helen suggested that we meditate one at a time, with the other one there as a witness. We had a little tape recorder with us, in case we received any 'messages.' I took the first turn, lying down on my back with my eyes closed. Sebastian, I've already told you that I'm not the world's most avid or accomplished meditator, in spite of my one spectacular experience. Well, I was mostly just lying there with the rocks grinding into my back and my thoughts flitting around aimlessly. Then after a few minutes I relaxed enough to see some hypnogogic imagery—the kind of pictures you see in your mind just before you fall asleep. I almost dozed off, and then I seemed to wake up again, but I was still seeing imagery. The various pictures had resolved into one—a white whirlwind, a dust-devil looking thing that extended up from where I was to a white object. At first I thought, 'Oh, a cloud,' until I concentrated on it. As I did that, I could see that the outline was smooth and round, like the bottom of a ..."

"Flying saucer!" Sebastian interrupted. "Come on, Will. Say it ain't so!"

"Actually, that's what I was thinking to myself. After I met Helen, I learned to accept metaphysical things like Tarot, stone energies, meditation, and even spirit guides, a little. But I drew the line at UFOs. I had never seen one and I thought the people who claimed to were mostly lunatics, as you said. So when I saw one riding a white tornado in my meditation on Bell Rock, I mumbled something like, 'Oh, no, anything but this.' Helen asked what I was seeing, but I didn't answer. I was still watching the inner vision of the saucer, trying to stay with it despite my negative reaction. Finally, I imagined I heard a voice in my head, and it said, 'Send the other one up.' Then the mental picture of the ship just broke up, like a bad TV signal, and disappeared. I opened my eyes, turned to Helen and said, 'It's your turn.'"

"Did you tell her what you had seen and heard?"

"No. I think I was testing to see what she would experience, and I didn't want to influence her."

"Well, what happened?" Sebastian asked Helen.

"I lay back, closed my eyes, and went quickly into a deep meditation," Helen said. "The first thing I experienced were tingling sensations running through my body like waves moving. They went up from my toes and out the top of my head. After a few minutes, I could feel myself letting go of my body, and it seemed as though I had slipped out and was sitting on the ground about three feet behind my head. I looked down at myself, and then at the landscape. I could see the sky and clouds, the trees and the desert around us, and the mountains in the distance."

"How did you experience your sense of yourself?" Sebastian asked. "Did you feel like a point of consciousness, or did you have some sort of body?"

"I've felt it both ways in my meditations, but in this case I had an astral body. It looked the same as my physical body, only shimmering and transparent."

"You seem so matter-of-fact. Have you had a lot of out-of-body experiences?"

"Of this type, yes. I've meditated for almost twenty years, and moving into the astral body is a fairly common thing in meditation. But what happened next went beyond what I had known before."

Sebastian nodded, "Please continue."

"As I looked at my physical body and the surroundings, I felt my spirit expand and become very large, growing up and up, with my feet still on the mountain. I seemed to be standing, growing larger and larger until I was taller than the mountains. I had the sense of three bodies—the physical one lying on the ground, the astral one sitting beside the physical, and this immense, expanded body that towered over the place. In this body, I identified with the consciousness of a Guardian, a spirit of the land and sky. I felt timeless, viewing this place over many centuries, and seeing in its history a procession of space ships, coming there to receive the vortex energy as some kind of fuel. As I watched them, it seemed that somehow the ground opened beneath them and a kind of light poured up from the earth into the ships. As I watched, I was filled with calm and serenity, a sense of knowing the benevolent nature of the beings who traveled in them. Then suddenly I was swept up towards one of the ships, and as I approached, a curved panel on the underside appeared to dissolve and I was inside. The 'me' inside seemed to have a normal-sized body, although I don't remember looking at it, and as I stood in the corridor, I was confronted by a pair of blue beings, a male and female, who greeted me as an old friend. For a moment, we 'talked,' exchanging a torrent of telepathic images and feelings. It was as though we were catching up on each other after a separation. The other beings were emanating a blue-white light, and I saw that I was glowing with that light as well. In that moment, I was aware of myself as this glowing being, as the mountain Guardian spirit, as the astral body and as my physical self, all at the same time."

"You saw *blue* beings and a blue-white light? Are you sure of that, or are you trying to nudge me completely over the edge?" Sebastian gripped the frayed arms of the chair and leaned forward towards Helen as he spoke.

"This is what I saw," said Helen. "The story of your dream made me think of it. I am not trying to tell you what it means."

"Is there more? I want to hear it."

"There is this much more: In the next moment, I lost awareness of myself in the corridor and saw a panorama of scenes from other planets and other lives, pervaded with the sense that I was viewing my own history. I could see myself working for the spreading of the Light through many incarnations and on many worlds. I had the sense of remembering my first choosing to come to Earth, many lifetimes ago, and forgetting who I'd been before. I recall feeling an overwhelming compassion for the great need of the earth and its people, and also a longing for the unlimited freedom I had known before coming here." Helen paused. Her eyes glistened with tears. "It was so glorious out among the stars. I had forgotten. And underlying that feeling was a deep, deep yearning for the Presence that *is* the glory of the universe. In the next moment, I found myself back in the ship, sitting before a radiant blue being that I recognized as my teacher. As I sat, I was flooded with energy and realized that I was being given the next part of my mission for this life. As the energy continued to rush through me, I grew closer in communion with the being before me, and I saw a glowing ball of light form at his heart. It grew brighter and brighter and moved toward me, and then into my chest. Next I felt a sort of inner explosion and everything I was seeing disappeared into light. I felt not so much that I was in the light as that I *was* the Light. I knew nothing else for what seemed an endless time."

"Where were you during all this?" Sebastian asked me.

"Sitting right beside her, listening to her describe it all, holding the microphone of our tape recorder."

"Was that the end of the experience, Helen?"

"No. After some time, I noticed a question forming in my consciousness. It was, 'Why is the Earth so important that so many are trying so hard to save it?'"

"Did you get an answer?"

"Yes. And after that, I returned to my physical self, moving backwards through the chain of spiritual bodies I had been in. I felt the whole vision recede and fade, although the emotional impact stayed with me. "

"Well, what was the answer to your question?"

"It was rather long. Will recorded it and we transcribed it later."

"May I read it?"

"Yes, if you like. I have a copy of it in the files." Helen went downstairs to retrieve the transcript. When she returned, she handed it to Sebastian. He was silent as he read these words:

*As I look at the universe, or this section of the universe, I see the Earth is on the outer circle of how far the Light has spread, and we need the Earth to be of the Light to continue the expansion. The Earth is a pivotal point, and if it turned to the darkness it would be like a black hole, a self-devouring emptiness. But if it turned toward the Light, it would emanate a brilliant radiance that would bring the Light to much more of the universe. Once we humans begin to know that we are one in the Light, we will no longer be able to harm another, or the being that is this planet Earth. She is like someone who needs to rest and be nurtured and healed. She is purging, but to purge so much is weakening her. She needs all those on Earth who are Light workers to create a web of Light that will hold her steady—a grid of energy through which even more Light can be poured in from higher sources. Without these grids, and energy vortexes like this place where we are now, it is not possible to send enough healing Light to the Earth. It is important for those who understand to consciously draw the Light down into and around our planet.*

*Our only purpose in all of eternity is to be one with and in the Light. We must ever expand the Light in our individual beings, so that everything we are and do is of and for the Light. Each breath we take, if we are conscious, draws Light into our being. Every word we speak in consciousness sends Light into the world. When we focus attention on another person, we can open a channel which creates a uni-*

*fying connection, a filament of Light. And if that being responds in kind, there is a great brilliance. As the Master Jesus spoke, "When two or more of ye are gathered in my Name, there am I." I AM. Because when the two truly unify in consciousness, for even a moment, a connection is made which builds the web of Light. Every acknowledgement of the Lightwork makes that connection. Every person with whom we make this link becomes a part of the network, when we each acknowledge being of the Light and working for the Light. It does not have to be complex and wordy and flowery. A few words, a few sentences acknowledging the Light are all that is needed. And at times all that is required is a touch or a look or even just seeing someone clearly for an instant.*

*There is great responsibility and there is great joy in spreading the Light.*

Sebastian set the paper down and stroked his beard thoughtfully. "That's lovely, Helen. And I certainly see *your* attitude towards life in those words, wherever they came from. In regards to my dilemma, your story raises more questions than it answers, but the similarities do make me less inclined to check into the nearest mental hospital. Unless you'd like to join me."

"No thanks," said Helen.

"Anyway," I added, "Goethe said that the earth is the insane asylum of the universe. What's the point of locking yourself up?"

"Touché. And besides that, I despise institutional food. Speaking of which, would the two of you consider submitting to more of my queries if I offered to ply you with pasta? You choose the restaurant. I'll pay."

We walked to our favorite Italian place, at the local waterfront, about ten blocks from the shop. The early evening was warm, and the sun was nearing the horizon. As we walked, we talked of the mundane events of the day, laughing and joking together, stopping to take in the fragrance of the blooming lilac bushes. Approaching the docks where the fishing boats were moored, we could hear the cries of the gulls and smell the salty air. We all agreed that we were hungry. I felt relaxed and happy, and I was glad that Sebastian seemed to have released the tension that had gripped him, but I wondered what his questions would be. After hearing his story and comparing it to Helen's, I had questions of my own.

We were well into our *pasta prima vera* before Sebastian picked up the thread of our previous conversation. He was on his second glass of wine, and I had thought he was going to let the matter rest. But he suddenly set down his fork with a clang on the edge of his plate and looked directly at Helen. "Was it real, Helen?"

She replied immediately, as though she had been waiting for his question, "What do you mean by 'real'?"

"Authentic, valid, actual, a true experience. Did you, and I, for that matter, communicate with genuine physical entities, or were we just imagining things?"

"I don't think I can answer that as an either/or question. To me, the experience I had was absolutely real. It was more genuine than most of my everyday life. It affected me deeply on an emotional level. It opened up what felt like memories of forgotten parts of my identity. It connected me with the Light at the source of my being. It even gave me an answer to my question. How real do you want it to be?"

Sebastian took a sip of his wine. "I understand what you're saying, Helen, but look—I woke up in my bed and my experience disappeared. You were lying down meditating on a mountain side. If you had opened your eyes, your vision would have vanished, too."

"I wonder," mused Helen.

"It didn't," I said.

"What?" they both asked, looking at me.

"Helen opened her eyes during her meditation, as she was describing the experience of being in the Light, and recounting the answer to her question."

"I did?"

"Yes, and you were gazing intently at something that I couldn't see. I was holding the microphone right in front of you and you didn't seem to notice it at all."

"It still doesn't solve my reality question," said Sebastian. He drank the last of his wine and put the glass on the table. "It leaves us both hallucinating, as far as I can tell."

"I've been thinking about that," I said. "The problem here might be the question of whether 'real' and 'physical' are the same thing. Take the experiences of shamans, for example. Ask them and they'll tell you that they walk between the worlds, and some will say, as Helen did, that the inner worlds are more real to them than this table where we're sitting. If an anthropologist observes a shamanic healing session, he may see the healer go into trance as he travels the inner domains. The body of the shaman goes nowhere, but the occupant of that body, when he returns, will tell the anthropologist of the journey he undertook to return the missing soul parts of the patient. If the patient gets well, doesn't that corroborate the shaman's story?"

"It could be the placebo effect," Sebastian said.

"Yes, but what *is* the placebo effect?" Helen asked. "It might be that the same aspect of spirit used by the shaman to enlist the healing power of his patient is also evoked, unwittingly, by the doctor who encourages *his* patient to believe a sugar pill will make him well. Affirmations, and also visualizations, work that way. It's our power of creation."

"So I could have imagined my whole trip with the gray guys and the blue being, and the blue-white light. And it could *also* be real at the same time? Is that what you're saying?"

"Maybe I am. I'm not even sure I believe that imagination is 'only imaginary,'" Helen replied. "Einstein said, 'Imagination is more important than knowledge.' Perhaps he meant that imagination is the creative edge where our perceptions are shaped. Regarding your experience, I could say that the whole thing was as real as the source of your nosebleed, some kind of crossover from another level of experience to the material one. Or as 'unreal' as the picture of the physical world that your brain generates from the data of your senses. Or considerably more real than the abstraction called 'money' that you will be using to pay for this meal. For which I thank you," she smiled. "The truth is, I don't know, Sebastian. But I was very interested to hear about your 'dream.' That reminds me, I think John Lennon said words to the effect that, 'The dream you dream alone is just a dream, but the dream we dream together is reality.' I believe there's something to that. If, as half the books in our store say, we, at some level, create our own reality, then there may be a multiplying effect when members of a group affirm and reaffirm the same picture back and forth to each other. That may be the main difference between the individual journey of the dreamer and the consensus reality we all agree to call the world."

"Could this relate to the quote from Jesus that came through to you on Bell Rock?" I asked. "'Wherever two or more of you are gathered in My name, there am I.' Couldn't that be referring to the conjuring power of shared beliefs?"

"It could be that," said Helen. "But for me it refers to the idea that the Christ consciousness, which is love, exists in relationship. When people gather or make a connection in the name of love, His consciousness is there."

"Okay, okay. I give," said Sebastian. "I just want to know, when two people like Helen and myself have inner visions of the same basic story, have we co-created the same imaginary world, or have we both stumbled into the same independently existing actuality?"

"That's a good question for all the UFO abductees," I said.

"And the Tibetan Buddhist lamas," said Helen.

"The quantum physicists are probably scratching their heads over that one." I said.

Sebastian yanked at his hair in mock agony. "Stop, stop!"

Helen laughed, "But we're just trying to tell you—"

"We ... don't ... know," I said.

Then Helen grew serious. "It's part of a great mystery. Something is going on, and we don't know what it is. We all decide what to take in and what to discard. I judge ideas and experiences by the responses of my heart and emotions. The images I see may or may not be illusions, but the feelings I have are real, to me."

"Well, *somebody* ought to figure all this out," Sebastian grumbled as we got up to leave.

"There's just the guy to do it," I said, pointing across the restaurant dining room.

"Where?" said Sebastian, and looking in the direction I was pointing, he caught sight of his reflection in the mirror.

For three weeks we saw nothing of Sebastian. The store was busy and we were involved in preparing to set up a stone and jewelry booth for the local waterfront festival. On the Friday before it began, just as we were getting ready to close for the day, a big RV pulled up and parked in front of the store. The driver started beeping the horn.

I called out to Helen, "Looks like a last-minute customer. Do you suppose our truck-driver friend with the spirit guides is on vacation?"

"We'll see," she answered, coming out from her desk in the office that adjoined the store's back room. "Whoever it is, I hope they don't take too long. There's a lot to do at home and we still have to set up the booth tomorrow morning at seven."

As we went outside, we heard the driver's door slam, and walking around the front of the RV came Sebastian. "Hey, you two. How'd you like to take a spin in my new home, a luxurious residential chariot which I have impatiently named *RV There Yet?*"

We quickly locked the store and got in. The RV glided away from the curb as Sebastian steered a course that took us on a circular tour of the town. He explained that he had received a call offering him a job teaching computer training seminars in a dozen cities in the desert Southwest and Rocky Mountain states. "They were going to pay all my airfares and hotel bills, which would have added up to more than the down payment on this slightly used mobile mansion, so I asked for the cash instead. The rent on my

apartment, which I have now vacated, was more than the monthly install-
ments, and I talked the software company into throwing in gas money. The
seminars are only on weekends, so there's plenty of time for me to drive from
one site to the next. And when I'm finished teaching I'm heading straight
for Sedona, to check out the reality of our shared hallucinations. After that,
it's parts unknown. It is my intention to put some *psi* into science, or failing
that, to debunk myself. The point is, once I get paid for this teaching gig, I'll
have enough money to spend the rest of this year doing what I want, and I've
decided to take on that job you gave me, Will."

"What job?"

"Figuring out what's going on with all this—" he made a sweeping gesture with one hand while holding the  steering wheel with the other. "My
dreams, Helen's meditation experience, the ETs, the stone energies and the
whole phenomenon of spirituality that's keeping stores like yours in business.
I'm back to the same question: Are these things real, or just wishful thinking?"

"But why can't—" Helen began.

"Don't take me there, Helen. I know you think we can have it both ways
at once, but you're horning-in on my dilemma. I'm a materialist scientist by
education and a mystical dreamer by accident. I'm not sure that there's room
for both of these guys in the same brain. We may be heading for a shootout
at the 'I'm OK, You're OK Corral.' So before my personalities split and I end
up at my mother's *alma mater,* I want to have a tilt at these metaphysical
windmills. I'll check in from time to time and let you know how, and what,
I'm doing."

"Why did you decide to attempt this on the road instead of going to the
library and studying?" I asked.

"To quote the fictitious guru Bokonon, who maintained that his entire
religion was made up of harmless lies, 'Unusual travel suggestions are dancing lessons from God.'"

"*Cats Cradle,* by Vonnegut, right?"

"Give that man a gold star," said Sebastian. "The whole journey is part
of my research. If synchronicity is for real, it ought to lead me exactly where
I need to go. If it's not, my boredom will be evidence of the meaningless ran-
domness of existence."

"I'm pulling for synchronicity," I said.

"Me too," said Helen.

"And look, fortuitously, if not by chance, we've come to the exact place
where you needed to go—we're back at the shop."

"When will you leave?" Helen asked.

"In the morning. My first job is in Denver next weekend." Sebastian stopped the RV at the curb. Helen and I hugged him as we said our farewells. That was our last contact until the arrival of the letter.

# — 4 —

Helen and I were still in the back room finishing lunch when the bells on the front door jingled again. The afternoon in the shop was as busy as the morning, so at the end of the day we brought Sebastian's letter home with us. Helen went upstairs for a shower while I made a big salad for dinner. We had agreed to read the letter together afterwards. Our rented house had a back porch deck looking out over the tidal river which divided the town. We took our bowls outside and sat in a pair of old white wicker chairs. The summer evening was cool and pleasant, and the setting sun lit the water and the trees with a golden glow. As we ate, we talked of the day's events at the shop. Afterwards we sat quietly for a while, listening to the soft drone of boats coming home from the day's outings.

I turned to Helen, "Well, are you ready to open Pandora's box?"

"Why do you call it that?"

"I'm not sure, but I've been on pins and needles about Sebastian's letter all day."

"I think you worry too much."

"I don't worry. I think ahead."

"About every possible disaster."

"And there are so *many* possibilities."

Helen jabbed me in the ribs. "Cut it out, for Heaven's sake," she said. "Do you remember what the last thing that came out of Pandora's box was, after war, hunger, fear and all those other dreadful qualities emerged?"

"Um ... tardiness? Ouch! Stop poking me. That's the spot where Eve came from, and we men have been vulnerable there ever since."

"It's Hope. The last thing in the box was Hope, you goof."

"Well, I *hope* you'll stop doing that long enough for me to get the letter and open it."

She smiled, "Since I want to read it too, I guess I'll have to. But let's go inside. It's getting dark."

We carried our bowls into the kitchen and left them in the sink. Helen retrieved the envelope from the counter top and took it into the living room. I followed and sat down beside her as she tore it open. Snuggled close on the sofa, we read together:

Dear Will and Helen,

Greetings from Sedona, crossroads of the Universe! Land of regal red rocks and scampering scorpions. Home on the range to Wranglers in Reeboks driving hot pink Cherokees (Jeeps, that is) full of sunburned seekers to the venerable vortexes. (Or is it vortices?) Sedona—the only town in Arizona with 112 *channels* and no TV station. This place imports so many spiritual tourists that the town motto is "There's a seeker born every minute." Was it like this when you were here? It's a mystical Mecca—just having been here lends one a certain reek of borrowed glory. Now, don't be offended. I know you like this place. Forgive me. You know how I go on.

But seriously folks, hi. I finished my seminars about ten days ago, and the soupy plot of my paranormal investigations is already beginning to thicken. I've started traveling to as many hotbeds of metaphysical repute as I can find. Testing your theories, one might say. And what's happened is as ambiguous as the upshot of all our discussions. Anyway, here goes.

Driving out here in my home on wheels, I decided to become a Tarot reader. In fact, I AM a Tarot reader. (Blame yourself, Helen, for giving me that deck of cards.) I started by practicing on myself, using the book I borrowed from you as a reference. Now, just for demonstration purposes, I'll ask a question and do a spread. "What do I need to know now about the journey I am on?"

Interesting ... The center is the ten of Pentacles, covered by the seven of Cups and crossed by the reversed five of Wands. The foundation is the reversed Page of Pentacles, the recent past is the three of Wands, the sky card is Temperance and the near future is the Page of Cups. The self card is the four of Wands, the environment card is Death, the hopes and fears card is the nine of Pentacles and the outcome cards are the nine of Wands and the Sun.

So what does it all mean? Well, here goes the novice who knows all. The ten of Pentacles at the center says I'm at a crossroads, and which way I'm going is anybody's guess. I mean, look at that card. There are four people and two dogs on it and the only ones looking in the same direction are the two dogs! And *they're* sniffing around some odd-looking old geezer in a coat of many colors. I had to cheat and look this one up in the book. It says that the pentacles are arranged in the form of the Kabbalah Tree of Life, indicating the card signifies a magical moment of which one's everyday conscious self may be unaware. The dogs, symbolizing the unconscious self, are the only ones who notice the old hermit/magician seated beside the gate. So I'm supposed to pay attention to hunches and feelings if I want to find the magic. Got all that?

The seven of Cups shows a bunch of weird illusions appearing before an astonished witness—me, I suppose—and the advice is to attempt to see beyond appearances to the real source of their creation. I can imagine that reinforcing the idea from the first card that I'm standing obliviously at an important turning point, looking in the wrong direction. Hey, that's insulting! If I want to be insulted, I'll go out in public. Darned these smart-alec Tarot cards anyway!

Oh, well, onward and upward. The reversed five of Wands tells me there's some kind of inner struggle blocking my vision, and that mania won't cure my myopia. Hold on. I'm getting a helpful message from my spirit guide, Al: "Cool calmness clears constipated consciousness." Crude but to the point, that's Al Literation. Wait, don't set fire to this letter! I'll be good, I promise.

All right, no more digressions. The Page of Pentacles reversed at the bottom tells me I've been playing hooky from what most people call "real life," including such considerations as money, security, and a home that can't be towed away. No surprises there. The recent past card shows that I've stopped watching my ships sail off without me. For better or worse, that time is over, and now I'm on board, sink or swim. Temperance in the sky position shows an angel of harmony and balance overseeing everything that's going on in my life, whether I know it or not. I guess it's nice to be blessed, but it's even better when you notice it. In the near future, the Page of Cups suggests I'm in for some pleasant surprises in the realm of emotions and/or spirituality, but that I'll feel like a beginner. (I think this may refer to Madeline, a woman I met here—more about her later.)

In the self position, the four of Wands shows me coming from behind castle walls, putting myself vulnerably out in the open. Could this have to do with my fearless plunge into the metaphysical madhouse of Sedona? If so, the portents are positive—everybody on this card looks happy.

The environment card ... uh oh. It's Death. And just when I was starting to have a good time. I ask you, why does the Grim Reaper always show up at inconvenient moments? It's like the way the phone always rings when you're in the bathtub. So what could this mean, Death in my environment? Am I in peril from some invisible threat, or is my presence dangerous to others? Well, don't worry about me—just be glad we're on opposite sides of the country. Do you think I should mention this when I meet people? "Oh, hello. My name is Sebastian, and this menacing presence over my left shoulder is Death. What? Do you really have to leave so soon?" No, I don't think this is going to help my popularity.

Well, the hopes and fears card is the nine of Pentacles, and it shows a very wealthy woman with a hooded falcon on her wrist. This must be a sign of my sublimated hope that discovering the keys to the kingdom of consciousness will make me wealthy as well as wise. Or perhaps it shows my sublimated fear that worldly success will hood the hawk of my inner freedom. Ouch, that one rings more true. Oh well, no danger of wealth sneaking up on me out here in the desert. My freedom is safe for now.

At last we come upon the outcome cards, and you couldn't find two more opposite ones. The nine of Wands shows a man who has been wounded, perhaps from acting irresponsibly in relation to the Wands energies of creative spiritual fire, and now he's a bit leery of them. He stands there peering out from under his bandage, as if wondering whether he should have stayed home and done laundry rather than entangling himself with such uncontrollable forces. Could this be me in a few days or weeks? Such ideas can drain the starch right out of one's resolve. But never fear! (That's what I would say if this were someone *else's* reading.) The final outcome is the Sun, a good omen if there ever was one. Old Sol fills the sky with warm rays, and sunflowers echo his blessings here on earth. A child sits naked on a white horse, arms opened wide in joy. Well, I promise not to show up at your house looking like that, but I won't complain if I start feeling that way. You know, now that I think about it, those two outcome cards fit together pretty well. I've read that one's first encounters with  spiritual energies may be more disturbing than enjoyable. That certainly fits my ET memories! But I've also read that the gods enter us through our wounds. (As Yeats wrote, "Nothing can be soul or whole, that has not been rent.") So in that scenario the Sun card goes well following that wounded guy. I guess one needs a hole in the head for the light to enter. If that's true, I'm well equipped.

Where do we go from here? I guess I'll just have to keep on and wait for the next installment in the serial. (Hey, did you know that those little elves, Snap, Crackle and Pop are dead? Yeah, murdered. They think it was a cereal killer. And he did it for Kix.)

So how'd I do? I think I said, and saw, more than I intended, but the cards are constantly tripping me up that way. If I don't want to know, I shouldn't ask, right? It's eerie, and exciting, how they always seem to make sense, and often answer a question more deeply than it was asked. Of course, perhaps the Tarot is nothing more than a suggestive blank slate, an ink blot pattern for the projections of my feral mind. On the other hand, if everything in the universe is connected to everything else, then looking at any part will give one information about any and all other parts ... if you know how to look. You could probably do it with chicken entrails, though it would be harder since chicken entrails don't come with hand-books for interpretation. And they're so messy. (Has the chicken industry thought of this? How much would they pay me for the idea? Seeing the future in your giblets beats the heck out of yanking on a wishbone.)

Einstein insisted that God doesn't play dice with the universe.

Quantum physics tells us that God does play dice with the universe, but He uses loaded dice.

Just so long as God doesn't get loaded and dice the universe. At least not while I'm in it.

But none of this quite addresses the *purpose* of this missive, which is the News of the Cosmos as Gleaned from the Crosscurrents of Consciousness in Sedona.

You both know that I came out here to take a plunge into the roiling pool of Mystical Experience and Holy Hogwash that makes Sedona the destination of choice for millions of metaphysical maniacs. After all, I'm a scientist studying to be a high priest—where else would I go? So I'm read-ing the newspapers and chatting with people in the bookstores and going to all the free workshops. This I can tell you. Earth changes are big, very big. It's almost redundant here to say that California is destined to sink beneath the waves of the Pacific. We're way beyond that. A guy told me yesterday that he's looking for investors to buy up stretches of Nevada desert to sell as beach front property. But wait, there's more. Bookstores are selling maps of the "Future North America," in which the Mississippi River is a saltwater channel over fifty miles wide, and there's a fjord that stretches from the West Coast almost to Denver. Some say this will be accomplished by garden variety floods and earthquakes, and others expect a pole shift, in which the earth will do a back flip, reversing the north and south poles, and causing a great deal of sloshing of the oceans. Either way, the apocalyptic consensus is that about eighty percent of the population will get killed off, leaving the rest of us to rebuild the world as a Planet of Light. Well, that should at least take care of overpopulation and pollution for a while. I haven't met anyone saying this who expects to be in the unfortunate eighty percent, but perhaps forewarned is forearmed. Speaking of which, once my Granola-of-the-Month Club deliveries are interrupted by the demise of civilization, should I have a basement full of guns and food, or should I have stocked up on crystals, essential oils and homeopathic remedies? It depends upon whom one asks. But I'll say this, I'd rather be marooned on a purged planet with the crystal crowd any day. The survivalists have that lean and hungry look, and I'm afraid they might see my community value in the form of protein, during the hardships of that first long winter after the End of Life As We Knew It. I trust your tribe will be among the saved, and that if I can crawl to your cave, you'll take me in. I'm no bodyguard, but I'd make a good human shield, and I can cook a little.

It's hard to find anyone in Sedona who's from Earth. I've met ETs, walk-ins, angels in human form, mediums, channels and shamans. In fairness, some of these people do claim Earth as their home, if only temporarily, but others don't even claim their bodies. I talked to a woman teaching one of the free workshops who claimed to be a "drop-in." That's a walk-in who only stays in the body for one to three months. Then she leaves and another one takes over. Every change means a new name for the body/person hosting this revolving door of consciousness. Right now she's Selena. Last winter she was Anara. (A lot of these names seem to end in "a". Maybe Latin isn't a dead language on the higher planes.) I asked her if her body felt like a motel, but she misunderstood me and thought I was asking her to go to a motel. She declined my ungiven invitation and told me that entities on the higher planes don't engage in sex. Well, that explains why I'm still here on Earth.

Now please don't get offended. I know I'm really heaping on the ridicule, but I just can't help it. It's like a carnival. There are self-styled extraterrestrials roaming the streets with glitter on their faces. (Stuff like this makes my own dream experience even more uncomfortable to contemplate.) I sat down on a bench outside one of the shops and asked my Tarot cards to help me understand the nature of this place. The card I drew was the seven of Cups—Illusions. As I mentioned in my reading, it shows a figure (me) confronting seven chalices floating on a veil of mist. Emerging from each chalice is the image of some desire or fear, but none are real. Yes, Helen, I remember when you told me about this card in Will's first reading—that it urges one to look beyond the illusions to the deeper reality behind them. So I asked what is behind the veil of the Sedona carnival and drew another card: The Star—Enlightenment.

How annoying! Just when I was ready to hop into *RV There Yet* and declare this experiment a failure, I drew that maddening card. Now I had to stay and try to see what, if anything, of value was behind all those absurd and entertaining visions. But I knew I couldn't wait for Enlightenment more than another twenty-four hours, so I decided to just try the next thing that came up. While I was sitting there a gust of wind blew my newspaper off the bench and sent it flying in pieces down the sidewalk. I went to retrieve it, and on the last sheet I noticed an ad for a Dr. Jordan, who was giving a talk on Government Abductions of ET Abduction Survivors. That didn't look much like Enlightenment to me, but I decided I had made my commitment and I had to keep it. At 8:00 PM sharp I was there.

But the Doctor wasn't. About twenty people gradually gathered at the hotel conference room where the talk was to be given, but no Dr. Jordan. I started chatting with some of the other folks, steering clear of two glitter-faced aliens and a woman wearing a multicolored chiffon dress and a tiara. At about twenty past eight, the man on my right, with whom I had been sharing my somewhat cynical views, glanced at his watch, mumbled about a yoga class and left rather quickly. I looked to my left past an empty seat at a pleasant-looking sandy-haired woman whom I seemed to recognize. After a moment I realized I had seen her working at a local health food store. She smiled, acknowledging that she remembered me too, so I started talking. I'll attempt to recollect the conversation for you.

"Do you think the Doctor has been abducted?" I queried.

"It's always possible."

"By the aliens or the government?"

"Given that choice, I'd prefer aliens."

"So would most taxpayers."

She smiled again. Nice. No makeup. Lots of teeth. "I met Dr. Jordan in the store where I work and over the last few months we've become friends. I even do some work for him, helping with his writing. I think his main interest is in the people who have had contact with aliens—helping them remember and come to terms with their experiences—but he's run into evidence about the involvement of the government, certain parts of it anyway."

"And what is their interest supposed to be?"

"That's something of an enigma, but the interest is definitely real. There are thousands of classified government documents about UFOs and their occupants, and even when people access them through the Freedom of Information Act, they come out heavily censored. Dr. Jordan says the government probably knows a lot about the ETs, but that they don't admit it because they're not in control of the situation."

"What do you mean by that?"

"In Dr. Jordan's view, the ETs may not be physical beings in the way we are—it's as though they're interdimensional. According to many reports, they seem able to appear virtually out of thin air, wherever and whenever they want. They can move through material objects like windows and doors without opening them. They can immobilize people and abduct them, and apparently track them down if they move or travel. When people are abducted and examined, the ETs can block their memories of what happened, although some can be recovered through hypnosis. Wherever they come from, these entities seem to be able to operate here in whatever ways they choose, and the government, even though it's been studying them for fifty years, can't stop them, or even anticipate their next move."

(I admit that this conversation was starting to make my nose itch, but I held back my own experiences and continued with the journalistic approach.) "And is this Dr. Jordan's analysis you're giving me?" I asked.

"One of several, actually. He says it's also possible that the government has been dealing with the ETs, trading cooperation for technology. In that scenario the secrecy is in place for military purposes. But that was one of his early theories. I don't really go along with it."

"What theory *do* you go along with?"

"The one he's writing about now, for his next book. I've been reviewing some of it for him on my computer at home. He likes to get the perspective of people who have personal experience with what he is writing about. I'm a pretty good proofreader, and I was very excited at the prospect of being the first person to read his new book."

"So, tell me about it."

"Dr. Jordan has been correlating the patterns of UFO abductee experiences, looking for similarities, and trying to guess what the agenda of the Visitors might be. There's a lot of contradictory evidence, but I think he's coming to the conclusion that they are trying to help us grow, seeding our evolution. Many of the abductees are getting that message, one way and another. Dr. Jordan says that the myths and stories of cultures all over the world are full of references to 'gods' and other beneficial beings which could easily turn out to be the ETs."

"But if helping us evolve is their agenda, why does he think the government would want to keep everything secret?"

"He doesn't know for sure, but I remember him saying that governments are in the business of control and security, and a real evolutionary leap might make the masses of people uncontrollable."

"Like the ETs themselves."

"Exactly. So he thinks some arm of the government, possibly the CIA, has been kidnapping UFO contactees and interrogating them, maybe drugging some of them, trying to find out what effects the Visitors' evolutionary efforts are having. He believes their goal is to hold back any breakthrough, so the power structure will stay the way it is. Dr. Jordan says the official ridicule of UFO stories has served to keep a lot of people quiet and to conceal the government's own interest in them."

"Well, I wouldn't put it past them. I've read a lot of conspiracy theories, and I'm convinced at least *some* of them are true. Do you think your friend Dr. Jordan is about to crack the case?"

"I don't know. But I know the ETs are real."

"How do you know that?"

"I've been taken by them at least ten times since I was six years old."

(I again felt a strong urge to confess my own recollections, but I held back. Maybe I was embarrassed, and anyway, I had only just met this woman. I went on with my questions.) "Uh, what's that like? I mean, do they scare you? Do they stick implants up your nose?"

"I don't have any memories like that. The experiences I've had are all spiritual. They're more in line with what Dr. Jordan calls 'seeding our evolution.' I think the ETs, whoever they are, are trying to help us find enlightenment."

That word again, from the Star card. And shades of the blue guy with that nifty spotlight. I had a little shiver of recognition. "Do you think they'll succeed?"

"I think enlightenment will succeed."

A burning question raced through my mind: "What's your name?"

"Madeline."

"I'm Sebastian. Do you think Dr. Jordan is still on his way here?"

"I'm not sure, but I doubt it. He's rarely late, although I've known him to miss appointments completely once or twice when he gets really involved in his work."

"Well, what are you doing after the lecture doesn't happen?"

"Climbing Bell Rock. There's a full moon. Want to come along?"

What else could I do? Synchronicity had struck.

We took separate cars and it was after nine o'clock when we reached the parking lot. Bell Rock loomed before us, frosted with the light of the full moon. Madeline got out of her car and led me quickly through the cedars and junipers, up to the base. I remembered from hearing your story that Bell Rock is one of the landmarks of the Sedona area, and it was starkly impressive—a tower of red rock sitting on a hummock of more red rock. If you squint your eyes and use your imagination, I guess it looks a little like a bell. Anyway, Madeline skipped up the paths like a mountain goat, with yours truly puffing along behind. After twenty or thirty minutes of increasingly difficult climbing, she stopped and sat down on a ledge that overlooked the landscape below. I sat beside her and gazed back towards the road. Our cars in the lot looked very tiny, and I was feeling a bit acrophobic.

"Watch out!" she said, lurching over my lap. She brushed something next to me off the ledge in a shower of gravel. "Scorpion."

I admit I jumped, but at least I didn't scream. "Oh, sure. That's what I always say when I want to lunge over someone's lap. Why didn't you mention that those things were running loose out here?"

"It slipped my mind. Look at that beautiful moon."

I looked. We sat for a while, just taking everything in and breathing the cool night air. Suddenly I saw two white lights coming over the horizon. "Look! Is that a space ship?"

"No," she said. "I would say that's a truck coming down the highway."

"Aw, you're no fun."

"Let's do a little meditation while we're here. We can just close our eyes and listen to our breath. And we can visualize ourselves surrounded in a cocoon of white light."

"Okay. I'll go for the cocoon. Should we sit any special way?"

"Just be comfortable."

That was the end of our conversation. She closed her eyes and started breathing deeply. Her legs were folded up and her hands were on her knees, the thumb and forefinger of each hand forming a little circle. I decided to try to sit the same way, but after a couple of minutes my knees ached, so I dangled my legs over the ledge and put my hands in my lap. I started to breathe deeply and slowly, matching my breathing to hers, and as I began to relax I tried to visualize myself sitting there with white light all around me.

My mind decided to bring up every stray thought and petty anxiety it could possibly imagine. I kept thinking I heard scorpions sneaking up on me, so I opened my eyes every few minutes, just to let them know I wasn't asleep. I tried to remember if I had locked the car. I imagined myself twisting an ankle on the way back down the trail. I wondered about Madeline's UFO experiences, and whether I was sitting here on a cliff under the full moon with a lunatic. Umm, oh yes, I mean a *fellow* lunatic. Every so often I would remember to meditate and I would start following my breathing and trying to imagine the cocoon of light.

Then something changed, and I can't say when it happened, because what happened was I stopped thinking. I sort of *became* my breathing, and I blended with Madeline's breathing, too. It was very pleasant, and very easy. For a while, all I knew was the sound and rhythm of our breathing, and somehow that sound and rhythm was me. Then I felt light inside my eyelids. I nearly opened my eyes to see where it was coming from, until I realized that the light was inside my head, not outside. As I paid attention to it, it became brighter. My breathing started getting deeper and a bit faster. Madeline's breath seemed to match mine, as soon as it changed. The light inside my eyelids grew brighter, and the pleasant feeling got stronger. I gave myself over to the light and to the rhythm of breathing. Then I started to feel a tingling at the top of my head— it moved downwards and merged with the light inside my eyelids, and continued down my spine until I was vibrating all the way to my tail bone. I felt rooted into the ground and charged with electricity.

Next, I could see myself sitting there with light all around me, beside Madeline, who also sat in a pool of light. There was even a connection between us where the light seemed to be pulsing and moving back and forth as we breathed. Right about then my thinking kicked back in and I got scared because I thought that if I could see my body it meant that I wasn't in it. Immediately I was back inside my body with a jolt, and I was thinking a mile a minute: "What *was* that? How did I do that? Did *she* do that to me? Are there ETs out here ready to abduct me? etc., etc." Of course, the thinking spelled the end of my paranormal experience, but I was excited about it anyway. I wanted to talk to Madeline and find out if she felt it too. As my thoughts raced, my breath went back to normal and the light in my head ebbed away.

After a few minutes I opened my eyes and shifted my legs around. I yawned and otherwise tried to subtly convey that I was back in my body and getting a little restless. Finally Madeline let out a long sigh and opened her eyes. "Hi."

"What was that? How did we do that? Did you feel that? Can you do that all the time?"

"I would say that we kindled our light, by breathing together and letting go. The power of this place makes it easier. I used to meditate a lot, but I had never had this type of experience. After I moved to Sedona and met Dr. Jordan, he showed me the vortex spots and brought me up here. He told me that one of the abductees he interviewed a few years ago, a woman from England, claimed to have been given instructions by the Visitors to come to Sedona and sit for a day at each of the energy vortexes. She said they used her body to ground higher vibrations into the earth, and that meditations done at those places would become exceptionally powerful. After she went back to England, Dr. Jordan visited the locations, and he maintained that he could feel a difference, especially here at Bell Rock. My first experience of the light cocoon came when I sat here with him. He suggested that I do this with others whenever it feels appropriate, and that his English interviewee told him the experiences will become stronger as more and more people have them."

I meant to ask more questions, but some sticky thread of ego got tangled in my web of thought, and instead I asked, "So you mean ... I'm not the first guy you've ... breathed with?"

She looked startled and then laughed. "Actually, except for Dr. Jordan, you are. The others were all women. Not that it matters." I sat silent and wondered if she could see my face turning red in the moonlight. Then she said, "We'd better be going back. It's getting late." We slid off the ledge and hiked back to the cars. When we arrived she unlocked her door and then came over to me. "It was nice meditating with you, Sebastian. If you liked it, I'd suggest giving it some practice on your own. And try it with others, too. Now, how about a hug good night?" It was a nice hug, not a bit sexy, but very warm. Then she said, "See ya'," jumped behind the wheel and was gone. I stood beside my rental car, watching the moon and listening to the chirping of the scorpions. I tried some deep breathing, but my thoughts and I remained inseparable. The magic was over, but I imagined that my aura was still tingling. Right over the pinnacle of Bell Rock, a single star hung huge in the clear desert sky. Then I remembered—the Star card, Enlightenment. Well, I'd had a taste of it. I slid into the car and drove back to the RV.

I should have gone to bed, but I was restless. I hate to admit it, but I felt as though there was *energy* surging through me. It made me jumpy, even though I felt happy. I tried to read more in the Tarot book, but I couldn't concentrate on it. I made myself a peanut butter and banana and sprouts sandwich and a cup of hot chocolate. That helped a little, but I was still wide awake. I thought about calling you two, but decided it was best to let sleeping lovebirds lie, or perch, or whatever. Finally, I elected to soothe my nervous neurons by composing this manic missive. I don't know what I'll be doing tomorrow, or next week, but once I've done it, I'll let you in on it. Until then, keep holding the fort. You never know when we might need one.

     Yours in giddy uncertainty,
     Sebastian

I turned to Helen. "What do you think of that?"

She furrowed her brow. "I just don't see how he could enjoy eating peanut butter with bananas and sprouts. Ouch! Hey, I'm supposed to do the rib-jabbing around here."

"You shouldn't tease a man who's hungry for answers. Is that the only part of his letter that interests you?"

"It all interests me, especially the way Sebastian is following the synchronicities. If he keeps doing that, I think he'll be learning a lot more than he expects."

"What about his experience on Bell Rock?"

"I'm certain it was very real. Just as ours was." She looked into my eyes and smiled. "You're still not sure, are you?"

"Well, I'm sure we had the experience, but I don't know how to classify it. I guess I want to be able to find the right mental pigeonhole to put it in, so I can feel comfortable thinking about it."

Helen smiled again and tugged on my sleeve. "Pigeonholes are for pigeons. Come on. Let's go to bed."

# — 5 —

The next morning, we drove to the store together an hour early, planning to do some cleaning and get a head start on the day. The golden sunshine was brilliant on the green lawns, white houses and multicolored flower beds we passed along the streets of our little town. A sea breeze brought in the fresh, salty ocean air, and we heard the rumble of fishing boats getting under way as we drove past the downtown docks. Helen turned to me and said, "I need carrot juice, and a muffin."

"Your command is my wish." I drove up a side street and parked in front of the local health food cafe and bakery, Leaven on Earth. We walked through the door and into a cloud of rich aromas—fresh hot bread, blueberry muffins, oatmeal cookies, coffee and fried potatoes. As my mouth watered, I felt my resolve to clean the shop beginning to wane. "You know," I said, "I only had a tiny little cup of yogurt for breakfast. I feel the need to fortify myself to face the tribulations of the day."

"And what would that require?"

"Umm. Home fries with melted cheese, carrot juice, tea, and a cookie for later should cover it."

"In that case, we'd better find a table."

We scanned the room, which contained about six tables, a showcase for the baked goods, and a counter with stools across from the grill. Two of the tables were occupied by local fishermen. Several more held tourist families, and at the back table a gray-haired woman in a flowered shirt sat alone sipping a cup of tea. "All occupied," I said to Helen, and we turned to sit at the counter. But at that moment the woman in the back held up her hand and waved to us.

"There's plenty of room here," she called, indicating the three empty chairs at her table. I looked at Helen and she nodded, so we placed our orders at the counter and walked to the back of the room. Halfway there, I recognized the woman who had beckoned to us. She looked older without makeup, but I had seen her in her flowered shirt the day before.

"Good morning," I said. "It's Ms. Entwhistle, if I remember correctly."

"Call me Radha. Isn't it interesting, I was just thinking about visiting your shop again today when the two of you walked in. Sit down."

I noticed the glitter of gems on her fingers. "Are you getting along well with your new rings?" I asked.

"Oh, yes indeed I am." She held up her hands to show us. "At first I couldn't decide which fingers to wear them on, but when I tried this arrangement, everything clicked."

"Are you going to the beach again today?" Helen asked.

"Actually, I had planned to go home, but I had one of those feelings I get sometimes, and I knew I needed to stay another night. And to visit your shop."

"Was there something else you were looking for?" I asked. "Helen and I were on our way in to the store to do some cleaning before we open. If you like, you can come with us and we'll show you whatever you want to see."

"No, no, it's nothing like that." She smiled broadly, making road maps of wrinkles in her face. "The reason I needed to visit was to say that you really ought to take me up on that channeling session I offered. Right away. Today."

A little stunned, I turned to Helen for a hint of how to respond, but she was looking at Radha. "You know," Helen said, "when Will told me yesterday about your offering a session on your way out of the shop, I wished that we could have arranged it before you left town. But I thought it was too late."

"And I thought it might never happen," said Radha. "But my spirit guides have a way of nagging me, and now here we all are together." She looked at me, "What do you say, Will?"

"No point in swimming against the river. Let's do it. But we have to figure out when."

At that moment, our food arrived and interrupted the conversation. For a few minutes, I devoted myself to home fried potatoes while Helen drank her carrot juice and Radha refilled her tea. I was bemused at the synchronicity of the situation and wondered about the significance of this meeting with Radha. Finally, I turned to her and said, "Helen and I don't have any help in the store, so it would be difficult to get together with you before evening. Will you be here that long, and would you like to join us for dinner?"

Radha pulled back her gray-streaked hair and smiled again. "Evening will be fine, but I won't trouble you for dinner. Should we meet at your shop about eight?"

"Would our house be just as good for you?" asked Helen. "We only live a few miles from here."

"Certainly, just give me the directions."

We sat talking with Radha for another half hour or so, discussing the local beaches and telling her about the old granite quarries where we liked to swim. She knew a surprising amount about the history of the area, particularly about the lives of eccentric and exceptional people. By the time the conversation slowed down a bit, we were almost late for opening the store.

"We've got to get to work, but we'll see you tonight," said Helen.

"Yes, thanks for getting us out of cleaning," I said.

"The dust will still be there tomorrow," Radha smiled. "I'll see you two at eight. Blessed be."

We hurried to the shop and opened the door at just two minutes after nine. It was another busy summer day, and I spent most of my time dealing with customers while Helen worked in the back room on bookkeeping and the scheduling of upcoming talks to be given in our workshop space upstairs. In the afternoon, she left for the local copying store and returned with a stack of printed flyers listing the events.

I read aloud the titles of the workshops she had scheduled, "Astrology and Archetypes, Morphogenetic Fields of Consciousness, Holotropic Breathwork—this looks like a heavy-duty month coming up. Do we know all these presenters?"

"We don't know any of them. They responded to our postings on the Internet, and I spoke to each one on the telephone. I thought we should branch out into some new areas."

"That's great, but we'd better address these flyers and get them in the mail, or no one is going to know what we're offering." We spent the rest of the day stuffing envelopes, in between waiting on customers. We finished about a half hour after closing time. On our way to the house, we dropped the envelopes in a mail box, and we picked up a pizza for dinner. At home, we again sat together on the deck, enjoying the end of the day while we ate.

After we had finished, Helen slid her wicker chair over next to mine, and she took my hand. We sat silently together, listening to the peaceful sounds of the gathering evening, watching the western clouds turn from white to gold, and on into deepening red. With the twilight came cricket sounds and the dancing lights of fireflies over the lawn. At the same moment, we both let out deep sighs of relaxation. Helen looked at me and smiled softly. I closed my eyes, feeling myself drifting in a pleasant glow of contentment. I listened to the evening breeze that glided through the tree-tops, mixed with the distant sounds of cars, boats and voices that carried across the tidal river below. Everything seemed to blend together into a kind of quiet song that carried me away and made me forget myself, as I descended into unintended sleep.

*My father opened the door and regarded me with pure delight. "William, Son, come in. Come in! I've been waiting for you." He motioned me across the threshold and threw his arms around me as soon as I was inside. I could smell his cigars and feel the scratch of his stubbly cheek as I embraced him. He was dressed in his double-breasted blue suit, and his gray hair was combed back. I looked around the room. It was our old apartment, the one where I had lived with him during high school. The ironing board was set up in the living room, and across the sofa lay my own blue suit, a clean white shirt, underwear, socks and a tie.*

*"Dad, what's going on?"*

*"Your clothes, that's what. I've ironed them all for you. Now you'd better wash and get dressed. There isn't much time."*

*"Much time for what?"*

*He looked puzzled. "Until your graduation, of course."*

*"Graduation? I haven't been to school for years. And you didn't come to my graduation anyway. You were sick, remember?"*

*"Well, I'm here for this one. Now stop arguing and get your clothes on. We don't want to be late."*

*"All right, but I hope you know where we're going." I picked up the clothes from the sofa and walked to the bathroom to change. As I took them off, I noticed that the shirt and pants I had been wearing were torn and soiled. I ran clean water in the sink and washed, drying afterwards with a thick white towel. It felt good to button up the crisp white shirt and put on the suit my father had pressed for me. I smiled into the mirror, and my reflection winked. That shocked me, and I kept smiling over and over, trying to make it happen again. Then I heard knocking at the bathroom door, and the sound of a voice that I thought was Helen's.*

*"Will, hello there! Will? Are you in there? Hello, Will?"*

"Hello? Is anyone there? Will, Helen? Are you there?" I was pulled out of my dream by the insistent voice. The evening was now fully dark and I stumbled over my chair as I jumped up. I heard Helen beside me as she murmured from the disturbance. She too had been asleep.

"Hello," I called. "I'll be right there. Is that you, Radha?"

"Yes," I heard her voice coming up from the driveway which ran down the slope beside the house and below the deck. "Are you all right? I've been knocking on your front door for ten minutes. I was about to leave, but I decided to try calling through the windows on the side of the house."

"I'm glad you did. We fell asleep on the deck. Just a minute—I'll meet you at the front door." I opened the kitchen screen and walked through the house to unlock the door before Radha reached it. In spite of the jolt of awakening, I felt groggy, still half in my dream. I was standing in the doorway, leaning on the frame and yawning, as she approached.

"Usually my arrivals are greeted with greater enthusiasm," she said.

"I'm sorry, I don't know what came over us. We ate some pizza and we were just watching the sunset and—"

"Don't worry. I'm just glad I wasn't pounding on the door of the wrong house. Hello, Helen." I turned and saw Helen walking slowly and deliberately towards us through the living room. She looked rather disheveled and bleary-eyed.

"Radha, come in," she said. "I'm sorry we didn't hear you. I just passed out next to Will, and I've been having the weirdest dream."

"You too?" I said. "I'd almost forgotten mine until you mentioned it."

Radha walked past me and into the house with brisk determination. "Well, let's get a teapot on and you can both sit down and tell me what kind of dreams were engrossing enough to keep you sleeping through my entrance. And then I'll do my show-and-tell for you."

Helen and I made our way into the living room after Radha, who was already turning on lamps and finding the chair that suited her best. I went into the kitchen to heat some water while Helen and Radha chatted about the events of the day. Radha had gone swimming at one of the granite quarries and had taken a tour of a nearby mansion that had once belonged to an eccentric inventor. I heard Helen telling about the speakers she had scheduled at the shop for the next month, and Radha seemed quite interested in the talks, especially the one on astrology. When I came in with the tea, Helen was just starting to relate her dream.

"I was with my grandmother," she said. "My father's mother. She passed away last winter. In the dream, she was wearing a deerskin dress and turquoise jewelry, and she was dressing me in the same way. Of course, she was half Native American herself, and she went to a lot of powwows, but in my dream she was preparing me for some sort of initiation. She told me how proud she was of me, and she promised she would be there to help me."

"What was the initiation?" Radha asked.

"I don't know. It was something to do with fire. A fire dance, or a fire bird ceremony. I've never heard of anything called that before. She told me that everyone would do the dance, but that I had to wait for Will. I was looking for him when I heard you calling and woke up."

"And where *was* Will?" Radha asked, scrutinizing me with a wry smile.

"At my old apartment from high school days, dressing for graduation. And Helen, you were in my dream at the end, trying to get me out of the bathroom."

"Sounds like real life."

"Ouch. Let's stick to dreams for the moment. You know, Helen, it's interesting that you saw your grandmother, because I saw Frank."

"You did?"

"Who is Frank?" Radha asked.

"My father. He died about a month after Helen's grandmother." I told them everything I could remember about my dream. When I was finished, Radha sat back in her chair and took a sip from her teacup.

"It seems my co-workers have preceded me." she said. "Perhaps I ought to get comfortable and let them complete their messages."

"Your co-workers?" I asked.

"Yes. The spirits of your father and Helen's grandmother, and perhaps others as well. I told you I am a medium, and I am here because my guides have brought me to you. With great insistence, I might add. Although I don't know the content, there is apparently some communication which it is vital for you to receive now."

I looked at Radha, and seemed to see her with new eyes. As she sat holding her tea in the glow of the table lamp, she no longer looked like just another gaudy tourist. There was dignity in her wrinkled face and her eyes were as bright and alert as an owl's. I wondered what knowledge lay behind those eyes, and what purpose had brought her to our home.

"Radha," I asked. "Would it be all right to tape the session?"

"Of course."

"Good. I'll be right back." I went to my desk, found the recorder, and snapped in a fresh cassette. I put it next to Radha on the table and clipped the little microphone to the neckline of her dress. "Just push this button when you're ready to begin."

Helen asked, "Is there anything you need? Would you like the lights off? Shall I smudge the room for you?"

Radha smiled and shook her head. "Perhaps you could just turn out the light overhead. The lamp will be enough, I think. And I'll clear the space with my bells." She opened her bag and brought out a pair of slightly domed, silver-colored disks, inscribed with symbols and bound together with a leather thong. Holding the thong, she struck the disks together three times, each impact producing a pure tone that reverberated through the room.

"Are those Tibetan chimes?" Helen asked.

"They are," said Radha. "And now, I'll be leaving for a while. The way I work is to step aside and allow the other beings to express through me. I'll be conscious of everything that happens, but I won't speak to you again until the session is over. Enjoy your communions." She pushed the button on the tape recorder, closed her eyes and began to breathe deeply. Gradually the breaths came slower and slower until her head nodded in what seemed to be sleep. As I gazed at her, it was hard to tell if the golden glow around her came from the lamp or from her body. I wondered if I was seeing an aura, and whether Helen could see it too, but I felt unable to break the silence. After several minutes, Radha's body jolted slightly, like a scarecrow being hit by a gust of wind. Her eyes remained closed, but her mouth began working, and small, unintelligible sounds came out. Then she spoke, in a strong, resonant voice that sounded almost like a man's:

"I am Anon, servant, bringer, emissary of the holy fire. The time of death and rebirth is at hand, and you are called." With those first words, I felt a warm vibration move into my body, and my calm was shaken. I reached my hand out to Helen's where she sat beside me, and she clasped it tightly. "I serve the Infinite One, and exist as both one and many. I appear throughout the manifest worlds as a midwife for planets at the cusp of birth into the Light. Your Earth is at the point of choice, so I and many more have come, to guard and guide the emergence. To help or hinder inner birth, each entity must choose. Now is the moment of the great transition, and each choice will affect the fate of all. Are you ready to choose?"

I had no idea what to say. I was still off balance from hearing this masculine voice come out of Radha, and from the odd sensations in my body. I turned to Helen, who was looking intently at Radha's face, and she said, "I am ready at each moment to choose the path of Light."

"And you?" The powerful voice was directed at me. The tingling in my body intensified. I felt awkward, yet I knew that I had to answer.

"I, uh, choose to go with her."

"Well spoken!" I thought I caught a hint of irony in the voice. "Though you do not know all of what your choice shall mean, I see that your souls have agreed, and the process will unfold. I come to herald a dawning, but before the Light comes there will be darkness, and then fire. The time of fire is the turning point. It can be the gateway to a golden age, or the funeral pyre of your world. This planet is the womb for humankind, as is the universe for all embodied souls. The birth contractions of the past five thousand years are coming to their climax. Here and now you can enact the conscious birth of the Divine into the world, but your future hangs by a fragile thread, and the outcome is uncertain. You have the opportunity to change the balance, all of you who have chosen to live at this time. If enough of you open to the holy fire, *all* will receive its purifying grace. If too many deny the opening, this world's light could blow out like a candle. I say, do not fear any death, for the end of fetal life is birth, and the end of embodied life is the renewal of the soul. Yet you should strive to live through the coming days, and to assist the holy fire. For the Infinite One yearns for awakening within this world. When you truly open to receive it, the holy fire ignites. Know that as you need the Divine, it also needs you. Know that infinite awareness, through infinite love, has sacrificed control of what will happen in this world, and has given that choice to you, its children, as to all sentient beings. Know that the mind of humanity connects to each and all, and that every individual choice affects the whole. Thus the holy fire may begin as tiny sparks in a scattered few, but from this it can spread throughout your race and become the Earthfire, the cleansing flame which consumes all that is corrupt and brings humanity to new birth. As you approach the critical time, you will find its sparks upon many paths. Rejoice in this, and breathe upon them. The dark fires of destruction also threaten to immolate your world. Do not feed them with your fear, but know they too can serve the Infinite One. I bring these words to those who can hear them. This is the message of Anon."

At this, Radha fell silent. Her body seemed to relax and her head drooped. The tingling in my body subsided as quickly as it had begun. As I exchanged glances with Helen, I released my grip on her hand and noticed that my palms were sweaty. We both turned back to Radha, who was breathing slowly and deeply. As we watched, her eyelids fluttered and she let out a sigh. Then she opened her eyes, yawned and stretched, picked up her teacup and took a sip. Finally, she looked towards us. "Whew," she said, in her normal voice. "This is the first time *that* ever happened."

"I was just about to ask you what did happen," I said.

"I think we were contacted by a master force, or some kind of interdimensional being. It wasn't a discarnate human, that's for sure."

"What was your experience? Could you see it?" Helen asked.

"Not exactly. At first, I was moving into the space where I normally go as a medium. I was aware of my spirit guides around me, and a number of discarnate souls. As I expected, both Will's father and your grandmother were among them, apparently waiting to speak with you through me. I could feel and see them both approaching, and I silently told my guides I was willing to allow them the connection. Then, as this was happening, I became aware of a bright light coming in. When I directed my attention to the light, it descended upon me. There was some kind of unspoken question about permission, and I granted it. For a moment I could still see my guides and the discarnates. Then the light moved into me and everything else faded away. There was a feeling of immense power, and joy. The next moment, I heard my voice speaking, which I assume is what you also heard."

"It wasn't exactly your voice," I answered. "It was very powerful and resonant, and it sounded male."

"Not to me," said Helen. "The voice I heard was different from Radha's, but it was female. I agree that it was strong, but to me it sounded like an ancient woman."

"Well, *I'm* feeling fairly ancient right now. Whatever that being was, it really blasted me," Radha said, while fanning herself with a magazine from the table. "And I'm very warm, too. I'd think it was a hot flash, but I haven't had one of those in ten years." She picked up the little tape recorder and pushed the rewind button. "Let's play this back and see who's right about my voice."

We waited until the machine clicked, and then Radha played the beginning of the recording. The words were the same ones we had heard, but the voice was clearly Radha's, without any special intonation.

"Now, how can that be?" I asked, looking at Helen and then back to Radha. "The words are right, but that's not the voice I heard."

"Nor I," said Helen. "But I was thinking, maybe the sound was connected somehow to the energy that was in my body. I'm not feeling it now, but I did while that entity was coming through."

"You too?" I asked. "I felt like I was vibrating the whole time Radha, or Mr. Anon, was talking."

"I think that's it," Radha interjected. "When the entity moved in, I felt rather overwhelmed, as though it were too big and too powerful to fit into me. Perhaps some of it occupied each of you as well, and you heard it speaking in both the inner and outer domains."

"And this has never happened before?" I asked.

"Not to me. Up to now, my spirit guides have been the only beings I have contacted, except for discarnates. Of course, I've read about master forces and angels, but this is my first encounter with one, if that is what it was."

"Could it have been a demon or something like that? I don't remember everything that was said, but it kept mentioning fire."

"It didn't feel negative at all," said Helen. "I was in awe, but I never had any fear."

"I didn't either," Radha replied. "And I can clearly remember sensing happiness from my guides when it arrived. For my part, now that I've had a few minutes to recover, I'm feeling quite well. And curious. I'd like to play back the rest of that tape, if the two of you are agreeable."

We listened to the tape three times, stopping after each time to discuss the message and its possible meanings. Radha felt that the experience was in part a spiritual initiation for Helen and me, and that our dreams of being dressed for ceremonial occasions by our deceased loved ones were an inner-plane purification and preparation. She made much of the fact that we were asked to choose a path, and that Helen unswervingly answered the challenge. (Radha told me I had been smart to tag along.) Helen recalled her experience at Bell Rock in Sedona, and said that the message from Anon agreed in many ways with what had come to her there. I kept returning to the images of fire and birth, wondering about the nature of their connection. It was midnight when Radha finally declared that she was getting too tired to think any more, and would have to leave. She told us she would be spending the night in the local motel and going to her home in western Massachusetts in the morning, but she promised to return for a weekend to attend one of the talks scheduled at the Missing Link. We strolled with her to her car and said our goodbyes.

After she drove away, Helen and I walked to the porch and listened for a moment to the night wind gusting through the trees. Clouds were moving in from the west, and as we watched, there was a flash of summer lightning. A few seconds later came the rumble of thunder. We went inside to sleep, not waiting for the storm that would soon arrive.

# — 6 —

The rest of the month was a pleasant time for Helen and me. We worked most days in the shop, tending to customers, ordering books, stones and jewelry, and taking reservations from people who planned to attend the evening workshops. On our days off we swam in the quarries and picnicked in the surrounding woods. Several times, we discussed Radha's visit and the enigmatic message from Anon, and we often wondered where Sebastian's adventures were leading him. But we had a business to run, and the last days of summer to enjoy, so we spent our time in those pursuits.

It was on the Monday afternoon of Labor Day weekend, when the store was packed with customers, that Radha's fax came in. We didn't find it until after we had closed the doors and locked the jewelry in the safe. I went into the back room to turn off the lights and noticed the sheets in the machine's wire tray. I picked them up and scanned the cover page.

"Helen, there's a fax here from Ms. Rhoda Entwhistle."

"From Radha? What does it say?" Helen hurried into the room and deftly snatched the papers from my hand.

"I don't know yet. But I'm hoping the person who just nabbed it will tell me."

Helen turned and smiled as she walked back out to the empty counters, "Maybe. You'll just have to wait and see." After a few moments, she called to me. "Will, come here. I think you'll want to read this."

I turned off the lights in the back room and joined Helen behind the counter of the empty store. The fax pages lay spread on the counter. I picked up the first one and began to read:

Greetings, my seaside friends!

I have thought of you often since our meeting, and not only because my beautiful rings are a daily reminder of your lovely store. Indeed, it is the evening we spent together that is still most vivid in my mind. The powerful being which came through me that night is unique in my experiences, and the message intrigues me as much now as it did when we were together. In fact, I've been doing a bit of research on some of your questions, Will, and that is the main purpose of my writing to you.

When we talked after the session that night, you asked about the images of fire and birth that the entity stressed in the message. The first thing that came to mind when I put those concepts together is the legendary Phoenix. The image of the Phoenix is that of a supernatural bird which periodically cremated itself in its nest and rose reborn from its own ashes. The myth evolved from stories of the sacred kings of Phoenicia, who were sacrificed in flames and believed to be reborn in heaven. The Egyptian god figure who evolved out of this was said to have risen to heaven in the form of the Morning Star, after his fire-immolation death and rebirth. So there, at least, is one parallel to the message we received together.

As I thought more about the fire imagery, I went to my library and started pulling books from the shelves on pure intuition. Have you ever done this? The results can be fascinating! One of my first selections was the 1901 classic, *Cosmic Consciousness*, by Richard Maurice Bucke. Within moments of opening the book, I came upon this quote:

"I was in a state of quiet, almost passive enjoyment, not actually thinking ... All at once, without warning of any kind, I found myself wrapped in a flame-colored cloud. For an instant I thought of fire, an immense conflagration somewhere close by ...; the next, I knew that *the fire was within myself* [italics by Radha]. Directly afterward there came upon me a sense of exultation, of immense joyousness accompanied or immediately followed by an intellectual illumination impossible to describe. Among other things, I did not merely come to believe, but I saw that the universe is not composed of dead matter, but is, on the contrary, a living Presence; I became conscious in myself of eternal life. It was not a conviction that I would have eternal life, but a consciousness that I possessed eternal life then; I saw that all men are immortal ... The vision lasted a few seconds, and was gone."

So what do you think? Is this an example of the "holy fire" that Anon purports to serve? And is Bucke's "living Presence" the same as the "Infinite One?" Although there is no mention of death and rebirth, there is Mr. Bucke's intimation of eternal life, which certainly touches similar territory. I wondered how many others have experienced spiritual illuminations connected with fire.

I found this instance in a book of poetry by W.B. Yeats:

> *My fiftieth year had come and gone,*
> *I sat, a solitary man,*
> *In a crowded London shop,*
> *An open book, an empty cup*
> *On the marble table top.*
>
> *While on the shop and street I gazed,*
> *My body of a sudden blazed;*
> *And twenty minutes more or less*
> *It seemed, so great my happiness,*
> *That I was blessed and could bless.*

I got shivers when I read that one! Doesn't it give you the same feeling of what happened to Mr. Bucke? And Yeats declares not only that he *received* grace from his fiery illumination, but also, while he was in it, that he had the power to bestow such blessings upon others. It reminds me of the part of the message about the spreading of the holy fire.

Maybe it was the phrase "holy fire" that made me think of it, but one book I picked out was *The Gospel According to Thomas*. This is one of the gnostic gospels, not a part of the Bible, that is a compilation of the "sayings of Jesus." When I opened that book, I came quickly to these quotes: "Jesus said: 'I have cast fire upon the world, and see, I guard it until the world is afire.'" And this one: "Jesus said: 'Whoever is near to me is near to the fire, and whoever is far from me is far from the Kingdom.'" So there it is again, the image of a spiritual fire spreading over the earth, just like the Earthfire that Anon predicted. And in the second quote, the fire is associated with Jesus himself, and thereby to what he calls the Kingdom. Do you think the energy of Jesus' expanded awareness could have been what he called the "fire," and that when the "world is afire," the energy will manifest as a global Christ con-sciousness? Could this turn out to be the form of the much-predicted Second Coming? It makes the ignition of such a flame sound most desirable, although one wishes there were more information on just how to do it.

Up to now, my interest in Christianity has been more as mythology than as religion, but the last thing I found, which is what finally prompted me to write all this to you, truly made me wonder. It came off the Internet, and I just discovered it today.

Have you ever heard of the Garabandal Prophecies? I hadn't, but the tone of what came through me at your house that night got me interested in other prophecies, so I decided to see what I could find on the Web. There's a lot out there, but I'll confine myself to this one for now.

The name Garabandal comes from the Spanish village of San Sebastian de Garabandal. The story goes that during the period from June 1, 1961, to November 13, 1965, a Lady, purported to be the Blessed Virgin Mary, appeared to four young girls of the village numerous times. Reportedly, the girls received messages for humanity. There were admonitions for prayer and sacrifice, and finally predictions.

According to the story, there will be a worldwide warning experienced by everyone on Earth, for the purpose of calling humanity to return to God. After this it is said that a great miracle will occur within one year of the warn-ing. It is also predicted that signs will appear and remain permanently at a pine grove near Garabandal and other sites of Marian apparitions. Finally, there is predicted to be a terrible chastisement during which up to two-thirds of humanity will die. The collective response to the warning and the miracle is supposed to determine the severity of the chastisement.

Now, normally I wouldn't be interested in this kind of doomsaying. I tend to think of dire warnings as the would-be prophet's attention-getting device. But a small detail of this one attracted my attention.

One of the four girls, Jacinta, has said, "The Warning is something that is seen in the air, everywhere in the world and is immediately transmitted into the interior of our souls. It will last a very little time, but it will seem a very long time because of its effect within us. It would be like fire. It will not burn our flesh, but we will feel it bodily and interiorly." She also describes miracu-lous astronomical phenomena, "like two stars—that crash and make a lot of noise, and a lot of light—but they don't fall. It's not going to hurt us but we're going to see it and, in that moment, we're going to see our consciences."

So isn't that interesting! Once again, the image of divine fire comes up, this time in a Christian prophecy. And this one is not as antiquated as the quote from Jesus. In fact, another of the girls, Conchita, said that she was told by the Virgin in 1962 "There will be two more popes after Pope Paul VI and that one of the popes will have a very short reign. After that will come the end times but not the end of the world." Well, it happens that the next Pope after Pope Paul VI, Pope John Paul the First, had a very short reign indeed— only about a month if my memory serves. If the rest of this prophecy is equally accurate, the reign of Pope John Paul II will be seen as the last before the onset of the end times.

Personally, I find all this quite fascinating. The Garabandal prophecies, though couched in Christian terms, seem to have some intriguing elements in common with our message from Anon. The worldwide "fire" predicted to be seen in the air and felt within our bodies as the Warning has implications that sound more ominous than the other references to spiritual fire, but I nonetheless find the message quite compelling. As I do the other examples from my afternoon at the bookshelf. What do you think? Coincidence or synchronicity? I choose the latter!

I trust my discoveries will pique your interests, and that all things are otherwise well with you both. As I send this, I am already on my way out the door to visit a client and friend of mine for a couple of days. His name is George Camden, and I must admit he is a bit of an old boyfriend as well as a friend— and I *do* mean old. But then, I'm no spring chicken either. At any rate, I hope to be in your store again soon, or at least to make it to the Astrology and Archetypes workshop next weekend.
Blessed be,
Radha

When I finished reading the last of the pages, I handed it to Helen, who had arranged the others in a neat pile on top of the counter. "We should talk about this ..." I began.

"Over dinner," she interrupted. "Let's go."

We locked the store and got into our car. We decided to drive around the peninsula to the other side of town where there was a little seafood restaurant overlooking the water. Helen held Radha's letter in her lap as we made our way along the meandering, tree-lined roads. The holiday traffic was heavy, and I had to keep my eyes on the road. Something had stirred up a turbulence of inner tension in me, and I grumbled at the other drivers as I tried to find a path through the congestion. Helen seemed unperturbed, as she gazed at the familiar scenery, pointing out flower beds and gardens that she liked.

"You're always looking for what's beautiful," I said, half in admiration and half in annoyance.

"Yes, it beats muttering at the traffic."

"I wasn't muttering at anything."

"Will Lerner, if you weren't muttering you were growling. Now which was it?"

I took a deep breath and shook my head, "Both, I guess. I'm feeling stressed-out all of a sudden. I thought it was because of the traffic— I hate this stop-and-go driving—but now I'm not sure what's the matter. How do you stay so serene, anyway?"

"It's simple, if not easy," she said. "Our feelings often follow our thoughts, so I try to think about what I love—like the flowers and gardens—instead of falling into focusing on what I dislike. It's harder when things are stressful, or when I'm around other people who are indulging in negativity, but I still try to do it."

"In spite of bad influences like me."

She reached out and touched my hand, "You're not a bad influence, sweetheart, but sometimes you give in to them. You know, all forms of consciousness are contagious—from road rage to nirvana. When we can remember to be positive, it uplifts not only ourselves, but also everyone around us."

"And when we're negative, we spread that everywhere, too?"

"Unfortunately, yes." A car behind us honked loudly, as if to confirm her answer.

"Wow, that's depressing," I said.

"If that's where you put your focus."

"And you've taken it upon yourself to singlehandedly uplift the world by paying attention to beauty."

"It's a lovely job, but somebody's got to do it." Helen smiled, "I'll let you help me with it, if you want to."

We were stopped in the traffic. I reached over and put my arm around her, drawing her to me for a kiss. "Yes, thank you. I'll do my best."

We drove on for a while in silence. I felt calmer, but I realized there was more bothering me than the traffic. "Helen," I said. "There's something else."

"What is it?"

"It's that fax from Radha. Up to now, I had put aside most of my concerns about the message from Mr. Anon, but this letter brings everything back, and underlines it."

"Mr. Anon?" she chuckled. "Why do you keep using that name, and what's bothering you about the message?"

"Oh, I don't know. I guess I do it because I'm trying to make Mr., uh, Anon, seem less intimidating, or more human. As for the message, I'm not sure I want to seriously contemplate death and rebirth just now, or a crisis that could incinerate the earth. And then Radha brings in this Garabandal prophecy with a divine chastisement that could wipe out two thirds of us. It sounds just like the earth-change predictions Sebastian mentioned in his letter. If this stuff isn't hogwash, it's scary."

Helen was still smiling at me. "You're such a worrywart! If the message from Anon was real, it means we could be headed for a global awakening, an enlightenment. We have to focus on that, not the frightening parts. And don't forget the other quotes Radha found. Those were all associating the spiritual fire with feelings of joy and blessedness."

I looked at her, seeing in her smile the confidence and strength with which she faced the world. Finally, I let go and smiled back, thinking to myself, "*I have married well.*"

The traffic began to open up, and by the time we reached the Fisherman's Shanty I felt both relaxed and hungry. We pulled into the gravel lot, where there were already about a dozen other cars and an RV. As we went in through the weathered screen door, I said to Helen, "It's early for this much of a crowd."

"It's the end of summer. I'm not surprised. At least there's not a line at the counter."

The restaurant was very casual. It had an open kitchen with chalkboard menus on the wall next to the cash register where we ordered our meals. There were three rooms furnished with tables and a few secluded booths, and outside there were picnic tables scattered about a seaside lawn. After ordering we found an outdoor table outside near the rocky shore, and we sat down to wait for our names to be called when the food was ready. The salt air blew in from the ocean, provoking sighs of contentment from Helen and sharpening my appetite greatly.

"If they don't call us soon," I said, "I'm going to jump in the water and catch my own fish."

"It's only been about five minutes. If you don't give them time to cook it, the fish on your plate might jump in himself and get away."

"Well, I suppose one bizarre image deserves another. But I'm starving."

Just then a woman's voice crackled over the loudspeaker attached to the building, "Lerner and Waters, your dinners are ready."

"And not a moment too soon!" I said. "Watching me starve before your eyes would not have been pleasant. I'll go get our tray."

"Don't forget the salt and ketchup."

I identified myself at the counter and was handed a large red plastic tray, laden with paper plates that were heaped with fresh fried haddock, french fries and onion rings. I added paper cups of water, packets of salt, plastic silverware and a bottle of ketchup, and I headed back to our picnic table. I sat down and handed Helen's dinner to her. Before tasting anything, she leaned over, closed her eyes and inhaled the aromas.

"Mmm ..." she said. "Smells delicious."

"*Is* delicious," I answered, swallowing my first bite. "And hot. Very hot. Ouch, where's my water?"

"Are you sure you wouldn't prefer beer?" chuckled a male voice right behind me. Helen looked up, and her eyes widened. I twisted around, although I already knew who it was.

"Sebastian!" we both called out in unison. And there he stood, a red-bearded bear with a beer can, his eyes twinkling with mischief and merriment.

There followed a short commotion of hugging and exclamation, during which I noticed that behind and to the right of Sebastian stood a woman I had not seen before. She was fair-complected and slender, with short, dark-blonde hair, and she looked to be in her early thirties. Remembering Sebastian's letter, I guessed this might be the woman who had taken him to meditate on Bell Rock, and I felt even more surprised to see her than Sebastian. The contours of her face were smooth and rather childlike, and her bright blue eyes radiated an unusual intensity. She stood patiently while we greeted Sebastian, and then he turned to her. "Maddie, these are my friends Will and Helen."

"And you must be the Madeline that Sebastian wrote about in his letter," said Helen, extending her hands. The two women lightly embraced.

"You can call me Maddie," she said, flashing a smile.

"Or the Mad-Woman of Sedona," Sebastian grinned.

"There's the cauldron calling the kettle black," she replied, giving him a knowing look.

"Cauldron? Is that a reference to my shape, or to my storage capacity?"

"Both. *And* to the inky pits of your devious mind."

"Well," I said. "I see you've gotten to know one another a lot better since that first evening on Bell Rock." At my comment, I noticed that both of their smiles immediately disappeared. "Um, excuse me, did I say the wrong thing?"

"No," Sebastian said hastily. "Not at all. Look, your dinner is probably getting cold, and we've just eaten. Is it all right if we sit with you while you finish, and then maybe we can go somewhere and talk?"

"That sounds perfect," said Helen. "You can fill us in on your journey, and we'll tell you our news, too."

"Okay," I said as we all sat down on the picnic table benches. "But I want to ask a couple of questions before we go anywhere. I suppose that's your RV out front. I should have recognized it. But where were you sitting? I didn't see you when we came in. And how did you know we would be here?"

"We were in one of the booths near the back of the first room, and we didn't know you were here until they called your names on the loudspeaker. Then I saw you pick up your tray, and we stealthily followed until the moment was right." Sebastian looked at me and grinned again. "As to our foreknowledge of your arrival, we didn't have any. In fact, we just got into town this afternoon and weren't planning to call on you until tomorrow, in the store. But apparently fate had other plans. Don't you two call it syn-chronicity?"

"Yes," I said, "and there seems to be a lot of that going around these days."

"Maybe too much," Sebastian answered.

"What?"

"Later," Sebastian said. "Later."

We sat together there for almost an hour, Helen and I finishing our had-dock and offering french fries and onion rings to Maddie, who politely refused. Sebastian found room for them between beers, claiming that talking gave him an appetite. We heard about their cross-country drive, and the mechanical idiosyncrasies of *RV There Yet*. It was clear to Helen and me that since Sebastian's letter these two had formed some sort of new relationship, but they did not speak of it. Nor did they make any reference to Sedona, or to their experiences there. At one point, Madeline mentioned having heard some of Sebastian's tales of political conspiracies, but he looked sharply at her and she dropped the subject. Sebastian asked us how the store was doing, and I started to recount our meeting with Radha, but Helen stopped me, saying, "Let's tell that story when we can sit with a cup of tea at the house."

Shortly after that, we all got up to leave. It was agreed that Sebastian and Madeline would follow us home in the RV and park for the night in our driveway. When we arrived, the sun was hanging low, just beginning to embroider golden edges onto the clouds in the western sky.

# ─── 7 ───

Sebastian sat sipping from the teacup Helen had just given to him, completely filling the easy chair that Radha had used on the night of her visit. Madeline sat cross-legged on the floor beside him, and I faced him from the couch. Helen glided among us with teacups and plates of shortbread cookies we had made the night before, finally coming to rest on the sofa next to me.

"All right," I said. "I want to know the whole story. What happened in Sedona, why did you come back here, and how did you two transform from breathing buddies into traveling companions?"

Madeline looked up at Sebastian and he leaned forward in his chair, reaching to touch her shoulder. She took his hand, as he glanced back and forth between Helen and me. Finally he spoke, "You remember my letter, right?"

"Yes, of course," said Helen.

"And you remember the lecturer who didn't make it to the talk where Maddie and I met?"

"Dr. Jordan," Madeline interjected. "And you and I had actually met before, at the natural foods store."

"That's right," Sebastian agreed. "I went looking for Maddie there the day after we meditated together at Bell Rock." He grinned, "I don't know if I was hoping for additional enlightenment or another post-meditation hug, but I didn't get either one. The manager told me she had called in sick. I asked him what was wrong, since she had seemed perfectly healthy the night before, and he said he thought she might be upset after learning what had happened to Dr. Jordan."

"What *had* happened?" I asked.

"That's what I wanted to know. The manager said there had been an accident. Dr. Jordan had apparently fallen from a sixty-foot ledge on Bell

Rock. His neck was broken."

"Oh my," Helen gasped. "When did it happen? Was it the same night ..."

"The same night we were there? Yes, it was. The body was found by hikers the next morning."

"A friend of mine who knew Dr. Jordan from his workshops heard the news on a police scanner and called to tell me," said Madeline. "I was shocked, and a little frightened. It spooked me to realize that he must have been lying there dead, quite close to where Sebastian and I were climbing— or that he might have still been alive."

Sebastian continued, "The store manager knew that Maddie had been on Bell Rock the night before, so I assumed she had told him about it when she called in sick. I asked him for her telephone number, saying I was a friend from out of town. He balked at that, so I said I had been with her at Bell Rock, and I really needed to speak with her. That raised his eyebrows, but he finally took me into the office and called Maddie himself. When he mentioned my name to her, she asked to speak with me."

"I was pretty upset," said Maddie. "Even though I had only known him a few months, I felt close to Dr. Jordan. He shared some of his ideas with me and showed me the breathing meditation I did with Sebastian, and I told him about my experiences with the ETs. That morning I kept remembering his stories about the government and the kidnapping of abductees. But I didn't want to get paranoid, and I needed to talk to someone. I was happy when I heard Sebastian's voice on the phone."

"I asked if I could come to her place, and she gave me the address," said Sebastian. "I bought a bag of fresh muffins from the store's bakery and drove over in my rental car."

"Muffins?" Helen questioned.

"Emergency rations, comfort food. I don't know—they smelled good, and it seemed like a good idea at the time."

Madeline continued, "We talked for the rest of that whole day. I guess you could say we pretty much told each other our life stories. I was surprised to discover how much we had in common—especially the experiences with the ETs. I'm fairly certain that Sebastian is an abductee, and that his mother was too, even though he still hangs on to his dream hypothesis."

"Well, you can't deny that all my stories end with '... and then I woke up,'" Sebastian replied.

"Sometimes with a serious nosebleed," she retorted. "Anyway, your dreams might be repressed memories. I've had a lot of those. Regardless, the longer we talked that day, the more I felt I understood why I had been drawn to invite this redheaded stranger to my favorite meditation spot, and to open up to him on an energetic level. When it happened, I thought I was just spreading the Light, but as I learned more about him, I felt destiny at work."

Sebastian smiled and looked to the ceiling, "Ah, destiny, so rarely my friend. This time I owe you one."

I glanced toward Helen and she reached over to touch my hand. Then she turned to Madeline and said, "I know the feeling. But tell me what else happened that evening. There was something, wasn't there?"

"Yes ... there was a telephone call. How did you know?"

"I didn't, really. I just sensed a tension of some kind."

"My wife, the psychic," I said.

"A guy gets no privacy around these spiritual women," said Sebastian.

"Hush up, you two," said Helen. "I want to hear this."

"Well, it was about eight o'clock that evening," Madeline began. "The muffins had been gone for hours and we were getting hungry. Sebastian suggested going to a restaurant, and I was in the bathroom getting ready when the phone rang. I ran out to answer it, and the caller was a man whose voice I didn't recognize. He asked me if I was a friend of Dr. Jordan. I said I had known him, and the man asked if I was aware of his death. I said I was, and then he asked what time I had gone to Bell Rock the night before. At that point, I started to get alarmed, and I asked the man who he was. He didn't give his name, but he told me he was an FBI agent investigating Dr. Jordan's death. He said he wanted to come and ask me some questions."

"I could see that Maddie was getting nervous," Sebastian said. "So I walked over to her and listened. When he repeated the question about coming to interview her, I shook my head and whispered, 'Not tonight.'"

"I couldn't have agreed more," said Madeline. "I told the man that I wasn't feeling well, and that the earliest I could see him was at work the next afternoon. He didn't sound happy, but he finally agreed to meet me at the health food store."

"We decided not to go out," Sebastian continued. "We called for Chinese food and I picked it up."

"I was really jumpy while Sebastian was gone," Maddie continued. "But I didn't notice his car when he drove back into the driveway, and when he knocked I nearly leaped out of my skin."

"I gather that the FBI man's call is what rattled you," I said. "But why did it bother you so much? I mean, it's a bit odd for the FBI to investigate an accidental death, but you obviously had nothing to hide."

"No, I didn't really. But ... it was a lot of things. The man on the phone wasn't friendly. He sounded cold, intimidating. And Dr. Jordan was always talking about secret agencies that were covering up the government/UFO connection and making people disappear."

Sebastian jumped in. "The fact that the doctor turned up dead enhanced his credibility with me. I mean, sure, it was reported as an accidental fall. We even called the sheriff's office to ask, and that was the coroner's preliminary conclusion. But what was Jordan doing climbing Bell Rock when he was scheduled to be giving a lecture? And there was another strange thing—his car was found with the keys in it, off the road near Bell Rock. And I wondered how the man on the phone knew that Maddie had been there the same night?"

"From the store manager?" I asked.

"Possibly, but that's fast work. I couldn't imagine how the FBI could even find out and get an agent to Sedona so quickly, unless they were already on the doctor's tail."

"Hmm, that's a point," I agreed. "Well, what did you do?"

"I volunteered to spend the night standing guard," Sebastian smiled.

"He was a valiant knight, a gentleman to the core," Maddie said.

"She means I slept on the couch. That's just how I gained her confidence. Once her guard was down, I began behaving like the beast I truly am, but that came later. The next morning I suggested to Maddie that she call the FBI and ask for the name of the agent working on this case."

"I told them I had an appointment to be interviewed, but that I needed to change the time, and I had lost the agent's name and telephone number."

"And did you get the name?" I asked.

"They told me there were no FBI agents on assignment in Sedona, or anywhere nearby."

"Uh oh," I murmured.

"You paraphrased my sentiments exactly," said Sebastian. "After that call I got a little scared myself, and I began doing my level best to convince Maddie to join me in an impromptu cross-country vacation."

"The idea seemed crazy," she mused. "But a part of me was practically screaming, 'Get out of there!' Still, I told Sebastian I had to go in to work and talk to my manager. So we drove to the store in Sebastian's car, and he bought provisions while I went to look for John. He wasn't in the office, and after waiting a few minutes I left him a note saying I would be in at noon. Then we drove back to my apartment.

"When we opened the door, I just about fainted. The place had been ransacked. Books were all over the floor, furniture was torn apart. My jewelry and a little cash I kept in my dresser drawer were strewn about the bedroom. My TV and stereo were untouched. The only thing missing, as far as I could tell, was my little computer."

"The one she used to help with Dr. Jordan's book notes," Sebastian said.

"But none of that was on the computer," Maddie continued. "When I proofed things for him, or read his chapters, I always worked on his discs, and I didn't keep copies. All I had was the most recent one, and that was in my purse. I hadn't even had a chance to read it."

"Did you leave then?" Helen asked.

"Yes. I took Sebastian up on his offer. We hurried to his RV with the groceries he had bought, plus some of my canned goods and a few clothes. I drove his rental car back to the agency, while he followed, and from there we took to the highway. I hadn't lived in Sedona very long, so I didn't have many friends outside of work. After a couple of days, I called John at the store to tell him there had been a family emergency, and that I didn't know when I would be back. I asked him to tell my landlord to put my things in storage and rent out the apartment. It's only been a few weeks, but it seems like years ago."

"Did the FBI man show up looking for you?"

"He did, whoever he was. John told me about it when I called. He said an older man, tall and heavily built, came into the store asking for me, and he showed John a badge. But at the time he had no idea where I was, and the man didn't come back, as far as I know."

"What about John?" I asked. "Was he the one who told the man you had been up on Bell Rock that night?"

"No, he said he never spoke to him before he came to the store looking for me. But anyone working in the store might have known, and told. John said he had mentioned it to a couple of the other employees who were talking about Dr. Jordan's death."

There was a silence. I glanced at Helen, as she gazed intently at Madeline, who sat with her knees pulled up against her chest and her eyes closed. I looked to Sebastian, who smiled grimly and gave a slight shrug. Finally, he spoke. "I'm sorry, you guys. We've taken a roundabout road, but from the moment we left Sedona, I knew we were coming here. Maybe I should have called and asked permission. I felt as though Maddie and I needed friends, allies. But I don't want to bring trouble down on you."

Helen slid off the couch and sat beside Madeline. She took a hand from one of her knees and squeezed it. Madeline looked up at Helen, and her eyes glistened with tears. Helen said, "I don't think either of you, or any of us is in danger right now. You are welcome here, of course. Maybe tonight you would like to sleep in the house, in our guest room. You can bathe and rest and just be still for a little while."

"That sounds good," Madeline murmured, smiling.

"And one more thing would be wonderful," said Sebastian. "Do you think it would be possible for us to, umm, do some laundry?"

Helen laughed and the tension was broken. "Yes, yes. Go out and fetch your clothes before you get in the shower. Will and I can help, but you'll have to do your own ironing."

"Ironing?" said Sebastian. "What's ironing?"

The women went upstairs while Sebastian and I walked outside to the RV. It was fully dark, and the stars winked brightly between the scattered clouds. Sebastian unlocked the door, turned on a light, and I followed him in. As he gathered clothes, towels and linens from the rear of the vehicle. I looked around. He had made some additions to the furnishings since giving Helen and me that first ride. A potted cactus adorned the dashboard, along with an assortment of crystals and a few brown feathers, all glued down with blue putty. On the walls were assorted bumper stickers with aphorisms like, "It's never too late to have a happy childhood," and "Just because you're paranoid doesn't mean they're not out to get you." Most noticeably, the kitchen table was occupied by a rather large computer monitor. At the keyboard sat an inflatable blue vinyl extraterrestrial about four feet tall.

Sebastian came lumbering out of the rear of the vehicle, arms full of laundry, and he caught me regarding the ET doll. "Will, I'd like to introduce you to our new friend. We picked him up hitchhiking outside Area 51, or was it Roswell? Anyway, he's life-size, very friendly, really knows how to handle a pair of tweezers, and he can be used as a floatation device in the event of a water landing. His name is Anon. Anon, this is Will. Stick out that hand of yours and give him three, or is it four?"

I had been smiling until he mentioned the doll's name. Suddenly, my thoughts spiraled into an inner whirlpool. I struggled to speak, and finally managed to ask, "Anon? Was that the name you said? Where did that come from?"

"I'm not sure. It was Maddie's idea. I figured she meant it as in 'anonymous'. It's kind of a weird name, though, isn't it?"

"You have no idea," I said, taking half the laundry from his arms. "Come on, let's go inside. We'll talk about it later."

I sent Sebastian upstairs to shower while Helen and I took the laundry to the basement. As soon as we were alone, I told her about the odd coincidence of the plastic ET's name. "How can something like that happen?" I demanded. "Sebastian and Madeline don't even know about what transpired here with Radha, and Madeline certainly couldn't have known anything about our situation when she named that doll."

"Synchronicities don't need logical connections, although by definition they have meaningful ones," said Helen. "Weren't you and Sebastian mentioning some others at the restaurant? To me, they can be the Universe trying to help us by drawing our attention where it needs to go. They can show us that we're on the right track, or sometimes the wrong one, by piling up these wild coincidences. I've also read about some synchronicities that just seemed to be playful, but I believe there is usually a message implied. Think about it, Will. What is a Tarot reading, or any oracle, other than a deliberate setting up of a synchronistic pattern?"

"Yes, that's true. But if you're right, what's the meaning we're supposed to get from this one?"

"Perhaps we need to pay closer attention to the message that came through Radha. Maybe more of that is moving into our lives. Also, it's possible that there's an important connection with Sebastian and Madeline, and that's why the name came to them." We finished sorting the clothes for the first load of wash and Helen turned on the machine. "Anyway, I think we should tell them about our experience and see what comes from that."

"Agreed. But do you think it was really necessary for them to run? Couldn't they have stayed in Sedona and straightened things out?" I asked.

"Are you serious?" Helen scolded. "Maddie's friend was killed, the man from the FBI was apparently a fake, and her apartment was ransacked, all within twenty-four hours—how much more danger should she have endured? If, in spite of appearances, it was truly an accidental death, it won't matter that Maddie left town. If it wasn't, why should she have stayed and become involved in it?"

"Do you think leaving town got her out of it?"

"I don't know. It may have. It should have. I hope it did. Anyway, I'm glad Sebastian came here with her. She needs to stop and re-center herself, and I think we can help with that."

"I thought it was nice of you to offer the guest room to Maddie, but what about Sebastian? He seems very protective of her, and I don't know if he'll want to sleep in the RV. Maybe the couch?"

"Will, you are so thick sometimes. They'll both be in the guest room. Can't you see they're in love?"

"Oh."

We climbed the stairs to the kitchen and busied ourselves loading the dishwasher and putting things away. The sound of running water from the shower upstairs had ceased, and we walked through the house turning off lights, preparing to go up to bed. As I turned toward the staircase I looked up and saw Sebastian, in my green bathrobe, coming down. Behind him was Madeline, in a pink flannel nightgown. Sebastian yawned and said, "As tempting as your guest room looks, we can't go to sleep yet. Maddie wants to know about Anon."

I glanced at the clock on the living room mantle. "Well, actually it's only a quarter till ten. That's not so late. Helen, can we make one more pot of tea?"

"Sure. And how about candlelight this time?"

"Good idea." I took matches and lit the two candles on either side of the mantle clock. Then I found two votives in the kitchen, lit them and placed them on the coffee table in front of the sofa. This time Madeline curled up in the easy chair and Sebastian reclined on the floor in front of her. While the water was heating, Helen came in and sat beside me on the sofa, and we began to tell our story about meeting Radha and hearing the message from the being called Anon.

The two of them listened without comment, although Madeline nodded her head at several points in the narrative. Finally, Sebastian asked, "Could we listen to the tape?"

"Oh, sure. Do you want to hear it now?"

"Please," said Madeline.

"I know where it is," said Helen. "Will, you get the teapot and I'll fetch the tape."

After I brought in the tea and cups and poured for everyone, Helen placed the little tape recorder on the coffee table between the candles and clicked the switch. Once again we heard Radha's voice conveying the words of Anon, challenging us to choose our path, foretelling a world crisis that would lead to destruction or renewal, or perhaps both.

Sebastian let out a long, low whistle. "Maybe you were right, Maddie."

"Will, what date was this tape made, do you know?" asked Madeline.

"I think we wrote it down on the cassette. Let me check. By the way, what were you right about?"

"We'll get to that in a minute. What was the date?"

I told her, and she leaned over Sebastian from her perch on the easy chair. "Where were we that day?" she asked him.

"On our way to Seattle, I think. Or maybe we were already there. What day of the week was it?"

"Monday," I said.

"Okay, so we were already in Seattle. We had arrived on Sunday. Maddie, wasn't Monday the day we went to the bookstores looking for that flying saucer book? We finally found it, at the same store ..."

"Where we bought our little blue friend!" she exclaimed. "And I named him early that evening. It could have been at the very time this tape was being made."

"Now I see why Will turned sort of green when I introduced him," Sebastian remarked.

"Indeed I did," I answered. "But I want to go back and ask what you think Maddie was right about."

"Oh, that," said Sebastian. "Well, I mentioned in my letter that Maddie claims to have been abducted by ETs numerous times."

"*Was* abducted. Since I was six, at least."

"Okay, was. For the moment. Well, since we vacated Sedona, we've been doing a lot of sharing of our experiences as we drove along, and Maddie's been filling me in on the spiritual component of her encounters with Whoever They Are. The messages she remembers from these episodes are not all that different from what's on this tape. There were warnings about the self-destructive path mankind has been traveling, and urgings to 'awaken' or strive for enlightenment. It made me recall my own ET dreams and even my poor crazy mother's ramblings. And I remembered your Bell Rock story too, Helen, which was so directly spiritual. Maddie says these Visitors are trying to help us evolve, to make some kind of leap of consciousness."

"I can see that," said Helen.

"Of course," Sebastian continued, "the usual question is that if these guys are real and they want to help us, why don't they land on the White House lawn and go on television with their message?"

"Maybe they've tried," said Madeline. "Dr. Jordan said the government knows a lot about them, and it won't admit anything."

"Or maybe they can't," said Sebastian. "Either because they're imaginary, or they're not physical."

"They're *not* imaginary," said Madeline.

"But they might not be physical," said Helen. "At least not at our usual level of density. Whatever our Anon was, both Will and I felt a powerful energy move into our bodies as the words came through Radha, and I guarantee you we weren't dreaming at the time."

Sebastian said, "As we've been traveling, Maddie and I have both been doing some reading in this field, and we've found some parallels. I started with Carl Jung's book called *Flying Saucers*. And I must say, Dr. Jung was much too clever to get caught believing *or* disbelieving in UFOs as material objects. But he made a point of the idea that saucers, with their mandala-like shape, could be spiritual symbols of wholeness and unity that emanate from the collective unconscious. Actually, I got the impression that Jung thought the whole phenomenon of flying saucers and extraterrestrial visitors is a product of the collective unconscious. Then at the end of the book he recounted the story of a man named Orfeo Angelucci, who in the early 1950s claimed to have met extraterrestrials and even traveled in their ships. His journey was full of mystical experiences and sensations of ecstasy brought on by mysterious energies. He even reported being shown all of his past lives and being told that Jesus was not actually the son of God, but was rather the 'Lord of the Flame,' an infinite entity of the sun. Jung suggests that it would be naive to take all this literally, but at the same time he acknowledges that Orfeo's story exhibits the classic form of a mystical experience. And it shows me that this stuff has been going on for a long time."

"For a very long time," I said. "You can go back to the Bible story of Ezekiel seeing a wheel in the air, or in African mythology to the Dogon people who say their ancestors came from the star Sirius. The amazing thing about the Dogons was that they knew Sirius was a binary star with a 'dark companion'—a dwarf star—long before Western scientists' telescopes were able to detect it."

"You know, Sebastian, we're getting back to the same question you raised when you were having those ET dreams," said Helen. "And I'm thinking that the problem is the idea that something has to be physical to be real. That's part of the programming we get as children—we're taught to ignore and disbelieve in all kinds of paranormal experiences, from out-of-body episodes to 'imaginary' playmates."

"Sebastian told me that, as a child, he *was* an imaginary playmate," said Madeline.

"And she believed me, until she realized I'd stolen that line from an imaginary character in a novel," said Sebastian. "Anyway, as I said, Maddie may be right—these saucer jockeys might be real, and they apparently have more to say to us than 'Take me to your leader', One thing is for sure—mystical and spiritual content is much more common in ET encounters than I ever realized until we started reading. Tell them about the book you found Maddie."

"It was an odd little incident," she said, "Sebastian and I were in a used

book store in Ashland, Oregon, on our way up to Sea
and the woman who owned the place was stocking boo,
She was sliding a book into place on the other side of the ope,
accidentally pushed one in too far and knocked a book onto the ,
feet."

"*The Andreasson Affair*," said Sebastian. "A subtle synchronistic suggestion from somewhere."

"Naturally I picked it up and looked at it," Maddie continued. "It was
pretty old, published over twenty years ago. It's the story of a woman from
right here in this state who, in 1967, apparently experienced contact with
extraterrestrials. Now, the author was a UFO investigator of the old style,
and some of his breathless excitement over ET technology seemed rather
silly to me. But the woman, Betty Andreasson, who recalled the episode
through hypnotic regression, had some very spiritual experiences. So spiritual, in fact, that the 'scientific' researchers listening to her were a bit embarrassed to report them."

Helen smiled her encouragement to Maddie, "Let's hear about them."

"As in many close encounters, the beings came into Betty's house, floating right through the closed door, and they spoke to her telepathically. Her
family members went into a sort of suspended animation while she interact-
ed with the ETs. It gave me a bit of a shock to read that the beings inserted
a long needle into her nose to retrieve some sort of tiny implant. It was so
much like Sebastian's dream. And they told Betty that they were doing that
to 'awaken' something. Another parallel to Sebastian's recollections was
that Mrs. Andreasson was put under a bright white 'cleansing light,' rather
like the blue-white light he remembers."

"But *my* light was ecstasy-inducing," Sebastian said, grinning. "I think
they have definitely improved the technology since Betty's day. I'm hoping
that the next time I'm abducted, they'll put me in the Orgasmatron."

Madeline scowled at Sebastian, "Can't you take anything seriously?"

Sebastian frowned back at her, "The day I take this completely seriously may be the day I follow in my mother's footsteps. I'm better off cracking
jokes. Excuse me. I'm going to get a beer from the RV." He stood up and
stalked out of the house.

Maddie stared after him, "I hope he's okay. He's so full of wisecracks, I
sometimes forget that he's under stress too."

"The dreams he had made him doubt his sanity," said Helen. "I think
those jokes are his shields."

"He'll be all right," I said. "If he's not back in five minutes, I'll go check n him."

"Please continue, Maddie," Helen soothed.

"I remember an odd moment in the book when Mrs. Andreasson tried to feed the ET's, and they told her they couldn't eat her food, that their food was 'knowledge tried by fire.' The leader told her that 'within fire are many answers' and that our race will find the answers through the spirit. Later they took her on some kind of journey that climaxed in a vision of a giant bird, like an eagle, that burst into flame and was completely consumed, and then reborn, right in front of her. While she was watching that in her hypnotic regression, she said she felt as though she were on fire herself, and she appeared to be in real pain."

"The Phoenix," Helen said.

"That's right," said Maddie. "That's what they called it in the book, too. Mrs. Andreasson looked it up in the encyclopedia, and her vision corresponded to it exactly."

"It also corresponds to what Radha wrote us about Anon's message," I said.

"What was that?" Madeline asked.

Helen and I spent the next few minutes filling Maddie in on the contents of Radha's fax and her speculations on how to interpret the cryptic words of Anon. While we were talking, Sebastian came back inside, beer can in hand. He went immediately to Maddie, whispering apologies and embracing her. Then he sat down on the floor again, leaning against her easy chair.

"So what did I miss?" he asked.

"More synchronicities," I answered.

At Sebastian's insistence, Helen retrieved Radha's fax so he could read it, while Maddie looked over his shoulder. At several points, they exchanged glances and nods. Finally, Sebastian looked towards Helen and me and said, "There are a lot of pieces here. The question is, do they belong in the same puzzle?"

"How could they not?" exclaimed Maddie. "The Phoenix shows up in Radha's fax and in the book I found, and it's implied in the message from Anon. And then there's the fact of the *two* Anons. How likely is that? And look at all this fire imagery, from Yeats' poem, from the *Gospel of Thomas*, and from those Garabandal prophecies—everything connects to the central vision from Radha's channeling."

"And I'm intrigued," said Helen, "by the details that connect Jesus to this spiritual fire. In the Gospel of Thomas that Radha quoted he says that to be near to him is to be near to the fire, and that he comes to set fire to all the world. Then in the book by Jung, the ETs say, almost offhandedly, that Jesus is—what did you call it Sebastian—Lord of the Fire?"

"Lord of the Flame," he answered. "Okay, I see how the pieces are fitting together, but to me they still don't make a picture. Or if they do, it's a pretty bizarre collage."

"I can't help thinking it's hopeful," said Helen.

In the next moment, before anyone else could speak, we heard a rush of wind in the trees outside, and a gust came in through the open windows, blowing out all four of our candles.

"Well, I *hope* that's not an omen," said Sebastian.

"Will, do you have matches?" Helen asked.

"They're here somewhere, but I can't see them. Give me a minute."

"Maybe," said Madeline slowly, "this would be a good time to go to bed."

"I second the motion," Sebastian's voice echoed.

"All in favor?" I intoned.

"Aye!"

"The motion is passed unanimously."

I woke the next morning with the sun streaming in across the bed and a pleasant breeze blowing the white curtains out from the window. Helen was already up and out of the bedroom, but I could hear her talking with Sebastian and Madeline on the deck below. I went to the window and called down to them, "Good morning! What's for breakfast?"

Sebastian looked up from the newspaper he was reading as he sat in a white wicker chair. Through a mouthful of fresh biscuit he answered, "Are you familiar with the phrase, 'Snooze you lose'? Helen has whipped up a veritable feast, but I fear it will be too late by the time you get here." With that, he put down his paper and leaned forward to the table where Madeline and Helen were seated, helping himself to more fried potatoes and fruit salad from the serving bowls.

"Don't worry, Will. We won't let him eat everything," Madeline said, smiling up at me.

"I'm not taking any chances. Just make him put down his fork while you count to ten and I'll be there." I hurried into the bathroom and washed quickly, then threw on shorts and a knit shirt and ran down the stairs barefoot. I walked through the living room to the kitchen and out onto the deck. Though it was only eight o'clock, the gray floorboards were already warm when I stepped on them. It was going to be a hot day.

I stood behind Helen's chair, leaning down to kiss her as she turned to me. "Wow, that was fast," she said. "What's your secret?"

"Teleportation," I said. "Inspired by fear of starvation. Is there any food left?"

"There's plenty. Now sit down and eat. I've been talking with Maddie and Sebastian, and you need to hear what we've got planned."

Helen explained that all three of them had been up since dawn, and that they had been strategizing about what Sebastian and Maddie would do next. Sebastian said his teaching seminars were over and he still had enough money to last a few months. He wanted to take time off and do more read-ing— he was still on his quest to find the key to his inner experiences. Madeline was at loose ends, since she had abruptly abandoned her job, friends and daily activities. Helen had suggested that they try to find a place to stay locally, and she offered to hire Maddie to work for us at the shop. "It doesn't need to be permanent," she said to me, "but we could really use some help through the holidays, and Maddie has quite a bit of knowledge about the stones and other metaphysical topics."

"It sounds great," I said. "Maybe this will allow us to take some time off, too, instead of working six days a week. What do you think, Maddie?"

"I'd like to try it, if Sebastian wants to stay here."

"I'll be happy anywhere there's a library, a bookstore and a modem. Well, maybe not in Will's driveway. And what about that? Is there anywhere I can park *RV There Yet* and maybe plug in a phone without calling down the wrath of the zoning board?"

I thought for a moment. "Sure, there's a campground, Dune Forest, just a couple of miles from here. It's usually full during the summer, but after Labor Day it thins out quite a bit. They have full hookups for RVs and I think some of the spaces even have phone lines. Helen, if you and Maddie go open the store, I could ride over with Sebastian and look into it."

And so it was decided, Sebastian and Madeline would stay. Right after breakfast, Sebastian and I took the RV to Dune Forest. It was near the beach, with several dozen parking spots for trailers and RVs nestled amid an old grove of scrub pine trees. Only about half the spots were occupied, and the owner was glad to take Sebastian's deposit for a three-month rental. After papers were signed, the owner drove us downtown and dropped us at the Missing Link. Then we took my car to a town twenty miles away where Sebastian had stored his vehicle in a rented space while he was traveling.

"I hope it's still here," he said, taking the padlock off the beat-up garage door. He pulled it aside, revealing a rusty yellow Toyota sedan of indetermi-nate age. "Ah, transportation," he smiled. "Point A to point B here I come."

After some coaxing, the engine rattled to a start, and Sebastian followed me back to the shop.

By the time we arrived, it was midday. Helen had been busy showing Madeline the basics of her new job, and now the two of them wanted to go out for lunch. Sebastian and I stayed behind to take care of customers, though so far the store had been fairly empty.

"That's the way every summer finishes here," I said. "The last weekend is a madhouse, and the next day it's a ghost town."

"Which do you prefer?"

"They both have their charms. But if we didn't get the madhouse, I definitely wouldn't welcome the ghost town."

"Well, that makes sense." Sebastian wandered through the store, picking up stones and setting them down, taking books off the shelf and reading the back covers, filling a cup with tea from the metal urn. Finally, he turned back to me. "So, what do you think of Maddie?" he asked, smiling.

"She's wonderful. I like her. And she seems to like you."

"Glad you noticed. Yes." He stopped smiling. "And I'm wild about her, too. I just hope I did the right thing bringing her here with me."

"You must have felt she was in real danger."

"I did. You would have too—her apartment was torn to shreds. But I also wanted her to be with me, and running away together accomplished that in a hurry."

"Are you saying *that* was your reason for leaving?"

"No, but the longer we've been out of Sedona, the more remote the danger seems to me, and sometimes I start to wonder whether I exaggerated it, or if it would have been better to stay there and go to the police."

"Excuse me, but are you the same Sebastian who believes in all those political conspiracies, the ones in which the police are always accomplices? And if not, what have you done with my friend?"

He gave me a wry grin. "It's interesting. I've discovered that believing such things in the abstract feels very different from confronting them in one's life. When it's personal, there's a tendency to want to deny that anything could be seriously wrong, because the other path could lead to panic. And it can make you imagine things." He shook his head. "I don't want to talk to Maddie about my suspicions now, when there's nothing to back them up. I just wish I knew more about that so-called FBI man—like whether he's going to show up here."

"Here? I don't think that's likely, do you? How would he know where to look for you, or Maddie, even if he cared?"

"I don't know. I guess it's a bit paranoid to imagine that we've been followed across the entire continent without our noticing it."

"Of course, 'Just because you're paranoid ...'"

"Doesn't mean they're not out to get me? Thanks, pal."

"Seriously, Sebastian, I don't know what to say about that situation in Sedona, but it looks to me like Maddie cares for you. If it happened in a cross-country flight from danger, real or imagined, I don't think it matters. When love shows up, you should follow the immortal advice of Yogi Berra."

"Who?"

"Yogi Berra, the baseball player. He said, 'When you come to a fork in the road, take it.'"

Sebastian laughed, "That's what I've been doing this whole year." He walked back to the bookshelf and began rummaging through the titles again. I spent time behind the counter, checking the jewelry inventory and noting things that we needed to order. A few customers came in to browse, but the store never got busy. After about an hour, Helen and Madeline returned, bringing sandwiches to Sebastian and me. After we ate, he and Madeline decided to go back to Dune Forest and set up housekeeping in the RV. Helen and I waved as they drove off in the rusty yellow sedan.

"Well, that's better," she said as we walked inside.

"Yes, things are settling down, and we're getting a new helper."

"We can use one, too. I've got tons of bookwork to catch up on, and there's that workshop to get ready for this weekend."

"Which one is it?"

"Astrology and Archetypes."

"That's a relief. Nice safe astrology. No extraterrestrials, no death and rebirth, no burning birds."

"We'll see," she smiled. "It may be more intense than you expect. Radha's planning to come, you know."

As usual, Helen was right.

# — 8 —

At 7:00 PM on the following Saturday evening, Helen, Maddie and I were setting up folding chairs in the apartment upstairs from the Missing Link, in preparation for the evening talk. We had received twenty-three registrations, but we always needed extra chairs for last-minute attendees, so we were prepared for about thirty. I put out jugs of cider and bowls of popcorn on a table against a side wall, while Helen set up a tape recorder. We didn't always record these informal evening lecture/discussions, but this speaker was a well-known astrologer and author who had consented to come to our shop because it was near an overnight stop on his current book tour. On another table, we had a stack of the speaker's books for sale, as well as order forms for the evening's tapes. We had closed the shop at six and gone out for a quick dinner before coming back to set up the workshop.

Maddie's first week working in the store had gone well. She and Helen became fast friends right away, and they spent the days plowing through piles of neglected record-keeping, as well as cleaning and restocking the shelves and displays. I noticed Maddie had a knack for understanding customers and helping them choose the book, stone or jewelry piece that was right for each of them. As I watched her finish aligning the chairs and lighting the sage bundle we used to purify the room, I marveled at how quickly she had become a part of our lives.

Sebastian had gone into a hermit mode. We saw him only once that week, when we gave Maddie a ride home and went in to say hello. He was cordial but preoccupied, sitting at his computer screen, the table piled high with books. He had promised to come to the shop to attend the talk, but we hadn't heard from him yet.

At about 7:20, the speaker arrived at the apartment's outside entrance, just after I had asked Maddie to unlock the door. Donald Lee was a slender man in his mid forties, with brown, almond-shaped eyes and long black hair which was tied back behind his head. When we shook hands, I felt he was a bit shy, but when I introduced him to Helen, he warmed to her quickly. She had read his books, and immediately started asking him astrological questions. Within moments, the two of them were in a rapid-fire conversation in a language I only half understood. When I was fairly sure they had forgotten my existence, I slipped away and went downstairs to the office to retrieve the workshop registration list and our cash pouch. It took a few minutes to find them, and by the time I made it back up the stairs the room was starting to fill. Half a dozen people were clustered around the refreshment table, and a few more had already chosen seats. Helen and Mr. Lee were still in deep conversation at the front of the room, and Maddie was near the back wall, talking to someone on the portable telephone we had brought up from the shop. I started circulating through the room, taking people's names and checking them off the list. Then I went back and spoke to Maddie.

"Who was on the phone?"

"I called Sebastian to make sure he was still coming. He had forgotten all about it again, but now he's on his way here. He's been so absorbed in his reading lately, I have to remind him to eat."

"That's pretty darned absorbed, especially for Sebastian. Say, would you mind pulling up a chair by the front door and taking people's names as they come in?"

"Sure, I can do that."

"Thanks. If they're not on the list, they need to pay ten dollars per person. Here's the list and the pouch. If Radha comes, tell her I said her ticket is on the house."

People continued to file in, filling most of the chairs, as well as the couch. I pulled the two old easy chairs to the back of the room, where I usually sat with Helen. It was almost seven-thirty, the scheduled time to begin, when Radha came in. I waved to her as she was giving her name to Maddie, and she hurried to greet me.

"Good gracious, William, it's good to see you!" she exclaimed, embracing me. "Thank you for the free pass. It seems like at least a year since I was here last. But then, time is always like that. We should probably measure it by experiences rather than days, don't you think? Where's Helen? I have to say hello to her before this business gets started. Ah, there she is. Is that the speaker she's talking to? Would you be willing to introduce me?"

Radha's verbal barrage subsided and I took her to meet Mr. Lee. They exchanged pleasantries and seemed poised to launch into an astrological discussion similar to the one he had been having with Helen, but then he glanced at his watch and turned to me. "Do you think everyone has arrived?"

"Almost everyone," I said. "I know of one more person who is on his way, but everyone else on the list is here, plus some extras."

"Well, I think I should get started. I have to catch a plane tomorrow morning."

I called the group to take their seats and introduced the speaker while Helen started the tape recorder. She motioned to me that she was going to sit in the front row with Radha and Maddie. The other chairs were full, so I returned to my seat in the back. Just as the speaker was arranging his notes at the little podium, Sebastian slipped in. I motioned to him to come back and take the chair beside me.

I had come to this evening's talk prepared to be bored. Although Helen and I had chosen our wedding date with help from her astrologer friend, and though I had received personal readings with accurate predictions, the language of astrology was mostly incomprehensible to me. Aspects, angles, progressions and transits—the words might as well have been incantations for all I understood them. So I was surprised to find myself listening closely as Mr. Lee moved through the beginning of his talk. When he mentioned the name of the great psychologist Carl Jung, I thought immediately of the book about flying saucers Sebastian had mentioned, but Mr. Lee was making a different kind of reference.

"Dr. Carl Jung was one of the geniuses of depth psychology, the discoverer of the collective unconscious and its population of archetypal forces. Jung's daughter was an astrologer, and there is evidence to suggest that Jung himself was aware and respectful of the fact that astrology can offer useful insights into the self and the events of life. This is no surprise, since Jung was the originator of the term *synchronicity*, which refers to coincidental events which are connected through meaning, though not through what we think of as linear cause and effect. In my understanding, synchronicity is at the very core of astrology, which, although it works well, is quite mysterious from the strictly rational Western point of view. In fact, as we look more deeply into the interconnectedness of all things which is implied by both astrology and the new physics, we may find that synchronicity is fundamental to the way things are."

Sebastian leaned toward me and whispered, "Mysterious is right. I was almost comfortable thinking of this synchronicity stuff as a once-in-a-while surprise. Now this guy says it's everywhere?"

"And every-when, from the sound of things," I answered.

Mr. Lee continued, "Astrology is defined in *Webster's Third New International Dictionary* as 'divination that treats of the supposed influence of the stars upon human affairs and of the foretelling of terrestrial events by their positions and aspects.' I would differ somewhat from that position. In my mind, it is not that the stars or planets are *influencing* events or people so much as it is that there are *correlations* we can observe between the inner and outer events of life and the positions of the celestial bodies. One way of describing this is to say that we live in a one-piece universe, in which the boundaries we have drawn between self and other, subject and object, inner and outer, are all artificial demarcations. In a one-piece world, everything is connected, so changes in one domain are reflected everywhere else. An individual can learn to notice the changing patterns in one area, and to relate those patterns to observable changes in others. If the same corresponding patterns are seen repeatedly, one has found a correlation that may have predictive value.

"In astrology, the ancients did much of this type of observation. They closely watched and recorded the movements of the stars and planets in the night sky, and noticed synchronous connections with the events of human life, both in the outer world and within the psyche. Astrology and astronomy were originally different aspects of a single science. In fact, Sir Isaac Newton, who 'discovered' gravity and formulated the laws of planetary motion, studied and wrote about both astrology and alchemy. In more recent times, astrology has been dismissed as a kind of superstition. However, quantum physics, arguably the most advanced branch of science, has given rise once again to the idea of a radically interconnected universe in which the observations and predictions of astrology may ultimately be recognized and validated.

"If we go back historically, astrological alignments can be correlated with the great developments and transitions in civilization and human thought. Let's take a single combination of planets to illustrate. Saturn and Pluto are two powerful outer planets, and the outer planets tend to influence humanity as a whole, generationally. In the domain of astrology, Saturn symbolizes discipline, structure, repression, conservatism, judgment. Pluto is power, the underworld, aggression, sex, death and rebirth. In 1914, the conjunction of Saturn and Pluto, in which they appeared to be at the same place in the sky, corresponded to World War I. In 1921 to 1923, they squared, meaning they were at a ninety degree angle to each other, and this period saw the emergence of Fascism. From 1929 to 1932, the two planets were in opposition to each other, one hundred and eighty degrees apart, and in that time we saw the Great Depression and the invasion of Asia by Japan. From 1939 to 1941 there was another Saturn/Pluto square, and that was at the beginning of World War II and the German concentration camps. Then in 1946 to 1948 there was another conjunction, and this post-war period included Stalin's takeover of Eastern Europe, the initiation of the Cold War, and the beginnings of the CIA."

Sebastian whispered, "Saturn and Pluto have a lot to answer for."

"But who'd want to mess with them?" I whispered back.

Mr. Lee went on. "The examples I just gave you were presented at a seminar taught by Richard Tarnas, one of the leading astrologers of our times. Mr. Tarnas also made a number of statements which powerfully express the implications of the observations and predictions we can make via astrology. The fact that the movements and positions of physical objects such as the stars and planets can be accurately correlated with events in the human world reveals that, in his words, 'The earth is a center of cosmic meaning.' Rather than being a random universe of unconnected objects and events, the cosmos is revealed to be an intelligent whole which is permeated with meaning.

"Another of Mr. Tarnas' ideas which resonated with me was, 'Astrology is not concretely predictive, but it is archetypally predictive.' In other words, astrology can't tell you exactly what will happen to you or anyone else, but it can illuminate the pattern of the *kinds* of things which might occur. So, for instance, your astrology chart can't tell you that you'll be hit by a truck on Elm Street next Tuesday, but your astrological transits—the elements of the birth chart affected by various alignments with the planets—can show you a pattern of energies that would suggest a period of being accident-prone."

Sebastian whispered again, "More synchronicity. This works just the same as Tarot cards."

"It's like you said in your letter from Sedona," I replied. "Chicken entrails would probably work, too, if you knew how to observe them."

"*You* can observe them if you want. I like this better."

"Shhh, let's listen."

Mr. Lee continued, "Does everyone here know what I mean by the word archetype? Let's see hands." About a dozen hands went up, including Radha's, Helen's and Maddie's. "About half. Okay, I'll say a few words about that. In his classic work, *The Archetypes and the Collective Unconscious*, Jung tells us that archetypes are the primordial types—universal images that have existed since the remotest times. They are seen as embedded in the structure of the shared soul of humanity which he names the collective unconscious. We can understand archetypes as forces of the psyche, the gods and goddesses of the interior world, powerful instinctual forces, and/or philosophical principles. The mythologies of all cultures, as well as the deeper dreams that we experience, can show us the outlines of these eternal forms. Beings such as the Great Mother Goddess, the pagan god Pan, and all the pantheons of gods and goddesses from the world's religions are expressions of archetypal principles. Astrology has identified a number of specific archetypal patterns, which appear to be intimately linked to certain planets and their movements. The first seven planets of the solar system were known to the ancients, who gave them the names of the gods whose traits matched the observed 'effects' of the movements of those planets. For example, the planet Venus is associated with the archetype of the ancient goddess of love and beauty Our own experiences with love and beauty, as they appear in our lives, can be understood through the placement of Venus in the birth chart and predicted through studying transits involving the planet Venus. The evidence that astrology is able to map and predict the interplay of archetypal forces in both individual and collective life shows us that the archetypes in a very real sense determine the *very possibilities* that are played out through our choices in life here on Earth.

"Stanislav Grof, one of the founders of transpersonal psychology, has said this: 'The world of archetypes, although normally imperceptible, is not entirely separate from our own. It is intimately interwoven with it and plays a critical role in creating it. In this way, it represents a supraordinated [higher] dimension that forms and informs the experience of our everyday life. The archetypal domain thus represents a bridge between the world of matter and the undifferentiated field of Cosmic Consciousness.'" Mr. Lee continued, "As a conceptual aid, we might place the archetypes roughly midway between ourselves and the Divine source, occupying a position like that of the Greek and Roman gods and goddesses of antiquity. Thus they set the stage and form the basic storylines of our world, and we act them out in a kind of improvisational play."

"See?" Sebastian nudged me. "I'll bet the Tarot cards are involved in all this. Think about the names of the major arcana cards—Temperance, Judgment, the Empress, the Fool—those have got to be archetypes too." He stood up, "I have a question. I use the tarot. My friend Helen up there in the front got me started. Do the Tarot cards have anything to do with this?"

"Yes, I would say that the Tarot, *I Ching*, and other divination systems, including astrology, work with the ordering principles of the archetypal forces. Both Tarot and astrology use the principle of synchronicity by assuming that a pattern observed in the physical world, be it the inexorable movements of the planets or the random shuffling of a pack of cards, can be interpreted in a way that will shed light on whatever questions we bring to them.

"That of course takes us to what I think makes astrology worthwhile. It provides a means for us to become conscious of the archetypal weather report—it can give us a moving picture of ourselves, our life situation, and even the state of our world—past, present and future. When we learn how to look at that picture, we can navigate better, riding the fair winds and weathering the storms.

"One of the most revolutionary ideas underlying astrology is that domain of the archetypes is somehow linked to our physical world. In the words of Richard Tarnas, 'The collective unconscious seems to be embedded in the cosmos itself.' Let me give you two instances that show how the material universe reflects archetypal meanings. I found them in this quote from astrologer Caroline Casey: 'The planet Venus—also the goddess of beauty and symmetry—has been identified by astronomers as the most perfectly symmetrical in its shape and orbit of all the planets. And Uranus, which is the planet that is associated with the trickster archetype—representing the maverick, the eccentric, and the energy of disruption—we now know is the one and only planet that rotates counterclockwise.'" So you can see here how the archetypal energies associated with these planets are mirrored in the physical attributes of the planets themselves."

"Now, that's amazing," I whispered to Sebastian.

"Amen. Two points for the Creator of the universe on that one."

Mr. Lee went on to describe the characteristic energies of each planet and the basic traits of the zodiacal signs. Sebastian took notes in a spiral notebook he had brought, and I borrowed paper from him to make some of my own. The evening passed swiftly as Mr. Lee illustrated his points with examples of famous people and historical events. As he built his case, I grew more and more intrigued, beginning to envision a profound interconnectedness between the inner and outer worlds. As he neared the conclusion, he began to discuss his thoughts on possibilities for the future.

Mr. Lee continued, "The Uranus/Neptune conjunction that started in 1985 has been a major influence towards consciousness expansion. The revolutionary energies of Uranus have acted to awaken and free Neptune's mysticism. The spread of the New Age mind set and life style, as well as the coming together of science and spirituality, are both manifestations of this combination of energies. The harmonious aspect of Pluto sextile Neptune has been in effect for most of our lives and may be responsible for the long period of spiritually oriented evolution we have been experiencing. By the way, this same aspect also happened during the Renaissance.

"As to what lies ahead for us all, I personally feel the human species has been going through something not unlike the birth process, and I expect that to continue. The acceleration of change on all levels during the 20th century—from the technological to the social to the spiritual—seems to be carrying us to some future point of discontinuity, a radical shift of consciousness that could be seen as the moment of our emergence into a new world. This acceleration seems to have coincided with the linking of several outer planet cycle crossings, in which their powerful collective energies tended to magnify one another.

"Having said that, it is difficult to see what astrological conditions would set the stage for a quantum leap of human consciousness, at least one of the magnitude I have been describing. At times I almost feel that such a shift would go beyond our traditional understanding of astrology. If that is true, the leap could happen virtually anytime. Another consideration is that the most powerful changes often occur in situations of crisis, so it might be incorrect to expect any kind of breakthrough to happen during harmonious times." He smiled, "After all, on the everyday human level, how many of us are likely to make significant changes when our lives are comfortable? And if discomfort is what is called for, the first decade of the new millennium, especially its latter stages, ought to offer us plenty. Moving through that period, there are numerous aspects coming up that in the past have been associated with economic depressions, social control and repression by governments, revolutions and struggles for freedom, attempts to transcend known boundaries, and the onset of war. The period from 2008 through 2011 is of particular concern, since it exhibits aspects I would tend to associate with an economic depression. But this kind of stress can also produce profound spiritual growth, as people turn inward for answers."

Mr. Lee took a sheet of paper from his notes. "My fellow astrologer, Norma Ream, has said this about the first decade of the twenty-first century: 'There is the excitement of discovery ahead. There are indicators of inventiveness and higher levels of creativity. Spirituality and science may still clash while witnessing phenomena that neither one can define or categorize. Health and healing may also take leaps of advancement relating to the greater general acceptance of more spiritual ideas. Intuition and increased sensitivity are likely to be a greater part of the theme of expanded human potential. By the end of the first decade of the 21st century, there are some potent eclipses that add to the increased energy of very slow planets changing signs. This is always a change of tone, so to speak, of how the energy is expressed. We will have the potent energy of adventure and pioneering spirit similar to the American 1760's . There is the drive to conquer, control and territorialize. The excitement to go beyond known boundaries might apply to deep sea or deep space exploration, or diving into the inner worlds. There is also the sense of strict and rigid control or structure. Those holding the traditional reins of power may try to tighten their grip. There will be stresses between those in power and those feeling the drive for freedom to explore new territory. The power structure or system may even use force in maintaining control. Economics could be dramatically transformed during this period. In fact, the whole system of productivity and material goods could also undergo a reformation. The years of 2010 to 2012 hold the potential for a radical shift of how we live our lives and what we do as a species. This time can herald an explosive evolutionary growth spurt. Technology and science are likely to have some incredible breakthroughs in the general understanding of life. Just as there have been leaps in understanding at key points in history, this will be the next really big stepping off point.'"

Mr. Lee said, "I generally agree with Ms. Ream's assessments, although I'm not sure we'll have to wait until the end of the decade before we see major breakthroughs in consciousness. That having been said, now I'll show you a preview of what's coming up." He went to the blackboard on the wall behind the podium and began drawing circular charts that sketched out the significant astrological configurations he expected to coincide with important events in the next ten years. Although I didn't comprehend the symbols, I understood enough to know that, from his perspective at least, the world was headed for what the old Chinese curse called "interesting times." I thought again of the words that had come through Radha: "Before the Light comes there will be darkness, and then fire." A shiver moved through me. I looked around the room at the familiar walls and furnishings, at the people who sat in rapt attention, and at Mr. Lee smiling as he explained and answered questions. I gazed out the window, and the night seemed somehow darker than usual. I felt a sense of the precarious vulnerability of the lives we all moved through with such unthinking confidence. I suddenly wished Helen were sitting next to me so I could put my arm around her.

A few minutes later, I heard Mr. Lee concluding his talk. I joined the audience in their applause, and then stood up to stretch as some of the attendees clustered around Mr. Lee while others gathered their belongings and prepared to leave. I walked to the display table and collected money from several people who wanted to buy his book. Sebastian had stationed himself at the refreshment table, where he stood, cider cup in hand, munching popcorn. Radha, Helen and Maddie were near the front of the room, talking among themselves and waiting for the crowd around the speaker to dissipate. When there were no more customers, I made my way through the maze of chairs and people, until I was right behind them.

"Will, what did you think of it? Wasn't he terrific?" Maddie asked.

"Terror-ific." I said, putting an arm around Helen's shoulders. "The next ten years could be a little tough, if this guy's right."

"There goes Will the worrywart," said Helen. "Give him a glass that's half full, and he'll not only say it's half empty—he'll fret about the rest of it evaporating."

"I don't entirely blame him," Radha remarked. "I've been coming upon quite a bit of material that appears more dire than the predictions we've heard tonight. However, I must say that I like Mr. Lee's attitude about future events. It takes courage to see a crisis coming and view it as an opportunity."

"Do you think he's right about the possibility of an evolutionary leap?" Maddie asked.

"I'm not sure," Radha answered, "but I've got an inkling ..."

"An inkling?" Sebastian grinned, as he came to join us. "Isn't that a baby ink? And you have one? I've heard they're awfully messy to carry around."

"Forgive me for doing this, Radha," I said, rolling my eyes, "but I'd like to introduce you to our friend Sebastian. What his jokes lack in quality they make up for in frequency."

"It's a pleasure," she smiled. "Your charming friend Madeline has already warned me about you. I consider myself immunized."

"Don't be so sure," he retorted. "Like any self-respecting, self-replicating virus, I know how to mutate."

"My pal, the mutant," I said.

"At the risk of raising the level of this conversation," Helen interjected, "I suggest we have a word with Mr. Lee. I think he's free now."

The speaker was signing his book for the last person who had been waiting. The crowd was gone, except for two people who were by the door. The three of them left together, and only six of us remained in the room. Helen held out her hand. "Mr. Lee, thank you so much for a fascinating lecture."

"Thank you for having me, and please call me Don. This was quite a sophisticated audience, especially in regard to the astrology. I appreciate it when I don't have to begin at square one."

"You would have had to for me," Sebastian said. "But I enjoyed it anyway. I may not know an aspect from an elbow, but I certainly agree with you about the upcoming repression of personal freedoms by governments. Except that I think it's already here."

Mr. Lee frowned, "It can always get worse. And it often does before it gets better."

"'Before the Light comes there will be darkness, and then fire,'" I murmured.

"Yes, I suppose you could put it that way," he said. "But what is the fire supposed to signify?"

"I wish I knew," I said.

"Will has brought you in at the middle of a very long story," Helen said.

"Actually, it involves us all," Radha continued. "If you'd like to hear it, perhaps the whole group of us could go somewhere for coffee. And I'm sure we're all bursting with questions for you as well."

Mr. Lee's cheeks colored and he cleared his throat. I thought I could see his earlier shyness returning. "Well, I'm not sure. You see, I have that plane tomorrow."

"Please, Donald," Radha cajoled. (I could have sworn she batted her eyelashes at him.) "It would mean so much to us. And, as my spirit guides always tell me, 'You can catch up on your sleep when you're dead.' Of course, they're liars. Nobody sleeps when they're dead. But never mind that. If you'll give us an hour, I promise we won't ask for more."

"Well, I suppose I could use a cup of something."

"Wonderful! How about everyone else? All coming? All right then, where shall we go?"

# 9

Rivendell's was a comfortable cafe within walking distance of the store. The building had once been a sea captain's house, a Victorian mansion, but now the rooms were filled with old oak tables and mismatched wooden chairs. The time was half-past nine, and there weren't many diners left in the place. Our group was seated at a round antique table in what had once been a parlor. Because of the late hour, we had the room to ourselves.

We all scanned our menus quickly, to make our choices before the kitchen closed. Desserts at Rivendell's were famous. Helen and I shared a chocolate mousse, Maddie ordered apple crisp, Radha chose baklava, Sebastian ordered a hot fudge sundae, and Donald Lee asked for a cup of espresso.

In a matter of minutes, our orders arrived. We all dug in, and the first conversation consisted mainly of delighted moans and exclamations of pleasure. Don sipped his espresso and looked around the table with quizzical amusement.

Sebastian raised his spoon and held it aloft as if it were a champagne glass. Smiling at Maddie, he proclaimed, "Here's to the two things that make life worth living, love and ice cream."

"Greek pastry and higher knowledge," Radha intoned.

"Umm, apple crisp and enlightenment," Maddie chimed in.

"Mousse and merriment!" Helen smiled.

Mr. Lee raised his cup doubtfully, "Espresso and astrology?"

"What do you say, Will?" Maddie asked.

I didn't answer immediately. I was stuck in a pensive mood, still thinking about the uncertain future the astrologer's talk had foretold. "Oh, I don't know ... There are lots of things that make life worth living." I turned to Radha, "Aren't you going to tell Don the story?"

"I surely am. I was just getting my strength up."

Radha began by explaining to Mr. Lee how she had met me and Helen, about the insistence of her guides that she do a channeling session for us, and about the surprising events of that evening. She showed him a written transcript of the message. He was particularly interested in the details about Anon— the different voices Helen and I had heard, the warm vibration that had moved into our bodies, and the vision of this radiant being that Radha had seen on the inner planes. He suggested that perhaps we had been contacted by some kind of archetypal entity. Sebastian and Maddie retold their tale of Bell Rock and their hurried departure, including the synchronous naming of their inflatable ET. When they finished, he sat back in his chair, arms folded, looking at each of us, and finally back to Maddie.

"You know, I've given some thought to the question you and Sebastian have been wrestling with—the nature of the Visitors. It's clear to me that something real is happening. Hundreds of thousands of people all over the globe are having encounters with these beings. And the themes of many episodes—warnings of planetary crises and urgings toward spiritual transformation—are remarkably similar, even among people who know nothing of others' encounters. Yet the physical traces of the contacts are often ambiguous, and some of the experiences people claim to have are impossible in the physical world as we know it."

"But they happen," Maddie said. "I've been with them, and they *can* come through closed doors and make you float out of windows. And they *do* want to help us become enlightened."

"Granted," Don said. "Your experiences completely fit the pattern. What I'm concerned with is not about the validation of your encounters— I believe you had them and they are real on some level. But I want to understand the *nature* of the events—how and in what domain such things are possible. At the moment, my best guess is that we are dealing with manifestations of an archetype, perhaps a very important one for our time. I can imagine both the Visitors and other figures from the archetypal domain as independent intelligences capable of bridging the inner and outer worlds, or of operating in each world from another dimension which transcends both. That's a description that can be applied both to Madeline's experiences with the Visitors, and to Will, Helen and Radha's encounter with Anon. For that matter, the same model fits many of the stories which have been told of meetings with gods, angels, fairies, demons, and all manner of other extraordinary encounters."

"I keep wondering if it's a matter of differing densities or vibrational frequencies," said Helen. "For instance, we're all aware of electromagnetic energies such as heat and visible light, because we can sense them. But ultraviolet and gamma rays are real, too, and they can affect us, even though our senses don't detect them."

"Right," Mr. Lee continued. "And the archetypes are normally undetectable to our senses, even though we can observe their influences. But people have reported encounters and even communications with archetypal entities, such as animal and plant spirits or the gods of various mythologies, which occur in nonordinary states of awareness. Such states have long been a part of human experience—they can be generated by special breathing, yogic techniques, the ingestion of psychotropic plants, or in many other ways. Western medicine and science have generally dismissed such experiences as hallucinatory, but the transpersonal psychologists have begun to show us the healing potential of these encounters, and their value to our understanding of the psyche."

"What do you think of the Visitors' messages?" I asked.

"That many of them make sense, wherever they come from, and that they sound familiar. Their prophetic aspects resonate with prophecies for our times from all kinds of sources. Have you ever heard of the Kalachakra?"

"No, what's that?"

"It's a path of Tantric Buddhist teachings, purportedly first taught by the Buddha at age thirty-seven, a year after his enlightenment. I don't pretend to understand the complexities of this teaching, but I did attend three days of a Kalachakra initiation given by the Dalai Lama in New York in 1991. While I was there, I learned that the initiates are given the opportunity to pledge themselves to the Bodhisattva path, that is, to strive for enlightenment but to refuse the bliss of nirvana until all other sentient beings become enlightened. It's a very selfless ideal, and I admired it greatly. But the reason I bring this up has to do with a prophecy. Between the lectures, I walked through an exhibit of Tibetan *thankas*, sacred mandala paintings. One in particular attracted me, and I read the explanation placard on the wall beside it. The painting depicted the rescue of the world by the Lords of Shambhala. The legend states that, in the time of the Kalachakra, there will be great evil and degeneration, and that the world will be in danger of being taken over by violent barbarians. At that time the great warrior Raudra Chakri and his heroic followers will issue forth from the mystical land of Shambhala and save the earth for the forces of Light."

"I've heard the name Shambhala before, but what is it, and where is it?" I asked.

"It is said to exist on multiple levels. Physically, its location is supposed to be somewhere in the south-central section of the former Soviet Union. However, it is also a 'pure land,' an ideal spiritual country existing in the same space but in a higher dimension. It's somewhat similar to the idea you expressed about the ETs, Helen. Anyway, the Tibetan teachings say that the entities on this extraordinary dimension can be contacted by pure-hearted devotees of this world, and when conditions are ripe, the mystical heroes of that higher domain can emanate forth to subdue the forces of evil."

"How would we know if the conditions are ripe?" asked Helen.

"Take a look around," said Sebastian, gesturing with his spoon. "The twentieth century is the most horrific in the history of the world. More people have died in wars, more destruction has been done to the environment in our century than in all the others put together. Weapons technology—nuclear, chemical, biological, to say nothing of the stuff I worked on—has put the whole planet's neck in the noose. It seems as though our knowledge has grown faster than our humanity—Pasteur's work has been turned to germ warfare, Einstein's breakthroughs have given birth to atomic weapons. How much more evil can it get? Don, tell me, what are those Shambhala guys waiting for?"

"The critical moment, I suppose. Or perhaps they have to be summoned by us. It may be that the Tibetans think so. One thing I learned touches on that—the prophecy I read says that this will happen 'in the time of the Kalachakra.' While I was in New York, I learned that Tenzin Gyatso, the fourteenth Dalai Lama, who gave the initiation there, is only the third Dalai Lama in history to offer the Kalachakra initiation. The seventh Dalai Lama gave it once, the eighth one gave it twice, but Tenzin Gyatso had given it *fourteen* times by 1991, and he has continued to offer it since then. He was also the only Dalai Lama to offer the initiation to laypersons. It was explained that in these degenerate times it was necessary to attempt to bring in beneficial energies in any way possible. In my own mind, I wonder if all these initiations aren't an attempt to call forth the 'Lords of Shambhala.' If there really is a 'time of the Kalachakra,' I think the Tibetans believe we're in it now."

"The Lords of Shambhala," Radha mused. "What a beautiful image it is—to see help unlooked-for emerging from an invisible realm."

"These stories are not new to the West," Don went on. "Madame Blavatsky, the Russian mystic who founded the Theosophical Society, popularized the legend in North America and Europe, beginning in the late 1800s. It was probably through her work that the author James Hilton learned of it and fictionalized it as the mystical land of Shangri-la in his novel *Lost Horizons*."

"Wasn't there a movie made of that?" I asked. "I remember an old black and white film about Shangri-la. I saw it on TV when I was a kid."

"That's the one," Don replied. "It's a classic that's still popular with movie buffs. You know, there was even a clip from it used in *Raiders of the Lost Ark*."

"There's another story where the barbarians are destroyed by supernatural forces," Sebastian said. "I wish that would happen in real life. It was so satisfying to see those melting Nazis at the end of the movie. I've got my own list of villains that need melting, but I can never find a fire-wielding, avenging archetype when I need one."

"Be careful what you wish for, Sebastian," Radha said. "Sometimes our desires are granted, in ways that we come to regret."

"But when they're denied, I regret that immediately. I'd gladly take my chances with instant gratification, given a choice."

Our waiter came to the table to ask if we were finished. No one wanted to leave, except possibly Don, who glanced at his watch. Helen, Maddie and I ordered herbal teas, Radha requested coffee, and Sebastian decided to have another hot fudge sundae and a beer.

"How can you do that?" Maddie asked incredulously.

"Life is short, ice cream is sweet, and beer is blissful," he retorted.

"Life *will* be short if you keep that up," she said.

"I'm afraid it might be anyway," he said, turning to the rest of us. "To tell the truth, I never expected to live this long. I grew up thinking a nuclear war would wipe us all out before I was thirty."

"It could still happen," Don remarked. "In some ways, the world is more unstable now than it was during the Cold War. Think of all the stories you read in the newspapers about the old Soviet nuclear weapons being smuggled out and sold."

"And their scientists are leaving Russia and going to work in countries that are less than crazy about the U.S.A.," I added.

"I'm more concerned about a collapse of the environment," said Helen. The natural world supports everything, but it's being systematically destroyed."

Mr. Lee frowned, "I agree with you, Helen, and I've been reading lately that some scientists believe we have less than ten years to turn things around before the damage done to the ecology is irreversible."

"That's the same thing the ETs are telling people," Maddie interjected.

"During one of my abductions, I was shown a screen with projections of environmental disasters—oil spills, smokestacks spewing pollution, dead fish floating in rivers, dumps with leaking barrels of toxic chemicals—and I was told telepathically that we only had a few years left before the damage was irreversible. Later I read that a lot of abductees have had very similar episodes."

"The voices of the inner world are practically shrieking it at us," said Radha. "And so are the voices of science and reason, but nothing seems able to stop the momentum of greed and blindness that is rolling us towards disaster. As I said earlier, I've been doing a bit of research since my last visit with Helen and Will, and there are a number of prophecies, some of them quite old, that point to the crisis into which we seem to be moving." She reached into her bag and produced a small notebook. "I've written down one with some predictions that interested me. Would you like to hear them?"

"Bring 'em on," said Sebastian.

"Yes," said Helen. "Let's listen."

"Is this going to worry me?" I asked.

"Without a doubt," Radha smiled. "But we can't let that hold us back, can we? I spent a day this week searching the Internet. There's a lot of rubbish out there, but it's also a place where one can find some very interesting materials that never appear on the news."

"You can say that again," Sebastian agreed. "The stuff I've been reading about political conspiracies is enough to make what's left of Will's hair stand on end."

I said nothing. Radha continued, "Ahem. I was about to mention that one of the more interesting things I found was an article on a prophetess named Mother Shipton. According the the article I discovered, her given name was Ursula Southiel, and she was born in 1488 near Yorkshire, England. She was around twenty-four years old when her gift of being able to foretell the future became known. As was typical in those days, she composed her prophecies in verse. Some of what she wrote was rather localized in scope, confined to her country and the relatively near future. However, a surprising amount seems to relate to our modern world. I'll just read you a few of her verses." She turned the page of the notebook and began reciting:

> Through towering hills proud men shall ride
> No horse or ass move by his side.
>
> Beneath the water, men shall walk—

*Shall ride, shall sleep, shall even talk.*
*And in the air men shall be seen*
*In white and black and even green.*

*A great man then, shall come and go*
*For prophecy declares it so.*
*In water, iron then shall float*
*As easy as a wooden boat.*
*Gold shall be seen in stream and stone*
*In land that is yet unknown.*

"When was this prophecy made?" Don interrupted.

"In the first half of the sixteenth century," Radha answered. "I don't know the exact date."

"That's fascinating. It sounds as though she foresaw the advent of automobiles, airplanes and steel ships."

"And scuba diving," Sebastian added.

"What about the 'gold in stream and stone?'" I said. "Could that be the California Gold Rush?"

"I'm not certain about that, but there's more I want to read to you." She continued:

*For in those wondrous far-off days*
*The women shall adopt a craze:*
*To dress like men, and trousers wear,*
*And to cut off their locks of hair.*
*They'll ride astride with brazen brow,*
*As witches do on broomstick now.*

*And roaring monsters with man atop*
*Does seem to eat the verdant crop;*
*And men shall fly as birds do now,*
*And give away the horse and plough.*

"How curious," said Helen. "She had a vision of women's future hair styles and clothes."

"The crop-eating monsters have got to be mechanized harvesting equipment," I said.

"Correct," Radha agreed. "Now, listen to this section."

*In nineteen hundred and twenty-six*
*Build houses light of straw and sticks.*
*For then shall mighty wars be planned*
*And fire and sword shall sweep the land.*

*When pictures seem alive with movements free,*
*When boats like fishes swim beneath the sea,*
*When men like birds shall scour the sky,*
*Then half the world, deep drenched in blood shall die.*

*For those who live the century through,*
*In fear and trembling this shall do.*
*Flee to the mountains and the dens,*
*To bog and forest and wild fens.*

*For storms will rage and oceans roar*
*When Gabriel stands on sea and shore;*
*And as he blows his wondrous horn,*
*Old worlds die and new be born.*

"The twenties were when Hitler was organizing the Nazi party," said Sebastian. "And he published *Mein Kampf* in 1924. I can believe that in 1926 he was already planning his attempt to take over the world."

"And the following stanza is a fair description of the World War II era," Radha added, "complete with moving pictures, submarines, airplanes and a dreadful amount of blood."

"I don't like where this is going," I said, reaching over to pick up Radha's notebook. "The beginning of the twenty-first century is supposed to fill the people—that's us—with fear and trembling. I don't want to live in a bog, or a wild fen, whatever that is."

"The last stanza sounds like the earth-change predictions," Helen mused. "I don't know how to interpret the reference to Gabriel, but that last line, 'Old worlds die and new be born' ... It's like the message from Anon, about the time of death and rebirth."

"Exactly," Radha assented, reaching to take back the notebook. "And it continues with a long description of a chain of natural disasters, apparently triggered by the earth's drifting through a comet's tail. She says, 'A fiery Dragon will cross the sky/ Six times before this earth shall die.' The encounter of our planet with the dragon's tail is supposed to set off floods, earthquakes, the shifting of oceans, and the pushing-up of new lands from the ocean floor. She predicts that most of the human race will be destroyed, and that a small band of people will begin a dynasty on the unsullied ground which has emerged from the sea."

"It reminds me of the Edgar Cayce prophecy of the rising of Atlantis," said Helen.

"Except that this one came four hundred years earlier," I said. "Radha, do you think all these disasters will actually happen? This Mother Shipton sure seemed to be precise with the predictions about modern technology."

"I don't know, Will. I hope not. We have certainly all heard a lot of 'earth change' forecasts, filled with dire warnings, but I've personally seen a number of deadlines go by with no cataclysms to show for them."

"I've often thought these things can be symbolic," Don said. "In the inner world, such as we see in dreams, visions of physical catastrophes can represent upheavals in the personal psyche. When we have thousands of people reporting such visions around the world, as we do now, along with the convergence of the same images in prophecies coming from various cultures and individuals through history, it may mean that we are due for a major shift in the collective unconscious. Rather than actual physical destruction, we might see a big change in the world soul."

"Well, I'd prefer that, I think," I said.

"There may even be a choice," he continued. "With the archetypal energies in astrology, I've seen over and over that the exact same patterns can show up in very different forms. When the client is aware of what's going on and is consciously working with the energies which are in force, the experience is usually more inward, and more graceful. When the client is unconscious or resistant, things often show up in his outer life in ways that are considerably more difficult."

"Inner transformation or outer destruction—that's the choice Anon foretold and it's the choice we ultimately have," said Helen. "We've been talking about the environment, for instance. If we change our inner attitudes towards the earth, we'll stop destroying it. If we don't, it may destroy us."

"I'm afraid I agree with that," Radha said, "but I still want to read you the end of Mother Shipton's prophecy."

> And before the race is built anew,
> A silver serpent comes to view
> And spews out men of like unknown,

*To mingle with the earth, now grown*
*Cold from its heat, and these men can*
*Enlighten the minds of future man.*

*To intermingle and show them how*
*To live and love, and thus endow*
*The children with the second sight—*
*A natural thing so that they might*
*Grow graceful, humble, and when they do,*
*The Golden Age will start anew.*

"A silver serpent!" Maddie exclaimed. "Carrying men 'of like unknown'—that must be the extraterrestrials. She sees them coming to live among us, bringing enlightenment to the people."

"Endowing the children with 'second sight'—activating their psychic abilities, bringing them into a state of grace. That makes sense," Helen mused.

I had latched onto Radha's notebook again and was scouring the pages. "Radha, do you have any idea what this phrase means: 'To mingle with the earth, now grown/Cold from its heat ...'?"

"Old Mother Shipton must have had one too many that day," Sebastian remarked, while draining his glass of beer. "How can anything grow cold from its heat? It's like growing sober from your drinking."

"No danger of your doing that," said Madeline.

"Hey, I only had one beer. It's the ice cream that intoxicated me."

Helen said, "Maybe 'from' is being used in place of a word like 'after'. The earth could grow cold 'after' its heat, like a hearth can grow cold after its fire."

"Fire," I muttered, almost to myself. "Before the Light comes there will be darkness, and then fire."

"Will, you've got it!" Radha exclaimed.

"What have I got?"

"The connection between this prophecy and the message from Anon. Mother Shipton's verse lays out the same pattern of destruction and renewal, death and rebirth, as the one we were given in your living room. She talks at length about the darkness of human depravity, and about the fiery dragon's tail that will sweep across the earth, with its wake of destruction. Then, with the spiritual awakening brought by the men in the silver serpent, the Light returns. And the return comes *after* the earth grows 'cold from its heat,' after the transmutation of the fire." She pulled the paper with Anon's words from her purse and unfolded it. "Look, Anon says the time of the fire can be a 'gateway to a golden age', and Mother Shipton says, 'the Golden Age will start anew.'"

"So what does that mean for us?" I asked.

Don frowned, "If it means anything, it means that people need to wake up. If that happens, we'll undoubtably see shifts of consciousness on the inner levels that will be reflected in positive changes in the outer world. If not, the outer world may force us to change or be destroyed. As I said, when a person is conscious, the energies of any transit, or transformation, go a lot more smoothly. But when the individual's mind is closed, the archetypes get his attention by hitting him over the head with crises in his day-to-day life. On a worldwide level, it *could* mean economic depression, war, epidemics, famines, or even natural disasters."

I turned to Radha, "Is that how you see it?"

"Regrettably, I'm afraid I must agree with Don."

"See?" Sebastian said to Maddie. "I knew I should be eating ice cream while the eating's good."

"Don't worry, Will," said Helen. "I know in my heart that the power of the Light is infinite. It can take the greatest evil and redeem it to an even greater good."

"I'll join you in that affirmation," Radha agreed. "And even that potential was addressed by Anon." She read from the page, "*The dark fires of destruction also threaten to immolate your world. Do not feed them with your fear, but know they too can serve the Infinite One.*'"

At that moment, the waiter approached our table. We were the only ones left in the restaurant. "Is everything all right?" he inquired.

"We're not sure," I said.

"I beg your pardon?"

"Oh, never mind. I'm sorry. I was on another subject."

"Will you be needing anything else?"

"No, I suppose we should be going. You can bring us the check."

We all left the restaurant together and walked back to the shop. There we thanked Don Lee and wished him well on his book tour. Sebastian and Maddie drove off to the RV park and Radha accepted an invitation to spend the night at our house. As we drove home, both Helen and I were quiet, reflecting on the thoughts and images that the evening's events had stirred in each of us.

# — 10 —

The next day was Sunday and the Missing Link was closed. We had made plans to visit Sebastian and Maddie that day and go with them to the beach. Radha was also invited to come along.

Around midday, the three of us rode together in Radha's car to Dune Forest. I sat in the back seat savoring the breeze from the open window while Helen and Radha conversed in the front. The September air was remarkably warm, and I was looking forward to what might be the final swim of the season.

We pulled into the long gravel driveway that led through a thicket of stunted pines to the campgrounds. As we approached, Maddie emerged from *RV There Yet*, waving and smiling, already in her bright blue swimsuit. Radha parked next to Sebastian's rusty yellow Toyota, and we all got out. Maddie embraced Helen, and beckoned to Radha and me.

"Come on, let's get going. Bring your bags inside. You can change here and we'll walk to the beach."

We all filed in after Maddie. Sebastian sat on the bench seat at the kitchen table, looking intently into his computer screen, stacks of books on either side of the keyboard. I read some of the titles—*Conspiracies, Cover-Ups and Crimes, The Seventy Greatest Conspiracies of All Time, The JFK Assassination, The Illuminatus Trilogy*. I picked up one of them and asked, "Catching up on your light summer reading?"

Sebastian started, "What? Oh, yeah. That's what I'm doing, yes indeed."

"Are you going to the beach with us?"

"Um, yes, but ... not right now. I want to finish reading something here and then I'll come out and join you."

Radha, Helen and I changed into our beach clothes and walked with Maddie along a trail through the scrub pines that led to Good Haven Beach.

The sand covered a wide expanse of ocean front, shaped in a crescent with two arms pointing out into the Atlantic. The sea breeze was fresh and salty, and the air was alive with the shrill cries of white gulls. The blue sky was punctuated with puffy clouds, and the strengthening sun warmed us inside and out. We chose a spot about fifty yards from the water's edge, and at least that far from the nearest neighbors. Helen and Radha laid out the towels while I set up the green beach umbrella. Maddie ran to the water, while the other women stretched out to sunbathe. I reclined with my head in the umbrella's shadow and opened the book I had chosen from Sebastian's table.

I must have read for at least an hour, because I had finished several chapters before I began to notice that my legs, unshaded by the umbrella, were slowly roasting. Helen and Radha had applied sun screen, and had been periodically turning themselves while Maddie cavorted among the waves. As I sat up, attempting to fold myself into the umbrella's shadow, she ran up from the surf and sat down in front of me.

"The water is so *cold*," she smiled, pulling a towel from the beach bag and wrapping it around her shoulders. "I love how it makes me feel—I just wanted to keep swimming and swimming. After a while I started cramping a little, though, so I thought I'd better come out."

"That's probably a good idea," I said. "But I think you've spent your time better than I did. My legs are sunburned and this book is giving me brain cramps."

She looked at the cover. "Oh, that one. Sebastian loves that book. He keeps reading me passages from it."

"Where is he, anyway? He said he was going to join us, didn't he?"

"He's probably lost in cyberspace somewhere. I told you I have to remind him to do everything these days. Maybe I should walk back and get him."

"That's all right. I feel like stretching my legs and getting out of the sun. I'll go see what he's up to."

Helen lifted her head, "Bring us back something to drink, would you, Will? I forgot our water."

"Will, dear," said Radha, still lying motionless. "I have some wonderful mint tea bags in the glove box of my car. Would you consider brewing up a batch of iced tea while you're retrieving Sebastian?"

"Why not? I'll be back in a long, slow flash. Don't get too cooked."

"I'll coax them into the water," Maddie said.

I picked up the book and headed back along the path by which we had come. When I reached the campsite, I went to Radha's car for the tea bags and then to the door of the RV. "Sebastian?"

"Come on in."

I entered and found Sebastian still seated at the computer. I pointed to it and said, "We were afraid you'd gotten lost in there."

"Sorry, I do tend to get absorbed." He turned to me and grinned. "What do you think of that book?"

"*The 70 Greatest Conspiracies?*" It's wild. I've been skipping around in it, reading the chapters that grabbed me. Do you believe all that stuff is true?"

"I'm pretty sure that a good thirty percent of the theories discussed in there are wrong, but I'm never certain *which* thirty percent. You've probably noticed the authors themselves don't pretend to be convinced by all the scenarios. But one thing I'm positive about is that *some* of them are for real, and that the government and the media have lied too often for me to trust them. Of course, the good stuff is not all in one book—I've got a pretty decent little library going here."

"I can see that," I said. "But I still have trouble believing those things really happen."

"My boy, you've been hanging around crystals and incense for too long. Would you like me to give you about three zillion examples?"

"Uh, sure. Half a zillion should be enough. Do you mind if I make some tea?" I asked, moving to the sink.

"No, go ahead. There's spring water in the fridge."

I took out the plastic bottle and filled a pan, threw in the tea bags and lit the gas burner. Then I turned back to Sebastian. "Okay, shoot."

"Unfortunate choice of words," he grinned, "but since you've shown a shred of curiosity, I'll gladly spill my guts, so to speak." Sebastian rubbed his beard thoughtfully and then turned towards me. "It's hard to know where to begin, but just to shake your faith in authority, let's start with some big ones that are well documented. Do you remember World War II? Of course you don't. Neither do I, but you studied it in school, correct?"

"I got an A in World History, as a matter of fact."

"Here's something I'll bet they didn't teach you. At the end of the war, our government made a deal with the vanquished Nazis' head of Eastern European intelligence, General Reinhard Gehlen, to use his corps of spies and SS men as *American* intelligence agents. In fact, Gehlen himself was imported to the States in the garb of a *U.S. general*, and he became a leader in the organization that evolved into the CIA. His 'ex'-Nazi spy network was America's principle source of information about the activities of the Soviet Union during the Cold War, and they systematically overestimated the Soviets' belligerence and war capabilities. It's frightening to think of how close we came to atomic war because our country's highest officials were listening to the whispers of 'ex'-Nazis."

"That's incredible. You say this is documented?"

"In the book you're reading now, plus half a dozen others. And that's just for starters. Some people might say that the grafting of Nazi intelligence onto the budding tree of the newborn CIA was a single unfortunate mistake, but the stuff I've been reading suggests an even darker picture. The early CIA was staffed by a number of former officers of the OSS, and those guys were well known for, shall we say, their freedom from normal constraints. As CIA director Richard Helms put it, 'We are not Boy Scouts.' Of course, by now it's a cliché that the CIA is frequently at the bottom of the dirtiest doings abroad, and sometimes here at home, all in the interest of 'national security.' Some writers suggest that the Agency has become a power unto itself, too big for even the President to control. You can go back to the JFK assassination, for one example."

"I've heard plenty of theories about that one," I said.

"I know what you mean, and from what I surmise, one of the few people I can be sure *didn't* shoot Kennedy was Lee Harvey Oswald. Anyway, after being embarrassed by the failed Bay of Pigs invasion of Cuba, Kennedy threatened to dismantle the CIA, and he fired the director, and his deputy. Coincidentally, the deputy's brother was the mayor of Dallas and could have been involved with the altering of Kennedy's motorcade route, sending him on the detour into the shooting zone where he was assassinated."

"So you think the CIA killed him?"

"Who can say? I'm sure they had a role in it, but there are so many motivated suspects in this caper, the tough thing is deciding who *wasn't* involved. And some of the theories are really wild. I've even heard one that maintains JFK was killed because he was about to go public with the government's knowledge about UFOs."

"That's a new one on me."

"And I'm suspicious of it, too. But there have been so many devilish plots and programs uncovered and half-uncovered in this conspiratorial world that it's difficult to rule anything out. For instance, did you know the CIA was involved with LSD back in the Sixties?"

"You mean they were taking it?"

"Yes, but that's not all. They were also using it in mind control experiments, under a program called MK-ULTRA. Here on American soil, during the 1950s and 1960s the CIA ran the program, utilizing drugs and electromagnetic fields on unwitting subjects, in an effort to produce people who would follow any directive, even against their own will—they wanted to cre-ate human automatons. One of the drugs that they tried was LSD."

"But that would never work for mind control. It's too expansive, and it opens people up to mystical experience."

"Under favorable circumstances, that's true. But many of the MK-ULTRA subjects were given LSD without their knowledge. Often the agency used prostitutes and their clients, and other unsuspecting victims. This skullduggery caused at least one suicide and uncountable bad trips. Later, of course, LSD got loose in the youth culture and the whole thing exploded. As John Lennon, my favorite Beatle, put it, 'We must remember to thank the CIA and the army for LSD. They invented it to control people and what it did was give us freedom.' Of course, not everyone agrees with Lennon about the freedom part. Some say the CIA deliberately put LSD on the streets in vast quantities to diffuse the left-wing political youth move-ment. And it may have worked. It's certainly true that the militant protests of the Sixties died out as millions 'turned on, tuned in and dropped out.'

"But I can't believe that expansion of consciousness is ever a mistake," I said. "Even if LSD did deflate the political revolution, it may have started the spiritual one that is still growing today. Think about all the people that got their first glimpse of the sacred on a psychedelic trip. It reminds me of what Helen said last night about the power of good being great enough to redeem and transform even the greatest evil to a higher purpose. Wouldn't it be something if your Nazi-infested CIA had actually played a part in start-ing a chain reaction that would ultimately bring enlightenment to the whole planet? Talk about unintended consequences!"

"And an unproven outcome, I'm afraid. Maybe I know too many ugly facts to share Helen's and Maddie's optimism. Look at what's happened since the end of the Sixties. LSD and the other psychedelics have all been crimi-nalized, and stigmatized by a deluge of media propaganda, making construc-tive uses of them impossible. Meanwhile, cocaine and heroin, which are decidedly *not* drugs of enlightenment, have joined guns as the bestselling black market products used by the CIA and its pals to finance their shadowy agenda."

"What do you mean? Are you saying the CIA sells drugs?"

"Are there any more back on the farm like you? Yes, that's exactly what I'm saying. For example, do you recall the war in Nicaragua in the 1980s?"

"Sure, during the Reagan years. Wasn't that when the Iran-Contra scan-dal was going on?"

"Precisely. Anybody who watched the news then knew about Oliver

North's 'neat idea' to sell overpriced missiles to Iran and use the money to help the anti-communist (i.e., mercenary) Contra fighters in Nicaragua. Less well known, but perhaps even more lucrative, was the practice of CIA planes flying from the USA to Nicaragua loaded with guns and coming back with big shipments of cocaine. During the Iran-Contra hearings on Capitol hill, protesters burst into the chamber demanding that Congress investigate the drug-running, but it was all hushed up. Other deals were made in places like Vietnam and Afghanistan, where the CIA was in alliance with local drug lords who were willing to assist in the agency's political agenda. And some black leaders in America believe the CIA dumped its drugs in the inner cities to simultaneously make money and erode the political power of blacks by turning them into addicts—another 'neat idea'."

I was beginning to feel uncomfortable. "You know, Sebastian, I don't really enjoy thinking about this stuff."

"Who does? But my theory is, if you know the ugly facts, they're less likely to sneak up and bite you. Anyway, I'd rather be awake and angry than asleep and oblivious."

"Yes, but how does this affect me? I don't take drugs, and I'm not planning to get involved in any wars either."

"Aside from issues of right and wrong, which are supposed to matter to citizens in a democracy, I think we're all affected by the structure of power that exerts a relatively huge amount of control in our lives. Think about the news media. One of the chapters in the book you're reading reports that the CIA has used hundreds of reporters, magazines and news organizations to carry out assignments. The authors name many of the best-known newspapers, as well as television networks and a number of news magazines, all lending themselves to the CIA for the avowed purpose of fighting 'global communism'—a menace blown out of proportion by the CIA itself. If the main sources of news are propaganda tools, how can we make informed choices about anything beyond our personal lives? You know, I've read enough books so that when I watch the TV news I can see some of the lies. But how many more am I missing?"

"Sebastian, you're starting to sound paranoid. Do you think the CIA is running the whole country?"

He paused, and his gaze seemed to turn inward. "No, I guess I don't," he said slowly. "It's just that it's easier to point to an organization than to try to see the whole landscape of power and control. When I make the CIA my villain it's as though the problem is localized, and I can get angry at that. But when I look at the larger picture, it's overwhelming."

"What do you mean by the 'larger picture'?"

Sebastian looked troubled. "Where to begin? All right, how about television? It's clearly brainwashing. Never mind that the news programs are all exactly the same, and that they perpetuate a false and self-serving image of America's place in the world. Never mind that the news focuses on negative and frightening events, while during the commercial breaks they sell pills for upset stomachs and insomnia—the whole thing is brainwashing. Children watch an average of over ten thousand commercials before they're old enough to comprehend the concept of advertising, and the possibility that all its wonderful promises might not be true. Is it any wonder they become standardized cogs in the consumerism machine? They see forty thousand murders on television by the time they're sixteen. Is it a surprise they're desensitized to violence? And scientists have found out that television itself, simply the process of watching the screen, short-circuits the brain development of young children in the area of internalizing images. It literally kills the imagination. People watch television instead of visiting their friends and neighbors, instead of doing something creative or reading something to expand their minds. It isolates us, makes us feel inadequate, increases stress, and cooks the brain into a stale soufflé."

"And you think all this is part of some sort of plot? Come on, Sebastian. What you're saying may be true, but I don't think you can seriously believe it's a conspiracy."

"Maybe not, at least not consciously, but that could be worse. I mean, I'm sure the political propaganda is mostly written in full cynical awareness, although it's even more frightening to imagine that the people who create it really believe it. I'm positive the pill pushers and deodorant sellers and their brethren have figured out that people buy more products when they feel anxious and insecure, so there's incentive to keep frightening and stressful images in front of us. As for violence and sex, we've become so numb by overexposure that what we're shown has to become more and more graphic to hold our attention. And attention is everything—you can't sell soap to someone watching the other channel. But what happens is people grow up in this environment and they don't know anything else. So they unconsciously indoctrinate their offspring and each other by constant repetition and reinforcement of the reality picture they've accepted. If a child reports seeing an 'imaginary' playmate, or a human aura, or anything outside the tight little fenced-in world we're educated to believe is the whole thing, her loving parents and teachers assure her it's 'just her imagination'. And they believe it, too. If the child persists, the parents become worried and may take her to a psychiatrist for a drug fix. Anything so they can stay asleep and not be unsettled by those reports from over the fence. You heard it here first—consensus reality is a conspiracy of zombies." He grinned. "Are you ready to have me locked up yet? That's what they do to heretics."

I shook my head. "I think we've crossed the line here between political conspiracies and the old 'what is reality' question."

"Don't you see? There isn't any line. Money and power flow from the packaging and selling of reality pictures. Hitler's whole trip was selling reality pictures. What did he say—'the bigger the lie, the more people will believe it'? He sold his people on hate and scapegoating because it made them feel better to see themselves as a master race. Joseph McCarthy did the same thing here with his anti-communist witch hunts in the 1950s. Once he sold them the fear, people were ready to destroy whomever McCarthy accused. The military-industrial complex sold us the domino theory in Vietnam, and for a while most of America believed that communism would take over the world if we lost there. Didn't happen, did it? But a lot of money was made and a lot of lives were lost while that game was played. This stuff goes on all the time at every level, and in this country the practice has become so sophisticated that it's getting harder to see. But the biggest product they all push is fear—fear of being destroyed by a foreign enemy, fear that you'll be rejected if you don't wear designer clothes, fear that you'll be lonely, hungry, bored, you name it. If you can scare people, you can control them, as Madison Avenue and Washington, D.C., know so well."

"I see what you're saying, but not every commercial, or piece of propaganda, is about fear."

"That's true. One of the other insidious ploys involves counterfeiting genuine human feelings and tying them to products or other false reality pictures. I saw a car commercial that tried to tell me people with a 'passion for living' chose that car. There were all kinds of beautiful images with it— standard TV stuff. Now, a passion for living is one of the things most people lack, but deep down they know they should have it. So they buy the car and they still feel empty, which sets them up for the next illusion. I tell you, Will, our souls are being invaded for the sake of profits and power, and our national mental illness is being exported to the whole world through the media."

Sebastian continued, "On the personal level, we fence in reality so we can live with the illusion that we are in control. The authority of government rests on the myth that *they* are in control. People willingly give up their freedom and their ability to think for themselves in order to be comforted by this illusion. Huge amounts of secrecy, which conceal incredible corruption, are justified on the basis that it's better for us not to know. And most people accept that willingly. It's so much easier to believe a comfortable lie than it is to take the solitary, terrifying path of trying to see the truth."

My head was spinning from Sebastian's mental leaps, but I saw a thread of logic running through them. After a moment, I said, "So I guess that's where you are, on the search for truth."

"Where else could I be? Tracing conspiracies is actually part of the same project going out to Sedona was. I want to be awake. I want my eyes open."

"Well, how much truth have you found?"

"Lots of pieces, lots of pieces. Fitting them together is the tough part. It's like trying to assemble a jigsaw puzzle in the dark. And every time I make a new connection, it leads to more questions."

"Such as?"

"Hmm. Well, there's the extraterrestrial stuff, for one thing. All my experiences, and Maddie's, and most of the ones I've read about could be explained most easily by assuming the Visitors are non-physical. People are most frequently abducted at night, from their beds. They float through walls, get beamed up to ships and do numerous things that defy the normal laws of physics. Afterwards, they find themselves back in bed, or in cars or some such place. I'm not trying to say people are dreaming all this, or that the Visitors are figments of their imaginations. Maybe they're archetypes emanating from the collective unconscious, as Don Lee said, or some other kind of ghost or spirit. One thing I'm sure of is that the domain of non-physical realities is mostly fenced off and ridiculed by the authors of mass consciousness, and that makes me believe there's a lot going on over there."

"I follow you," I said. "But if you're right, what new questions does *that* pose for you?"

"The one that's bothering me now is this—if the ET visitors are non-physical, why was the *government* ever interested in UFOs? The spirit world is supposed to be outside their domain. If ETs are either hallucinations or manifestations of the inner world, then the whole thing ought to be of no interest to spies, generals or presidents. But it's clear that they have been interested. Project Blue Book was an Air Force program that for many years recorded and analyzed thousands of UFO reports. That shows a strong interest in the phenomenon. Yet Blue Book ignored the most famous UFO incident of all—the 'crash' at Roswell, New Mexico, in 1947. Why leave that out, unless Blue Book was really a cover-up posing as an investigation? And then there's the Robertson Panel."

"What's that?"

"It's mentioned in the book you were reading. It was a group of scientists brought together by the CIA in 1953, chaired by Dr. H.P. Robertson, for the purpose of evaluating UFO reports. The panel met for five days, looked at all the most credible UFO cases, and dismissed every one of them."

"Well, that doesn't sound much like a conspiracy."

"I agree. But they also went on to recommend that the government attempt to squelch reports of UFOs, and even to mount an anti-UFO 'education' campaign. They suggested using psychologists 'familiar with mass psychology' and even brought up the idea of recruiting Walt Disney Studios to make anti-UFO cartoons. The panel went on to suggest that UFO enthusiast groups be placed under surveillance because of 'the possible use of such groups for subversive purposes.' There was at least one named operative who did so—CIA psychological warfare specialist Nicholas de Rochefort, who infiltrated and undermined the National Investigations Committee on Aerial Phenomena, an early civilian UFO group. Why bother with all that if the phenomenon didn't exist?"

"Surveillance of UFO groups. My God, Sebastian. It reminds me of that lecture you tried to attend in Sedona when you met Maddie."

"'Government Abductions of ET Abduction Survivors,' a talk that was never given by one Doctor David Jordan, due to his untimely demise. The more I read, the more my kooks come home to roost. And the happier I am that we left Sedona."

"You're thinking of the phony FBI man again."

"I've never stopped thinking about him." Sebastian paused. He seemed to be struggling with what to say. "I used to know somebody on the inside of that world. He wasn't a very nice man, but he knew something about power and this reality game I've been talking about. One night we were out drinking together and he said something about it. I've never been sure whether to attribute it to honesty or alcohol, or both. Anyway, what he said was, 'By the time you begin to comprehend the game, you're a player. Then it's too late to opt out.' Sometimes I wonder if I've already passed that point." He looked at me, and I saw pain in his eyes. "Do you think I'm crazy, Will?"

I didn't answer immediately. I turned away from Sebastian and took a few steps towards the front of the RV. Through the windshield I saw a flash of color. Someone was running down the beach path and had passed the front of the vehicle. I went to a side window and recognized Helen dashing towards the door. "Oh, hell, I forgot about the tea," I said.

Helen reached the door and yanked it open, gasping for breath. "Will, Sebastian, come quickly. There's been an accident. Maddie's drowned."

# — 11 —

I was pushed to the floor by Sebastian as he rushed past me. An inarticulate groan of anguish came out of him as he leaped from the threshold to the ground and hit it at a dead run. I had never seen a man of his size move so fast. In another second, he was out of my field of vision, sprinting for the beach. Helen stuck her head inside the door and looked at me, "Will, come on, we've got to get back to her. Now!"

I pulled myself to my feet and hurried down the steps, "Then she's out of the water? Is she—is she dead?"

"I don't know. Radha is giving her CPR." She caught my sleeve and we started running back down the path.

A knot of people had gathered at the water's edge where Radha knelt down over Maddie's body. Running across the soft sand, I felt as if we were moving in slow motion. As we approached, I could see Sebastian on his hands and knees beside Maddie, saying something into her ear. Her chest rose and fell as Radha alternately blew into her mouth and pushed on her abdomen to force out the air. Running toward them, I felt my own heart pounding with exertion and fear.

"Has anyone called an ambulance?" Helen shouted when we were a few yards away.

"They're on their way. I just called," said a woman in the little crowd, holding up her cell phone.

"Maddie, Maddie, hang on," Sebastian pleaded softly, tears streaking his face.

"Will," said Helen, turning to me, "I want to try to channel some healing energy into her right now, so I'm going to put my hands under her shoulders. I want you to get down and massage her feet."

Helen began rubbing her hands together briskly, as I had always seen her do before giving a healing. She had had a gift for hands-on healing since she was a young child, and had used it to help me recover from my chronic back pain. I had come to take her talent for granted, but I had never seen her use it in a situation like this. Quickly, I stationed myself at Maddie's feet and began to rub them. Helen knelt above Maddie's head and slipped her hands, palms-up, beneath her shoulders. Radha continued the CPR, and Sebastian, holding Maddie's limp hand, kept calling to her.

The minutes dragged by as we four strained to save her, nearly oblivious to the onlookers around us. I pushed my thumbs hard into the arches of her feet, hoping to provoke some response. My breath came in gasps, and I felt light-headed. Although I had almost no awareness of the crowd, everything about the five of us there was etched into my mind. I felt the gritty sand caked on Maddie's toes, in contrast to the smooth pink polish on her toenails. I saw the strain in the muscles of Radha's back as she pushed for each exhalation. I perceived the grave concentration in Helen's face as she knelt, eyes closed, a few feet away from me, her hands under Maddie's back. I heard the fear in Sebastian's voice as he clutched Maddie's hand and begged her to breathe. Most excruciating of all was the silence we endured after each push from Radha, as we strained to hear a sign of life.

My light-headedness increased, and the scene took on a dreamlike quality for me. I continued to rub Maddie's feet and to listen for any hopeful sign, but I felt as if I were watching everything from a distance. It seemed almost like a movie, and I became emotionally detached, unworried, like a viewer who knows he is only watching projected images. Sebastian's voice sounded metallic, as if it were coming through a tube or an old gramophone. I felt my body getting very warm, and my hands tingled.

Suddenly there was a bright flash inside my head, and I lost consciousness. Or I should say I lost awareness of the scene around me. I seemed to be in a boundless space, permeated by gold light. I had no body, but I felt myself as a sphere of energy. Somehow, I was unsurprised by my surroundings, as though I knew them. Within and without, there was a sense of imperturbable joy. In the next moment, I noticed the approach of another entity, and I suddenly knew her as Maddie. As quickly as I recognized her, I felt her voice inside me, singing or laughing in merriment. Before I could respond, a harmonic chime resonated and a tremendous force pulled us down through a descending corridor or tunnel at incredible speed. There was a jolt, and I felt my face pushed into the wet sand of the beach. I heard voices and someone coughing repeatedly. I opened my eyes and saw Maddie sitting up with Sebastian and Radha holding her. Helen was kneeling beside me.

"Will, you fainted. Are you all right?"

"Maddie's alive!"

"Yes. She's just regained consciousness."

Maddie looked at me and smiled weakly, "Hi Will. We're back, huh?"

Just then the ambulance people arrived with a stretcher. The crowd was asked to disperse and Maddie was strapped down and carried off, with Sebastian walking beside her. One of the medical technicians asked me if I felt ill, and I told him I was all right. A minute later, I heard the siren and glimpsed the flashing red light as the ambulance sped away. Helen helped me to my feet and we walked back to our towels, which Radha was already beginning to fold and put away. When I reached her, I touched her shoulder, and as she turned, I embraced her. "Good job, Radha," I said. "You brought her back."

She held me at arm's length and looked into my eyes. "Good job yourself. Where did you go?"

"I don't know, but I think I was with Maddie."

Helen interrupted, "We should hurry to the hospital now. We can talk on the way."

As we drove, I asked Helen and Radha what had happened while I was with Sebastian.

"Madeline wanted to go back in the water, and she insisted that Helen and I join her," said Radha. "It seemed like a good idea, as we were becoming rather warm in any case."

"Maddie ran in ahead of us, and she took off swimming out toward the big rock that juts from the water on the left side of the bay," Helen said. "It must be at least two or three hundred yards out there. We were watching her, but we got into the water gradually because of how cold it was. We were just starting to swim around a bit when she reached the rock and climbed up on it to wave at us. We waved back, and she dived in, swimming in our direction."

"I must say that I let my attention wander at that point," Radha continued. "I lost sight of her until I heard her crying for help."

Helen said, "She was still at least a hundred yards from us when I heard her. She was screaming that her legs were cramped. I could see her thrashing in the water, and then a big wave hit her and she disappeared."

"I looked, but there was no lifeguard," said Radha.

"It's too late in the year," I said. "Not enough people at the beach."

"And no one else on the beach seemed to have heard her," Helen went on. "So I called to Radha and we both started swimming out to where we had seen her."

"I was a lifeguard myself, forty years ago," Radha said. "However, my swimming has become rather rusty. Helen reached her first."

"She was floating face down next to a half-submerged boulder. The only thing I could imagine was that she hit her head on it when that wave washed over her," said Helen. "When I got to her, I pulled her face up out of the water and tried to clear her throat, but she was unconscious, and the waves kept hitting us. I was really terrified. The next thing I knew, Radha was there, and she got Maddie turned on her back and started towing her to shore."

"Helen and I did it together," Radha said. "I'm not sure I would have been strong enough to manage it alone. When we got nearer the shore, where we could touch the bottom, a couple of young men who had noticed us came running out to help, and we got her onto the beach quickly from there. I immediately started with resuscitation while Helen ran for you and Sebastian."

"Thank God you got to her in time," I said.

"Indeed," Radha replied, looking back over her shoulder at me. "Now, I insist you tell me what happened to you."

I described to Radha and Helen what I had experienced when I fainted. As it turned out, both of them had felt odd sensations at about the same time.

"While I was working on Maddie, I kept trying to get a sense of where she was. Initially, I thought I was aware of her for a moment, and then I felt nothing," Radha said. "I was worried she had already passed over. Usually, the spirit stays close to the body right after death, but as hard as I tried, I couldn't feel her. I could hear you panting down by her feet, and then you made some kind of gasping sound and fell into the sand. I was alarmed, but there was no time to think about you, Will. At that same moment, an intense shiver ran up my spine, and then I was really afraid we had lost Maddie. But I kept up the CPR, and I quickly became aware that my hands were getting very warm. For some reason, her abdomen seemed to be radiating heat."

"As I had told you, I was trying to channel healing into Maddie's body, and I felt a big flow of energy moving through me," Helen continued. "I was totally focused on her, and I kept my eyes closed. I have to admit I didn't even realize it when you fainted. But what I did notice at about that time was something very much like what Radha mentioned. You know that when

I channel healing my hands get warm—it's an effect of the energy. But while I was working on Maddie, I suddenly felt the flow of energy reverse. It was as though *she* was channeling healing into *me*, and my hands became very hot while that was happening. Next there was a powerful burst of energy that went through my whole body. I opened my eyes and saw you lying in the sand. Then Maddie coughed, and in another moment she was breathing on her own. We sat her up, and I went over to make sure you were all right."

"It appears to me that whatever we felt was the same energy that knocked Will out of his body," Radha said.

"Is that normal?" I asked. "I mean, I've never been around someone who has almost died."

"Well, I was present at the deaths of my parents, and of course my work frequently brings me into contact with spirits of the deceased," Radha said. "I've beheld and experienced many strange and beautiful things, but I can't recall any sensations quite like these."

"That makes two of us," Helen agreed.

"Three of us," I said.

Radha spoke suddenly, "Now that I think of it, though, I do remember reading about something a little like what happened to Will. I believe it was Raymond Moody, the near-death experience researcher, who wrote about it. He was discussing deathbed phenomena that corroborate the reports of near death experiencers. He wrote that in some cases when people are dying, a loved one at the deathbed has a spontaneous out-of-body experience and journeys part of the way to the next world with the dying patient. There they say their goodbyes, and the departing soul moves on while the loved one returns to the body."

We drove on until we reached the local hospital. Radha parked the car and we all walked inside. After a few questions at the information desk, we were on our way to Maddie's room.

"They say she's in satisfactory condition," I said. "I wonder how long she'll be in here. I'm anxious to ask her what happened while she wasn't breathing, and whether she really was aware of me in that space with all the gold light."

"Will, please don't push this," Helen said. "We all want to know, but this may not be the time to satisfy curiosity. It's important for us to be there for Maddie and to support her in whatever way she needs."

We took an elevator to Maddie's floor and hurried through the corridors until we reached the room. Sebastian was sitting in the chair next to the bed where Maddie lay asleep. His face was drawn, but he smiled when he saw us.

"She's going to be okay," he whispered. "She got a bump on the head, maybe a mild concussion, but the CPR came soon enough to avoid brain damage. The cold water helped save her from that, too."

"Has she been conscious?" Helen asked.

"Yes, she fell asleep a few minutes ago. I'm thinking about waking her up soon, though. I've heard you're supposed to keep concussion patients alert, although the doctor didn't seem worried."

"I'd like to do another healing on her," said Helen. "If you'll let me use that chair, Sebastian, I'll work from there."

"Sure, I'll get a couple more chairs."

"I'll go with you," I said.

We left the women in the room and scouted the hallway for chairs. There were none in sight, so we went to ask at the nurse's station. The nurse on duty wasn't sure where to find any, and she sent us to the housekeeping office, where we were informed that there were no extra chairs on that floor. Finally, we gave up and decided to go back to the room.

"Are you all right, Sebastian?" I asked as we walked.

"What? Oh, sure. I'm okay. I just got really scared, that's all. I feel so responsible for protecting Maddie—I have since we left Sedona—and I thought I'd lost her. The other thing is, I love her, and I hadn't really told her, not in a serious way. I'm always joking."

"I'm sure she knows how you feel."

"Well, I hope you're right."

When we arrived in the room, Maddie was already awake. Helen and Radha sat on either side of the bed, and there were two more empty chairs at the foot. Maddie grinned at us, "Hey, guys!"

"Hey, yourself," I replied. "Where did all these chairs come from?"

"I retrieved them," Radha said. "Madeline told me where to find them."

"There's a whole bunch of them in the waiting room," Maddie explained. "We're probably not supposed to take them, but I could see you two weren't getting anywhere."

"How could you see that?" Sebastian demanded.

"I followed you. That nurse was not a bit helpful, and the man in house-keeping should have known about the chairs in the waiting room."

Sebastian and I both gaped at her. "How did you know that?" he repeated.

"I told you, I followed you. I was floating up by the ceiling watching you when Helen, Will and Radha came in. I decided to tag along when you went looking for chairs. By the way, I love you, too. That's one of the reasons I came back."

I had not seen Sebastian blush before, nor had I witnessed him at a loss for words. Maddie watched him with amusement, and finally burst out laughing. It was almost the same sound I had heard when I encountered her in the space of golden light.

"Madeline has been telling us some of what she underwent this afternoon," Radha announced. "She woke up while Helen was doing her healing work, but apparently her connection with her body is still rather loose. We had all better be careful what we say from now on," she added, with a wry smile at Sebastian. "Maddie, dear, do you feel strong enough to talk some more, or would you rather rest?"

"No, I'd love to talk. I'm feeling good, and very happy now, and I want to tell about what happened." So the four of us sat in a semicircle around Maddie's bed and listened as she related the story of her brush with death.

"I was intent on swimming out to that big rock—showing off, I guess. The water was cold and the distance was further than it looked. I was really huffing and puffing by the time I got there. When I reached the rock and climbed up on it, the wind made me even colder, too cold to stay and rest. So I waved to Helen and Radha and dove into the water to swim back.

"That was a mistake. I should have stayed on the rock until the sun warmed me up and I recuperated. I got a cramp in my left calf almost immediately, but I massaged it and it relaxed pretty quickly. So I started swimming again and everything seemed okay. The waves were higher than they had been earlier, and they were lifting me up and down as I made my way towards shore. The water must have been ten or fifteen feet deep, and the swells were at least half again that high. After each wave passed over me, I could feel myself being pulled backwards, so I swam that much harder. That was my other mistake. I was starting to get fairly close to Helen—I must have been two-thirds of the way back—and I was trying to go a little faster. Well, I got on the back side of a wave and started swimming hard, and suddenly both my legs cramped and so did my stomach. I panicked. I started screaming for help and thrashing my arms all over the place. I was doubled up with pain and paying no attention to where I was or anything else. The waves were still coming in and when one of them hit, I went under. I struggled to the surface to get a breath, but then another wave took me down and I must have hit my head. The next thing I knew, I was looking down on the water from five or six feet above it. I felt totally calm and peaceful. I wondered what was floating around underneath me—it looked like a rag doll washing back and forth in the waves. Then I thought, 'Oh, I know. That's my body. Look at that sunburn on my back.'

"It sounds strange, but I was completely unconcerned about whether I had drowned. I didn't even think about it. I just hovered over myself, and pretty soon Helen and Radha reached my body and started towing it to shore. I remember thinking, 'They should be careful, it's dangerous to swim way out here.' Anyway, I followed them back, and I even started getting a little bored with the whole scene. Then I realized, 'My God, I must be dead' and there was a real moment of alarm. Then I thought about Sebastian, and quick as a flash I was in the RV, and you two guys were talking about conspiracies. I tried to get your attention—I yelled both of your names really loud, but you couldn't hear me. That's when the fear came over me again, and I thought, 'I have to get back in my body right now!' Immediately, I was looking down on myself again, on the beach. Radha was pushing on my stomach and then bending down to my face, over and over again. I tried to will myself back inside, but I couldn't do it."

Radha interrupted, "Was Helen still there at that time?"

"Yes, and then she ran away."

"That's what I thought. I felt a glimmer of you when I first started the CPR, but then you were gone. What happened?"

"Well, I was really frightened when I couldn't get back into my body, and I felt mournful. I started grieving over my lost life, and that I wouldn't be able to be with Sebastian. But in the next moment I saw a kind of dark tunnel appear in the air in front of me. It was spiraling around, like a whirlpool, and I thought it looked very interesting. As I watched, I was soon concentrating on it completely, and then I was suddenly inside it, traveling at high speed through total darkness. After going what seemed to be a great distance, I saw light ahead of me. It was very beautiful and I wanted to go to it. When I arrived, I saw that the light was coming from a being, or maybe I should say that the light *was* a being. It's hard to explain, but I found myself looking at something, or someone, that seemed like a living light, and the space around her was *created* by her luminescence."

"It was female?" Radha inquired.

"Not like we are—I don't know. I just thought of it as *her*."

"How did you see yourself?" I asked.

"Like a ghost. I had a body, but it was a see-through version, and it was kind of shimmery. And when I approached that being of light, her radiance went right through me. I could feel it in my heart— it made me want to cry, with a feeling that included grief, but was mostly joy. It was the brightest light I've ever seen, but it didn't hurt my eyes. I couldn't see her face clearly, but it seemed to me that she smiled, and when that happened I felt as though I was receiving the most complete love that could ever be. It was like my parents, my grandmother, Sebastian and my best friend from sixth grade all rolled into one—and it was more than that. I could have stayed there forever in that light, and I wouldn't have missed my life enough to bother me. She let me just bask in it for a while, and then she spoke to me."

I regarded Maddie. She looked pale in her hospital gown, her face showing traces of exhaustion, but her eyes were shining. "What did she say to you?"

"She asked me a question. It might have been, 'What have you done with your life?' or 'How much love have you given?' There weren't words exactly—it was more of the feeling behind words that she communicated. I tried to answer, but I received another thought from her, something like, 'We shall look together.'

"Then she waved her arm and all around me I saw my life. From my birth to the moment I drowned, it was all there. It was like a thousand movie screens going at once, whichever way I looked. Everything was visible, but the most prominent scenes were the ones where I had a strong emotion, whether it was love, fear, anger, sadness or happiness. It seemed as though the negative moments had a 'charge' that I needed to release or neutralize somehow. I felt I was being encouraged to understand and forgive people who had wounded me, and to let go of the anger that caused me to hurt others. Standing there in the radiance of her light, I was able to do it. I see now that it's something we all have to do—and it's better if we do it while we're still here."

There was a silence. Then Radha asked, "Was there anything else that happened, dear?"

"Yes. After the review of my life, the being said, 'Now I have more to show you.' And I felt that I was lifted up in the air, that she and I were flying together. At first we were in clouds that were illuminated with gold light from some source I couldn't see. It felt lovely and peaceful in that place. Then we descended again, and looking down I could see beautiful geometric architecture, a city laid out in a circle with streets radiating from the center. The buildings were all translucent white and glowing from within. As I was looking at them, we swooped down into the structure in the center of the city, a huge, perfectly round domed building. We dropped in through an opening in the dome, and I found myself seated on a white stone bench, facing the center of this enormous room, where a huge crystal sphere sat on a white stone pedestal. I couldn't feel the presence of the being of light with me anymore, but as I looked around, I could see a lot of other ghosts, or transparent people like myself, seated on other benches, all facing the sphere."

"Did it seem solid, like a rock crystal?" I asked.

"It did at first. Actually, I had the urge to go and touch it, but I somehow knew that wasn't permitted. Anyway, I hadn't been sitting long before things started happening. First there was a deep resonant hum from below that echoed through the entire building. Then I heard chimes from above my head, at first very delicate, but then louder and louder, until the intensity of the two beautiful sounds became almost too much to bear. Just when I felt it was going to make me explode, the sound stopped, and the crystal sphere began to spin on its pedestal. In a few seconds, light started coming out of it, and it began to look like a fiery sun. I could feel my emotions building up to a peak—hope and grief, fear and love all mixed together. Then there was a burst of energy, like an explosion in the sphere, and a ray of gold light came straight out of it and went right into my chest. It was like fire, and it spread through my whole body. For a split second, I looked around and saw that the same thing was happening to all the other people on the white benches. Then the fire reached up to my head and I just ... I just turned into light."

I had closed my eyes as I listened to Maddie's description, remembering the meditation in which I had seemed to travel through space to the golden sun and had found its image in my own heart. When Maddie stopped speaking, I opened my eyes and looked at her. Tears were streaming down her cheeks, but her face seemed luminous in the dimly lit hospital room. Helen clasped her hand, and Radha gazed at her intently. Sebastian was holding his head in his hands.

"Would you like to rest now, dear?" Radha asked quietly.

"No. No, I want to finish telling you. When the fire reached my head, I felt obliterated by it, completely consumed. I couldn't see the room anymore—there was nothing except the brilliant light, and the remaining fragment of myself that could observe it. I think the emotion I felt would be called ecstasy. I felt like a minnow swimming in an ocean of sacred water, or a raindrop falling into the sun. There was no choice but surrender, and yet to surrender was to feel total freedom and joy. I let go, and for a time there was only light. But it wasn't golden any longer. Now it was a pure, clear white light, existing in a void of utter silence. There was no time or space, only light. I felt that I was nothing, and yet I was identified with the whole universe. In the next moment, I was back in the golden space, and I heard a voice speaking in my mind. It said something like, 'Bearers of the flame, return to life. Seed the harvest of the Light.'"

"After that, I knew I was on my way back to my body, and that I would live. I felt full of happiness, but also a reluctance to leave the peace and beauty and sacredness of this place. Then I ran into Will, a perfect little sphere of energy, but it was unmistakably him. I was so surprised that I laughed, and I thought to myself, 'Here's my welcoming committee. Someone must have known I'd be having second thoughts about coming back.' I decided as a joke I would sing 'Somewhere Over the Rainbow' for him, but before I could get through a line there was a *whoosh*, and the next thing I knew I was coughing and sputtering, and my chest *hurt*." She paused. "I think you all know the rest."

Radha was smiling at Maddie, and Helen was slowly stroking her hand. Sebastian appeared lost in thought. I wanted to ask more questions, and to tell Maddie about my own past vision of the fiery sun in my heart, but the time didn't seem right. Finally, I said, "Maddie, we're all very glad you're safe, but now I'm thinking Helen and I should go home and give you a chance to recuperate."

"Will's right," Helen said as she stood up and leaned over to embrace her. "We'll talk more tomorrow, or when you come home."

Maddie leaned back against the slanted mattress of the hospital bed and sighed, "But my story. You believe me, don't you?"

"Yes, I do," said Helen.

"Completely," Radha replied.

"I have to," I said. "You spotted me in there." Sebastian seemed not to have heard. Finally I asked him, "Do you need a ride to the RV?"

"What? Uh, no. I think I'll stay here with Maddie. I'll sleep in one of these chairs, or in the waiting room. The doctor said they plan to release her in the morning. Could we call you for a ride then?"

"Sure. We'll be in the store after nine."

Helen, Radha and I left the hospital and drove back to our house. Radha refused our invitation to come inside for tea, saying that she was tired, and feeling hot and flushed. "It must be the exertion and excitement of the day," she said. "Or perhaps I took too much sun. In any case, don't worry about me, I'll be fine. But be sure to take good care of young Madeline, and your friend Sebastian as well. I sense that he's almost as shaken up as she is. I may visit again on Saturday. I'm thinking of taking in the next evening talk at your shop. I hope you'll phone me if Madeline has any difficulties, or if any-thing interesting happens."

After Radha left, we went inside and ate a simple meal in the kitchen. Both of us felt exhausted, and after eating we went upstairs to bed. As we lay there, Helen grasped my hand and squeezed it. She said, "I was worried about you when I realized you had fainted. I'm glad you're okay."

"I'm glad you didn't drown trying to save Maddie. You know, I hadn't thought about it, but you did help save her life, didn't you? How does that feel?"

"Mostly like a relief. And I'm grateful."

"What do you think about her story?"

"I believe it. It's beautiful."

"I wanted to ask her more about it. It seems so fantastic—even the fact that we somehow met when I fainted—but I can't deny that it happened. And she knew all about my walk down the hall with Sebastian."

"I'm most intrigued by her visit to the luminous city," Helen said. "I've seen visions like that in my meditations, but always from a distance. I've never been close to such a place."

"She said she felt reluctant to come back. That surprised me."

"I've read accounts from other near death experiencers who say the reason we aren't allowed to be conscious of what lies on the other side of death is that if we were, no one would choose to stay alive."

"I would, as long as you were here."

Helen turned onto her side and kissed me. "I love you."

"I love you, too."

We lay there silently for some time, and finally I heard Helen's breathing move into the slow, regular pattern of sleep. I looked at the moonlight on the wall and remembered the space of golden light in which I had briefly been immersed. What would the world be like, I wondered, if people weren't afraid to die? How much tyranny, how much violence and destruction would never come to be? How much misery and grief would never be felt? I tried to imagine myself back in the golden light, and in the places Maddie had described. As I descended into sleep, I felt myself getting warm, and I saw a rush of luminous images that seemed to flow into me from a well deeper than memory.

# — 12 —

The next week went by quickly. Maddie was released from the hospital on Monday, and she spent the next several days at Dune Forest with Sebastian. We heard nothing from them, except one telephone call from Maddie letting us know she planned to come back to work in the shop the following week. When Helen asked her about Sebastian, she said, "He's working at the computer a lot at night, but when he's not doing that he's being very loving towards me. And I'm falling more in love with him, too. I think what happened Sunday made us realize how much we care about each other. Anyway, we're both planning to come to the talk on Saturday night, and I'll be back to work on Monday."

After closing the shop at six on Saturday, Helen and I arranged the chairs and tables in the workshop room and then drove to the Italian restaurant a few blocks away for a quick dinner. When we returned, the first attendees for the evening's talk were already standing by the stairs leading to the side door that opened into the workshop room. We unlocked the door and turned on the lights, as the people filtered in. We greeted those we knew and encouraged all of them to partake of the fruit juice and snacks we had laid out on one of the tables.

A few minutes later, Maddie and Sebastian arrived, and we greeted one another affectionately. It seemed that our friendship with them, like Maddie's bond with Sebastian, had been deepened by the life-and-death experience we had shared a week before. When Radha came in a few minutes later, the same wave of emotion moved through us all again, and I saw tears in Maddie's eyes as she and Radha hugged each other. This time, the five of us all chose seats together in one of the rows, and my upholstered chair in the back of the room was left vacant.

Kathleen Riley, the speaker for the evening, came through the door five minutes before her talk was scheduled to begin. She was a tall, powerful-looking woman of about fifty, with long red hair and bright green eyes. Like Don Lee, we had recruited her via the Internet and had never met her before. I was struck by her vitality and intensity. She walked, talked and gestured at high speed, and with constant enthusiasm. When Helen and I greeted her, she shook hands with us, as well as Sebastian, Maddie, Radha and two or three of the other people at the front of the room, all while unloading notes and pictures from a large hand-woven bag that apparently served as her briefcase. She apologized for almost being late, explaining that she had spent the afternoon photographing flocks of migratory birds at a wetlands sanctuary, and that she had lost track of the time. In spite of that, she said, through good fortune and "creative driving," she had made it to the shop, and when the clock read seven-thirty, she was standing at the front of the room, notes in hand. I turned on the tape recorder, nodded to her, and returned to my seat as she began.

"Good evening. As you can see, I am *not* Rupert Sheldrake. Nonetheless, I've come to talk to you tonight about an area of study that is almost synonymous with his name—morphic resonance and evolution.

"My name is Kathleen Riley and I'm a biology teacher at Huntington High School in Boston. I first came into contact with the works of Rupert Sheldrake in 1989, because of a question from a student. She had been in a serious car accident the previous summer and had gone through what is known as a near-death experience. During part of that episode, she viewed herself and much of the activity of her resuscitation from a vantage point outside her body. How, she wanted to know, was that possible if the mind, as we've been taught in biology, is contained in the brain?"

I looked down the row at Maddie, who was whispering to Sebastian. What a synchronicity, I thought, for the talk to begin this way.

Ms. Riley continued, "I looked in the school library, as well as on my own bookshelves, for information relating to that question. A friend referred me to Raymond Moody's book, *Life After Life*, from which I learned that my student's near-death experience was not unique—it is estimated that literally millions of people have had them. But I was looking for some reference which would relate to the question on a more biological level. If the phenomenon of mind is only a result of processes going on in the physical brain, then out-of-body experiences must be classified as hallucinations. But my student had heard the voices of her doctors and viewed the entire resuscitation process from a perspective several feet above her unconscious body, and her memory of what happened  was accurate. This, too, according to

Moody's book, is not uncommon. So I went looking for a biologic
that would allow for such experiences.

"Aldous Huxley once said that the brain acts less like a thought factory
than it does a radio. We may 'tune in' to ideas more than we actually con-
struct them. Moments of inspiration that seem to come to us 'out of the blue'
are a good example of this. I was recounting the concept to one of my fellow
teachers, who said, 'If you like that kind of stuff, you should read Rupert
Sheldrake.' The next day, he brought me a copy of *The Presence of the Past*,
Sheldrake's book on morphic resonance and what he calls 'the habits of
nature'. In reading it, I found that Sheldrake had constructed a model which
could account for such diverse phenomena as instinct in animals, the inheritance of acquired characteristics, and the apparent 'group minds' of species
such as honeybees, termites, and certain types of birds. Within the same conceptual framework, he also offered insights on human learning and memory,
cultural inheritance, myths, rituals, magic, the collective unconscious, the
mystery of creativity and the nature of the soul. It seemed to me that his concept of invisible 'morphic fields' of mind and memory could even underlie
such phenomena as my student's out-of-body experience. As I read the book,
I began to believe I had found the bridge her question had inspired me to
look for, and it has taken me beyond where I expected to go.

"Before we proceed, how many of you know what I mean by the term
*morphogenesis*?" Two hands went up. "Well, if we look to the roots of the
words, *morph* means form or shape and *genesis* means coming into being.
Therefore, *morphogenesis* is the coming into being of form. In Mr. Sheldrake's
theory, the way things come into being in the present is vitally influenced by
the way things have been in the past. As an example, if you walk through
the woods for the first time, you leave evidence of your passage—a trail. On
your next trip through the same woods, you may notice your previous trail
and have the tendency to follow in your own earlier tracks. After a few trips,
the trail has become a path, and it is increasingly likely that you and any
others going through those woods will follow that path. As this continues
and builds on itself, your original trail becomes *the* path through the woods
and is finally made into a road. This idea is key to Sheldrake's concept of
*morphic resonance*, in which causal influences from the past affect present
and future activities. This type of influence can and does occur on every
level from atoms to galaxies, from animal instincts to human group behavior. Mr. Sheldrake puts forth the idea that nature has habits rather than laws,
and that what we think of as laws of nature appear to be unchangeable only
because these habits are so well established. But as we all know, habits can

be broken, so this model of existence is open-ended, offering us a universe in which, theoretically, anything can happen."

Sebastian leaned toward me and whispered, "I wonder if I could be put in jail for breaking the laws of nature?"

"Didn't you hear her?" I shot back. "There aren't any laws. I think you're just one of nature's bad habits."

"My pal."

"Quiet, you guys," Maddie shushed us.

The speaker smiled in our direction and continued, "Sheldrake's term *morphic field* refers to the invisible field within and around a unit or form or organization—such as an atom, a galaxy, an animal species or a human group—which organizes the structure or activity patterns of that unit. As a conceptual aid, I like to visualize a magnet and its surrounding field and a plate of iron filings. The invisible magnetic field organizes the pattern into which the filings and magnet will align themselves. Morphic fields are shaped and stabilized by morphic resonance with previous similar patterns of activity from the same kinds of morphic units. For example, when scientists growing crystals create a new form, it is in the beginning rather difficult to grow the new form. But as this is done successfully more times, it becomes easier and easier to produce the new form. According to Sheldrake, what has happened here is that morphic resonance has made an invisible 'path through the forest' for the new crystal form, and nature gains a new habit."

I raised my hand, "I know from selling crystals here in the shop that the same species of crystal, such as a quartz, often grows in different characteristic shapes in different localities. An Arkansas quartz point looks very different from a Madagascar crystal, and both of those look quite unlike a quartz crystal from Herkimer, New York. Is that because of morphic resonance?"

"According to me, it is. And it's interesting to note that the growth patterns you're talking about are called 'habits' by geologists. My intuition tells me that there may be localized morphic fields in each area which influence the probabilities of how each new crystal is likely to form, even though no 'law' says it has to follow the local pattern."

Kathleen continued, "I think we should get out of definitions now and look at this through the lens of a story. How many of you know the fable of the Hundredth Monkey?" Eight or ten hands were raised. "All right then, I'll tell it for the rest of you. Even though this is a fictional tale rather than a scientific observation, and although Sheldrake doesn't use it in his book, I think it's instructive."

"I know this story," Helen whispered to me. "There was a book about this—I must have read it twenty years ago."

Ms. Riley apparently heard Helen, because she nodded to her and said, "That's right, the story was popularized in a book about nuclear disarmament. Anyway, here's how it goes: There was an island in the remote Pacific, populated by a certain species of monkey. Although other groups of monkeys of the same species lived on nearby islands, there was no way for the monkeys to get from one island to another. The groups were isolated. All of these monkeys lived by digging up and eating the wild sweet potatoes which were abundant on the islands, and each day the monkey tribes on each island would arise and go about their regimen of digging up and eating the sweet potatoes. Now, on a particular day, one of the monkeys had carried his sweet potato near the water's edge to eat, but instead he dropped it into the water. Quickly, he ran to retrieve it, and by the time he did, the water had washed the dirt off the sweet potato. When he ate it, the monkey thought the clean sweet potato tasted better than the ones with dirt on them, so the next day he purposely washed his sweet potato before eating it. Although some of the monkeys seeing this odd new behavior screamed at him and ostracized him, a few others tried it for themselves, and were soon washing their sweet potatoes on a daily basis. Like many helpful innovations, this one began to catch on, and soon dozens of monkeys were down at the beach every day, washing their sweet potatoes before eating them.

"Now about the time the hundredth monkey converted to the sweet potato washing method, a mysterious thing happened. Suddenly, on a single day, *all* the monkeys on the island went to the beach and washed their sweet potatoes before eating them. And stranger than that, the monkeys of that species on the neighboring islands began to do the same thing, even though they had never seen what the monkeys on the first island were doing.

"The idea behind this fable is that there is a group mind or collective field of consciousness shared by all members of a species, and that the spread of new ideas and behaviors through a species can occur by means of this field, even without contact or communication between species members by any physical means. Sheldrake's work on morphic resonance puts forth the idea that such fields are real, and that they underlie much of what we experience in the physical world.

"Sheldrake gives a real-life example of a phenomenon much like the hundredth-monkey story. It concerns the behavior of birds known as blue tits. In Britain, starting around 1921, blue tits began to be observed pulling the caps off milk bottles and drinking the milk. This habit spread, slowly at first, and then more rapidly, over areas in Britain and Western Europe.

Because blue tits rarely travel more than a few miles from their birthplace, it seems likely that the rapid spread of this behavior to areas separated by many miles could be due to the creation of a new pattern in the birds' group mind, or morphic field, analogous to the sweet potato washing in the fable of the hundredth monkey. Interestingly, during World War II, milk bottles practically disappeared in Holland, another country where the blue tit phenomenon occurred. However, when the war was over and deliveries started again, the milk bottle opening by blue tits in Holland resumed and became widespread much more quickly than it had happened originally. Furthermore, the short life span of this species suggests that few if any of the birds which had learned the habit before the war could have survived the intervening years. This means that the rapid spread of the bottle-opening habit after the war was revived by birds who were not yet born when the habit ceased, and who could not have learned it from older birds. Sheldrake, as I understand him, postulates that the information, or memory, persisted not in the brains of living birds, but in an invisible morphic field or group mind which is somehow shared by all the members of the species.

"According to Sheldrake's theory of formative causation, in which the morphic field is the key concept, such fields may underlie all types of phenomena from the movements of subatomic particles to the cultural patterns of human societies, and perhaps to the very 'laws' of the universe. One revolutionary implication of these ideas is that if the laws of nature are not eternal, but are actually habitual, they are open to exceptions and are susceptible to evolutionary change."

The audience sat engrossed for over an hour, as Kathleen Riley spun out the story of Sheldrake's revolutionary concepts. She took the group on an historical tour of the evolution of Western science from its roots in ancient Greek philosophy to the present-day indeterminacy of quantum physics. She explained that the fact that properties of subatomic particles are now expressed in probabilities undermines the concept of eternal laws and supports the idea of the habits of nature. She delved into biology, recounting experiments that seemed to show the transfer of learned information from one generation to the next in ways unexplainable through genetics. She gave examples of the apparent group-mind behavior of flocks of birds making instantaneous maneuvers in unison. She recounted Sheldrake's tales of termites, unable to see or physically communicate with each other, that nonetheless built highly complex tunnel structures which met and matched one another perfectly. I began to understand that here was a scientific paradigm which might validate the idea of a minded cosmos, a conscious uni-

verse in which self-aware life was not an accident but an evolutio_al, _
I was reminded of Don Lee's quoting Richard Tarnas' statement that the collective unconscious seems to be embedded in the cosmos itself. I squeezed Helen's hand and whispered, "This could bring everything together—the inner and outer worlds, spirit and matter. It gives consciousness a meaningful place in the universe, instead of being a cosmic accident."

Sebastian butted in, "A cosmic accident, that's what my father used to call me."

Helen smiled at him. "He should have called you a serendipity— that's a *happy* accident."

Ms. Riley next launched into the presence of morphic fields in the human world. Pacing as she spoke, rapidly gesturing as she made her points, she was clearly a presenter whose subject excited her, and her intensity was contagious. "Myths," she said, "are prime examples of the existence of morphic fields of human consciousness. Joseph Campbell was perhaps the best-known writer to point out the similarity of mythic themes throughout human cultures, even those isolated from one another in space and time. For many years scholars have tried to explain how these often uncanny similarities could be accounted for by trade, war or other physical contact. One example I am aware of is the story of the frog prince. Most of us know it from the European fairy tale in which an ugly frog befriends a young princess who eventually breaks his enchantment by kissing him, or in some cases by throwing him against the wall. When the enchantment is broken, he becomes a handsome prince who marries the princess. As I said, we know this as a European tale, but the startling fact is that a version of this story occurs in cultures throughout the world. I saw one version in Bali, enacted as the 'Frog Dance'.

"Some occurrences of this type are attributed to contacts by traders and explorers. However, many such correspondences have not been satisfactorily explained by these means, and the frog prince story is one of them. One theory has been that the very nature of the human psyche gives rise to these mythic images, as in Jung's concept of the collective unconscious. The same theory could also be expressed by positing that the *morphic field* of human consciousness is where the patterns of our myths are held. They manifest through us again and again, on all parts of the globe, because we are all connected to that field. The French anthropologist Claude Levi-Strauss has said that myths tend to live themselves out through human beings, without our knowing it. If that is so, morphic resonance may account for it better than any other theory we now have."

A young man in the audience raised his hand. "I thought a myth was something untrue, like a lie. Could you explain what you mean by a myth?"

Ms. Riley flashed a smile. "I'll try. Dr. Jean Houston, another luminary in the field of mind research, has put it this way: 'A myth is something that never was, but is always happening.' The idea is that the story of a myth is not literally or historically true, but it describes a pattern which is expressed through human events. For instance, many people inwardly feel the call to the hero's journey, a myth of separation and sacrifice, of striving, failure, ulti-mate success and return to the community. Some embark on this journey without consciously knowing it, but they nonetheless go through all its stages. Others experience it vicariously, through admiration of sports heroes or other cultural icons. Whether we enact the myth ourselves or participate as spectators, it speaks to us on a level we can feel, even if we cannot artic-ulate the feeling. This inner emotional resonance to the patterns of myths is, I think, strong evidence for the existence of morphic fields of human con-sciousness. The conscious or unconscious repetition of a mythic pattern strengthens its morphic field, and the stronger morphic field makes further repetitions even more likely.

"In the sphere of human activity, ritual is something of which we are all aware. Sheldrake quotes the definition of ritual as follows: 'formal actions following a set pattern which expresses through symbols a public or shared meaning.' Religious rituals such as the Christian mass and marriage ceremo-ny, secular rituals like the swearing-in of public officials, and cultural rituals like Halloween and Thanksgiving are familiar to all of us. Many rituals are associated with stories which depict the original act commemorated by the ritual. Thus the performance of rituals connects us with the past and invokes its presence."

Kathleen Riley paused and then read from her notes, "Indeed, as Sheldrake says, 'The effectiveness of rituals is believed in all cultures to depend on their conformity to the patterns handed down by the ancestors. The gestures and actions should be done in the correct way. But why is the effectiveness of rituals so universally believed to depend on their close simi-larity to the way they have been done before? The idea of morphic resonance suggests a natural answer. Through morphic resonance, rituals really can bring the past into the present. The greater the similarity between the way a ritual is done now and the way it was done before, the stronger the reso-nant connection between the past and present performers of the ritual.' When I read that, one of the little mysteries of my life was solved. I was raised Catholic, and I remember the days when the mass was spoken in Latin rather than English. When the change to English was made in our church, my mother said, 'It just doesn't feel the same,' and I knew what she meant. Something magical and numinous was missing, which had been present in the Latin mass. When I read Sheldrake's book, I realized that changing the mass to English must have weakened the connection of present performances of the ritual to the morphic field built up by all the times it was said in Latin in the past."

Helen raised her hand. "What about the chanting of mantras? Is that another example of the same type of thing?"

"Yes, exactly. The idea of morphic resonance validates the contention of many spiritual traditions that the repetition of holy words can invoke spiritual powers. For example, the Sanskrit words often used as mantras, when we repeat them in present time, can bring on powerful spiritual experiences, perhaps through morphic resonance with uncounted billions of purposeful repetitions of those words, spoken by millions of spiritual seekers through the centuries. Even if the words weren't 'holy' to begin with, the morphic field of human purpose has made them so."

"Are there negative instances of morphic fields?" Sebastian asked.

"In relative terms, yes. An obvious example is Nazi Germany. The destructive 'group mind' that overtook thousands of people in the crowds at Hitler's speeches, and which existed more generally throughout World War II Germany, is in my view a clear instance of a morphic field which led to horrendous human consequences. On a more mundane level, fads, crazes and even financial booms and panics can be seen as consequences of changing flows in the morphic fields of various societies. Their 'negativity' exists in terms of their results, and the values by which we assess them."

Ms. Riley nodded toward my raised hand. "My question is, do different morphic fields ever interact with one another, and, if they do, how does that work?"

"Sheldrake writes about 'nested hierarchies' of morphic fields, giving as an example the multi-leveled morphic fields of one's own body. For instance, there are morphic fields relating to the behavior of the subatomic particles which make up the atoms, which in turn have their own fields, which constitute the body's molecules with *their* fields, on up through the living cells, tissues, organs and the complete human body. At each level of organization, morphic fields are associated with the functions that occur on those levels, and they work relatively harmoniously, *within* one another. I have personally speculated that disharmony in the morphic fields of any level of one's being may be the precursor to dis-ease."

She paused and looked through her notes, seeming to be momentarily uncertain about how to proceed. Finally she gave a slight shrug and went on. "I want to answer your question fully, but I must tell you that this is my own idea, not Mr. Sheldrake's. A particularly dramatic example of what I see as the interaction of morphic fields involves a ritual we call fire walking. Now, I had long been puzzled by the stories I had heard of various tribes and societies around the world who have incorporated the ritual of fire walking into their religious ceremonies. In particular I was struck by something recounted by Joseph Chilton Pearce in his book *Evolution's End*." She looked down at the notebook she had placed on the podium and read, "In Sri Lanka, a local god Kataragama has for millennia been honored by fire walking ceremonies. As Chilton Pearce reports, 'Walkers are carefully selected by the temple priests and prepared for three weeks. The walk takes place in the central courtyard of Kataragama's temple. The recessed fire pit, six feet wide and twenty feet long, creates enough heat to melt aluminum on contact. Onlookers can't stand closer than twenty feet for any period. Yet, hundreds walk the fire each year; some rush across, others stroll or sit, some women pour handfuls of coals over their hair and face with no sign of discomfort or damage. Each year an average of three percent of the walkers fail, however, most of whom die in spite of the attendants with long wooden hooks who try to get them out of the pit. The cotton clothing worn doesn't scorch or singe, except in the three percent, whose clothing and hair burn at the moment of their failure.'

"What does this amazing story have to do with morphic fields? In my view, the reason the story surprises us is that the fire walkers seem to defy our concepts of the 'laws of nature'. Heat that melts aluminum must also burn any flesh it touches, so goes the Western materialist view. And it must certainly burn cotton clothing. For these fire walkers to survive unharmed, the 'laws' of nature must somehow be suspended. However, if the 'laws' of nature are probabilistic, if they are actually more like habits, if they are fields of morphic resonance, well-worn pathways of the past, then they are susceptible to exceptions and alterations. In this case, I think that a highly concentrated field of morphic resonance exists around the fire walking ritual, and that this field is capable of temporarily taking precedence over the 'laws' of nature, when and where it is performed. Notice that the ritual is consciously executed in a way that would tend to enhance its morphic resonance: The walkers are prepared and conditioned by the priest for three weeks, the ceremony is performed the same way it has been for millennia, and the protection of the deity is invoked. The walkers believe they will be protected by

Kataragama, they know the fire walk has been successful in the past, and they invoke the presence of the past through the preparation and the ceremony itself.

"One could look at the underlying pattern of this phenomenon and see a recipe for the conscious creation of new morphic fields. If we could learn to use that skill, I think our potential might be bounded only by our imaginations. Such stories suggest that invisible entities such as mind and spirit may claim primacy over the material domain, or at least be unbound by it, when we de-hypnotize ourselves from our limiting beliefs. Looking back from such a perspective, my student's out-of-body experience might be rather easily understood. If invisible morphic fields are the repositories of mind and memory, and if our link to the body is analogous to that of a television broadcast to its receiver, then clearly damage to the receiver does not alter the program being broadcast. Mind may not be a product of the brain so much as it is something which makes use of the brain to mediate its contact with the physical world."

Within the next few minutes, Ms. Riley concluded her talk and thanked us all for attending. I was eager to persuade her to join us at Rivendell's for dessert, as we had prevailed on Don Lee a week before. Her presentation had germinated questions in me, and I wanted to have them answered.

Ms. Riley was agreeable, and a short time later six of us sat together at Rivendell's, at the same table we had shared with Don Lee a week before. Once again the fireplace crackled behind us as we ordered our desserts and began to discuss the ideas raised that evening.

"Kathleen, I've been musing about the fire walkers in Sri Lanka," Helen said. "As you described it, in addition to the rituals of preparation, they invoke the protective deity, and ninety-seven percent of them are able to cross the fire pit unharmed, in apparent defiance of natural laws."

"Of nature's *habits*, I prefer to say."

"Yes, I understand. Well, that story reminds me of how I go about the hands-on healings. I begin by calming and centering myself, rubbing my hands together to raise the energy, and asking inwardly for attunement with the Infinite. Then I try to imagine myself standing outside my body and watching the Light move through me and into the other person. Reflecting on it now, I can see the steps are a kind of ritual, always performed in the same way, and the faith with which I follow them is something I never question. As to the effects, people almost always feel better after one of my healings, and sometimes the problems go away completely. Would you describe something like that as making use of morphic resonance?"

"I haven't looked into spiritual healing specifically, but what you describe does fit in with what I've been reading about prayer. The phenomenon of prayer—the attempt to communicate with the Divine in order to influence events on Earth—is universal to almost all religions. From that fact alone, you could infer that people believe it works. And now scientific studies have been done which seem to corroborate that conclusion. I read about one in particular in which volunteers were given a list of names of heart-attack patients to pray for. None of the patients were known to the people who were praying, and there was a control group of patients who were not put on the prayer list. As an added control, none of the patients in either group were told about the praying. When the results were calculated, the patients for whom prayers were said did much better than the other group. The prayed-for group had fewer deaths and quicker recovery times. Similar results were reported in experiments when people prayed for plants to grow or for seeds to germinate. Whatever the mechanism, it appears that prayer does work, and for those who prefer not to postulate an anthropomorphic God, morphic resonance is a promising explanation."

"But how does that relate to Helen's healings?" Maddie asked.

"I'm looking at Helen's healings and the prayers as efforts to attune to a 'higher force', and to bring that force to bear on behalf of someone's well-being. A morphic field can be viewed as a 'higher force', in the sense that it is generated by the collective energies of an entire group or species. There may even be a morphic field holding the essential pattern of the whole and healed human, and spiritual healers may simply be attuning themselves and their clients to its frequency. Whether that is exactly what happens or not, the model of the invisible morphic field provides a conceptual framework showing how one person or group may influence the experience of others without having any physical contact with them."

Looking a little confused, Radha asked, "You say this concept is a means of avoiding believing in an anthropomorphic God, but when I communicate with the spirits of people's deceased loved ones, they often refer to God, with great reverence and appreciation. And what about the ecstatic emotions people experience when they feel in touch with the Divine in meditations, or in near-death experiences like Madeline's? Are you saying it's all just a lot of invisible fields?"

"Not at all. As a scientist, Sheldrake leaves open the question of the existence and nature of the Divine, and that is also my position. As far as I'm concerned, morphic fields may simply be God's means of doing things. They might even be the dwelling places of the spirits you contact, just as the field of the collective unconscious is the abode of Jung's archetypes."

"What about faith?" I asked. "Helen is always telling me that I have to hold the vision of what I want firmly in mind until it comes into being. She says that's what faith is—visualizing the goal while keeping oneself in a positive state of expectant hopefulness. Does that kind of thing fit into your ideas about morphic resonance?"

Kathleen looked thoughtful. "Yes," she said slowly. "I can see it in terms of how one might create a morphic field around the vision you want to bring into reality. Since morphic fields are believed to be built up by repetition of actions, the repetition of thought, as in holding your vision, might work in the same way. To enhance the effect, I might suggest creating a physical ritual to go with the thought."

"Of course," Radha said. "That's a common magickal practice. When one wants to manifest something, one visualizes it as clearly as possible and grounds it into the physical world through a ritual. It can be as simple as writing down the essence of the vision or lighting a candle while doing a verbal affirmation. And it's true that repetition is believed to increase the power of one's efforts."

"I think the whole domain of magick and shamanic work is related to morphic fields," Kathleen said. "The magician's efforts to influence events and people without direct physical contact assume some connecting link or field. And shamans report that they dive into the inner ocean where our souls reside, and where the gods can be contacted. My hypothesis is that they have learned to consciously travel through the morphic fields of the human group mind, or collective unconscious, and to influence the energies there. This may be how their cures work. And have you heard of shamans shape shifting—'turning into' animals? Perhaps they have discovered a means of attuning to the morphic fields of the various animal species existing in their environments, and identifying themselves with those energies."

"I want to ask another question," I said. "Do you believe in the story of the hundredth monkey?"

Kathleen turned to me from across the table. "I'm not sure what you mean, Will. As I said, the story is a fable, not a scientific observation, but I do believe it shows a clear picture of how morphic resonance can operate."

"Well, on the way over here after your talk, Helen told me that the book she read about the hundredth monkey was an allegory, showing how higher consciousness could spread through the entire human race if a critical number of people achieved it. And I'm wondering about that, partly because of things that have been happening here with us." I told her about Radha's message from Anon, and asked Radha if she had brought her written copy of it with her.

"Yes, I believe it's still in my purse from last week." She pulled the wrinkled paper from her bag, unfolded it and read the text aloud to Kathleen.

Kathleen listened intently, her green eyes fixed on Radha, her hands absently clasping and releasing one another. "That's fascinating," she said. "I don't know what the 'holy fire' could be, but there are some clear references to what I would call the human morphic field. What was that phrase about the collective mind again?"

Radha looked over her shoulder and read, "'Know that the mind of humanity connects to each and all, and that every individual choice affects the whole.'"

"I could have written that myself. Now, what was that earlier line about the holy fire being received by everyone?"

"'If enough of you open to the holy fire, all will receive its purifying grace.'"

"I suppose that could be describing something similar to the way an idea crystallizes and spreads through the collective mind when enough individuals embrace it," Kathleen agreed.

"Like washing sweet potatoes!" Maddie exclaimed.

Kathleen laughed, "Yes, exactly."

"So do you think it's possible for higher consciousness to spread that way?" I asked.

Kathleen was silent. Finally Helen answered, "I think it is, Will."

"So do I," said Maddie.

"Of course it's possible," Radha said. "It's evolution. It's bound to happen. The only question is when."

"It had better be soon, or not at all," Sebastian said. "I don't want to be the one to throw ants on the picnic, but I'm remembering what Don Lee said—that some scientists don't think we have much time left before there's a severe environmental collapse. Is that true, Kathleen?"

"Unfortunately, I'm afraid it is. Of course, you can still find 'experts' who say there's nothing to worry about, but many of them are working for the industries doing the damage."

"That's just it," Sebastian agreed. "It blows my mind that corporate people are out there committing ecocide, knowingly lying about the consequences of what they're doing, hiring so-called experts as apologists, and going home at night to spend quality time with their families. How can they sleep, or look in the mirror?"

"It's a human trait," I said. "Look around—it's everywhere. What about the people who are involved in all those political conspiracies you told me about? Don't you suppose they think of themselves as the good guys, and the people who oppose them as villains or fools? Inhuman acts are possible when you first dehumanize the victim. That's why protest has to be nonviolent. If you give them an excuse to demonize you, fighting your enemies can actually make them stronger."

"And violence makes you *become* the very thing you hate," said Maddie.

"It's sad," Helen said. "Sometimes it seems as though our whole species is mentally ill. And while we're trying to figure out how to diffuse the most violent dimensions of our relations—the wars and atrocities—the earth is being poisoned."

"It seems to be going on everywhere at once," Kathleen agreed. "I've traveled a great deal, and it has sometimes discouraged me to see how deeply the self-destructive habits of people are embedded in their psyches and their cultures. As an example, people in Central America are burning down the rain forests to clear land for farming, and they can't easily stop, because their economic survival is so precarious. On the other hand, if this destruction continues, eventually the forests will be gone and all the land will become infertile from this non-renewable style of agriculture. At that point, the farmers won't survive, and ultimately we may not either. I can see all that, but it's hard to imagine making enough of an impression to convince a farmer to cease the activity that feeds his family."

"But if the monkey story is right, we won't have to do that," said Maddie. "If enough people can maintain and act from a higher state of awareness, everybody will catch on through the morphic field, and no one will act destructively. Isn't that the underlying message of your talk, Kathleen?"

"That's an implication," she admitted. "I hope it happens that way."

"What I like about the idea is that we can change the world by changing ourselves," Helen said. "I've always felt that the choices we each make have an effect on the whole."

"I don't think we have to do it all alone, either," Maddie said. "There's help being offered to us from the higher levels. The ETs, whether they're physical or not, are trying to wake us up to the danger we've created for ourselves. And consider all the other ways messages are coming to us from the spiritual domain—the apparitions of Mary, the entities like Anon that come through in channeling, the spirit guides who work with people like Radha. On an everyday level, just think about the incredible level of spiritual yearning that millions of people are feeling all over the world—that's a call to the Divine, and it's being heard. Then there are the people like me who nearly die and have a glimpse of the higher realms, and we come back knowing that the beings there want us to live in love and spread the Light." Maddie repeated for Kathleen the story of her inner journey during her recent brush with death. "When I drowned, my brief disconnection from the body allowed me to suddenly see that there are loving beings all around us. We can't see them with physical eyes, any more than we can see ultraviolet light or gamma rays, but I believe they are aware of us, and they care what happens here."

Kathleen nodded as Maddie spoke, and was silent for a moment after she finished. Then she said, "This brings me back to the beginning of my talk tonight. The student I mentioned also experienced a life review—seeing a panorama of the experiences of her lifetime, in the loving presence of what she called her 'guardian angel'. When I discovered the concept of morphic resonance, I wondered if the life review reported in near-death experiences might occur because the individual's consciousness has left the physical body and entered the morphic field where memory is held. But I don't have an explanation for the guardian angel, and I certainly can't tell you the meaning of what happened in that crystal temple."

"The meaning is, we're being helped to find the Light," Maddie smiled. "And we're being asked to spread it. And we can succeed. Your talk about the morphic fields makes me more sure of that than ever, because now I see how it can connect and grow invisibly among us all."

Sebastian put his arm around her. "Life with an optimist—it's a challenge, but it's never boring."

Our conversation went on late into the evening, touching sometimes on the thoughts and wishes each of us held most dear, and at others upon the doubts and concerns that worried us. As I looked around this table of friends, their faces seemed to shine in the glow reflected from the hearth's fire, and my heart was stirred. In the warmth of the moment, I felt that each person at that table, and each person on the earth, was an emissary of the Light, an expression of the infinite love of the Divine. At one point, I tried to express what I was feeling. All the women smiled, but Sebastian shook his head.

"If you met some of the people I used to know, you wouldn't say that, Will."

Finally, we paid our bill and left Rivendell's, hugging and saying our goodbyes in the parking lot outside. Then, alone and in pairs, we departed, moving along our separate paths.

# — 13 —

On Monday morning, after Helen and I had opened the shop, Sebastian called to tell us Maddie couldn't come in to work as planned. "She's got a fever again," he said. "Her temperature kept going up and down all last week, but we didn't worry about it, because it never rose much above ninety-nine, and it was always normal when she woke up the next morning. Today it's over a hundred and it has been all night. She says she doesn't feel too ill, but I'm thinking of taking her back to the hospital if this doesn't clear up soon."

"And how are you doing yourself?" I inquired.

"Actually, I'm not so great. I've been getting flushed and feeling a bit faint, off and on, for several days. I've been trying to tell Maddie we're just suffering from the heat of passion, but I'm not a hundred percent sure it's true."

"You know, Helen and I have been a bit under the weather too. She says she's getting hot flashes, which she has never had before, and I'm having night sweats. It sounds as if we might all be coming down with the same bug."

"How badly do you need help in the store? Maddie can't make it, but I'll come in and make a stab at your customers if you're desperate."

I consulted briefly with Helen before answering. "We're okay for today—the customers can go unstabbed. We'll see how Maddie is tomorrow."

On Tuesday, Maddie was back to work and all of us were feeling better. We spent the week dealing with the store's everyday concerns, catching up on bookwork and taking care of customers. In the evenings, I started reading about the next weekend's workshop topic, Holotropic Breathwork. At the suggestion of the presenters, David and Maureen Edwards, we had ordered a number of books by Stanislav and Christina Grof, the originators of the technique, and I was taking home a different one every night. From what I grasped through reading, the workshop promised to engage us in an intense process of self-discovery. The combination of special breathing, music and bodywork that the Grofs had developed was known for evoking experiences from deep within the psyche. All that week, I felt a growing eagerness, mixed with a slight but gnawing anxiety. There was a half-conscious sense of approaching some kind of threshold, but I couldn't see its outlines clearly.

On Friday afternoon, about half an hour before closing time, the store was empty, and I sent Maddie upstairs to the workshop space to set up chairs for Saturday evening's talk. Helen was working in the office, and I decided to start adding up the day's receipts. I was at the little table behind the rear counter, with my back to the door, when I heard the telephone ring. Helen picked it up in the office. In another moment, the bells on the front door clanged as it was shoved open. I looked over my shoulder to see two men walk in.

They did not look like our typical customers. Both of them were dressed in black suits with white shirts and black ties. One appeared to be about sixty years old, and the other in his early thirties. The older man was tall and husky; the younger one was of medium height with an athletic build, and he wore sunglasses. Perhaps because of their unusual clothes or because of the way they had pushed the door open, I felt immediately apprehensive. I quickly slid the money into an envelope and dropped it behind the table. Then I turned and watched the men walk around the store.

They moved through the room from shelf to table, picking up things abruptly and setting them down hard. They didn't appear to be shopping— the items they handled seemed chosen almost at random, and they didn't show a particular interest in anything. I found their presence strangely menacing, and I wondered whether there was going to be a robbery or an assault, or if I was imagining things. I thought to myself, "These are either police or criminals, and whichever they are, they're definitely not friendly." Remembering Helen's stories about how she put psychic protection around herself, I visualized myself surrounded with white light, and I fervently hoped it would work.

As I watched, the older man chose a beautiful, delicate quartz crystal cluster from one of the shelves and held it up to his companion. "Look at this. Here's a pretty one," he said. Then he opened his hand and let the cluster fall to the floor of the shop, where it smashed to pieces.

"Oops, sorry," he said as he turned to me with a menacing gaze. "You know how it is, accidents happen. Are you William Lerner?"

A chill went through me, but I answered, "Yes, I am. And that crystal you dropped is ninety-five dollars. Who are you?" I came out from behind the counter and knelt to pick up the broken pieces.

He looked down at me, as he reached into his jacket's inside pocket and pulled out a black leather wallet. "FBI," he said, flashing a badge in front of my face. Then he pulled a hundred-dollar bill from the wallet and tossed it on the counter top. "There's the money for your little crystal, Mr. Lerner." He turned to his partner. "Stevens," he said, "show him the picture."

I stood up as the younger man approached, holding out a color snapshot of a young woman standing beside an older man. I knew who the woman would be without even scrutinizing the photograph. I tried not to show that I recognized Maddie, and concentrated on the image of the older man. "Who is he?" I asked.

"That's the late Dr. David Jordan," the older man replied gruffly. "But I want to know if you've seen the cute little girl with him. Do you know her?"

I kept looking at the picture, shaking my head, trying to avoid looking into his eyes. "No, I can't say that I do. Of course, a lot of people come through here during the summer season. I couldn't swear I've never seen her. Is she in some kind of trouble?"

"She might be. Right now, we just want to talk to her. Her name is Madeline Starkey, of Sedona, Arizona, and the local hospital records show she was taken there a week ago last Sunday after a swimming accident. One of the nurses thought she mentioned this shop."

I forced myself to look up and meet his gaze, as I prayed that Maddie would stay upstairs, "No sir, I don't know a woman by the name Madeline Starkey. Of course, anyone who's ever been here could have mentioned the store's name, but that wouldn't mean we knew the person."

The younger man spoke up. "Did you say 'we'? Who else works here?"

"My wife. She's on the telephone right now. When she gets off you can speak with her if you like, but I'm sure she'll tell you the same thing. Uh, by the way, I didn't see your identification, sir. And I didn't get a clear look at yours either," I said, turning to the older man. I was amazed to hear myself challenging them, but the words seemed to come from some deeper part of myself. I went on, "If I could just get your names and badge numbers, I'd appreciate it. One can't be too careful, you know."

The younger man hissed an expletive, but his companion said, "Never mind that. We'll leave our card. Here you are, Mr. Lerner. If you meet anyone who might want to talk with us, especially Ms. Starkey, just give them this." I took the card without looking at it and slipped it into my pocket. He placed a heavy hand on my shoulder and looked down at me with a contemptuous smile, "Always try to choose the right friends, Mr. Lerner. One can't be too careful, you know." He guffawed at that remark, and the two men turned and walked out the front door.

I rushed to the door and locked it behind them. Then I started back towards the office, only to see Helen walking out to the front. "Locked up already?" she asked. "I thought I heard customers out here with you."

"They weren't customers," I said faintly.

"Well then, where did this hundred dollars come from? And what's this broken crystal on the counter?"

I quickly told Helen about the two men, and about their interest in Maddie. "They said they were from the FBI, but they never really showed me their identification, and I had a very bad feeling about them."

"I'm glad you lied to them, Will," she said. "They weren't who they pretended to be, I'm sure of that. We'd better get upstairs and talk to Maddie about this right now. Do you think they're gone?"

"When I went to lock the door, I saw a black van pulling away from the curb across the street. I'm guessing that was them."

"Well, let's take a deep breath and compose ourselves before we go upstairs. We don't want to frighten her unnecessarily. Now that I think about it, we should probably all get out of here before we do anything else, in case those men come back."

We climbed the stairs from the back of the shop up to the workshop space. Maddie had finished arranging the chairs and was setting up the book-selling table. We told her we were ready to leave and offered to take her home. Then we went back downstairs, quickly shut the jewelry and the day's receipts into the safe, made sure all the doors and windows were locked, set the alarm and left the building.

As we drove across town, I told Maddie about my confrontation with the two strange men, and her face grew increasingly troubled. Finally, she blurted out, "It must be that same man who tried to interrogate me in Sedona— the one who claimed to be from the FBI. But why would he follow me this far, and how could he have found me all the way back here on the East Coast?"

Helen said, "They seem to have known about your hospitalization. I wonder if that has anything to do with it."

"Oh, damn! Of course it does," she exclaimed. "When I checked out, I paid with my charge card, because I don't have insurance. That's got to be

it. I hadn't used my card since I left Sedona. Sebastian paid cash for everything. Oh, I feel so stupid!"

"Maddie, please, it's not your fault," Helen tried to soothe her. "And
blaming yourself won't fix anything. Right now, I'm wondering if it's safe to
take you home. What do you think? From what Will says, the men seemed
to believe your home address was still in Sedona."

"That would make sense," she said slowly. "I haven't changed my billing
address with the charge card company, and the hospital could have taken my
address from the identification in my billfold, after Radha brought it when
you all came to see me. Or maybe Sebastian was smart enough to give my
old address. I suppose the RV park will be as safe as anywhere. Besides that,
we've got to tell Sebastian what's happened."

A few minutes later, we turned into the long driveway running to Dune
Forest. When we reached *RV There Yet*, Maddie noticed that Sebastian's car
was missing. We waited while she checked inside the camper.

"He left a note," she said when she came back outside. "He's gone to
Boston for the afternoon, and maybe the evening. After what you've told
me, I'd really prefer not to stay here alone. Is it okay with you two if I come
over until Sebastian gets back? I'll leave him a note and he can pick me up."

"Of course," said Helen. "You can have dinner with us."

"But wait," Maddie said. "Those men knew Will's name. They probably
know where you live, too. Maybe this isn't such a good idea."

"They may not know," I said. "Our house is listed under the landlady's
name, and so is the telephone. She used to rent it only part of the year, and
when we moved in, we just kept everything the same. So depending on how
thorough these guys are, we could be relatively safe."

Maddie sighed, "Let's cross our fingers and hope for the best. If worse
comes to worst, I guess I'll just talk to them. I'll run back and leave Sebastian
a cryptic note." She dashed to the RV and returned quickly. She climbed
into the car, and said with a slight smile, "I wrote to him, 'You'll find me
where Anon came calling; Come and get me, quit your stalling.' Do you
think he'll figure it out?"

"Nobody else could, that's for certain," said Helen.

"Let's go cook some dinner," I said. "Paranoia makes me hungry."

After eating, the three of us sat together in the living room. During the
meal, we had kept our conversation on lighter matters—events at the store
during the past week and discussion about the Holotropic Breathwork workshop to begin the next evening. It was as though we had made an unspoken

agreement not to mention what must have weighed most heavily on all our minds. By the time we brought in our tea and sat down, I felt I needed to say something to break the tension I was feeling.

"So what do you think? Do we decide to forget about those two bizarros in the shop, or do we flee in terror?"

Helen smiled, "What do you say, Maddie?"

"Well, I ran away once before," Maddie said. "And that time I found romance and new friends. Maybe I should try it again."

Helen looked at her sharply, "Are you serious?"

"No, I'm joking, I guess. I don't know *what* I ought to do. I'm afraid of those men, but running away doesn't seem like it's going to work, and I don't really know what they want from me. Maybe a conversation will clear everything up, but I'm not sure whether I could face them without Sebastian. I hope he gets back soon."

"He's probably on his way," I said.

"I just wish there were something I could do to know more about what was going on, and what I *should* do," Maddie sighed.

"I have an idea," Helen said suddenly. "Let's consult the *I Ching*."

"I've heard of that, but I've never done it," Maddie said. "What is it exactly?"

"The *I Ching*, which means 'book of changes', is an ancient Chinese oracle," Helen explained. "It works using synchronicity, the same as the Tarot and astrology,"

"So how do you do it?" Maddie asked. "Do you just read the book, or are there cards, or what?"

"There are two main ways of consulting the *I Ching*," I said. "One involves repeatedly separating and counting a handful of sticks, actually yarrow stalks. Helen knows how to do that one, but I don't have the patience. The easy method I use is to toss three coins onto a flat surface six times. The way the heads and tails fall is translated into a succession of six lines called a hexagram, and the *I Ching* explains what each of the sixty-four possible hexagram patterns means."

"Will left something out," Helen continued. "When you throw the coins, you must hold in mind the question you wish to have answered. Just as in Tarot, concentrating on the question focuses the power of one's consciousness in a way that connects the so-called random tosses to the pattern that symbolizes your situation. After you have thrown the coins and formed the hexagram, which you draw on a piece of paper, you look it up in one of the interpretive *I Ching* manuals, and use that as a means to launch into your own understanding."

"We use the *I Ching Workbook*," I said. "It's really well organized and the interpretations are written in Western terms, so you can understand them easily. We have an older, more literal translation too, and it sounds authentically Chinese, but it can be hard to figure out."

"Well, I want to ask a question," Maddie declared. "Where's the book?"

Helen went upstairs to retrieve the *I Ching* manual and writing materials, while I dug in my pockets for pennies. When she returned, the three of us sat on the floor and opened the book.

"These are the ways the coin tosses are translated into the lines of the hexagram," Helen said, pointing to a diagram. "Solid lines are 'yang' and broken lines are 'yin'. You can see here that there is something additional—if you throw all heads or all tails, that line has extra energy which tends to change it over time into its opposite, so those lines are called 'changing lines'. If your throws include any of these, you end up generating two hexagrams instead of one—one for the past-to-present and one for present-to-future. Also, the more open-ended your query, the more information the oracle can give you. Do you have your question?"

"Yes."

"I suggest you write it down and record the yin and yang lines below it on the page. Then we'll look up the answer."

"Okay, here goes." Maddie wrote hurriedly in the notebook, then closed her eyes and spoke, "What do I most need to know about my situation and those men who were in the shop?" Then she picked up the three coins and shook them vigorously, tossing then onto the rug between us and recording each throw in the notebook as Helen directed. After the sixth throw, Helen scanned the patterns of the two hexagrams Maddie had drawn, and opened the book in her lap.

As she silently read, Helen's face furrowed. Maddie and I watched her with growing concern. Finally, I asked, "What did she get?"

"The hexagram for *Danger*, leading to the one called *Critical Mass*," Helen said. "I'm going to read you the parts that strike me; then you can go through the whole thing if you want to."

Helen turned the pages from one section to the other as she read through the interpretations. Finally she spoke, quoting from the book: "'The situation is one of real Danger, caused by and manifested in the affairs of man. The Danger that confronts you is brought about by your immediate environment. It will take skill to overcome the difficulties, but managed properly, this time of challenge can bring out the very best in you. Do not avoid confrontations in any difficult or threatening situations; you must now meet and overcome them through correct behavior. Hold to your ethics and principles, and do not for a moment consider compromising what you believe to be right. Acting with integrity and confidence is the key to surmounting the Danger.'" Helen went on, "The next section advises you on how to deal with danger in different aspects of life—you can read that yourself. Then here at the end is an interesting part: 'Beyond making you inwardly strong, familiarity with Danger, like the near brush with death, can instill in you a profound awareness of the life force and the mysterious nature of the cosmos. Such heightened awareness can bring new meaning, determination and richness into your life.'"

I turned to Maddie, expecting her to look frightened, but I saw instead her face focused in concentration. "It all makes sense," she said. "I was afraid when you told me about those men, but deep down I knew that I shouldn't run away. And the part about the near brush with death gives me the shivers. I mean, it's been less than a two weeks since I *had* one of those."

"It's possible that this whole answer is about that," I said. "Remember the first of the two hexagrams is about past-to-present situations. It could be describing what's already happened."

"That makes sense," Maddie agreed. "And it's absolutely true that the near-death episode made me more aware of the 'mysterious nature of the cosmos'. I know you remember the story I told in the hospital after my experience, but I haven't had the chance to fill you in on the dreams I've been having since then."

Helen was looking at the book and shaking her head. "I'd like to agree with you, Will, but I don't think this is saying the danger is past. The changing lines usually refer most specifically to what is going on now, and they have additional interpretations. Listen to this. 'Third line: You are surrounded by Danger and you do not understand it. Any action will only make matters worse. Maintain your principles and wait for the situation to reveal itself.'"

"Well, that's less encouraging," Maddie said.

"But it stresses the same advice," Helen insisted. "Stay put and deal with whatever comes. And it's reinforced by what the book says about the other changing line. 'Fourth line: Take the simple and direct approach to solving your problems and overcoming difficulties. Strive for clarity of mind.'"

"I try to do that anyway," Maddie said, "but sometimes I think there's more striving than clarity. So, what about the future?"

"Critical Mass," I said. "If I remember correctly, that's an intense one."

"As the name implies," Helen agreed. "Here is what it says: 'In an atom, when Critical Mass is reached, it is a time when several heavy particles are occupying the same space, thereby creating extraordinary events and cata-strophic chain reactions. In much the same way, the current situation is becoming weighted with a great many considerations. There are numerous decisions pending, the air is full of ideas with all their ensuing multifarious possibilities, and the ponderous affairs of the people around you are pushing into the foreground. All of it is important, serious and meaningful, and all of it is coming to a head right now. Your environment is rapidly becoming the meeting ground for many of the major circumstances affecting you. There is a lot going on, the situation is excessive and may reach Critical Mass soon.'"

"I've had that sensation all week," Maddie said. "It's hard to explain, but since that Sunday when I ... drowned, I've felt as though my life has a new momentum, as if I've become part of something huge that is trying to hap-pen through me. What else does the book say?"

Helen began reading again, "'Look for an avenue of escape. Prepare to make decisions about your next move. You will need your wits about you to successfully make this transition, perhaps into an entirely new mode of life. When experiencing Critical Mass in personal relationships and inner devel-opment, you must realize that this may be a time of crisis. You should mar-shal your forces and penetrate the meaning of what is happening. When sev-eral significant things come upon you at once, you must be prepared to take a stand and rely on the resilience of your character to see you through. If it should happen that you must face this alone and, in fact, renounce your entire milieu, you should do so confidently and courageously. Times like these bring to light the true fiber of the Self. A person who is prepared for such momentous times will survive them unscathed and emerge even stronger.'"

Maddie nodded her head and sat quietly. Finally she said, "I think I understand what that means for me, even though I don't know what's going to happen." She turned to me, "Will, I'm ready to answer your question now. I don't think we should flee in terror *or* forget those two men, at least not yet. But I won't be surprised if they come back, so we should prepare our-selves."

"How do you propose we should prepare?" I asked. "Guns?"

"Weren't you listening to the *I Ching*? Integrity, confidence, courage and resilience. No giving in to fear, and no compromises. You know, I think it was important that you surrounded yourself with white light when those men were in the store. In fact, why don't we all do that together right now, to call in some extra protection?"

"Good idea," said Helen.

The three of us sat cross-legged on the floor facing one another, holding hands in a tiny circle. At Maddie's suggestion, we closed our eyes and visualized a ball of pure white light surrounding each of us, glowing brighter and brighter, and ultimately merging into a larger sphere that encompassed all three of us. As we sat silently together, I could feel tiny tingles, like electricity, flowing through all of our hands. The only sounds came from our breathing, which eventually synchronized, bringing stronger surges of energy into my body. I wondered how long we should continue, but decided to keep my eyes closed until someone else spoke or let go of my hand. I kept imagining the sphere of light around us, and feeling progressively more open and expanded. Suddenly, as I watched, the inner vision changed, seemingly of its own volition, and the sphere began to grow until it covered the house, the city and the surrounding lands. I saw us in the center of a huge globe of light that kept growing until it encompassed the entire earth, ultimately blending with the light of the stars and bathing all of space in pure light. Unexpected bliss poured through me, and I felt tears running down my cheeks. It may have been the tears that made me aware of my body again, because the moment I noticed them the light faded and I found myself looking at the darkness behind my eyelids. Helen squeezed my right hand lightly and I opened my eyes. She and Maddie were both looking at me quizzically.

"Where did you go, Will?" Maddie asked softly.

When I answered, both of them agreed that they had felt an energy moving through our hands. Helen said, "I didn't have the sense of leaving or expanding, but I heard music, incredibly beautiful music, like voices and instruments blended together."

"I felt like a lightning rod," Maddie said. "To me, it seemed as though there was electricity pouring into me from the earth, and into you guys, too."

"Many thanks," I said. "Feel free to send any extra juice you have in our direction."

"That certainly was an unusually powerful meditation," Helen remarked.

"Yes, it was," Maddie agreed. "Maybe we should continue this on a daily basis. We could sit together in the store before we open."

"I'm for that," I said. "Especially if it fights off those men in the black suits."

Maddie looked serious, "I don't know if it will fight them off so much as take us beyond them. At least that's the feeling I've been getting from my dreams."

Helen brightened, "Yes, tell us about what you've been dreaming, Maddie."

"It seems as though I've been in school. Every night this week, I've dreamed myself back into that huge round room in the luminous city I visited when I almost died."

"The room with the crystal sphere?" I asked.

She nodded. "Yes, but I haven't experienced the same things. The sphere didn't rotate or send out rays of light, and I haven't heard the deep hum or the chimes. But now there are teachers, and a beautiful chanting that is an undercurrent in the air, although I don't see whoever is singing. Maybe it's something like what you were just hearing, Helen. The teachers stand on a platform that goes all around the sphere pedestal, and they speak and gesture, and I see pictures in my mind."

"So it isn't only you there?" Helen inquired.

"No. I think there is at least one person on each of the white benches, and there are hundreds of benches in the room."

"What are they teaching you?" I asked.

"It's hard to remember. You know how dreams can be. But I do recall, in last night's dream, seeing images of people touching each other, clasping hands or hugging, and then seeing golden light emerge from the points of contact. And then I saw the earth from space again, this time from the night side, so it was a black disc hanging among the stars with the sun hidden behind it. As I looked, I could see little spots of light appearing all over the land masses. And then I was back in the room and the teacher held up his hand and there were warm vibrations in my chest. I felt so happy, so absolutely full of joy when I was there in the room taking all this in. And I've been waking up tingling all over, with hot surges of energy moving up and down my spine. The other day I woke up, rolled over, kissed Sebastian and said, 'Good morning, sweetie. I'm learning evolution.' I'm not exactly sure what I meant by that, but it made sense to me at the time."

"It's interesting you mention the energy surges," Helen said. "I've had a lot of hot flashes last week and the first part of this week. At least I suppose they were hot flashes, but I've never had any before."

"And I've had night sweats," I said. "I thought I was getting the flu, but the sweats went away after a couple of days."

"Well, I haven't noticed either of you on the white benches, but I don't look around that much. Have you had unusual dreams too?"

"Not that I remember," Helen replied.

"No, just the usual chaos," I said. "I'm back in college and it's final exam week, and I realize I've missed almost all my classes, and then my book bag turns into a suitcase full of doughnuts, and I can't find my room to change clothes so I have to take the test in my underwear."

"That's more than I needed to know," Maddie chuckled. "Maybe you *were* getting the flu."

We talked on into the evening, and our hearts were lighter. The feeling of menace from the two men faded from my mind, and I felt, like Maddie, that I could face whatever lay ahead. Around eleven, Sebastian called from the RV and arranged to come and pick her up. She insisted that Helen and I go on to bed while she waited, and a little while later I heard the door close as she left.

On Saturday, the store was really busy for the first time since the Labor Day weekend. As a precaution, Maddie stayed in the back room, doing office chores for Helen, while the two of us worked the front of the shop, dealing with a constant flow of customers. At least a dozen of them told us they planned to come back that evening for the workshop. At closing time, Radha arrived with dinner for us all from the local pizza shop. We brought in chairs and sat together in Helen's office, sharing the food and catching up with each other's news. Radha had spent most of the week seeing clients and giving readings. She listened with interest to Maddie's dreams, and to my story about the two strange men.

"I think your light-shield must have worked, Will," Radha said. "It's amazing to me that they left after asking so few questions."

"It seemed strange to me, too. But I was even more astonished that I had the courage to challenge them," I said. "That's not normally one of my strong points."

"Perhaps your higher self was coming through, to protect Maddie and Helen," she replied. "Things work that way sometimes. Once I was walking in New York City, and two muggers approached me. They demanded my money and threatened to kill me. I was terribly alarmed, but from somewhere in me a calm, strong voice came through and said to them, 'You can't kill me. Now, get out of here before you get into trouble!' And would you believe it, they stopped in their tracks, looked disoriented and took off in the other direction! I've assumed since then that my spirit, or perhaps one of my guides, spoke through me and was strong enough to command, or at least confuse, the minds of those muggers long enough to scare them off."

"I hope that's what happened here yesterday, but I can't say those two men seemed overly frightened when they left."

"But they departed when you wanted them to go, that's what matters. I think you have access to more power than you realize, sir." She turned to Maddie, "You know, dear, those dreams you've been having are simply marvelous. And they remind me ..." She was silent for a moment. "Oh, yes, I remember. One of my clients and closest friends—his name is George Camden—was telling me this week about going through something quite similar. He's quite psychic himself, and has managed to make a great deal of money in the stock market. He is also a meditator, very deeply involved, probably at it for at least twenty years. I invited him to come to the talk this evening. He may even go through the all-day session with us tomorrow. Anyway, lately in his meditation sessions, he's been seeing visions of the earth, as if from space. 'But it gives light,' he told me. 'It has a golden corona, just like the sun.' Those were his exact words. Of course, I thought of the channeling session I did for Helen and Will, and the predictions from Anon, about the spreading of the holy fire all over the earth. It seems to fit right in with your dreams as well. These are exciting times, I say."

Just then the telephone rang, and I picked it up from Helen's desk. I immediately recognized Sebastian's voice. "Hello? Is this the Missing Link Taxi Service? I'm missing a few links myself and I need a ride."

"What's the trouble?"

"The Toyota is on strike. I've tried everything from jumper cables to threats, but it won't turn over. I think it's the starter. I was planning to be there for the workshop tonight, but I'm going to need help to make it."

"That's no problem. I'll lend Maddie the car."

"Would you mind coming yourself? Then we can talk on the way back."

"Sure, okay. How's twenty minutes?"

"I'll be ready."

I quickly finished my slice of pizza, jumped into the car and headed for Dune Forest. A few minutes later, I pulled off the driveway and onto the grass beside Sebastian's camper. The old yellow Toyota, with its hood propped open, was pushed up against the engine compartment of the RV. Sebastian stood between the vehicles, dressed in shorts and a black-smudged T-shirt, wrapping a set of orange jumper-cable wires into loops over his arm. He grinned and nodded as I got out of the car. "Glad you could make it. You're earlier than I expected." He tossed the bundled wires into the car's trunk, then closed the hood and walked to the door of the RV. "I need to change clothes. Come on in for a minute." I followed him inside and sat down on on the sofa next to Anon, the blue vinyl ET.

"I hear you've had a run-in with some men in black," Sebastian called from the bedroom.

"That's one way to describe them," I said.

"Actually," he said, as he walked into the room, still pulling a blue knit shirt down over his head, "I was hoping you would describe them to me in detail."

"Why?"

"I'm afraid I know who they are."

I sat on the sofa, retelling the episode of the day before, while Sebastian paced the floor in front of me. He stopped and looked at me intently as I described the older man.

"What color were his eyes?"

"Brown."

"When he talked to you, did he ever do this?" Sebastian stood directly before me and placed his hand heavily on my left shoulder.

"Yes, That's exactly what he did."

"Was he wearing any jewelry?"

"Actually, yes. I noticed his ring when he came into the shop. It stood out because it was the only colorful thing on him."

"Do you remember what it looked like?"

"Yes, I looked right at it when his hand was on my shoulder. It was on his index finger, a thick gold ring with five clear stones, diamonds I presume, and some symbol in the middle."

Sebastian had picked up a pen and a pad of paper from the computer table and sketched rapidly. In a moment, he held the drawing up for me to see. "Was this the symbol?"

"Yes, I believe it was."

"Oh, hell!"

"What? Do you know who it is?"

"It's got to be Garth. Garth Lemay from Morgoth."

"Morgoth?"

"The Morgoth Corporation, to be precise. Garth Lemay works for the Morgoth Corporation, and I've known him for two years."

"So he's a friend of yours? Well, that's a relief. I didn't know what to think. None of us did. Have you told Maddie? She was worried because they were looking for her."

"I didn't say he was my friend." Sebastian resumed his pacing, talking almost to himself. "When I was working at the defense plant, my father-in-law-to-be introduced me to a lot of the people in various departments, getting me ready for my promotion. I also met the security people who guarded the plant, and one of them was Garth Lemay. He was the supervisor of security at one of the buildings I couldn't get into—top secret weapons development, I was told. When I first met Garth, he was friendly to me, and we went out drinking together a few times. I figured he was trying to get chummy with the boss's future son-in-law, even though his orders came from elsewhere. I never took much of a liking to him, but I was still attempting to fit myself into the corporate mold, and the guy was an interesting conversationalist. He seemed knowledgeable about a lot of topics, especially certain unofficial activities going on at the plant, and elsewhere, too. He's one of the main reasons I believe in conspiracies."

"Because he believed in them?"

"Because he was *part* of them. Have you ever heard of the Morgoth Corporation?"

"I don't think so."

"Well, most people haven't. But they're the largest private security firm in the United States, maybe the largest in the world. Who do you think guards Uncle Sam's nuclear weapons manufacturing plants?"

"The army?"

"Try again."

"Uh, the Morgoth Corporation?"

"Brilliant deduction! Now you can add to that the security of most private defense contractors who manufacture missiles or other heavy ordnance, plus nuclear power plants, nuclear waste sites, oil pipelines and reserves, assorted U.S. embassies, Cape Canaveral and Area 51—the top-secret military site often associated with UFO activity. Morgoth also owns a chain of private prisons, if you'll pardon my pun."

"I'll ignore it, but are you saying a private company guards all those places? I thought the American military would handle a lot of that."

"That's what most people believe. But the Morgoth Corporation, which employs over 35,000 armed personnel, has spent the last thirty years gobbling up contracts until they're practically a power unto themselves. And of course in many ways, they are like another arm of the government—of the intelligence community to be exact. The board of directors is loaded with alumni from the CIA, the FBI and the Pentagon. Garth Lemay told me Morgoth might as well *be* the CIA, for all the difference it makes. He said he got his job with Morgoth when he 'retired' from the 'Company', as the CIA is affectionately known by its agents. He also told me Morgoth takes the jobs that are too sensitive, or too dirty, for the CIA.

"When I was working at Pantheon, and Garth and I were occasional drinking companions, he sometimes talked about his old CIA days, and about the Morgoth Corporation. He told me he had spent a number of years working in Central and South America—his dark complexion and black hair helped him blend in—and that he had enjoyed 'a lot of fun and games'. When I asked about that, he said, 'The good stuff—drugs, guns and mind control'. Of course, I had no way of knowing what, if any of it, was true. Sometimes I figured he was just bragging. But other times he hinted that the government knew a lot about UFOs. That interested me, because of my mother, and later because of the dreams I started having. Garth said that the people in UFO organizations were mostly 'useful idiots'—people who didn't really understand what was going on, but who served the government's purposes. He also intimated what I've since read— that agents like himself have infiltrated a lot of those groups, and actually have been leaders in some of them. I once asked him if he knew what UFOs were really all about. He leaned over the table, put that huge hand on my shoulder and said, 'Son, if I told you that, I'd have to kill you,' and then he laughed that ugly laugh of his. You know, I think it was Garth Lemay as much as anything else that made me lose my stomach for that job at Pantheon, and where it was taking me."

"So what has this got to do with any of us now? Are you really saying this Lemay was one of the two men in the store yesterday?"

"I think I am. As to what it has to do with us, I'm still trying to understand that myself. But I've been looking over my shoulder for Garth Lemay since Maddie and I left Sedona. Will, I've never mentioned this, but I've suspected for some time that Lemay was the 'FBI man' who wanted to interview Maddie in Sedona after Dr. Jordan's death."

"After yesterday, I can see why, but what made you think that before?"

"When Maddie got that telephone call from the 'FBI man' wanting to interrogate her about Dr. Jordan, I was standing next to her, trying to listen, and the voice on the other end of the line sounded a little bit familiar. I didn't immediately make the connection, but it kept bothering me. What finally made it click was when Maddie called the FBI and they told her they had no agents in the area. It was like the moment when you meet someone out of their usual context, and you know you should recognize him, but you don't, and then he says something that triggers your connection with him, and you instantly know who he is. As soon as it hit me that the FBI man wasn't a real FBI man, I suddenly thought of Lemay. That kind of subterfuge was common in his stories. He had told me about 'covert ops,' where he claimed to have posed as various government officials in Central and South America, and I thought, if he could do it there, why not here? My suspicions increased when Maddie got the description of the 'FBI man' from John, the manager of the natural food store where she worked. He said the man who was looking for Maddie was tall, black-haired and burly, and he also mentioned that the man was wearing a dark suit and a gold ring. That's a fair description of Garth Lemay. But by the time we heard all that, her apartment had been ransacked and we had already left town."

"I'm curious why you didn't go back and talk with the guy, if you knew him. Wouldn't you have been able to help Maddie establish that she was innocent and not a witness to anything?"

"I wasn't anxious to see Garth Lemay again under any circumstances, least of all these. We hadn't exactly parted on good terms. Towards the end of my employment at Pantheon, I got the feeling Garth was trying to recruit me. When we went out drinking, he told fewer stories and asked a lot more questions. He wanted to know all about my future father-in-law, personal things like who his friends were and whether he had a mistress. Once he invited me on an 'unofficial' tour of the top-secret weapons building that his men were guarding at the plant, but I told him no thanks. Another time, he tried to coax me to go with him on an 'interrogation mission' to Florida. He told me we would 'knock some heads, get laid, and make ten grand apiece.' I refused, saying I was about to get married, and he just laughed. He called me 'Mama's boy,' and that really made me angry, because I had told him about my mother's mental illness.

"The last time I saw him, he came into my office to let me know he was being transferred 'out West.' I remember he showed me his ring and asked me if I knew what the symbol on it meant. When I said I didn't, he said it was the insignia of the Knights of Seriphos, a 'multinational fraternal organization' whose members included, he told me, many of the most powerful men in the world—presidents, prime ministers, heads of the CIA *and* the KGB, generals, religious leaders, chairmen of the board, and 'a lot of very rich bastards'. He told me that the Knights of Seriphos had originated in feudal times and that their power had grown steadily through the centuries, until now no government could control them. 'But governments have to listen to us," he said, "or we'll take them out." Garth claimed it had taken him over fifteen years of 'patriotic service' before he was invited to join. 'But now,' he said, 'I'm in with the movers and shakers, and they take care of their own. You know, son,' he told me, 'if you don't wield power in this world, you're nothing. And you don't *get* power unless you choose the right friends.

You had a chance to make a friend on the inside, but you screwed it up. If you keep working here, you'd better watch your ass. Otherwise, go get a job in a grocery store and drink a six pack on Saturday nights. See you in a hundred years, pal.'

"With that, he walked out of my office and I haven't seen him since, although I must have come pretty close to running into him in Sedona. I'm guessing he was involved in Dr. Jordan's death on some level, and that's why he's looking for Maddie. I'm just hoping he doesn't know about me being with her."

"Because you're afraid of him?"

"No ... well, yes, I suppose I am, but that's not the reason. I don't want him to think she knows more than she does because I'm with her. He was so used to being involved in plots, he imagined that he saw them everywhere. He used to rave about conspiracies of 'the liberal media and the college professors,' all poisoning the minds of the young and making the 'real patriots' look bad. Lemay at his best is bad news, and I don't like the idea of his being around Maddie."

"Have you told her about all this?"

"I started to, but she didn't want to hear it. I tried to suggest that the two of us, or at least Maddie, take a plane to Oregon, where she has some relatives, but she was determined to stay here and deal with it. So now I'm just hoping I'm wrong and that the whole thing will go away. What else can I do? I have no way of getting in touch with Garth, even if I wanted to."

"Hey, I forgot to mention the guy left his card. Did Maddie tell you?"

"No, she didn't. Do you have it with you?"

"I think so. These are the same pants I was wearing yesterday," I said as I fished in my pockets. "You know, I haven't even looked at it yet. It probably has his name right on it. Here it is, in my back pocket." I pulled out the card and stared at it in confusion. It was pure glossy black on both sides—there was no name, nor any other writing. "This doesn't make any sense. Maybe this isn't the right card." I held it out to Sebastian.

"Oh, hell."

"What? What's the matter?"

"The black card. Now I know it's Lemay. He told me he used to hand out black business cards with no printing on them when he wanted to intimidate people in Central America. He said, rather proudly, that after a while the practice earned him the nickname, 'Dark Angel', and people started saying that the cards themselves presaged a visit from the Angel of Death."

I had reached out my hand to take the card back from Sebastian, but I quickly dropped it to my side. "You know, I don't really need that. You can keep it if you like."

Sebastian grinned wryly. "I know just how you feel. And now that I think about it, I do want to keep the card. If I run into Garth, I'd like to shove it in his face and ask what the hell he thinks he's doing passing these out to my friends."

I looked out the window, half expecting to see a black van blocking the path to my car. "What should we do now?" I asked.

"Go back and listen to the lecture, of course. What else is there to do?"

As we drove to the shop, I asked Sebastian, "So, if this *was* your ex-pal Garth Lemay, why do you think he's chasing Maddie?"

"Well, it obviously connects to her friend Dr. Jordan, but I don't know exactly how. In his books he claimed the government was covering up the truth about UFOs, but that's not so revolutionary. Dr. Jordan was more tuned in to the spiritual side of things than your average conspiracy-monger, but it's hard to see why that should matter to the government, or to Morgoth."

"There must be something more important, and more recent, that Dr. Jordan discovered or suspected," I said. "I mean, you think he was murdered at Bell Rock, don't you? If that's true, someone must have wanted to silence him quickly."

"Before his new book was finished," Sebastian agreed. "And the only thing missing from Maddie's ransacked apartment was her computer. Somebody must have wanted to make sure Jordan's book notes were kept under wraps."

"But didn't Maddie say the files weren't on her computer?" I asked. "Didn't she say she kept everything on discs?"

"Yes, but she had given them all back ... except the last one."

"Which was in her purse!" I exclaimed. "If Maddie turns it over to Lemay, maybe that will end the whole mess."

"Give it to Lemay? Before I look at it? You've got to be kidding!"

"You mean you haven't read it yet?"

"No, Maddie's computer was a Macintosh. Mine's an IBM. I couldn't read the disc, and after Maddie and I were on the road for a while, I more or less forgot about it."

"Didn't she read it?"

"No, she hadn't yet. He had just given it to her."

"We have a Macintosh in the store, you know."

"Which I hope you'll be lending to me this very night. I promise you, Sebastian the sleuth will burn the midnight oil!"

"Are you sure you want to know this stuff, Sebastian? It might not be healthy."

"I need to know. I have to protect Maddie, and maybe I can do it better if I understand more about why these guys are chasing her. Besides, I'm darn curious, aren't you?"

We rode on for a while in silence. Sebastian's story of Garth Lemay had unsettled me almost as much as the appearance of the two men the day before. I found myself glancing behind us to check whether our car was being followed, and scrutinizing parked cars along the way to see if they were occupied by a pair of black-clad men waiting for us to go by.

Sebastian noticed what I was doing and nodded, "I know how you feel, but I'm trying not to indulge in paranoia. As Maddie says, she's innocent and ignorant, as far as Lemay's possible interests are concerned. If he comes back, he'll discover that very quickly, and that should be the end of it. She says the I Ching consultation last night helped her solidify her thoughts, and she's determined not to run from rumors of danger, at least not until she finds out that the danger is real. If she's going to stand firm, how can I do less? Now, let's talk about the workshop."

For the rest of the drive, we discussed my impressions of Holotropic Breathwork, based on the reading I had been doing. By the time we reached the shop, I had calmed down again, and both of us were ready to listen to the evening's presentation.

# — 14 —

David and Maureen Edwards were standing at the refreshment table chatting with half a dozen of the workshop attendees when Sebastian and I arrived. They were a married couple in their fifties. He was tall and thin, with a mop of curly gray hair and a mischievous grin that lit up his face as he bantered with Radha and Maddie. Mrs. Edwards' most arresting features were her penetrating blue eyes and the earthy laugh I heard in response to her husband's jest. Unlike David, Maureen was built more heavily, "rounded and grounded" I later heard her say as she described herself to someone. Her dark brown hair was streaked with gray, and as I approached I could see networks of laugh lines around her eyes. I liked both of them on sight.

I introduced myself and Sebastian, letting them know I had been reading about Holotropic Breathwork in several books by Stan Grof, as well as one he wrote with his wife Christina. The Edwards told me they had trained with the Grofs, receiving certification as Holotropic Breathwork facilitators after completing a three-year training program. I wanted to ask them some questions which had come up in my reading, but I hadn't spotted Helen in the room, and I was anxious to find her. I excused myself and went downstairs to the back room of the Missing Link.

Helen was in her office, picking up the remains of the pizza and paper plates left from the impromptu dinner party. Her back was to me, so I knocked softly on the door frame to let her know I was there. She started, and then turned to me and smiled. "You're back. Just in time for K.P."

I walked to where she stood, took the paper plates out of her hands and embraced her. Hearing Sebastian's story about Lemay had made me feel the vulnerability of myself and all that I loved, and had helped me to realize afresh how precious Helen was to me. Not seeing her when I entered the room upstairs had caused a little rush of anxiety, and when I found her I felt compelled to take her in my arms. When I relaxed, she held me at arms' length and looked at me quizzically. "That was very nice, but you still have to help me with K.P. What's going on? Did you miss me that much in one hour?"

It was a question that required a long answer, or none. "I just love you, that's all," I said. "Let's get the trash picked up and we'll talk after the lecture."

A few minutes later we climbed the stairs to the workshop room and found a pair of chairs in the second row. Sebastian, Maddie and Radha were in the row right behind us. Radha's client and friend Mr. Camden had arrived while I was downstairs, and was seated next to Radha. He was slender and elegantly dressed, with snow-white hair, and he looked at least ten years older than Radha. When I turned to shake hands with him, he smiled warmly, showing the many well-worn lines in his face, and said, "It is a pleasure to meet you. Radha has spoken about you and your wife so glowingly that I looked forward to this moment, as much as to this evening's presentation."

"Well, I hope we can live up to our press releases," I said. "It's good to meet you, too." Mr. Camden then turned his attention to Helen, and the two of them launched into conversation about the Missing Link, the types of stones and books we offered, and our evening workshops. As I listened, I gathered that this old gentleman was well-versed in many of the spiritual and occult traditions, and I hoped there would be time to chat with him later.

There were about thirty people attending the talk, although Sunday's breathing session was limited to twenty. When the presenters made their way to the front of the room and asked everyone to be seated, I switched on the recorder and returned to my chair.

After introductions, David Edwards began to explain the concept and practice of Holotropic Breathwork. "The word holotropic, coined by Dr. Stanislav Grof, comes from two Greek words— *holos*, meaning 'wholeness,' and *trepein*, which means 'moving toward.' So the work we do involves a special kind of breathing that helps us in moving towards wholeness."

"It's interesting," Maureen interjected. "There are so many connections between the breath and the spirit. In fact, the word *spirit* comes from the Latin word *spirare*, which means 'to breathe.' *Respiration* means literally to *re-spirit* ourselves. *Inspiration* refers to the breath of spirit coming *into* us and giving us a new understanding. And of course, if we're going to bring our ideas into reality, that requires *perspiration*, working *through* spirit." She smiled at the chuckles from the audience. "We all know that breath is life itsel‚ ..⌣ can go for weeks without food and for days without water, but none of us can go for more than minutes without breathing. In Hinduism, the breath is intimately linked to *prana*, the vital life force which permeates the universe. In his autobiographical book on Kundalini, the evolutionary spiritual force, Gopi Krishna asserts that, here on earth, the cosmic vital energy, or *Prana Shakti*, uses oxygen as the main vehicle for its activity. He also points out that both air and water, the two essential requirements for earthly life, contain oxygen as a main element. From Western science, we know that oxygen is certainly a key to life. Oxidation is the means by which we digest our food, and every cell in our bodies requires oxygen for its functioning."

Radha leaned forward and whispered to Helen and me, "No physical fire can burn without oxygen. Maybe *prana* is connected to the holy fire in the message from Anon."

Maureen continued, "Various kinds of special breathing and breath control have been used for evoking non-ordinary states of consciousness in spiritual systems going back thousands of years. The yoga of Hinduism is most widely known for using a number of different kinds of regulated breathing for inducing shifts in consciousness.

"The type of breathing used in Holotropic Breathwork is not so specialized or rigidly programmed as some types of yogic breathing. It is simply a deeper, faster breathing than what one would normally do. The main goal of this breathing is to move a large volume of air through the lungs, which will enrich the supply of oxygen throughout the body. When that happens, an inner force is activated, the subconscious opens, and we experience non-ordinary states which have great potential for our healing and evolution."

David picked up the narrative at that point. "A number of years ago, when he was conducting his research on the transformative and healing potentials of psychedelic drugs such as LSD, Dr. Stanislav Grof discovered the consciousness-altering effects of this special type of breathing. In the psychedelic sessions, Dr. Grof functioned as a 'sitter' and therapist while a subject took the drug and went through the ensuing inner journey. As one might imagine, a great deal of unconscious material emerged in these sessions, including many deep emotional issues, and Dr. Grof's function was both to observe and to facilitate the resolution of such issues. As he reported in his lectures during our training, sometimes in the psychedelic sessions important material surfaced late in the sessions, as the effects of the drug were wearing off. In one such situation, Dr. Grof spontaneously discovered that directing the subject to breathe in a way similar to what we now use in

Holotropic Breathwork had the effect of re-energizing the subject's psychedelic state, allowing for the working-through and resolution of the material
which had emerged late in the session. Later, Dr. Grof discovered that the
*breathing alone*, without any drug stimulus, was capable of opening the por-
tals of the psyche and initiating powerful inner experiences. After the ending of his studies with psychedelic drugs, Dr. Grof and his wife Christina
worked to develop the process they have named Holotropic Breathwork. In
addition to the special breathing, it involves the use of emotionally evocative music, a special kind of bodywork, mandala drawing and group sharing
of experiences. Those of you who join us tomorrow will have the opportunity to experience firsthand some of the personal and transpersonal domains
which can open within us through the breathwork."

He paused, "How many of you have read Dr. Grof's description of the
perinatal stages?" I raised my hand, and noticed that several others did so as
well. "Now, who would like to explain them to the group?" All hands
dropped. David's wide grin spread across his face, and he continued, "I get
that response everywhere I go. Well, I want to emphasize that tomorrow in
the breathing sessions and the sharing, we don't want to analyze each other's
experiences. But at the same time I do want to give you a brief description
of some of the imagery and dynamics that can emerge in this kind of inner
work. What I'm going to say will be short and oversimplified, and I refer
those of you who want the full description to read Dr. Grof's books, *The
Holotropic Mind* and *The Adventure of Self Discovery.*

"Dr. Grof describes three major domains of the psyche which can be
accessed through exploratory techniques such as Holotropic Breathwork—
the biographical, the perinatal and the transpersonal. The biographical level
refers to events occurring in our infancy, childhood and later life. This is the
area most accessible to conscious memory, although the more painful events
have often slipped into the subconscious. The perinatal level of the psyche
relates to the trauma of biological birth and the emotional attachments we
may have because of our birth circumstances. The transpersonal level takes
us beyond the usual limitations of our bodies and individual identities into
the collective unconscious and the unlimited domains of the universe itself.
All of these areas are accessible and may spontaneously arise in the non-
ordinary states of consciousness induced in Holotropic Breathwork.

"One fascinating phenomenon which many of you may have experienced, if you have done this type of work before, or if you have ever utilized
psychedelic drugs for inner exploration, is an automatic internal focusing on
key issues, which becomes activated in non-ordinary states. As Dr. Grof

writes, 'It is as if an "inner radar" system scans the psyche and the body for the most important issues and makes them available to one's conscious mind.' How many of you have had such an experience?" At this, half the people in the room raised their hands, and the buzz of whispers that arose made me think most of us were surprised to see how many others had noticed this phenomenon in themselves. David continued, "This 'inner radar' can bring to our awareness information, memories and experiences from any of the three realms, depending on what is most important and what carries the strongest emotional charge for each of us.

"The process of self-discovery and healing available through Holotropic Breathwork can indeed take one on a journey which leads through *all* three realms, if enough time and energy are given to the work. Frequently, in the beginning we re-experience important biographical material from early childhood and infancy, later going into biological birth itself and the perinatal stages connected with it. Ultimately, we can move beyond our personal history into the transpersonal realms of unlimited experience. In these domains we can interact with or experience ourselves in the past, present or future, as plants, animals, other people, gods, stones, planets, stars or even the cosmic creative principle itself. We can go through our birth or give birth, be a murderer or a victim, swim among a pod of dolphins or fly with the eagles, be a single atom or the entire universe. Our inner experience of the transpersonal domain knows no limits. Although we often see a progression of experiences in breathwork sessions which starts with the biographical, moves to the perinatal and then on to the transpersonal, these steps can occur in any order, they can overlap one another, and they can happen simultaneously in the same session. It is primarily the 'inner radar' of one's own unconscious which selects the appropriate materials from the psyche. The Grofs have come to appreciate and trust the wisdom of this inner guiding principle, and I want to encourage each of you who will be breathing tomorrow to trust that principle in yourselves.

"Now, before we go on, I'd like to spend a little time defining the perinatal stages, because many of you are unfamiliar with this concept, and because perinatal material so frequently arises in Holotropic Breathwork. The word perinatal is derived from Greek and Latin terminology, and means literally 'near birth' or 'around birth.' Dr. Grof has found that psychological perinatal phenomena occur in four distinct patterns, which he calls Basic Perinatal Matrices, or BPMs. The first of these refers to our experiences in the womb and is characterized by sensations of oceanic bliss. The second relates to our experiences when birth contractions begin, before the opening of the cervix, and is often represented by feelings of confinement and a sense of 'No Exit.' The third perinatal matrix pertains to our movement through the birth canal, and is frequently felt as a violent struggle of death and rebirth. The fourth stage, when we leave the mother's body, signifies the completion of death and rebirth and relates to our cessation of existence as a fetus and the beginning of life as an autonomous human being."

David went on to describe in detail the phenomena we might experience in Holotropic Breathwork, as they related to each of the perinatal matrices. He pointed out that some of us might feel as though we actually were in the womb as fetuses, either enjoying the blissful union of the gestation time or undergoing birth as we had experienced it. He mentioned that people in the non-ordinary states engendered by breathwork often took on body postures and movements typical of infants undergoing birth, and that their experiences carried the feeling of present-moment events rather than memories. He noted that not all experiences of the perinatal matrices presented themselves in literal terms. Sometimes they were played out symbolically, as in the case of someone in the second matrix seeing himself confined within dungeon walls rather than the walls of the uterus. He warned us that the emotional content of many breathwork experiences was often very powerful, and that by opening ourselves to the process we were allowing the emergence of unconscious material that could take us in unforeseen directions. He reiterated, however, his belief that the process was a healing one, and he encouraged us to trust our "inner radar" to bring us what we most needed to see.

Maureen, who had been sitting in a chair behind David at the front of the room, stood up at this point and took over the narrative. "I believe Holotropic Breathwork initiates or accelerates the evolutionary process of each individual who does this work. Wherever you are, whatever healing you need, the guidance of your inner knowing takes you to that experience. If you need to relive your birth, you do that. If you need to recall repressed memories of childhood abuse, you do that. If you need to experience oneness with the Source of all being, you do that. Generally in our introductions we try to cover the concerns arising from the potential for difficult or painful experiences which may come up in breathwork, but please don't think that this is all about reliving old pain. We've seen hundreds of people go through incredibly joyful and peaceful experiences. But in those cases, there is seldom any difficulty for the breather, and the experience easily resolves itself. It is in the more painful cases that people sometimes need help, and that's why we tend to focus on them. I also want to suggest that you not try to avoid a negative or frightening episode, should it arise, because the resolution of such experiences often brings the most growth and the greatest satisfaction. As I've heard Dr. Grof say regarding such experiences, 'Never pass up a chance for death and dismemberment.'"

Nervous laughter moved through the audience. Sebastian called out a one-word question, "Whose?"

"One's own, of course," Maureen chuckled. "When I was going through my training, I had one session in which I hadn't been doing the breathing for more than five minutes when a whole jungle movie started playing inside my head. I saw myself as a young girl in India, maybe two or three hundred years ago. I was going to get water from the river, carrying an earthen jug, and on the way back to my village, I was attacked by a tiger. I fought desperately, and my sitter, the partner who watched over me during the session, later told me that, as I lay on my mat in the workshop space, I was writhing around and doing a lot of screaming. On the inside, the tiger ultimately overpowered me, killed me and ate my body. Curiously, my death didn't put an end to my awareness. I could see the whole scene as if from the outside, and I could also feel myself inside the tiger's stomach. I went into a kind of dual consciousness in which I was within the powerful tiger and at the same time I was a disembodied awareness looking down compassionately on the whole scene. Then my two consciousnesses reunited and I *became* the tiger, running through the jungle, coming to a tall cliff which faced the setting sun, and leaping off. I felt myself flying through space and falling towards the sun, but before I hit the ground, I merged with the sun and became one with its radiant awareness. I experienced a feeling of joy and power unlike any I had ever known. When the session was finally over, I came away with a new level of confidence in myself, a deeper trust for the process of life, and a diminished fear of death. After that, I understood why Dr. Grof encourages breathers to go into the most difficult or fearful elements that come up in their sessions. Going *through* such inner encounters liberates us from the hold they have over us and frees us to function on higher levels."

Radha raised her hand. "This is all fascinating, but I'm wondering, could you tell us a bit more about the actual process we'll be experiencing tomorrow?"

"That was my very next point," Maureen smiled. "Tomorrow's workshop will start at nine A.M. and it will probably last well into the evening. There will be two breathing sessions of about three and a half hours each—one in the morning and one in the afternoon. Before leaving here tonight, everyone who will be doing the breathing tomorrow must choose a partner. That partner is your 'sitter' and he or she will stay beside you, giving you his or her full attention during your breathing time. In the other session, you will be the sitter for your partner. The sitter's job is to be there to monitor the breather's situation, to give assistance in the form of tissues, drinks of water, and help getting to the bathroom, as well as anything else the breather might request. In addition, the sitter is there to call *our* attention to anyone who gets into a particularly difficult spot and may need help getting through it. David and I will be there particularly to offer bodywork to breathers who have pain or other physical symptoms. Often the energies associated with emotional wounds or blockages can constellate during breathwork in particular parts of the body. Through physical manipulations that consist mainly of putting pressure on these areas, both the pain and the emotional attachments can often be released."

David stood up and began to describe the arrangements of the room and other aspects of what we could expect on Sunday. "Each breather will lie down on a mat on the floor here in this room. Maureen and I have brought ten mats with us, which will be enough for everyone, but we recommend that you bring blankets, sheets, pillows and whatever else you need to be comfortable. You may also want cushions for when you are the sitter. At the beginning of each session, we'll do a brief relaxation exercise, and then the music will start. We haven't talked much about the music, but you'll hear what it's all about tomorrow. In essence, the evocative music we play during the breathing sessions is meant to assist in bringing you into the non-ordinary states of consciousness. It is loud, and it's probably not anything with which you're familiar. We use a lot of sacred music from other cultures, as well as electronic music, classical, drumming and other material. During the session, we encourage you to simply focus on the breathing and let the music carry you wherever your inner radar wants you to go.

"When you begin, remember there is no right or wrong way to do the breathing—the prime directive is to move a lot of air through your lungs. With that, you begin your journey. When you are finished in three hours or so, you can go downstairs to the back room of the Missing Link where there will be tables set up with paper and art supplies for mandala drawing. We encourage you to do a drawing, or more than one, after your session, because it helps you to complete and integrate the experience. Most people draw some type of representation of their inner journey, but there are no rules. Just pay attention to whatever wants to be expressed, and let it come out. Tomorrow evening, we'll have a sharing session and we'll each show our mandalas to the rest of the group." He continued with details regarding food and other logistics for the day, and then asked if anyone had questions.

A woman behind us raised her hand. "It sounds as though this breath-work can create some very powerful experiences, but how safe is it?"

David replied, "My short answer usually is that nobody has ever died from breathing." He smiled at the laughter from the group. "Seriously, though, there are some medical contraindications, including pregnancy, epilepsy, severe heart disease or other cardiovascular problems, a history of severe emotional disorder or past psychiatric hospitalization. We have med-ical forms for all the breathers to fill out before we start tomorrow, and any-one with questions should speak to us before going home tonight. As regards other concerns, Maureen and I have facilitated over a thousand people doing Holotropic Breathwork, and one of our main objectives always is to keep the environment safe and supportive. We'll stay with it as long as it takes for everyone to come to completion, and we want sitters to call on us anytime during the session if a breather needs help or wants bodywork."

Maureen added, "The help we'll be offering is not usually to get you out of a negative experience. We'll encourage you to go *into* your experience and move through it, no matter how horrific it may seem. And if you experience physical pain or tension in the body, we'll put pressure on that area and ask you to tense it even more. The way we see it is that whatever symptoms come up can be resolved best by allowing ourselves to feel them fully. So you might have a pain in your back and David or I will press on it hard while you try to intensify it. As feelings arise, you're free to yell, scream, curse, what-ever."

"We do have a magic word, though," David said. "The magic word is STOP. If you say that, we'll back off and renegotiate. Anything else you say we'll assume is part of the drama you're playing out. So if it becomes too much, say 'STOP', and we will."

The questions continued for another twenty to thirty minutes, as people brought up their queries about details of the coming daylong session. Finally, Maureen and David brought the evening to a conclusion, encouraging those returning the next morning to get a good night's sleep. Radha's friend Mr. Camden said good night to her and to us, promising to return the next day for the breathing sessions.

Helen had invited the David and Maureen, as well as Radha, to spend the night at our house. I was worried about Sebastian and Maddie, after what he had told me regarding his old acquaintance, Garth Lemay. But when I spoke to him after the end of the talk, he assured me that they would be all right. "Even if Garth was here yesterday, that doesn't mean he knows where

Maddie and I are camped, and I can be a very light sleeper when I'm paranoid. Do me a favor, though—if the phone rings in the middle of the night, take the call. I'd hate to have to speak my last words to an answering machine."

Radha volunteered to drive Maddie and Sebastian to the RV, while Helen and I put the chairs away and helped the Edwards bring in the mats and stereo equipment for the next day. About twenty minutes later, we set the alarm, locked the building and drove across town, leading David and Maureen to our house.

When we arrived, Radha was already waiting outside. We quickly showed the Edwardses to our bedroom and set up Radha in the guest room. Helen and I unfolded the couch in the living room.

When the house was quiet, we turned out the lamp next to the sofa bed and lay down to rest, but before I could close my eyes, I had to tell Helen about my conversation with Sebastian. As we lay there in the dark, she listened quietly until I had told the whole story, including Sebastian's parting joke about their safety that night.

"Humor is his shield," she said. "I've always seen that about him." Both of us were silent for a few moments, and then Helen spoke again, "I don't know where this is all going, but it certainly corresponds to what came up last night when Maddie threw the *I Ching*."

"*Danger* and *Critical Mass*," I mused. "This is making me jumpy, even though it's not my problem."

"How can you be sure it isn't?" Helen asked. "I have the feeling that whatever involves Maddie and Sebastian is going to affect us too."

"I know. How can you see that and not be worried?"

"What's the point of worrying about the unknown? You can't do anything about it until it arrives."

I didn't answer, but I lay awake in the dark beside Helen for a long time before sleep finally came.

# —— 15 ——

An autumn storm blew in off the ocean during the night, and the morning arrived gray and wet. Gusts of wind rattled the windows, and the rain beat against the glass. The house felt cold, and when Helen and I woke up we found ourselves curled together in a ball under the blankets. We dozed until the mantle clock struck seven, and then we got up, re-folded the couch, and I built a fire in the hearth while Helen mixed batter for breakfast pancakes.

While Helen was working in the kitchen, Radha came downstairs in her robe. She embraced me lightly, nodded approvingly at the fire and said, "Dreadful weather. It chills one to the bone just looking at it. I must brew a cup of tea before I can face the shower."

Helen called out, "The tea is steeping as we're speaking. Come into the kitchen and keep me company."

Radha padded into the kitchen, and I went upstairs to the guest bathroom to shower and dress. When I came out, I heard stirring in our bedroom, so I knew David and Maureen were awake. I went back to the kitchen to tell Radha the bathroom was free, and started gathering the pillows, blankets, water bottle and other paraphernalia we planned to take to the breathwork experience. The smell of fresh blueberry pancakes was a comforting antidote to the sound of the wind and rain that blew against the house.

In a short while, we were all seated around the big kitchen table. David and Maureen gave high praise to Helen's pancakes, as well as the scrambled tofu and vegetables she had prepared. David looked at my plate and cautioned me, "If you're the first breather, we advise eating a light breakfast. Very few people throw up during the breathwork, but a heavy load in your stomach can literally weigh you down."

"I'm on the second shift," I said. "Helen is breathing this morning, and I'm taking the afternoon session. I'm filling up now, since I'll probably skip lunch."

After breakfast, we all got into our cars and drove back to the shop. No one else had arrived yet, so we went inside and helped David and Maureen finish arranging the workshop space. I joined David in setting up his stereo equipment and placing speakers in the four corners of the room. Helen and Radha, under Maureen's direction, were taping black plastic over the windows, to keep light in the space to a minimum. While David was testing the sound system by playing snippets from the music he would use for the morning session, I went downstairs to the store office and called Sebastian.

The telephone rang and rang. I told myself they must already be on their way to the shop, but my worries flooded into me immediately. Finally, as I was about to hang up, someone picked up the receiver and said, "I hope this is important."

"Sebastian! It's Will here. I was calling to see ..."

"If we made it through the night? Yes, the worst disturbance up until your call was the rain on the roof."

"I'm sorry, I just wanted to check on you. Where were you anyway? I must have let the phone ring a dozen times."

"In the shower. Have you ever tried to take a really good shower in an RV? It isn't easy, or quick. Maddie's out walking on the beach— don't ask me why, in this weather. By the way, when is Radha picking us up?"

"Oh my gosh, that's right! I forgot about your car. I guess we all did. I'll go upstairs and remind her right now, and if she isn't up for it, I'll come myself."

When I let Radha know we had forgotten Sebastian and Maddie, she blushed and immediately volunteered to go and get them. While she was gone, the other breathwork participants started to arrive, and Maureen directed them to lay out mats wherever in the room they wanted to be for the morning session. Helen and I chose a spot near the middle of the rear wall, and she spread two blankets over the mat, placing her pillow at one end. I made a space for myself to sit on the floor beside her, setting a cushion against the wall, with a bottle of water and a box of tissues beside it. The other pairs of people were creating similar spaces for themselves. David finished testing the stereo and went around to all of them, checking in and answering questions. Maureen moved through the room, passing out boxes of tissues and little plastic trash bags, "just in case." She also offered ear plugs and blindfolds to those who wanted them.

By the time Radha returned with Sebastian and Maddie, all the others had arrived. Helen met them at the door and quickly helped them set up their mats, blankets, pillows and other supplies. Radha's breathing partner, her white-haired friend Mr. Camden, was waiting for her, with his mat neatly made up and ready. After a few minutes, Maureen asked everyone to take their places and make final decisions about who would breathe and who would sit during the morning session. She advised breathers to make agreements with their sitters about whether they wanted to be touched, what hand signals would indicate the need for a drink of water or a tissue, and if they wanted to be reminded to breathe.

"As you move into your inner process," she explained, "you may forget to do the deep breathing. In some instances, because of the increased levels of oxygen in the body, people will completely stop breathing for up to minute or so. It hasn't been found to be dangerous, but it's best to decide now whether you want any intervention by your sitter if something like this happens."

A soft murmur of conversation filled the room as breathers and sitters made these arrangements and took their places. Helen lay down on the mat and I propped myself against the wall beside her. I looked around and saw that Sebastian was lying down to take the first session, and that Radha was in the far corner of the room sitting next to her reclining partner. She caught my eye and winked solemnly. Maddie was kneeling, whispering to Sebastian with her back to me. I watched the other participants, some of them familiar faces from the shop and others strangers to me, arranging themselves and getting comfortable. Suddenly, I had the feeling that the room had become a kind of vehicle, and that all of us were in some sense embarking together on a voyage into the unknown.

David had stationed himself at the controls of the sound system, and Maureen paced slowly around the room, exchanging a few final words with each set of partners. Breathers were reminded to "move a big volume of air", and the sitters were admonished to give our breathing partners our full attention and to be ready to help them as needed. At last Maureen picked up a microphone and began by leading the group through relaxation exercises in which we all lay down and systematically clenched and released the muscles in every part of our bodies. At the end, she said, "Sitters, take your places. Breathers, have a good journey." And with that, the music began.

All around the room, those on the mats began to breathe deeply and rapidly, as powerful rhythms welled out of the speakers. The breathers' eyes were closed, some covered with blindfolds, and their partners sat beside them, watching and waiting. Helen's face was calm, and the blanket over her rose and fell with each cycle of respiration. I didn't recognize the music, but it reminded me of Africa, of drum trances and dancing. David had turned the volume up, as he said he would, and the high intensity and rapid tempo of the piece seemed to flood the breathers with energy. Certainly they all appeared to be moving a great deal of air through their lungs. For a moment I thought about how odd this scene looked on the surface, and I wondered what might soon be happening in the inner worlds of the participants.

The first piece of music continued for perhaps five minutes, and then it faded out and another took its place. This one seemed to me to have come from the Middle East. There were male singers, possibly Arabic, chanting in a language I did not know, accompanied by an unfamiliar orchestra of horns, strings and bells. This song had a yearning quality to it, and I imagined it as some kind of prayer or invocation. I watched Helen, as her breathing became even deeper, and the expression on her face went almost blank. I had seen her like that before, when she sat in deep meditation. I looked around at the other breathers. Some were still, and completely shrouded under blankets and sleeping bags. Others had begun to writhe and undulate on their mats. A few made sounds, little sobs or moans. Maureen walked slowly and gingerly about the room, looking down into the faces of the breathers and their partners, while David surveyed the scene from his chair beside the stereo controls.

The breathing continued and the music evolved, next into an other-worldly cascade of electronic sounds. This synthesizer music contained no voices or recognizable instruments—its tones and almost mathematical patterns made me think of outer space, or a kaleidoscope of intertwining dimensions. It continued for some time, transforming from heavenly, chime-like tinkling to deep, severe, slamming rhythms. The room began to feel electrically charged, as though some atmospheric disturbance were building. The breathers continued, and some of them grew louder, groaning or crying out spontaneously. Helen's respiration was deeper, but slower now, and her face remained expressionless. I kept my eyes fixed mostly on her, occasionally glancing about the room to see the sources of cries heard, or stirrings caught by my peripheral vision.

The music moved on, through transformation after transformation. There were powerful, uplifting orchestral selections and several strange chants. I heard a young woman's beautiful voice singing in Gaelic and an old shaman croaking a peyote song. There were many more pieces played that morning while the breathers journeyed, and they seemed to have been cho-

sen to run the emotional gamut. But as time passed, I had less opportunity
to reflect on the music, because more began to happen with the breathers,
and Helen started to show signs of distress.

We were near the halfway point in the session when Helen began to
weep. Two or three of the other breathers had already gone through periods
of deep sobbing, and one woman had moved from that stage into screams of
rage, but through all that, Helen had stayed calm and quiet. As I gazed at
her, I thought she must be deep within herself, since she showed no reaction
to the disturbances around us. She made no sounds, but at a certain point, I
noticed tears leaking out of the corners of her eyes. Then her breathing
became rough and uneven, and I saw her face contorted into a mask of
anguish, as her chest heaved in silent spasms. Finally, she drew a very deep
breath, and she began to cry out loud. She wept and wept, though she continued the deep breathing and kept her eyes closed. It frightened me to see
my strong wife, my closest friend, in such a state. I wanted to touch her or
speak to her, but we had agreed I would do neither of these unless she asked
me. So I sat silently beside her, not knowing what was transpiring within her,
yearning uneasily for her to get through this part of her journey, whatever it
was.

As I was watching Helen, I heard a great shout come across the room
from Sebastian. It was no word—it was almost an animal roar. It happened
at a moment when Helen was at what seemed to be a peak of emotional
intensity. The music, too, was strident, a symphonic piece that seemed to
push even my own feelings to the brink. After the shout, Sebastian began to
moan, and his cries blended with those of others in the room. In the next
moment, the music suddenly changed into a sweet and soft evocation of
peace, but the laments of the breathers continued. As I listened there in the
dimly lit space, it seemed that the gentle music and the grieving voices
blended together into a single song that encompassed life in all its beauty
and suffering. Though I had tried to stay centered and objective, my com-
posure began to falter. My own eyes filled with tears, and I felt powerful emotion welling up within me. I sensed that, in another moment, I would suc-
cumb and join the breathers in their hymn of pain and release.

I regarded my wife and remembered that I was supposed to be there for
her, as witness and helper. It was not the time to give myself over to whatever was happening around or inside me. With an effort, I pulled myself back
and tried to still the forces that were threatening to erupt within me. I took
a sip of water from our bottle. I looked at Helen, who had begun to weep
more quietly. The lines of her face were beginning to soften. I glanced

around the room and saw David and Maureen circulating, whispering to sitters whose partners seemed to be most distressed. They appeared unperturbed by the turmoil around them, their faces showing calm and focused attention, compassion without pity, and looking at them helped me regain control of myself.

The music played on, but after some time its tone began to change. It began to feel softer. As I watched, Helen's expression lost its distress as well. She no longer breathed rapidly and deeply. In fact, it seemed to me that she didn't breathe at all. Once again I fought the impulse to disturb her, leaning over to see or hear the slightest evidence of respiration. Several times I was on the verge of touching her cheek to see if she would respond, wishing that she had agreed to have me remind her to breathe. Each time, I was held in check by a barely perceptible exhalation. Helen was alive and breathing, but her mind was far away from where I sat beside her.

At last, the songs and chanting, rhythms and dances were replaced by a sound far older than the first human cry. From the speakers in the four corners of the darkened room where the ten voyagers lay beside their witnesses, the recorded sounds of ocean waves on an invisible beach washed over us all. Like the breathing of the Earth itself, the rhythm of the surf cycled endlessly, bearing the gift of peace. Helen, her eyes still closed, took a deep breath and let it out in a soft sigh. She brought her arms up from her sides and draped them across her chest, rocking slightly side to side. I felt myself begin to relax as well. There was a sense of relief, as though I had come through some long dark passage, even though I had not been one of the journeyers.

The music was over, but the gentle roar of the ocean went on and on, calling everyone back—to their bodies, to their lives, to the world we all shared with one another. Where Helen's face had been a blank slate or a mask of suffering, it now shone with peaceful joy. Though she had not opened her eyes, she reached from beneath the blanket and took my hand. I gave hers a slight squeeze in answer.

Around the room, the return progressed at different rates. I saw two breathers sitting up with open eyes, embracing or whispering with their sitters. Several others were still deeply immersed in their journeys, shouting or sobbing, and one was laughing. David and Maureen were both bent over a woman whose body was twisted and tensed in apparent pain. As they pushed against her abdomen, she screamed, then panted and tensed again. Radha's partner Mr. Camden was sitting, eyes closed, in the yogic lotus position. Sebastian lay curled on his side with his back to me, while Maddie crouched down beside him. I returned my gaze to Helen and kept my vigil, listening to the endless surf, holding her hand and waiting for her eyes to open.

I sat like that for several minutes before I noticed how hot my hand was. It took a few more moments for me to realize the source of the heat was Helen's hand. I scrutinized her face, wondering if the radiant glow I had seen was actually the flush of a returning fever. "Ah, *well*," I thought to myself. "*When in doubt, worry.*"

I looked around the room again, wondering what inner experiences had brought up such apparently powerful emotions for so many of the breathers. Listening to the lecture the previous evening, I had prepared myself for self-generated technicolor adventure movies, but not for pain and grief. What had caused Helen to go through her catharsis of sobs, and what had made Sebastian wail like an animal? I glanced down again at Helen, and found her gazing up at me.

"Woolgathering?" she asked softly.

"What?" I whispered. "No, I was just looking around and thinking ... Hmm, I guess that *is* woolgathering. But never mind that—how are you? What happened?"

She raised my hand to her lips and kissed it. "I'm not ready to talk yet, but I'd appreciate it if you would help me get up and go downstairs. I need to use the bathroom, and I want to sketch something, but I feel a little unsteady."

Carefully, I helped Helen to her feet and held my arm around her as she walked to the stairway. I went down just ahead of her, and she kept a hand on my shoulder for support. While she was in the bathroom, I stood outside like a sentinel, and when she came out I walked her over to the long table where Maureen had laid out colored chalk, crayons and big sheets of paper. I noticed that each sheet was inscribed with a large circle, the primal form of the mandala. Two of the other participants were already there, one of them sketching busily.

Helen sat down, selected several colors and immediately began to draw. I decided I shouldn't just stand there looking over her shoulder, so I walked out of the back room and into the store's retail space in front. I turned on the lights, chose a book from the shelf and sat down in one of the two reading chairs. The sky outside was still gray, and the cold rain lashed against the plate glass windows at the front of the shop. I opened the book at random and began to read.

The book was *On the Way to Supermanhood*, by Satprem, a disciple of Sri Aurobindo, and his companion, known as Mother. Among the words I read were these: *"In fact, the first effect of Truth as it touches a new layer is to produce a frightful disorder, or so it seems. The first effects of mental truth when it touched the primates must have been traumatic, we can assume, and utterly subversive of the simian order and effectiveness; a peasant has only to take a book for the first time for all his bucolic peace to be upset and his sound and simple notion of things to be thrown into turmoil. Truth is a great disturber."* I remembered Radha's notion that one can view randomly chosen passages in books as omens, giving oneself a glimpse at the meaning of events through the workings of synchronicity. I wondered if what I had just read was an answer to my question about why there had been so much sound and fury during the breathing session. I read the words again, speaking them softly under my breath. As I was repeating, *"Truth is a great disturber,"* a hand touched my shoulder from behind.

"I hope I'm not disturbing *you*," Helen smiled.

"Not at all." I stood up and put the book back on the shelf. "I was waiting for you to finish your drawing, and I didn't want to look over your shoulder, so I came out here."

"Well, it's done," she said, holding up a rolled sheet of paper which was secured with a rubber band. "Now I need a hug, and maybe a kiss, too." She reached her arms toward me and we embraced. Then she buried her head against my shoulder and sighed. "Will, I don't know how to begin telling you about it."

"Chronologically is always good," I said.

"I'll try that and we'll see how things go," she agreed. "I think I'm one of the first ones to finish, so maybe we have a little time." She quickly walked to the back room doorway and glanced in. "Yes, there are only a few people downstairs so far." We sat in the two reading chairs and she began to describe her experience.

"I was a little nervous before the session started. I don't know why. It was a bit like the feeling I used to have when I climbed the ladder to the high diving board as a girl—I felt both eager and afraid. Anyway, I was glad to do the relaxation exercises, and tensing my muscles before releasing them really helped me to let go. By the time the music started, I was calm and centered.

"I remember the drumming. It was so loud, it practically took me over, but I used the rhythm of it to get myself into the breathing. I tried to make it as deep and rapid as I could, and it wasn't very long before I was in an altered state. My body began to tingle, and I felt myself falling deeper and deeper into darkness."

"I noticed that your face went blank," I said, "so I assumed you had gone inside the way you do in meditation."

"It was like that at first. The darkness wasn't uncomfortable at all. I've been there many times. I floated in that space and waited, and before long I heard the voice of one of my spirit guides. She was asking me a question, offering me an initiation. Through my thoughts, I conveyed my acceptance of the invitation, and the next thing I knew I was looking at my parents in the church on their wedding day. I was hovering over them, and I sensed that I was the spirit of myself before incarnation, viewing the couple through whom I would take birth.

"In the next moment, I had a glimpse of my mother and father, newly married, engaged in physical love. I felt a great deal of curiosity, but I was also aware of some sort of electromagnetic pulsing energy moving through me and connecting me with them as well. Then there was a great surging explosion and I was filled with ecstasy and light. In the next moment, I felt myself pulled down through a long funnel and compressed into something incredibly small. Then there was a period of oceanic peace. I seemed to be some sort of sea creature, floating and growing quietly in a dark underwater cave. There was such blissful comfort in that space. I had no sense of time, and no need for anything else. It seemed I could have gone on forever like that.

"But then there was a change. Suddenly, the walls of the cave closed in on me like a vise. And there was a strange new sensation— pain. My bliss evaporated in an instant, and I was filled with shock and fear. And, Will, it was the most utter terror, because I didn't understand what was happening and I didn't even know what I was afraid of. It was simply sheer pain and panic."

I nodded my head. "It sounds like the second perinatal stage Dr. Grof writes about, when the birth contractions begin."

"Yes, it does, but I have to tell you I didn't think of that then. I was total-ly involved in the experience, and it went on for a long time. The contrac-tions, if that's what they were, grew stronger and even more painful. I felt I was being crushed alive. And there was no way out. My mind started flash-ing on scenes that felt like past lives—I was a prisoner in a medieval dun-geon, an inmate at a Nazi concentration camp, a quadriplegic soldier in a hospital bed. The images kept coming in waves with the pain, and I had an incredible sense of despair."

"At one point, you started crying," I said. "Was it during that part?"

"It could have happened then. I don't know. I wasn't aware of crying until a bit later in my experience. In any event, the next thing I noticed was a feeling of rage coming out of my despair. I knew I deserved to live, but it seemed I was going to be extinguished before taking my first breath. It was such a strange emotion—I felt murderous, absolutely out of control. It was as though I were filled with an intense will to live that would have gladly mowed down anything or anyone in its path in order for me to survive. Then I could feel myself moving, but it was like being shoved through a meat grinder. I know I was sobbing by that time, in this strange mix of hopelessness and fury. I started seeing images again; this time there were scenes of terrible devastation. I saw armies clashing with swords and spears, and others with guns and rockets, villages destroyed by carpet bombings, earthquakes opening great fissures in the ground. And there was a feeling of tremendous heat. There was fire coming out of my hands and my abdomen felt like it was going to explode. I was beyond crying then. All I could do was gasp and groan. The feelings were so intense, a stray thought in me wondered about David's statement that nobody ever died from breathing. And then suddenly I was through it. If I cried then, it was from relief."

"I think I could tell when that was happening," I said. "And it seemed to me that when you were in the most distress, some of the others were, too. I even started to feel overwhelmed with some emotional force that seemed to be sweeping through the room."

"Was that when Sebastian shouted?" she asked. "I can remember hearing that, even though I don't recall the music or anything else that was going on then."

"Yes, it was about that same time," I said. "But what happened with you after that?"

"After the breaking point, whatever it was, I found myself bathed in a soft gold light. It was more than light, really. It was an *atmosphere* of gold. There was a feeling of such profound peace, and I rested there for a while. I felt like I was a tiny bird gliding over the ocean, floating in an atmosphere of light and stillness. I didn't move. I think I scarcely breathed."

"I thought you had *stopped* breathing," I said. "I was bending over you, trying to decide if I had to touch you or speak, or if I should call David and Maureen."

"I'm happy you didn't, because I wouldn't have wanted to miss what I experienced next. After resting in the gold light, I decided to try to go to the inner temple where I meet my spirit guides when I meditate. I started in on the breathing again, and the gold light dissolved into darkness. It felt as if I had dropped down inside the earth. It wasn't frightening at all—I felt total-

ly safe and protected, and there was a sense of a benevolent feminine presence all around me. After a bit, I saw a small light in the distance. I thought
it was my temple, so I moved toward it. When I began to see it more clearly, I realized I was somewhere else. I was standing at the edge of a great bonfire, and there were people there, painted but otherwise naked, dancing
around the fire. They were singing, too. It wasn't in English, but I recognized
it as a song of praise and devotion to the Great Goddess. As I watched, I was
suddenly drawn into the circle, and I was dancing and singing the song with
all of them. I could feel the heat of the fire moving through my body as I
gave myself fully to the ecstasy of the dance. I had the feeling that the
Goddess had descended into the fire itself, and that she was warming all of
us with her energy. I kept dancing, singing and praising her, and I watched
the sparks of the bonfire rising into the sky. And as I watched, the rising
sparks turned into the stars, and I was suddenly dancing among them, dancing the Milky Way, dancing the Universe. I felt fire pouring out of my hands
and my heart, but this time the feeling was one of intense pleasure and happiness. And then I became a star myself, and my singing became the singing
of the stars and the galaxies, loving and praising the Living Light."

I looked at her and saw the echo of that light still shining in her eyes. I
had no words to say.

Helen smiled at me in my awkward silence. "The next thing I knew, I
was falling back in a great spiral, down, down through the layers of reality,
back into myself, into my body, back to the earth."

"Were you sorry to leave that space?"

"No, I knew I was coming home. And I didn't feel I was leaving that
other glory completely behind me. There was a sense of bringing a seed of it
back here with me, and a knowing that the focus for me is to manifest the
Light here on earth, not to fly away and escape. Anyway, when I was starting to feel grounded again and was at least ninety percent back in my body,
I heard the ocean wave sounds being played, and I became aware of my physical being, in exquisite detail. I sort of hugged myself, because I was happy
and because it felt good to notice the sensations of my own skin. I reached
and found your hand, and that sensation was just as wonderful. A few minutes later, I opened my eyes, and there was my beloved— woolgathering."

"I guess you caught me. But I was actually very attentive, most of the
time. You'd have had a hard time staying completely focused for three hours
yourself, with all the wild noisy stuff going on. I'm surprised you could concentrate on what was happening to you."

"The breathing must have really put me into another level of consciousness," she said. "Once I got going with that, the only things I noticed were Sebastian's yell and some of the music."

"May I see your mandala drawing?"

She unrolled it, and I immediately recognized her journey. There in the center of the circle was the bonfire surrounded with dancing figures, its sparks flying up into the sky and changing into stars. And there was Helen as a crayoned stick figure, dancing among the galaxies. Further from the center, in a radiating spiral, were the cloud of gold light, the dark void, and the images of destruction and entrapment she had described. At the furthest perimeter were the beginning scenes of her parents and a little sphere of light that depicted her as a spirit hovering near them. Around the whole circle she had shaded in a shell of black, surrounded on the rest of the page by dozens of sunbursts of yellow, silver and gold, connected by intertwining yellow lines.

"Wow! That's fantastic," I said.

"Well, of course it's really crude, but I guess you can recognize the story. The cloud of darkness around the circle represents the negativity of our incomplete awareness, the ignorance of the Divine that pervades the human world. And outside that is the web of the Living Light, which is reality."

"So, um, where am I in all this?" I asked, "You've got the whole universe in there. Where am I?"

She looked at me quizzically and grinned, "Why, you're the invisible binding force that holds everything together ... by worrying!"

"No one appreciates my hard work. Worrying is difficult."

"But you are appreciated. The forces of fear and uncertainty think you're doing a great job. And I love you, so there! Now, I'm starving. When do we eat?"

I put my arm around Helen and we walked into the back room, where several more breathers were now seated, drawing their mandalas. Radha stood at the end of the table beside her friend Mr. Camden, who was working intently on his sketch. When she saw us, she leaned down and spoke to him and then came toward us.

"My goodness, that was powerful, wasn't it?" she said in an excited whisper. "Will, could you feel the energy in that room? It reminded me of the time I visited the King's chamber in the Great Pyramid. I was with a metaphysical tour group, and we bribed the guards to let us in at midnight. When we were all assembled, we had the lights turned out and we did a chant together. In a matter of minutes, everyone could feel the rising of the *Num*, the spiritual presence in the place. Well, it was astonishing, let me tell you, but no more so than what just happened here. Will, you haven't answered me. Could you feel how much energy was building up in that room? I wasn't even doing the breathing, but if I closed my eyes to blink I could see my spirit guides, and I could feel the presence of many more entities around us. And they seemed so *excited* and *pleased* by what we were doing, don't you think?"

When Radha's torrent of words subsided, I tried to answer, describing the sense of rising and falling emotions I had felt swirling around and within me. "I can't say I was aware of entities around us, but *something* was aroused in there. I could feel it."

"How about you, Helen?" Radha asked. "What was it like for you doing the breathing?"

Helen briefly recounted her story to Radha, also showing her the mandala drawing. While they were speaking, my attention wandered about the room. After a moment or two, I realized that most of the participants had come downstairs, but I still hadn't seen Sebastian. Just as I was about to excuse myself to go up and check on him, he and Maddie came down the staircase. She was trying to steady his bearlike frame as he swayed back and forth, gripping the hand rail. I walked over and offered my arm as he moved toward the drawing table.

"Welcome back," I smiled.

Sebastian looked distant and serious. "Sorry, Will," he said. "I can't talk yet. I need to write something down, and then I have to draw."

Maddie greeted me, but she also seemed rather withdrawn, as she ushered Sebastian to a seat at the table next to Radha's partner. I turned away and went back to Helen and Radha.

We talked for a few more minutes, until the last of the participants made it down the stairs. Then the three of us went back up and helped David and Maureen to straighten the room and begin laying out the potluck lunch. Radha and I put the spring water and fruit juices on the table. Helen had brought two loaves of banana bread, plus an assortment of cookies, crackers and cheese. "This looks good," I said, "but I hope the other people remembered to bring their contributions, or it won't go far."

"Don't worry, they didn't forget," said Helen. "There are at least a dozen dishes in the refrigerator. Why don't you go get some of them and put them out on the table?"

After the room was rearranged and the food was set up, Maureen went downstairs and told the group that lunch was ready whenever they were. Gradually, they made their way back to the workshop room and within a short time the space was filled with the pleasant buzz of multiple conversations. I noticed, with some surprise, that no one seemed to be discussing their breathwork experiences. I mentioned it to David as I stood next to him in the lunch line.

"That happens frequently," he said. "I think it may be that breathers crave grounding after these intense sessions, and the food and normal conversation help with that. Also, the inner journeys can be so personal that it's hard for people to bring them up casually. Anyway, we'll have a group sharing this evening, and that's where the stories usually come out."

At the lunch table, I limited myself to fruit juice and a handful of grapes, remembering David's words of caution about eating before breathwork. Looking around, I could see that some of the other participants were following that same advice, but those who had breathed in the morning session were loading up their plates. Helen was no exception, and I sat on the floor beside her as she plowed through a small mountain of food, both of us chatting with Radha and Mr. Camden.

Radha had been talking about her technique of pulling books from the shelf and opening them at random as a way of divining information to answer questions. I mentioned that I had just made such an attempt, and recounted as much as I could of the quote from Satprem's book.

"Ah, Sri Aurobindo!" Mr. Camden exclaimed, smiling. "A very amazing man he was. Do you know much about his philosophy?"

"I haven't actually read any of the books about him," I admitted. "But I got the sense that Satprem was saying humanity may be heading for an evolutionary leap. Does that come from Sri Aurobindo?"

"Indeed it does, and I quote: 'Man is a transitional being; he is not final. The step from man to superman is the next approaching achievement in the earth's evolution. It is inevitable, because it is at once the intention of the inner Spirit and the logic of Nature's process.' I believe that comes from the very book you took off the shelf. I've been an amateur student of Aurobindo for over twenty years."

"I've read a bit about him myself," said Radha. "As I recall, he was a native of India, but was schooled in the West, wasn't he?"

"Correct," Mr. Camden replied. "In England. But he came back to India and became a revolutionary, a poet, and ultimately a mystic. However, he wasn't typical of those who say the goal is to escape the earth and go into the disembodied bliss of Nirvana. Aurobindo believed that the purpose of human evolution was a complete transformation of ourselves in *this* world, the world of matter. And his yoga shows it. Unlike traditional kundalini, which tries to raise one's energies from the bottom up, Aurobindo's practice attempts to open the crown chakra and pull the divine energies *down* into the body, into the material world."

"That makes sense to me," Helen said. "I've always felt that we're here to ground the Light on Earth, not to leave the body and escape, and that message came through loud and clear in my breathing session. As you describe it, Aurobindo's method reminds me of the meditation on Bell Rock that Sebastian had with Maddie. Do you remember it from his letter, Will?"

"Yes, I do. He should be in this conversation." I looked around. "Where is he, anyway? And where's Maddie?"

"I don't believe they've come upstairs yet," Radha replied.

Just then I saw Sebastian's head, and then the rest of his body bobbing into view as he ascended the staircase and entered the room. Maddie was right behind him. He gave me a weak smile and a little wave, and then turned toward the food table. Maddie came over to us.

"He's had a rough time," she told us. "He hasn't been willing to talk much about what he saw or felt during the breathwork. I know the process opened up something frightening, but he won't say what it is. I'm just trying to be with him and get him grounded. I'm hoping the food will help."

"Did he tell you anything?" I asked.

"Some, but I don't think I should talk about it. It's his story to share, or to keep to himself."

"Of course it is," said Helen. "But you should probably go back to him, Maddie. And you should have something to eat, too."

She looked over her shoulder. "Maybe a bite. I'll see if he wants to come sit down over here."

A few moments later, Maddie returned with Sebastian, and the six of us sat together talking while they ate. Sebastian was friendly and smiling, but he seemed fragile, as though the wrong word might push him into tears. He didn't discuss what he experienced in his breathing session, and no one broached the subject. When they finished, Helen and I went to put away the leftover food and take care of the trash. David and Maureen were at the front of the room, answering questions and passing out tissues and blindfolds to those who wanted them for the second breathing session. Around the room, pairs of partners were setting up their mats with pillows and blankets and arranging their seating cushions. Helen and I returned to our spot just before Maureen called the group to get ready.

I lay down on the foam mat and pulled the cotton blanket up to my chin. Helen sat leaning against the wall beside me, in the same place where I had stationed myself next to her. All around us, the other breathers and their partners were situating themselves and whispering last-minute agree-ments. I turned to Helen and she smiled down at me. I reached from under the blanket and squeezed her hand. She bent towards me, and I spoke to her softly, "I feel like an astronaut on the launching pad."

"Excited?"

"Nervous."

"Don't worry. Just ask for what's highest and best to come to you, and trust whatever unfolds."

"All right, but if I stop breathing, I mean totally, give me a jump start, okay?"

"Absolutely. Don't forget you married me permanently. I'm not letting you get away."

"That is strangely reassuring," I said. "Okay, I guess it's time to make myself relax."

"Just let go," she replied. "Let everything go."

At that moment, Maureen spoke into the microphone, once again lead-ing the breathers in tensing and releasing all the muscle groups, encouraging us to visualize ourselves being gradually flooded with light, from our toes to the tops of our heads. I closed my eyes and listened to her soothing voice, and as I did, I felt the tension flowing out of my body and mind. I surren-dered to the imagery of light filling me, allowing all the muscles to relax. I followed her voice as she instructed us to begin breathing a bit faster and deeper than usual, gradually increasing the volume of air and the frequency of the breath. I heard people around me beginning to breathe with stronger and stronger intensity, and I pushed myself to do the same. In the next moment the music came on, and my journey began.

# — 16 —

I had expected that within minutes of beginning the breathing I would lose awareness of the group and my environment, finding myself in some inner landscape, as Helen had. Not so. For quite some time, practically everything I experienced was physical. I lay with eyes closed on my mat under a light blanket, pushing the air in and out of my lungs, listening to the powerful music and the sounds of the other breathers around me. A portion of my mind was disappointed, thinking things like, "Where are the visions? What am I doing wrong?" But I decided there was no other choice but to continue. I focused on my stomach, trying to make it rise and fall as steeply as possible, to maximize the flow of air. I willed myself to breathe a little faster, in rhythm with the pounding drums that throbbed from the stereo speakers. Another stray thought came, "How can I possibly keep this up for three hours?" I pushed that idea aside. A stubborn part of me was determined, visions or no visions, to see the process through to the end.

The music progressed, moving through several permutations, each with a different emotional tone. As I breathed, thoughts came more rapidly, and from various places in the mind. Trivial worries and concerns, random memories from recent days, conversations with Helen—it seemed as though my brain was dumping its leftovers into consciousness. I remembered Sebastian's description of his attempt to meditate on Bell Rock in Sedona, and recalled my own early efforts. I decided not to concern myself with whether I was doing it right, and kept on with the breathing.

I must have finally relaxed, because I seemed to have lost consciousness. I was brought back by the light touch of Helen's hand on my shoulder, and I gasped. I opened my eyes and saw her looking down at me. "What happened?" I whispered.

"You stopped breathing, so I touched you. Are you okay?"

"Yes, I guess I fell asleep." The sound of the music and the breathers around me had not abated. It was hard to believe I had dozed off, but I had no other explanation. "Well, I'm going to give it another try," I said, and with that I closed my eyes and began again.

As I pushed the pace and depth of my breathing once more, I recalled the reading I had done about the connection of breathwork to reliving birth. I wondered what it would be like to experience that. Almost as soon as the thought came, I found myself descending into total blackness, something deeper than the darkness behind my closed eyes. As I went down, I found myself losing consciousness again. It was like falling asleep against my own will. As I reached the bottom of the blackness, my awareness sank. I came back to consciousness with a startled gasp. Apparently I had stopped breathing again. The same thing happened three more times. The music playing in the room was a slow, dirgelike orchestral piece, and it seemed to be a part of the force that kept pulling me down into darkness.

At the bottom of the fifth descent, everything changed. Instead of falling into unconsciousness again, I found that the utter blackness was dispelled by a light from above. At the same moment, the music changed to a strong, harmonious instrumental song of triumph. I felt I was being lifted up from the stifling darkness and brought into the light. My breath came much more easily, and I felt an unexpected smile on my face. I pushed myself to breathe yet more deeply, and relaxed into the music.

As I listened, I noticed others in the room, not only breathing now, but sobbing, moaning and crying out with powerful emotions. The atmosphere seemed charged, just as it had in the first session. I listened and wondered what the others were going through.

I slipped into a hypnogogic state, in which images floated up in rapid succession, as they sometimes do just before sleep. Initially, I saw a pattern of deep violet light, pulsing and changing shape before my inner eye. Then there were multi-colored geometric forms, moving and shifting into one another. I watched these in fascination, and in a few moments they were replaced by more recognizable visions. I saw a rapid succession of faces, first my father's face, then his father's and then a procession of others I didn't recognize, though I felt they were moving backward in time. After dozens, or perhaps hundreds of faces passed by, they became more and more primitive, until they transformed into apelike features. The thought came to me, "Oh, I get it—the theory of evolution," and I chuckled silently. In the next moment, the process reversed, and the faces flashed before me, now moving from past to present at high speed, blending together almost like a moving picture. Suddenly the movement stopped, and I saw a ring of five faces— Helen, Sebastian, Maddie, Radha, and at the center the blue vinyl extraterrestrial, Anon. As I puzzled over its unexpected appearance, the flat plastic face changed into a living one, with blue-gray skin and large, penetrating eyes. As I looked, the tiny mouth smiled, and a shock of astonishment jolted me. Then the faces all disappeared, and I nearly opened my eyes. Instead, I kept on with the breathing, waiting to see if the visions would return.

The music continued to flood the room, and my thoughts and emotions flowed with it. A selection of otherworldly synthesizer sounds came on, and for a moment I found my consciousness suspended among the stars. At first, I saw only uncountable blazing diamonds scattered in an endless void. Then I seemed to turn, and before me there was the earth, its vivid colors in stark contrast to the velvet blackness around it. As I gazed with inner vision, its thin aura of atmosphere seemed to ignite and expand, surrounding it with a golden corona like the sun. I felt a flash of fear, thinking to myself, "The world is burning." Then a clear voice above me laughed softly and said, "*No, it is awakening.*" A wave of awe washed over me, and the word *Earthfire* formed in my mind. I thought to myself, "It's real ... I'm seeing it."

At that moment, I was drawn back to the room and awareness of my body. My hands were tingling. There was an intense sensation of pins and needles and of electricity. Without my willing it, the tips of my thumb and forefinger touched one another, forming a circle, and apparently a circuit as well. Immediately, the flow of energy in my hands increased and began to move steadily up my arms. I noticed that the same energy was now also in my feet and was flowing into my legs as well. There was a feeling of vibration surging throughout my body, accompanied by a rising, quiet excitement. Though I didn't comprehend what was happening, something in me wanted it to increase. I pushed my breathing harder.

My hands seemed almost on fire. It felt as though energy were coming out of them as well as going into them. I wanted my whole body to be electrified with this strange power, so I began to move my hands over my abdomen and chest. Stopping at each chakra, my hands automatically were drawn into specific positions or gestures, and as they shifted into place, the chakras opened and more energy poured into and through me. I began to notice certain movements or positions which increased the intensity, and others which slackened it. I kept breathing deeply, willing the energy to increase and moving my hands in rhythmic synchronization to the flow. Now it was throughout my body, seeming to feed upon itself. I felt it pour from the top of my head, and there were other fountains streaming from my hands and my chest. With each breath, there was more.

I noticed that I was crying. Tears trickled down my cheeks, and I was overwhelmed with an odd mixture of gratitude and regret. I sensed that the energy coursing through me was some gift of grace, some purifying divine dispensation. I understood nothing about it, but I knew that it was good. At the same time, I felt a heavy weight of sorrow, as it came to me that this boon had always been available, and it had taken me half a lifetime to become aware of it. A luminous presence seemed to hover near me, yearning towards me but unable to speak. In a flash of intuition, I saw that the presence was my own soul. And I felt the patience, the hoping, tender forbearance with which it had always waited for the chance to express itself in the world through me.

Something in me let go, and the luminous presence moved inside me. My trickle of tears became a river, and I sobbed with grief and joy. The inner fire transformed to inner light, and the flower of sweet release opened in my heart. Wave after wave of love, of sorrow, of aching happiness washed over me, as I lay there letting the tears come.

I wept longer and more deeply than I could remember ever having done before. It was as though a dam had burst and the reservoir of all the grief of my life had been released. I saw flashes of childhood memories, glimpses of my father's death, and many more moments of lesser pains and fears which had been pushed down below the surface of consciousness. I had always believed such things were gone as soon as I forgot them, but I suddenly saw that the presence I now understood to be my soul had been carrying them for me. And with each pain that I repressed, I unknowingly had pushed away the core of my own being. What I had thought of as my self, the lord of my world, was only the empty husk of what I truly was and might have expressed. With each breath, the revelation came to me more fully. With each breath, the depth of grief increased, and through my mourning sobs it was released.

As I allowed more of the emotions and tears to flow, their intensity was magnified, as were the tingling fire and light that electrified my body. I was taken aback, feeling almost overwhelmed, but I held to the rhythm of the breathing and kept moving my hands in the strange gestures, building the energy ever higher. I was pulled by a feeling of necessity—now that this door, whatever it was, had opened, I had to take the experience as far as I could. And I knew also that what I was feeling was not only pain but the cessation of pain, not only sorrow but the ending of sorrow.

I let go on some even deeper level, and the flood rose higher. But I noticed that there were no more personal memories involved. My grief was unconnected now to any cause I knew, but it became stronger and stronger. I had surrendered, and I simply let it come, no longer trying to analyze or understand. From somewhere, there was such need for the cry of this with-held pain that I knew it was right to let it come. And so I wept, in anguish and in liberation, feeling now like a simple vessel, an instrument through which something greater is made manifest. It seemed that I had gone beyond myself, and the soul of the world was crying out through me, in wave after wave, expressing some of its great sorrow through my tears.

Gradually, the waves of sobs subsided, the fiery energies ebbed away, and I became aware of ocean waves. I folded my hands across my chest and listened, breathing softly now. The ocean sounds came through the speakers in the workshop room, and I kept my eyes closed, letting them pull me back. Deep peace slowly filled me. After some time, I reached for Helen's hand, and she clasped mine. I opened my eyes and saw her looking down at me with tender care.

"I love you," we both whispered at the same moment.

I sat up carefully, blinking and looking around the darkened room. Nearly half the participants had already finished and gone downstairs. About twenty feet away, Maureen was massaging Maddie's back while Sebastian looked on. David was working with a man a few steps away from us, holding down his shoulders as he arched his back and groaned in anguish, twisting his head from side to side in some inner struggle. Radha and Mr. Camden were not in sight.

"I need to go down to the bathroom," I said softly to Helen. "It's your turn to steady me now." I stood up gingerly and immediately grabbed her for support. I was light-headed and a little dizzy.

"Careful," she cautioned, pulling my arm around her shoulders. "Let's take this one step at a time." She walked me slowly to the stairs, and we went down together.

In the bathroom, I took care of the body's needs and then stepped to the sink to wash my face. As I looked in the mirror, I had the odd sense that someone else was looking back. It was still my face, but the eyes seemed different. "The eyes are the windows of the soul," I said to my reflection, "and all those tears washed them for you. So, how is it in there? Clearer anyway, I'll bet. We let out a lot of old stuff, didn't we?" I sighed, almost expecting an answer. "I guess we're still in a bit of an altered state, aren't we? Well, listen, Soul, I want you here, and I promise I'll never force you out again. I love you." I held my hand up to the glass, and our fingers nearly touched. I smiled and turned to the door.

At the drawing table, several breathers were busily working on their mandalas. I had no plan for what I was going to try to draw, but I sat down across the table from Radha and took a sheet of paper from the pile. Radha looked up and nodded to me, but said nothing, returning her attention to her picture. After a few moments consideration, I started sketching. At the center of the circle, I drew the earth with a corona of golden light. Above it floated a baby, or a fetus, and hands were reaching down from the sky to lift it up. Below the planet and facing it, I attempted some crude caricatures of the faces of my friends and of the smiling alien. At the bottom of the circle, I drew myself, lying on the mat, with electric sparks of energy and fire surrounding me. It was a pathetic rendering of the intense experiences I had just been through, but for some reason I liked it anyway. When Helen came over to me, I stood and held it up for her.

"So there it is," I said. "Michelangelo must be quaking in his grave."

"Quaking in his *boots*, or maybe *rolling over* in his grave," Helen corrected me, smiling. "Although I have my doubts about either one." She inspected the drawing. "This is really interesting. Are you going to tell me about it?"

"Yes, I'd like to. Can we go back out in front and sit in the reading chairs?"

"Why not? I think we still have some time before dinner."

Helen led the way to the front of the store, and we sat down together in the dimly lit room. It was completely dark outside, and rain continued to beat against the plate glass windows. I recounted my breathing experiences to Helen as completely as I could. She listened attentively and refrained from interrupting the story. At the end of the tale she said, "It's beautiful. I could see you were going through a lot, and I could feel the energy radiating from you, especially towards the end. The hand gestures were rather amazing—they seemed so precise, I wondered if they were *mudras*."

"Mudras?"

"Yes, I think that's the Sanskrit name for sacred hand movements that are practiced in Hindu meditation and ritual. I've seen them in pictures of statuary from India, and I'm sure you have, too."

"Yes, you're right," I agreed. I looked down at my hands and tried to make my fingers repeat the positions they had assumed during the breathwork. "You know, the energy was moving my hands without my help. I can't even remember most of what I did. But hey, maybe that's where the mudras came from in the first place. I wonder if this energy was part of what those statues and the Hindu stories were about."

"*Prana*," Helen said. "Divine life force energy. Maureen mentioned it in the talk last night."

"Maybe that was it," I said. "It could be that prana is even part of what Earthfire means. When I saw the vision of the earth surrounded by the golden light, I felt as though I really grasped it for a moment. I'm starting to think again about the night when Radha came to the house and got the message from ... Mr. Anon."

"Speaking of which," Helen replied, "what do you make of that vision of the plastic Anon changing into a living alien?"

"I don't know. I wondered if I was seeing the 'real' Anon, whatever that would mean. I just don't know, but the biggest shock to me was seeing him smile. For a moment, I believed he was actually looking at me."

"How about the voice telling you that the earth was awakening? Do you know who that was?"

"I don't, but it reminds me of the voice I heard in meditation a couple of years ago—the one that said, 'The Light you seek without is identical to the Light within you.' Remember?"

"Yes, of course I do. I can't wait to talk with Radha about all this," Helen said.

"Me, too." I was quiet for a moment. "You know, this whole business is so overwhelming when I think about it ... it's amazing I can even discuss it. Yet I'm sitting here with you, feeling relatively normal, talking about these utterly outlandish things that have happened to me. I mean, I think I was just in contact with my soul. Shouldn't I be rolling on the floor or speaking in tongues or making prophecies or something?"

"I like what you're doing now," she smiled. "You're integrating these profound experiences into yourself."

"I hope you're right, and it's not just that I'm shallow or schizophrenic."

Helen eyes twinkled with mischief, "Don't worry, honey. I've never thought you were shallow."

"What about schizophrenic?"

"I don't know. That's a question you'll just have to ask yourselves."

"Oh. Har, har, very funny."

We kept on talking until we heard Maureen's voice from the back room calling to us, "Everybody's finished. Are you folks ready to come upstairs for dinner?"

When we climbed the stairs, the lights were on and we found that David and Maureen had straightened the workshop room and arranged the foam mats in a circle, as well as having set out food and dishes on the serving table. Several of the attendees were standing in line with their plates, while others were seated on the mats, eating and talking with one another. I saw Maddie and Sebastian sitting on the floor next to Radha and Mr. Camden. Sebastian waved to me, and I motioned that Helen and I would join them as soon as we served ourselves.

Helen placed herself between Maddie and Radha, and I sat down opposite her between Sebastian and Mr. Camden. I found I had worked up an appetite, and the others had as well. At first, our talk was about the good food, with only perfunctory references to our breathwork experiences. Finally, the pace of both conversation and consumption slowed, and Radha said to me, "Will, you must tell me about your breathing session. Did you experience anything unusual?"

"*Everything* I experienced was unusual," I answered. I started to launch into a description of what had happened, but was interrupted when David Edwards stood up in the front of the room and tapped his glass with a spoon to get our attention.

"All right everyone, if you're ready we'll form a circle now and we can all share our experiences. Don't forget to bring your mandala drawings with you."

I turned to Radha, "I guess we'll be doing this as a group. We can talk more later if you like."

"Agreed," she replied, as she glanced absentmindedly around the room. "Now where did I leave my drawing?"

Within a couple of minutes dishes were put away and everyone was seated on the circle of mats. David and Maureen said a few words of introduction, inviting everyone to choose the time to hold up their mandalas and say something to the group about their breathwork sessions.

We all sat silently for a moment, and then a young man in a tie-dyed t-shirt across the circle from me raised his hand. I had seen him in the store several times before with some of his friends. One of them was the young woman beside him, who smiled as he began to speak. "In the first part, I was listening to the music and getting in sync with it, doing the deep breathing and everything. And the next thing I knew, I was on this island. It was like this total paradise, with fruits hanging off the trees and warm sun and butterflies everywhere. And I was walking around the whole place, eating the sweet fruit and exploring my little kingdom. Everything was blissful until this storm blew in from the ocean. I was climbing the mountain—a volcano actually—in the center of the island, and I had just reached the rim of the crater when the storm hit. All of a sudden there was thunder and lightning, and I slipped and rolled down into a crevice inside the crater. I was wedged in really tight. I couldn't move, and I was suffocating, and this toxic sulfur gas was seeping up all around me. And then there was some kind of tremor—the volcano was starting to erupt. I was really stuck, you know, and the tremors in the ground were pushing the crevice walls closer together. I struggled to get loose, but there was no way out. I began to get panicky because I couldn't breathe, and it seemed like I was going to die there.

"Then there was a really big tremor, and the crevice opened. I started to pull myself out so I could stand up, and then I felt the heat underneath me. The crevice had opened to a lava flow, and it was rising up underneath me. The tremors had turned into real earthquakes, and the whole crater was filling up with hot, red lava. I knew I had to get away before I was burned alive.

"I forced myself to climb back up to the crater rim, but the molten lava was right behind me. It bubbled up over the top of the rim on both sides of me, but I was on this little rock ledge, so it didn't quite get to me. I stood there and watched while the lava rolled down the slopes and burned up everything on my island, from the forests on the slopes of the volcano all the way to the beach. The lava even made the water boil in the blue lagoon. It was so close to me on the crater rim that I felt like my blood was boiling, too. I was sure then that I was going to die. I started to scream from the pain and the fear of dying—and also, you know, I was pretty mad about it. Then there was another really big tremor and the ledge where I was standing gave way and started to slide down into the lava. While it was falling, I took a big leap and just dived into the hot lava. For a few seconds, I was totally on fire, and then it seemed like I *was* the fire.

"The next thing I knew, I was flying. I had turned into this wild, multi-colored bird. The lava didn't burn me then. In fact I had just taken off out of a pool of molten rock like it was my nest or something. I flew away from the island, gliding for miles and miles over the water. I was like totally free, and I felt so great. It was really trippy. Anyway, this is the drawing I made afterwards." He held up his mandala—a vividly colored depiction of a lush tropical island surrounded by blue water. At the top of the volcano's cone, a huge rainbow-colored bird sat on the crater as if on a nest.

"Do you know the legend of the Phoenix?" Radha asked the young man.

"You mean, like in Arizona?" he asked, grinning. Radha quickly told the tale of the mythical bird and its symbolic theme of death and rebirth. "That's so cool," he said. "I'd never heard that story, but it came to me anyway."

"This sort of thing happens often in Holotropic Breathwork," said

Maureen. "We can make contact, even when we aren't aware of it, with the archetypal and mythological realms. There are a number of cases in which people in breathwork have experienced inner reenactments of myths from obscure cultures about which they knew nothing. I'd like to point out one other thing as well. Your experience on the island is a very complete symbolic recounting of the perinatal stages of consciousness we talked about last night. One could say that the island paradise you described in the beginning corresponds to the first perinatal stage of fetal life in the 'good womb'. The second stage of birth, in which contractions have begun but the cervix hasn't opened, the 'no exit' stage, is analogous to your being trapped in the crevice. The third perinatal matrix, in which the cervix has opened and the fetus moves into the birth canal, is particularly powerful and difficult. It is often associated with clashing energies, pain and images of catastrophe. Your vision of the island being destroyed by lava and the fall of your ledge down the side of the mountain is classic symbolic imagery for this stage of the birth process. And at the end your plunge into the lava and rebirth as the rainbow bird depicts the typical imagery of the fourth perinatal matrix, which frequently begins with fire and consummates with death, rebirth and resurrection. We don't often see such a complete experience of all four of the perinatal matrices in a single breathwork session, let alone your first one. Thank you for sharing your story. Now, would you be willing to pass your mandala around so everyone can see it?"

"Sure, that's cool."

Several more participants spoke to the group and showed their drawings. Helen recounted her inner visions, much as she had told them to me. Her mandala elicited numerous expressions of appreciation, as did her descriptions of the Great Goddess' bonfire and of dancing among the stars. After Helen finished her story, Radha cleared her throat and spoke.

"As I mentioned when we all introduced ourselves, I make my living as a medium, so I am accustomed to meditation and various non-ordinary states of awareness, and I have some talent for attuning to the vibrations of others in order to shed light on their situations. However, this evening I journeyed in a new direction within myself.

"During the first few minutes of the breathing session, I saw my spirit guides around me. This was no surprise, because I had felt their presence this morning during the first session. But then I suddenly lost all awareness of them, my body, and this room, and I found myself disembodied, flying down a geometric corridor or tunnel at what seemed to be a great speed. The walls of the tunnel were translucent, and I caught glimpses of various landscapes and scenes as I went by them. Suddenly, I stopped moving down the tunnel and was pulled through the wall into one of the scenes. In the flash of an instant, I recognized that I was within the body of a young woman, indeed I *was* this young woman.

"She, or I, was an apprentice priestess in one of the dynasties of old Egypt. Apparently, I had the gift of prophecy, because an older priestess took me alone with her into a dark chamber and demanded that I tell her the future of some member of the royal house. I went into trance and my voice was taken over by a spirit entity who gave the answers. Apparently, the message was not to the liking of the older priestess, for when it was finished and I came out of trance, she insisted that I do it again. I protested, explaining that the words were not mine and I could not change them. She screamed and threatened me, and I tried to escape, but the door guards caught me.

"When she was convinced I would not or could not change the prophecy, the older priestess commanded the guards to kill me. I was strangled first, and then my throat was cut.

"Upon death, my awareness rose from the body and was pulled back into the translucent tunnel. I traveled further down the lighted corridor, and was suddenly stopped again and drawn into another life. This time I was a man, an early Christian in the ancient days of Rome. In this life I spent many hours speaking fervently to other Roman citizens, trying to teach my doctrine of the one true God. My reputation came to the attention of authorities, and I was imprisoned. My death came in the Coliseum when a lion mauled me and tore out my throat.

"This was the pattern of a least a half-dozen lives. When I spoke my mind or tried to spread my ideas, I ran afoul of others who were stronger, and I was put to death. I was suffocated by a jealous husband, drowned by the Puritans, left to die of pneumonia in a dungeon by the Inquisition. And the fascinating thing to me is that in this lifetime I keep running into the same kinds of issues. When I chose to claim my calling and become a professional medium, my minister husband divorced me, and virtually all my health problems have centered on the throat, or the lungs. I'd say it's clear that my karmic challenge is to find a way to bring forth my truth without becoming a victim. By the way," she said, turning to David and Maureen, "am I correct to assume that the imagery from my journey is mostly coming from the second perinatal matrix?"

"Yes, I'd say so," David answered. "Images of suffocation and drowning are typical for that stage. And it's interesting from my perspective to see what a large percentage of people with second-matrix issues are involved in work that involves speaking or teaching. It's as though we're drawn to work in the areas of our past difficulties."

"For many years, especially in my teens and twenties, I hid my gifts," Radha said. "I was afraid to talk about the things I saw and heard intuitively. It has taken years of effort for me to get beyond that fear." She looked down at her hands. "Even now, I sometimes shy away from seeing too deeply. At least I did until recently," she said, turning her eyes to Helen and me. "And as I look at what has just surfaced in today's session, I am tempted to think there are further limitations to transcend." For a moment, her face looked tired and drawn, but then its lines were set again in brisk determination.

"There was one more vision in my journey," Radha continued. "It was this." She held up her mandala. The circle was divided in half, with a vertical line down the center. The left side was a dark gray room with a woman holding herself against the door dividing the two sides. Beyond the closed door, the right side of the circle was filled with brilliant flames of orange, yellow, red and gold. "There were many cracks in the wall," Radha said, "and the flames came in wherever they could. As I stood at the door, in my mind's eye, I both desired and feared to open it. I didn't know whether the fire was dangerous or safe, healing or destructive. I wanted to trust it, but I felt afraid. Yet I ultimately knew I must open the door. And this was no past life—the woman at the door was me." She handed her mandala to Mr. Camden, who passed it on around the circle.

After a brief silence in which everyone looked around to see who would speak next, Maddie smiled shyly and began, "I didn't really see much in the way of visions, and that surprised me, because my life has been full of visions lately." She gave a brief description of the near-death experience she had gone through when she almost drowned, and some of the dreams which had come to her since then.

"I'm also a UFO abductee," she continued. "So with all that going on, I came to this workshop expecting to go consciously to the crystal temple with the energy sphere, or to see the ETs, or to at least visit some past lives, as Radha did. Instead, I stayed right here in my own body the whole time. I followed the relaxation exercises at the beginning, and when we visualized the light filling our bodies, that part did happen very vividly for me. In fact, it never went away. I spent the whole three hours breathing my brains out and listening to the music, filled to the brim with white-gold light. At first it felt wonderful, but as the time passed, I started feeling hotter and hotter. The light intensified, and so did the heat. I thought I might be coming down with a fever, and I almost gave up on the breathing. But then, just for a moment, I heard a voice inside my head. It said, 'Ground the energy. Bring the flame to Earth.' After hearing that, I decided I was supposed to act as some kind of lightning rod—I had been told something similar during my near-death experience—so I kept on with the breathing and hoped I could bear the increasing heat. It felt as though I was on fire. At the peak of the session, I also had some very wild electrical energy zooming up and down my back-bone. I felt all lit up like a Christmas tree, and I almost wondered if people in the room could see me glow. I asked Sebastian afterwards, and he said no, but he could feel me radiating heat. He said I was hot enough to toast marsh-mallows." There were chuckles from the group, and Maddie beamed.

"That's about it, except that towards the end I developed a muscle spasm in my back, and Maureen helped me with it. When she was pressing on it the pain was *very* intense, and my mind flashed on everything I've ever been afraid of. I felt these intense shudders of fear move through my body. Then all at once the muscles released and the sensations of fear evaporated in an instant. At that point, the light just exploded in me, and I moved into total peace and bliss. I'm still in it, a little bit. I guess I don't really want to com-plain about not seeing visions, but I couldn't make a very interesting man-dala." She held up her drawing, which appeared to be a sketch of her own face at the center of a huge golden flower. "The petals are supposed to be light rays," she explained.

I looked at Maddie and she smiled in my direction. "I guess I should go next," I said. "It seems I got my share of visions, and Maddie's too." I recounted to the group the story of my breathing session—the descents into darkness and being lifted into the light, the evolutionary time travel, the faces of my friends and the alien, the vision of the earth, the encounter with my soul, and the fiery energies which had electrified my body. At the end, I held up my mandala and passed it around the circle. Afterwards I asked if others in the group, besides Maddie, had felt anything similar to the tingling energies which had coursed through me. About five or six people nodded in acknowledgement.

I turned to Maureen and asked, "What about the times I went into the darkness and stopped breathing? I remember your mentioning that people do that sometimes, but do you know why?"

"There could be a number of different reasons. Did you say this hap-pened when you were recalling your birth?"

"I wasn't recalling it. I was wondering about it, actually."

David asked, "Do you know the circumstances of your birth?"

"Some," I answered. "I was born Caesarean, and my mother and I both almost died. The placenta came out first, and she hemorrhaged. The doctors had to work fast to get me out before I died from lack of oxygen." I paused. "Wait a minute ... Do you think the plunge into blackness in my vision was like the fetus losing consciousness during the birth?"

"I've seen it before," David said. "Especially when anesthesia was involved."

"And what about—oh, I see. The vision of being raised into the light could be the doctor reaching in to get me after the incision was made for the Caesarean."

"Yes," Maureen said. "But don't forget that these experiences resonate on many levels. Just as Radha's visions were of circumstances with a common theme, visions in breathwork can symbolize the essential myths of our beings. Your physical birth in this life may not be your only experience of being lifted from darkness into light."

"That's true," I replied slowly. "In a sense, my whole session was about that. And I was surprised at how mingled the emotions were. I felt such unbounded pain and grief, and it led to so much joy."

"That's one of the things we learn in this deep inner work," David said. "The opposites are the two sides of one coin. In extremes of pain and grief, we sometimes laugh. In the highest moments of bliss, we often weep. Death and rebirth work the same way—they don't come separately."

"What about all the fire?" I asked. "It was in my vision, and in my body, too. And so far everyone who has spoken has mentioned it in some form." I looked around the room and saw many heads nodding in agreement. "Is this fire something that comes up in all breathwork, or is this group unusual in that respect?"

David looked to Maureen and leaned toward her. She whispered something to him, and then he sat up straight and turned his gaze to me. "On one level, this has to do with the perinatal states. The transition between the third matrix, in which the fetus is moving through the birth canal under tremendous stresses, and the fourth matrix, in which delivery occurs and the crisis reaches successful resolution, is frequently characterized by images of fire. In this stage of the actual physical birth process, mothers often report the sensation that their entire genital areas are on fire. In Holotropic Breathwork, people reliving this transition stage commonly experience visions of consuming fires. Typically, these seem to consume everything that is rotten or corrupt in us, preparing us for renewal and rebirth. The transition between these third and fourth stages is the peak of the crisis, the moment of most intensity, in which we are forced to let go into death-rebirth.

"As far as this group is concerned," David smiled, "it is somewhat unusual for the fire motif, or any other, to show up so widely. Just for my curiosity, can we get a show of hands of those who had some imagery or sensation of fire in their sessions today?"

Everyone in the room raised their hands—everyone except Sebastian. There was a brief murmur as people looked around at one another, and then Sebastian spoke. "I'm not ready to say anything about what happened when I did the breathing, but I have a question for you," he said, looking to David and Maureen. "You say the visions and experiences people have in this process resonate on many levels of our reality. I'm wondering if we can take that beyond ourselves. For instance, do the perinatal stages apply metaphorically to nations or species as well as individuals?" I noticed Radha looking up abruptly when Sebastian asked his question, focusing her gaze intently on the two presenters.

Maureen nodded, "Yes, I believe they can, but would you tell me the context of your question?"

"Well, I've been thinking about this idea all day. If you look back at human history, you can compare it to the perinatal stages. The relative lack of restriction of primitive times—the era of hunter/gatherer tribes and early agriculture—could be compared to the first stage. Next, the stresses created by the rise of nations and boundaries, laws and patriarchy, might signify the second stage. Then if you look at the chaos and destructiveness of recent history, especially the twentieth century, with its horrific wars, environmental pillaging, and the threat of total annihilation in nuclear war, it appears to my mind at least to be the time of the big crisis, comparable to the third perinatal stage. If you had to point out humanity's current place in the 'birth' process, what would you say?"

David looked at Maureen, and then turned back to Sebastian, "Pretty much the same thing as you, it seems. We've discussed this before, together and with others in a number of fields. It looks to us as though the human race is collectively at the last stages of the third matrix, the period of transition."

"The time of death and rebirth," Radha murmured softly, her gaze fixed straight ahead, as if seeing something beyond the room where we all sat. "The moment of the holy fire."

The group sharing went on into the evening, and the stories varied widely, though the unifying image of the fire was present in them all.

Radha's partner, Mr. Camden, described his encounters with archetypal beings and deities, in which he identified with Prometheus, who stole fire from the gods. "But as I was being bound," he said, "flames blazed from my body, burning the ropes and melting the chains, and I was freed. It was quite remarkable."

The mandalas circled the room, and at last everyone had told their stories, except Sebastian. All eyes turned to him, but he shook his head and looked at the floor. "I can't do it," he said. "I'm sorry." Maureen and David assured him that they understood, and went on to ask each of us to keep in confidence the stories others had told. They passed around a sheet for everyone to write down names, addresses and telephone numbers, so we could reconnect with one another if we wanted to do so. There were a few questions and finally a closing ceremony, punctuated by hugs all around. Gradually people began to locate and gather their things as they prepared to leave.

Sebastian, Maddie and I helped Maureen and David pack up the mats and stereo equipment, while Helen, Radha and Mr. Camden washed dishes and straightened the workshop room. When the other attendees were gone and the Edwardses were ready to leave, I called Helen and we walked out to their van to say goodbye. The rain had finally stopped and a few stars could be seen through the breaking clouds. I enjoyed the night's cold freshness, but Helen shivered, and I put my arm around her. The four of us stood together on the sidewalk, the clouds from our breath mingling in the air.

"Thank you both for everything," Helen said. "This day was so powerful for all of us, I don't think it will ever be forgotten."

"Not by me, anyway," I said.

"We love this work," Maureen said.

"You must," I agreed. "Otherwise you wouldn't be able to stand it—I mean the intensity of it."

"Well," David mused, "for me it was either do this or teach philosophy to college freshmen. I think I took the less frightening alternative."

"Don't listen to him," Maureen interrupted, laughing. "He gets giddy after every workshop. Now, seriously, I hope you two will hang on to our telephone number and call us if you have any problems or issues that come up regarding the breathwork, or even if you just want to talk. And let us know if you decide to schedule another event or to attend one of ours."

There were a few more parting words and several hugs, and at last they started the van and drove away. Helen and I turned and walked back inside, intending to say good night to our friends and go home. Sebastian, however, had other plans.

# — 17 —

By the time we were back inside, the others had almost finished washing the dishes and rearranging the furniture in the workshop room. In spite of the cold outside, Helen wanted to leave the door open for a minute to air out the space. She started to remove the black plastic from the windows, but Sebastian called out to her from across the room.

"Helen, wait a minute. Let's keep the windows covered a little longer."

"Why?"

"I was hoping you all would agree to stay awhile. I want to talk about my breathwork session, and some other things."

"You want to talk about it now?" I asked, surprised. "Why not an hour ago?"

"The time wasn't the problem," he answered. "It was the audience. I'm not usually shy— a fact to which the world will testify— but this is very private stuff, and some of it scares me. I only feel comfortable discussing it with friends I can trust."

"Perhaps I should be going, in that case," Mr. Camden said.

"No, no, it's all right," Sebastian protested. "Any friend of Radha's is a friend of mine, Mr. Camden. And besides, I'd like to get your point of view about my story."

Mr. Camden smiled, bringing his many well-worn wrinkles sharply into focus. "If I'm going to be elevated to the rank of trusted confidante, perhaps you should call me George. That goes for everyone."

In a few minutes, the six of us were gathered in a circle of chairs set around a table we had pulled to the center of the room. Helen had turned out the overhead lights, so the room was lit only by a floor lamp in one corner and two candles she had placed on the table. She carried in a tray with

coffee for Sebastian, a pot of tea, some cups and a plate of homemade cookies left over from the workshop food. Sebastian fidgeted, drumming his fingers on the table, sipping repeatedly from his too-hot coffee and shifting his
weight from side to side in his chair. When Helen finally sat down, she said.
"All right, we're ready. Tell us what happened."

Sebastian sat in silence, the light from the candles on the table flickering across his face, making his red beard look like fire. He clasped his hands
together and looked down at them. Then he took a deep breath, as though
summoning his strength. "So," he asked, looking from face to face around
the table, "how many of you believe in hell?"

No one answered. Finally Mr. Camden asked, "Do you mean as a place
or a state of mind?"

Sebastian turned to him, "After today, I'm not sure what the difference
is. Let me ask the question another way. How many of you believe in evil?"

I raised my hand and looked around. Mr. Camden followed suit, After a
moment, Helen said, "I think of evil as the conscious denial of the Light.
Many bad things are done out of ignorance, but evil is a choice. Sebastian,
why are you asking this?"

"Because I think I saw evil, or hell, or hell-on-earth today, and I'm trying to figure out how to talk about it."

She reached across the table and touched his clasped hands. "Just start
at the beginning. Don't worry, let it come out."

Sebastian took another deep breath and shuddered slightly. "Okay," he
said. "Here we go."

At that moment there was a loud knock on the door. Maddie stifled a
shriek, and I jumped up from my seat. Adrenaline coursed through me, and
I thought immediately of the two black-suited men who had been in the
store a day earlier. Before approaching the door, I turned to Helen and gestured toward Maddie. Helen nodded and whispered, "Maddie, why don't you
go into the bathroom for a minute?" Maddie got up and hurried down the
stairs.

"Maybe you should go, too," I whispered to Sebastian.

"No. I want to face them," he said.

I turned back and walked to the door. "Who's there?" I demanded.

A familiar male voice answered, "It's us, David and Maureen. Can we
come in for a moment? We forgot our microphone."

Radha, Helen, Sebastian and I all sighed with audible relief, while Mr.
Camden looked on in bewilderment. I opened the door and the Edwardses
came in, smiling and apologizing for bothering us. Maureen strode to the

window sill where the wireless microphone had been overlooked as they were packing. "Sorry about this," she said, looking at the group seated around the table. "I hope we didn't disturb you."

"Not at all," Sebastian replied, turning in his seat to face Maureen. "In fact, I take this as a synchronicity. I was starting to share the tale of my breathwork experience with my friends here. Maybe your arrival means I'm supposed to tell you too— that is, if you have the time and inclination to listen."

Maureen looked at David, who glanced at his watch and shrugged. "As Maureen says, I'm always energized after one of these workshops. I could stay up all night, and we don't have any commitments tomorrow. Besides," he grinned, "it's our duty and pleasure as facilitators to listen to every story. I didn't think we'd get the chance to hear this one."

Maureen was already pulling two chairs over to the table. "Now he's going to have to thank me for misplacing that mike," she declared, smiling.

Mr. Camden still appeared mystified. Looking back and forth between me and Sebastian, he asked, "Were you two expecting someone else when you heard that knock?"

Radha shushed him, "We'll talk about that later, George."

"All right, but I was just wondering when young Madeline was going to be let out of the bathroom."

"Omigosh," I said. "I forgot. I'll run down and get her."

While I was retrieving Maddie, Helen had apparently given some suitable account to Mr. Camden and the Edwardses, although I was sure she hadn't gone into the full explanation of the situation. When we returned to our seats at the table, the conversation quieted and we all turned to Sebastian once again.

"From the moment I stretched out on the mat, even before the music started, I was uneasy," he began. "I felt as though some dark shadow was trying to come to the surface. While Maureen was leading the relaxation exercises, I started seeing flashes of imagery—people's faces. Most of them looked terrified, but some were enraged and others were crying. All of them were tinged in blue, like an El Greco painting. The flashes were sporadic, and each one disappeared so quickly I could almost believe I hadn't seen anything. I didn't recognize any of the faces, though it seemed as if I should. Then when the African drum music came on and I started the deep breathing, I saw one image of all the faces bound together in some kind of net. I felt as though I was falling, free-falling toward the web of faces, and when I reached it, the whole thing shattered into a million pieces.

"After that, I seemed to be underwater. When you told your story, Helen, I recognized some similarity there. But it wasn't blissful where I went. I was in darkness, and it was an oily, unwholesome place, like a polluted, stagnant river with a foul taste in the water. I couldn't see anything, but I could feel the presence of evil, hungry entities around me. I felt vulnerable to them, and thought that I must hold very still to keep them from noticing me. But they were aware of my thoughts, and they sent sly, menacing intentions back at me.

"Every so often, a wave of fear washed through the entire space, and every time it happened I was overwhelmed by it. Imagine the whole world suddenly becoming terrified, and think how you would feel in that moment. After each of those waves, there were periods when the dark water seemed to grow even murkier, and I felt poisoned. Another time, I sensed that the sinister presences around me were pleased by some event that they anticipated. I perceived an emotion I would now call despair permeating my world, and I thought my death was near. But the feeling eventually passed, leaving me to exist as best I could. At one point, there was a pain, as if I had been pierced by a huge needle, and after that I think I lost consciousness for a while."

I looked around the table. All eyes were glued on Sebastian, who stared down at his hands as he spoke. He paused for a moment. The flickering candlelight made me feel almost as though we were some tribe gathered around a campfire to hear the story of a shaman's visit to the other world.

"Were you aware of the music?" Radha asked.

Sebastian shook his head. "No, I never heard any of it after the first few minutes. Wherever I went, it was a long way from here. I mean, on some level, I always knew I was doing the breathing, and I suppose I could have stopped. But that thought never occurred to me. I wanted to continue. I wanted to see whatever was coming."

"The seeker of truth," I whispered to him.

He nodded. "The next thing I remember was coming to consciousness because of pain. I had a terrible headache—it felt as though my skull was in a metal vise. My arms were wrapped tight across my chest, and breathing had become difficult. Inside, I was still in the darkness, but I could feel the evil entities circling all around me, looking for my vulnerable spots. Their circling continued, faster and faster, until the dark space seemed to turn into a whirlpool. I felt myself being pulled helplessly down into the black vortex, and I quickly realized I wasn't alone there. Besides the evil presences which had surrounded me, there were human beings, terrified people who were also caught in this maelstrom. Maybe they were the same people I had first seen as faces trapped in the web, I don't know. In the next moment, the darkness gave way, and I began to see visions of tremendous suffering. I saw people being massacred in wars, cities wiped out by plagues, women and children being raped and tortured. I observed a nuclear power plant explosion that sent radiation over thousands of square miles, killing people and animals in a wide radius. I saw the insides of hospitals where thousands more were suffering. I viewed towns being suffocated by poison gas, and families being murdered by roving bands of scavenging bandits. There were natural disasters too—floods, earthquakes, tidal waves and terrible storms.

"As I witnessed all this horror, there was a change in my perspective. Suddenly I was no longer simply watching—I became identified with the sufferers of everything I saw happening. I felt their pain and experienced their emotions. I somehow *was* every victim of all of this overwhelming landscape of anguish and death. I saw that the whole earth was caught up in some terrible pattern of destruction and was on its way to being engulfed and pulled irretrievably into darkness."

Sebastian paused for a moment and Helen spoke, "I was aware of the same thing during my experience with Will at Bell Rock in Sedona. If the people on Earth were to turn away from the Light, there would be something here like a black hole, a consuming vortex of negative energy."

Sebastian nodded and said darkly, "That's exactly where I was." He shook his head, "We may all be there soon, at least that's how I was feeling. The visions were so frightening, I nearly opened my eyes to make them stop. But I sensed that there was something else I needed to see, so I kept on with the breathing, though I felt like there was a thousand-pound weight on my chest.

"I moved back into total darkness, and I perceived the menacing beings swirling around me again. My energy started to dissipate, and I felt exhausted. I seemed to be dropping downwards, moving into a deeper blackness. Then suddenly I began to see shapes and movement, and I found myself watching the same scenes of pain and destruction all over again.

"But there was a difference. This time there were shadowy figures, like gray ghosts, scurrying around throughout all the carnage, exulting in it and somehow feeding off of it. At every murder, a pack of them seemed to leap onto the victim, and the killer as well, draining them of something I thought of as 'life essence'. In the war scenes, there were hordes of them, screaming obscenities into the ears of soldiers on both sides, encouraging them to kill. They eagerly drank in people's suffering, but they were even more rabid to tap into human cruelty. The crowds of them around the most horrific scenes of brutality were huge and frantic. I was confused at first, but then I realized I was seeing demons. They were all over the earth, working in a frenzied passion, to pull it into oblivion.

"As I concentrated on the demonic beings, the scene changed into situations more like those in everyday life, and I saw these shadow creatures doing their work everywhere. In arguments and angry confrontations of all kinds, they found their food. Every type of fear and anxiety was their wine. They gleefully consumed all kinds of self destruction, from one man's alcoholism to the entire planet's cancer of pollution. Even a person's decision to say an unkind word was a tidbit for them.

"As I watched all this, I felt a sinking sense of hopelessness. There were legions of these entities, eagerly seizing upon every morsel of suffering. They were constantly shrieking into every human ear their demands for destruction. Of course, most people never heard them consciously, but that's not the level where their work was done. They seemed to attack people on a subconscious level—through feelings, most often fear and anger. I could see no way for us to defend ourselves against them.

"I wondered if there was some entity or organizing force behind these swarming vampires, and as soon as the question rose in my mind, the vision changed. I saw the landscape open, like a cross section, and below the surface I sensed a horrible presence in the darkness. Now the demonic beings looked like a billion ants teeming over the tortured surface of the earth. And from each one came a thin gray stream, going down under the ground. I knew somehow that the stream was the 'life essence' stolen from the living world, and I saw the streams twist together into a huge tornadic swirl, siphoning down into the maw of an invisible malevolent power. As I watched, I was pulled down into the subterranean chamber. I felt as though everything was burning, but there was no light. There were horrible noxious smells, and endless screaming and wailing. I became one of an uncountable number of piteous souls, bound in agony. In the next moment, there was a flash of red lightning, and for a split second I saw the being whose hell this was. It was animal and man-shaped—a wild-eyed god with a skull necklace. Its huge mouth was always turned upward, ravenously consuming the negative energy of the whole suffering world.

"In that same lightning flash, it seemed that it saw me. Its huge red eye looked right into me, and my heart stopped. That's when I yelled. In the next moment, I was paralyzed. I couldn't move my arms or legs, and I felt as if I was going to suffocate. At the same time, huge energies were traveling through my body, similar to electricity, but not pleasant like Will's. I thought I was being roasted from the inside out. Then I felt myself falling, falling down into a deep pit.

"I landed on a ledge on the wall of the abyss. It was a narrow platform circling the entire perimeter of the cavernous space, and there were numerous incomprehensible machines stationed all around it. I crept to the precipice to look down over the edge, and one of the gray demons leaped up at me from below, screaming hideously. I jumped backward and fell against one of the machines along the wall. There was excruciating pain in both of my hands, and when I looked I saw that they had been impaled on sharp levers that protruded from the mechanism. I tried frantically to free myself, but my efforts only succeeded in pulling both of the levers downward an inch or two. When I did that, I heard a deep, dull roar emanating from farther down in the pit, and as I hung suspended by my wounded hands, dozens of the demons came out of the shadows, laughing and clapping, shouting in exaltation. In a moment, I understood why. The abyss was actually a nuclear missile silo, and by pulling the levers I had accidentally launched the missile. This is what the demons had wanted, but they apparently required a human being to do the deed. The roar became deafening, and I saw the cylindrical metal body go past, just before I was burned by the flames from the rocket engines. Hundreds of the demons clung to the shaft of the missile, gleefully riding it to its rendezvous with Armageddon. And I was left alone, burned and crucified on the launching mechanism. I surrendered to a black despair, and I waited for death to come. Then my thoughts blinked out, and I knew nothing.

"Eventually, I heard the ocean waves coming through the stereo speakers, and I pinched myself to make sure I was real. I opened my eyes and saw Maddie, and she helped me come back. My body was covered with sweat, and I was really shaken. I kept rubbing my hands together—it was hard for me to believe there were no holes in them." Sebastian turned to Maddie and asked, "Do you know where my drawing is?" She quickly brought it to him from their little pile of belongings against the wall. He removed the rubber band and unrolled it on the table top. In dark red. he had sketched the outline of a monstrous body with a grotesque, beastlike head. The mouth was tilted upward, swallowing a whirling tornado. Behind the head, a bolt of jagged red lightning stretched across the mandala circle. Everything else, both within and without the being's body outline, was shaded in black. "I had to draw this to get it out of my mind," Sebastian said. "I was seeing it every time I closed my eyes. My friends, I give you the god of hell. From what

I saw, I think he's making a bid for *all* the local real estate, *and* the people on it. I'm embarrassed to admit I'm starting to sound like a fundamentalist, but I can almost sympathize with their point of view now. Come on, everybody, talk me out of this. Tell me where I'm wrong."

For a moment, we were all silent. Then Mr. Camden spoke, "I'm not going to say you're vision is wrong, Sebastian. I hope it is, but it reminds me of something the poet William Butler Yeats saw in a vision of his own."

"I've read some Yeats," Sebastian said. "Which poem are you thinking of?"

"It was called *The Second Coming*. Let me see if I can remember how it goes." The old man closed his eyes and furrowed his brow. Then, slowly, he began to recite:

> *Turning and turning on the widening gyre,*
> *The falcon cannot hear the falconer;*
> *Things fall apart; the centre cannot hold;*
> *Mere anarchy is loosed upon the world,*
> *The blood-dimmed tide is loosed, and everywhere*
> *The ceremony of innocence is drowned;*
> *The best lack all conviction, while the worst*
> *Are full of passionate intensity.*
>
> *Surely some revelation is at hand;*
> *Surely the Second Coming is at hand.*
> *The Second Coming! Hardly are those words out*
> *When a vast image out of* Spiritus Mundi
> *Troubles my sight: Somewhere in the sands of the desert*
> *A shape with a lion body and the head of a man,*
> *A gaze blank and pitiless as the sun,*
> *Is moving its slow thighs, while all about it*
> *Reel shadows of the indignant desert birds.*
> *The darkness drops again, but now I know*
> *That twenty centuries of stony sleep*
> *Were vexed to nightmare by a rocking cradle,*
> *And what rough beast, its hour come round at last,*
> *Slouches towards Bethlehem to be born?"*

Just as Mr. Camden finished speaking, the doors and windows were rattled by a strong gust of wind outside. All of us were startled, and I shivered involuntarily. Then I said, "I see what you're saying, George. That poem gives me the same fearful feeling as Sebastian's story, and some of the images are similar, too. The 'widening gyre' is like the whirlpool Sebastian saw."

"It's interesting," Helen commented. "Both of those images are spirals, which I normally see as beautiful motifs of the cosmic design, but in these visions they're negative and dangerous, like shadows of themselves."

I nodded and continued, "The first part of the poem paints a bleak picture, but it's one I can see in the world around us—the drowning of innocence, the ambivalence and passivity of good people, and the crusading fervor of the worst. Isn't that the same sort of thing that was feeding the demons you saw, Sebastian?"

"Absolutely," he agreed. "And at the end, when the poet mentions the 'rough beast' that 'slouches towards Bethlehem to be born,' I get an echo of the horror I felt when I saw the demon god."

"I don't understand," said Maddie. "I thought the Second Coming was a Christian belief about the return of Christ. Isn't that supposed to be a good thing? And what does *Spiritus Mundi* mean?"

Mr. Camden smiled gently, "The *Spiritus Mundi* is the spirit of the world. Yeats must have sensed that his vision had a significance beyond his individual being, as I think Sebastian's may. As for the Second Coming, you're correct about its traditional meaning, but I think Yeats saw a different myth taking shape in the world, a myth from the shadow side. I believe he feared, as I do, that our times are fated to see not the return of the loving Jesus, but the arrival of his dark brother."

Radha looked at her friend with disapproval, "Gracious, George, you're not being very positive, if I do say so. I think we should hear from David and Maureen. After all, they know about breathwork, and they can probably interpret Sebastian's story better than Mr. Yeats!"

David smiled, "I'm making no promises, but I'll share what comes to mind with you anyway. Sebastian, some of the images from your story do fit within the framework of the perinatal matrices. For instance, the unpleasant, polluted waters you mentioned are sometimes associated with the first matrix, but in its negative form, known as the 'bad womb'. Even the feeling of being surrounded by malevolent entities and the sensation of being poisoned can be a part of it. The waves of emotion you felt could be feelings transferred to the fetus from the mother, although terror is a rather unusual one. Do you know anything about your mother's pregnancy?"

"Yes, I know a little bit about it. Actually, that was the period when she first began to talk about being visited by extraterrestrials. She saw some B-grade science fiction horror movie with my father, and it gave her a series of nightmares. She would wake up in the middle of the night insisting that the aliens had made her pregnant, or that they were going to take her baby. Sometimes she would cry and say she didn't want to lose *another* baby to them. That was odd, because she did have a miscarriage the year before, but she had never mentioned aliens. My father of course didn't understand this stuff, and he ascribed it to what he called 'typical pregnant hysteria'. Anyway, my mother apparently smoked and drank a lot during the pregnancy—so much so that her doctor asked her to tone it down. But she couldn't shake the nightmares, and she used the alcohol and cigarettes to try to calm herself. Even as she did all that, she worried about injuring the fetus—me, that is. From what I've heard, she also considered having an abortion, but finally decided against it, which I'm pleased to report. Anyway, once I was born and she saw that I didn't have green skin or tentacles, she quieted down and went back to normal for quite a few years. At least that's what my father has told me."

"That's fascinating," Maureen said. "The research in holotropic breath-work has shown the images of pollution or poison in the womb can be correlated with the mother's taking in toxic substances such as alcohol, cigarette smoke, or drugs. The waves of overwhelming emotion you felt could also have come from the mother, and what you've said about her emotional state strongly indicates that possibility. But as to the source of her upsets—I have to say we've never dealt with anyone whose bad womb experiences had extraterrestrial connections."

"But Dr. Grof ran into it," David added. "He mentions it in one of his books, although he doesn't go into it in detail."

"You know," Maddie interjected, "I think Sebastian's mother must have had some repressed abduction memories, and they were set off by the movie she saw. A lot of female abductees report having fetuses taken from them." She turned to Sebastian. "You mentioned feeling pain as if you were stabbed by a huge needle. Maybe you were given an implant when you were a fetus, so they could keep track of you. They use big needles for that sort of thing."

Sebastian shook his head, "All this analysis is good, but what about the other parts of the visions? I feel as though I really saw something— a piece of the truth of what is going on here on earth. Don't tell me those gray demons and that huge devil are nothing but symbols from my birth trauma. They were more than that. I could feel it. I can *still* feel it."

Helen was nodding, "I don't usually like to talk about these things, but I think you're right, Sebastian. Sometimes during healing sessions, I've seen or sensed entities like those you described. Often there's a negative presence clinging to the client, like an energy vampire, feeding off the person's distress. It can even feel as though there's an ill will involved, trying to keep people trapped in negative, self-destructive patterns."

"That's exactly what I saw," he agreed. "But they weren't just attached to a few people. There were hordes of them all over the earth, and it seemed to me they were draining 'life essence' from practically everybody."

"Yes," she acknowledged. "The negative forces are pervasive here. When I visualize them, I see a dark cloud, almost like a gray shell around the planet. I tried to draw that image on my mandala today. From my perspective, the addiction to fear and other kinds of negativity runs through so much of human activity that simply being here is painful for a sensitive person. And there's always some stimulus trying to draw us into the vicious circle of negative beliefs that acts like a self-fulfilling prophecy. It's very much like the whirlpool you saw in your vision, Sebastian. I do my best to stay out of it, and to avoid contributing my own energies to it. For that reason, I don't watch the news on television or go to violent movies."

"That's the way she is," I interjected. "She's always trying to 'hold the pattern' of the positive point of view. Even when I'm yelling at the traffic, she's looking out the car window at the flower beds. I used to accuse her of being unrealistic, but now I'm starting to wonder how much I've been 'feeding the demons'."

Helen touched my hand and smiled softly, "It's not an easy thing to stop."

"But I wanted to bring up something else," I continued. "When Helen was talking about people's addiction to fear, it reminded me of that conversation about conspiracies we were having just before Maddie's swimming accident. Do you remember it, Sebastian? You were talking about a sweeping conspiracy among the government, the media, the corporations and the advertising industry, all set up to control the masses by building up and catering to their fears. At the same time, you said they were selling a false sense of security to people by offering a picture of reality that portrayed the government and other institutions as having more knowledge and control of reality than they really have. What was it you said—'our souls are being invaded for the sake of profits and power'?"

"And the American brand of insanity is being exported to the rest of the world through television." Sebastian nodded sadly. "Today I saw it on a deeper level. I'm not sure anymore whether these people realize what they're doing, even at the higher levels of power. Maybe it's just that they—and all of us to some extent—suffer from a kind of species insanity, driven by greed and hunger that isn't even our own—the greed and hunger of all those demons."

David, who'd been listening intently and looking indecisive about whether to break into the conversation, leaned forward in his chair and spoke, "I've read that all the gods and demons live within us, and that's how I tend to see the things that come up in breathwork. But whether that's true or not, it doesn't absolve people of responsibility for their actions. I agree with Helen's definition— evil is the conscious turning away from the Light."

"Garth Lemay," Sebastian muttered under his breath.

"What did you say?" Maureen asked.

"What? Oh, nothing. I was thinking about someone I knew a long time ago. He dabbled in mind control, or at least he said he did. I was just wondering if he knew the true face of what he was serving."

When Sebastian mentioned Lemay, I looked up sharply. I was about to mention the two men who had been in the store on Friday, but Sebastian silenced me with his eyes. I could see he wasn't ready to bring that set of worries into the open yet.

Mr. Camden spoke. "Has anyone here read a book called *Shikasta?*" No one answered. "It's a novel by Doris Lessing, and it touches on a number of the points we've been examining here. I can offer you a little summary, if you'd like."

Sebastian looked grateful for the change of subject. He picked up one of the cookies from the tray and sat back in his chair. "Lay it on me, George. What kind of a book is it?"

"Well, I suppose the book would be considered science fiction. The story presents itself as a set of records kept by a race of benevolent extraterrestrial beings from the star Canopus. They are a civilization of colonizers and facilitators of higher intelligence who go around the universe seeding the evolution of various species. Shikasta is their name for the planet Earth, and the story concerns its sufferings and redemption.

"The Canopeans are spiritually oriented beings who seem to exist on a dimension above ours, but they can dip down into our world as well. They viewed Shikasta/Earth as an incredibly fertile and beautiful planet, very promising for the development of the primitive humans which they found there in the distant past. In the beginning, their program of speeding our evolution went well, and there was a feeling of Paradise on Earth. This increased exponentially when the Canopeans initiated 'the Lock,' an energetic connection with their own planet which brought about a great infusion of love and oneness on Shikasta.

"However, the seeds of disaster (which literally means 'bad-star') had already been sown. A species of evil space renegades from the planet Shammat, the rivals and enemies of Canopus, had infiltrated the planet and were awaiting their opportunity to corrupt and transform the positive energies of Shikasta into the negative vibrations upon which they fed. Their chance came when an unfavorable interstellar alignment, an unexpected dis-aster, disrupted the flow of sustaining energy from Canopus. At that moment, the feeling of Paradise on Earth ended, and the poor inhabitants suffered as though they had literally been expelled from heaven. (I think the author means to suggest that the many human myths of 'the Fall' might have stemmed from such an occurrence.) As the demonic extraterrestrials from Shammat did their work, the humans and the planet itself experienced progressive degeneration and an increasingly violent history. Because of the failure of 'the Lock,' the Canopeans could do little to halt or even slow the destructive process, at least until the celestial alignments became more favorable. Meanwhile, the pirates of Shammat gorged themselves on the energies of pain and suffering emanated by the planet and its creatures. The feeding became a frenzy, as the fertility of the planet was twisted to generate an abundance of disharmony. The balance became so skewed that even the evil ones found it difficult to hold themselves together, and Shikasta lurched towards a cataclysmic war. The Canopeans tried everything they could, even incarnating as humans in an attempt to influence events and minimize the destruction. There were some small successes, but in the end the war came, and huge numbers of people were wiped out. Then afterwards, the stellar alignments shifted and the benevolent energies of Canopus could be received once again. The people who had survived the wars awoke as if from some insane nightmare, and they suddenly all knew what they must do. Following that inner sense of knowing, they began to rebuild their world, abandoning their old cities to begin anew."

Maddie had been listening intently to Mr. Camden's story. "That is so much the way things are here!" she exclaimed. "And the Canopeans are just like the ETs who are helping us to reach enlightenment."

"They're like the blue ones, maybe, but not the Grays," Sebastian said. "From what I've read and personally hallucinated (I hope), the Grays don't seem to be from anyplace like Canopus *or* Shammat."

"Now that you bring that up, there was another extraterrestrial breed in the book, and they rather resembled the ones you call the Grays," Mr. Camden replied. "They were a race from Sirius, an emotionless species of scientists. They were nominally allies of Canopus, and were thus allowed to be present on Shikasta, but their lack of feeling led them to perform numerous breeding experiments and genetic manipulations on humans and animals. The experiments caused additional suffering and seemed to be without any higher purpose."

"That could be the Gray ones, all right," said Sebastian. "Or their fictitious brothers. I wonder if Doris Lessing was abducted herself."

"I'm sure she was aware that her book was more than pure fiction," Mr. Camden said. "In her introductory remarks at the beginning, she mentioned her belief that it was possible for people to tap in to the overmind or collective unconscious. I took that as an implied statement that she had done so, and it appears that way to eyes like mine, and perhaps Maddie's." He smiled at her and then turned back to Sebastian. "Perhaps the extraterrestrial parasites from Shammat are a metaphor for the the gray demons from your vision."

"Or vice versa," Sebastian grimaced. "To me it confirms the fact that, in some way at least, they're real."

"I want to go back to George's story for a moment," Radha interjected. "What about the redemption of everything? That's where I would like to focus."

"Yes," Helen agreed. "Maybe we should look at the positive side."

"The positive side of what?" Sebastian asked.

"Of what we think and feel is going on in the world, and where it's taking us," Helen said. "We've been pulling together a lot of information and receiving a number of clues these past few months. Now you're saying the vision you had during the breathwork feels as though it's about something greater than your personal story, and I agree. But all of our other visions and experiences may signify something more as well. Perhaps we should pool our thoughts and try to get a sense of the larger picture. My intuition tells me the time is right, so I suggest we consider burning a little midnight oil and putting our heads together."

"And our hearts," Maddie chimed in.

"And our stomachs," Sebastian added. "Is there any other food around here besides these cookies? Otherwise, I plan on eating all of them myself."

There was a short break while members of the group buzzed about the space, picking up notebooks, using the bathroom or standing up to stretch. Everyone had agreed to stay together and brainstorm for awhile. Sebastian and I raided the refrigerator and brought out more leftovers from the workshop, which we placed on a small table, alongside a pitcher of water and glasses. Mr. Camden had gone downstairs, and he returned with two books he had apparently found on the store shelves. Radha and Maddie walked outside for a few breaths of fresh air at the same time David went out to lock his van. In a few minutes we were all back at the table.

For the benefit of Mr. Camden, David and Maureen, the rest of us recounted the significant events of the past couple of months. Sebastian told the story of his recurring dreams of experiences with the ETs and his subsequent trip to Sedona. Maddie recalled her meeting with Sebastian, the events at Bell Rock, the death of Dr. Jordan and her own near-death experience. I noticed David's eyes widen as she described the call from the 'FBI agent' and the ransacking of her apartment. Mr. Camden nodded as I spoke of meeting Radha and of the message from Anon that came through her in our living room. At that point, Radha pulled the paper from her purse and read the transcript to the group. Afterwards, she and Helen related some of the main points from the previous workshop on astrology and archetypes, as well as the one on morphogenic fields.

Helen turned to me and said, "You're next, Will."

"Next to do what?"

"To finish filling in David and Maureen and George. Tell them about what happened here Friday."

I glanced at Sebastian, who nodded almost imperceptibly. Then I recounted the sinister visit of the two men in black suits, including their questions about Maddie and my denial of having seen her. I was about to go into my conversation with Sebastian about Garth Lemay, but when I looked to him he shook his head slightly, so I cut my explanation short.

When I finished, David said, "I don't understand what motivates people like that."

"Well, there's money and power, for starters," said Sebastian.

"Money I can understand," Maureen remarked. "But why anyone would want power is beyond me."

"It's a strange thing," I said. "When I look at myself and think about when I've pushed for power over someone else, even in a small way, like winning an argument, there was always a feeling of something I'd call 'negative satisfaction'. In me, it's a type of ego pleasure, a kind of ugly counterfeit of real happiness."

"And it is easily achieved, if one is willing to dehumanize the other, or simply to withdraw compassion," Mr. Camden observed.

"Some people have no compassion to withdraw, so it's even easier for them," Sebastian said.

"I'm not so sure about that," Helen disagreed. "I don't think it's possible to be alive and have no spark of the Light within oneself. It may be buried and twisted, but I believe it is the source from which we have all emerged. When I read a statement like that of Jesus admonishing his followers to love their enemies, I think about that little spark of Light."

"And our work is to find those sparks and fan them into flames," Radha said. "First within ourselves and then in others. I've known it practically all my life, but it seems more important now than ever. I'm reminded of what Anon said through me at Will and Helen's house—that the holy fire begins as tiny sparks in a scattered few, but that it can grow into something that cleanses and renews the world."

"Yes," Helen agreed. "Remember the quotes from Jesus in the *Gospel According to Thomas* you sent to us in your fax?"

"Indeed I do, and I can recite them: 'I have cast fire upon the world, and see, I guard it until the world is afire.' And the other one: 'Whoever is near to me is near to the fire, and whoever is far from me is far from the Kingdom.'"

Mr. Camden had been thumbing through one of the books he brought up from the store shelves. "You know," he said, "there is an interesting parallel to what you're discussing in this book about Sri Aurobindo. It is from the Hindu perspective, but I believe it refers to what you are calling the 'holy fire'. The word used here is the Sanskrit word for fire, *Agni*. Incidentally,

Agni is the original root for such English words as *ignition*. He turned a few pages, searching for the paragraphs he wanted. "The Hindus speak of three types of fire in the physical world—ordinary fire or *jada Agni*, electric fire or *vaidyut Agni*, and solar fire or *saura Agni*. It is interesting to note that their ancient seers understood that solar fire, atomic energy, is fundamentally different from the other varieties, thousands of years before our scientists discovered that fact. In any case, behind all of these outer manifestations there is 'the fundamental *Agni*, that spiritual *Agni*, which is everywhere.' Sri Aurobindo's disciple Mother describes it as an atmosphere of 'warm gold dust.' The ancient Hindu holy text, the Rig Veda says 'other flames are only branches of thy stock,' meaning that all types of physical fire derive from the spiritual *Agni*. Both Sri Aurobindo and the ancient Hindu holy men, the rishis, linked the experience of the spiritual *Agni* to the inner transformation of rebirth and enlightenment."

Maddie eyes shone with wonder. "Mr. Camden ... George, I know what they're talking about. I was in the atmosphere of the 'warm gold dust' part of the time when I was out of my body after I almost drowned. Will was there, too, when he fainted. And Helen felt the atmosphere of gold in her breath-work session today."

"I know, Maddie," he smiled. "And there is more here that will speak to you. Satprem, the author of this book, says this: 'Indeed the whole universe from top to bottom is made of a single substance of divine Consciousness-Force; and *Agni* is the element of force or energy in consciousness ... It is a heat, a flame, at whatever level we feel it. When we concentrate in our mind, we feel the subtle heat of mental energy or mental *Agni*; when we concentrate in our heart or in our emotions, we feel the subtle heat of Life-Energy or vital *Agni*; when we plunge into our soul, we experience the subtle heat of the soul or psychic *Agni*. There is only one *Agni* from top to bottom, a single stream of Consciousness-Force or consciousness-energy or consciousness-heat taking on different intensities at different levels.' On the next page, he quotes again from the *Rig Veda*: '*He tastes not that delight* (of the twice born) *who is unripe and whose body has not suffered in the heat of the fire; they alone are able to bear that and enjoy it who have been prepared by the flame.*'"

"You know," Radha said, "I'm reminded of the other quotes I sent in that fax you mentioned, Helen. There was the experience reported by Richard Maurice Bucke, where he thought at first a huge fire must have erupted nearby, only to discover moments later that the fire was within himself, and in that instant of recognition he moved into a state of ecstasy. The other one was described in the poem by Yeats. As he sat alone in a shop, his body suddenly seemed to blaze, and he was filled with a sense of blessedness that he felt he could also bestow upon others. I believe this sort of thing has happened for thousands of years to people all over the world."

"And it's happening now, to all of us!" Maddie exclaimed. "Think about what went on today in the breathwork. Everyone had some kind of experience with fire. And when I almost died, I went to the crystal temple where a whole group of people or souls was being instructed and ignited with what must have been this same spiritual fire or *Agni*. I remember the teacher at the center of the room telling us telepathically, 'Bearers of the flame, return to life. Seed the harvest of the Light.' And today, during my breathing session, I felt I was being used as some kind of lightning rod to ground a lot of fiery energy."

"So the Hindu rishis declared that the spiritual *Agni* engendered 'the delight of the twice born,'" Radha mused. "That makes me recall Anon's saying that the time of death and rebirth is at hand, and that the time of the fire comes just before the time of Light."

"It's fascinating to see how this pattern manifests on so many levels," Maureen said. "In the perinatal domains, as we go through them individually in Holotropic Breathwork or other non-ordinary states of consciousness, the fire imagery shows itself at the end of the third stage, which corresponds to the moment of peak physical stress and emotional intensity, just before birth. At the moment of birth, the beginning of the fourth perinatal stage, the fire transforms into light, as the baby emerges from the birth canal. Inwardly, that's the moment when a successful transition brings a sense of victorious joy and transcendence."

"And I think Sebastian was right when he suggested humanity is collectively at a stage akin to the end of the third perinatal matrix," David added. "It's as though we've reached the breaking point for the old way of life, and some radical shift has to happen soon. It's not simply a matter of 'relaxing into' death and rebirth, as if that were possible. We're facing the necessity of rebirth or death. If the process doesn't complete itself, the fetus dies. The trouble is, as a species, we've never done this before, so how can we know what to do?"

"Sri Aurobindo called it 'an adventure into the unknown'," Mr. Camden said. "And Satprem says that as soon as *one person* achieves the transformation, the conditions will change for everyone, because the trail will have been blazed and the way will then be known."

"It reminds me of the hundredth monkey story," Maddie said. "At the beginning, one individual sets the new pattern, and others add their energy to it by following."

"And when a critical mass of people does it, it will crystallize in the group consciousness of the entire human species, and we will all experience the transformation," Helen said. "At least that's the way I'm seeing it intuitively."

"Those were among the words that came through from Anon," Radha added. "'If enough of you open to the holy fire, *all* will receive its purifying grace.'"

"I can see how it fits in with what Kathleen Riley was saying in her talk on morphic resonance," I said. "But can we really be sure Satprem is writing about the same thing we've been experiencing?" My question sounded more like a hope than I'd meant it to. I was recalling my breathwork experience of a few hours earlier, seeing the golden corona around the earth and being told by the inner voice that I was witnessing the light of planetary awakening. I suddenly realized that I desperately wanted that vision to come true. I was no longer a neutral observer, if I had ever been one. As Sebastian had said, I had become a player and it was too late to leave the game.

"To borrow from the old parable, I believe we are all blind men touching the same elephant," Mr. Camden replied. "And it is the commonalities in our reports that make me think so. Listen to Satprem's description of the symptoms of the holy fire: 'When *Agni* burns in our mind, in moments of inspiration, we know it creates a great tension, an almost physical heat; when it burns in our heart, in our moments of soul, we know that our breast feels like a red-hot hearth, so hot that the skin can change color, and even an inexperienced eye can notice a sort of burning radiance around the yogi; when Agni burns in our vital, in moments when we summon the force or open up to the cosmic world, there is a sort of concentrated pulsation at the level of the navel, almost a tremor of fever throughout the body, for a large amount of force is entering a tiny channel; but then what about the warm gold dust, *this wine of lightning* in the cells of the body? *It begins to seethe everywhere*, says Mother in her simple words, *like a boiler about to explode.*'"

"My goodness," Radha said. "If we've been connecting with this *Agni*, that could explain all the post-menopausal hot flashes I've been going through."

"*And* the fevers everyone came down with after my swimming accident," Maddie added. "Maybe the energy that entered me in the crystal temple went into the rest of you because you were touching me."

"Yes," Helen agreed. "I remember as I was sending healing energy into your body, I suddenly felt the flow reverse, and a very warm vibration moved into me. And you're right, Maddie. Will and I both had fevers afterwards."

"Even before that," I interjected, "I remember a feeling of heat moving into my body when that entity Anon was speaking through Radha."

Sebastian had been silent for several minutes. Finally he said, "I have a question to pose. If these references about *Agni* from the ancient Hindu sages, and about Jesus' holy fire from the *Gospel of Thomas,* and the experiences of Bucke and Yeats are all referring to what was called 'Earthfire' when Radha did that channeling, and even if that *is* the same energy Maddie and some others are experiencing, what makes us think it's going to change the world? It has apparently been known, if not widely, for thousands of years, and from what I can tell, the world has been heading more towards hell than heaven."

"I think it's a matter of reaching critical mass, as Helen said," I answered, surprised at my own enthusiasm. "Look at the hundredth monkey story. There was a period of time between the first monkey washing the sweet potato and the moment when the hundredth monkey did it. During that time, as more of the monkeys began to copy the new behavior, nothing extraordinary happened to the group at large. I can just imagine some potato-washing monkey asking, 'What chance is there that what we're doing will change the monkey world? There are thousands of monkeys all over the Pacific, and most of them will never even hear about our innovation.'"

"That's right," Maddie chimed in. "But when the hundredth monkey started washing his sweet potatoes, the group mind of the monkeys reached critical mass, and suddenly they all 'got it'."

"And who's to say whether the process of human transformation will take another ten years, or ten months, or ten minutes?" Helen said. "When the balance shifts, it could happen in an instant."

Radha had unrolled her mandala drawing and was gazing at it. Suddenly she looked up and said, "I agree with you Helen, and I must say that I believe we are very close to the moment of the great change, whatever its nature may be. It seems to me that the world has been building toward it for my whole life. Think of the eruption of interest in every kind of metaphysics and spirituality, especially in the last thirty years. And this occurs at the same time that the old religions are losing their hold, particularly in the more advanced nations. The esoteric secrets of every path are now published in paperback and available everywhere. More people are seeking self-realization than ever before, and the lack of a sense of meaning or higher purpose in the modern technological world probably helps that along. We listen to astrologers like Mr. Lee telling us that the stars are aligning for transformational times. We hear a biologist like Mr. Sheldrake suggesting that even the laws of nature are mere habits, which can be overturned by shifts of consciousness. Knowledgeable people like David and Maureen agree that our species is in the throes of a collective birth ..." She sighed, "And I find myself contacted by a being called Anon who declares that the time has come for the emergence of the Divine into the world." She held her drawing up for us to see. "This vision came to me today—I saw myself in a gray room, with only a thin wall separating me from the holy fire. The wall is full of cracks, and the fire seeks to find its way in through every possible opening. I believe our time is different from any other. We will not need to coax the Earthfire into our world— if we simply offer it a channel, it will come. When enough holes have been made in the wall, it will burn through."

Mr. Camden had been searching through the second book as Radha spoke. "I have one more quote to offer from Satprem, and I believe it relates to what Radha is saying." He looked down and began to read, "'Man has a self of fire in the center of his being, a little flame, a pure cry of being under the ruins of the machine. This fire is the one that clarifies. This fire is the one that sees. For it is a fire of truth in the center of the being, and there is one and the same Fire everywhere, in all beings and all things and all movements of the world and the stars, in this pebble beside the path and that winged seed wafted by the wind. Five thousand years ago, the Vedic Rishis were already singing its praises: "O Fire, that splendor of thine, which is in heaven and which is in the earth and in its growths and its waters ... is a brilliant ocean of light in which is divine vision ..." The Rishis had discovered that fire five thousand years before the scientists—they had found it even in water. They called it "the third fire," the one that is neither in flame nor in lightning: *saura agni*, the solar fire, the "sun in darkness." It is this Fire which is the power of the worlds, the original igniter of evolution, the force in the rock, the force in the seed ... No species, even pushed to its extreme of efficiency and intelligence and light, has the power to transcend its own limits by the fiat of its improved chromosomes alone. It is only this Fire that can.'" Mr. Camden glanced up from the book. "As I understand it, the 'solar fire' is, on one level, atomic energy. Therefore it is everywhere in matter—in rocks, water, seeds, and in our own bodies—in everything which is made of atoms. On a deeper level, it is the force of consciousness that lies behind all matter and all energy in the universe. It is the holy fire of divine desire that brings light and life into the void. If the predictions of Anon come to pass, perhaps this solar fire, the *saura agni*, will somehow merge with our human consciousness."

"Solar fire," Sebastian mused. "That reminds me of something. Helen, do you remember the letter I wrote to you and Will from Sedona?"

"Yes, of course," Helen said.

"Then you may also recall that I did a Tarot reading for myself, to show off how good I thought I was. I think the question I posed was, 'What do I need to know about the path I am on?' As I was listening to George just now, I remembered that one of the outcome cards from that reading was The Sun. Maybe I'm supposed to eventually connect with this solar fire, or Earthfire, or whatever it is. I hope so. Of course, the other outcome card showed a wounded man. I'd be willing to skip that part."

"Do you have any idea what that might signify?" Mr. Camden asked.

"Actually, no. I've been inordinately healthy for months, but ..." He hesitated, and then spoke, "But there's been someone following Maddie, and maybe me too, since we left Sedona—and for some reason I thought of him when you asked that question. I wasn't sure whether to bring it all up tonight, but I guess I want to." Sebastian told the story of his past connections with Garth Lemay, and of his conclusion that Lemay was the 'FBI man' who had attempted to interrogate Maddie in Sedona, and who had come into our shop looking for her two days earlier.

"Do you have any idea what he wants from Maddie?" Maureen asked.

"Not exactly, but it has something to do with her friend, Dr. Jordan." Suddenly, a look of incredulity crossed Sebastian's face, and he slapped the palm of his hand against his forehead. "I can't believe it! I forgot all about reading the disc!"

"What disc?" asked Mr. Camden.

"The disc of Dr. Jordan's notes, the last one he gave to Maddie before he died. I was going to pop it into Will and Helen's computer here last night and find out what was on it—the disc is for MacIntosh and my computer is a PC—but somehow I let it slip my mind. Some big slip that was," he muttered. "Sigmund Freud and J. Edgar Hoover could have both wiggled into it at once." He looked at me, "Listen, Will, I don't want to break up the party, but would it be all right if I sneaked down to your office and checked it out right now?"

"Of course," I said, "but I'd like to look over your shoulder, if you don't mind."

"Yes, I'm curious as well," said Mr. Camden.

"I think we should all read it," Radha declared.

Sebastian shrugged, "Why not? If misery loves company, anxiety must be crazy about it. Let's go."

The six of us of us followed Helen and Sebastian downstairs to her office, and we crowded around the computer as she turned it on and slid in the disc which Maddie had handed to her. Helen clicked the mouse to open the disc, and we saw the titles of three files:

Agents of Transformation: The ETs and Human Evolution
Agents of Control: Governmental Suppression of Information
Breakthrough: Threshold of the New World

"Okay, Sebastian," Helen said. "Where do we go from here?"

"Let's do it from the top down," Sebastian answered. "Maybe Dr. Jordan intended them to be read in order."

"I think that's true," Maddie agreed. "That's how he usually liked to work. He was a very organized man."

Helen clicked the file to open, and there, crowded into the little office of the Missing Link in the middle of an extraordinary night, the eight of us began to read the dead man's last notes.

Agents of Transformation: The ETs and Human Evolution

[Note to Maddie: This section is not 100% complete. I will add more material later in the places indicated. For now, just read it and make any necessary corrections, and let me know what you think.]

As I have written elsewhere, I began my investigations into the phenomenon of alien abductions when I was still practicing as a medical doctor. A patient, a friend of a friend, came to me with small lesions and little scoop-like scars she could not explain, and she complained of nightmares. The lesions and scars healed rapidly, but the nightmares continued. Although I was not a psychiatrist, I offered to put her under hypnosis, which I had learned to administer during my stint as a navy doctor, to see if we could get to the source of the nightmares and give her some relief. It was during that afternoon that my world began to change.

Under hypnosis, the patient recalled what has now become known as a classic UFO abduction experience. Floating out of her bed, through the wall of the house where she had grown up, she found herself immobilized on a table inside what appeared to be a ship. She was surrounded by short gray humanoid beings with oversize heads and huge black eyes, and these beings subjected her to an unusual and sometimes painful "medical" examination. When she looked into their strange eyes—a terrifying and yet mysteriously attracting experience for her—she experienced what she described as telepathic communication with the beings. She reported that pictures formed in her mind—cities devastated by nuclear war, oceans choked with polluted waters, dead forests filled with leafless trees, farm lands turned to empty deserts. The message which came to her with the pictures was a warning that mankind must radically change its course, or the earth would soon suffer the cataclysms she had been shown. Again, this type of report has become almost typical in the abductee literature, but I worked with this patient in 1973, in what now seems like another age. Untypically, the woman's nightmares were not about the abductions themselves—they were about the visions of devastation she had been shown. She believed the warnings of the alien beings and felt compelled to find some way to involve herself in activities that would help to avert the environmental disasters.

In those days, I would normally have referred this patient to a psychiatrist, but she was fearful of being institutionalized or put on tranquilizers, and because she was my friend's friend, I agreed to keep seeing her. We continued to work with hypnosis, and over the next six months the story of her abduction experiences unfolded. I recounted these in detail in my first book, so I will not go into them here. However, I will use elements from this first case, which shares key characteristics with so many of those detailed by other investigators, to illustrate the points I want to make about the connections between alien contacts and what I can only call the process of human spiritual evolution.

As abduction researcher Dr. John Mack, to whom all investigators in this field owe a great debt of gratitude, has stated, one of the most powerful aspects of what abductees go through in the process of recovering memories and integrating their experiences is what he calls "ontological shock," the dawning of the understanding that in some sense their experiences are real, that they are not delusions or dreams, that they truly "happened." The jolt to one's world view when one can no longer hold on to the idea that such experiences are only fantasies or dreams can literally shatter one's concept of reality. The woman who was my first client declared, when she first entertained this possibility, that she wasn't sure she wouldn't rather have been crazy. As her doctor and confidante, I admit I had similar feelings at the time.

[Maddie: In this section, I am going to go into case histories from my own work, and that of other researchers. I wonder if you would be willing to allow me to write about your experiences?]

As the above cases seem to show, the shock of confronting the actuality of episodes of alien contact can simultaneously shatter one's sense of reality and open one's consciousness to what seems to be a deeper domain of powerful spiritual dimensions. It may be that the shock brings about a type of "ego death" such as Dr. Stanislav Grof has reported in his investi-gations of altered states of consciousness. In my understanding, the "ego death" is a kind of breakdown or annihilation of the everyday personality or "local self," in the aftermath of which normally unconscious dimensions of soul and spirit can emerge into consciousness. Encounters with alien beings seem to so overwhelm the boundaries of one's everyday world view that such ego death/rebirth moments are often experienced. Some abductees even believe that part of the intended purpose of the abductions is to bring about these inner openings of awareness. In the wake of such moments, many abductees express a sense of awe and wonder, and some espouse the conviction that they are in some sense one with the alien beings and/or with all of creation. As one young woman stated it, [this is you, Maddie] "They're putting us in the fast lane on the road to enlightenment."

Indeed, a number of experiencers have expressed the idea that the alien agenda involves an effort to bring about spiritual awakenings not only in the abductees themselves, but also in humanity at large. Many say that looking into the visitors' eyes brings a powerful awareness of soul, and sometimes a feeling of merging identities. Generally, the aliens are not seen as being godlike or divine in themselves, but rather as messengers or emissaries whose mission is to bring awakening to humanity. (Note: Not all experiencers believe this, and some think this is only part of the aliens' agenda.) For those who see the visitors facilitating a connection between humans and the divine, they are reminiscent of the beings typically known as angels, who also are intermediaries between humanity and the Source. In the views of a number of abductees who have worked to integrate their experiences, humanity has lost its connection to that Source, and this loss has allowed us to act in the multiplicity of destructive ways which have led to the current planetary crisis. In order to save our race and the planet—which many experiencers say matters far beyond the earth itself—these entities, who retain their Source connection, have reportedly embarked upon an urgent mission to help us "raise our vibrations," expand our awareness, regain our connection to Source and turn away from the path of self-annihilation.

Some abductees believe the aliens have additional motives, such as the re-invigoration of their own energies through contact with human emo-tions or the genetic creation of a new hybrid alien/human species. Some report that the Source consciousness mourns the estrangement of humanity from Itself, and that our awakening will in some sense help to heal a wound or rip in the fabric of universal consciousness. A common thread in the more spiritually oriented abductees is that the inner growth and consciousness expansion they experience are not for themselves alone, but are intimately connected with a universal awakening for humanity at large. One woman expressed it by saying, "It is important for us (the abductees) to go through this, because what happens through us is happening for everyone."

Abduction episodes can include unusual physical sensations, such as feelings of electrical energies or strong vibrations coursing through the body. Some experiencers believe that these sensations signify energy shifts whereby their physical and/or "astral" bodies are raised to a higher level, so they can move into the dimension in which the visitors exist. Others say the aliens normally inhabit an even higher vibrational level, and that they must lower their vibrations in order to connect with humans on the physical plane, or even the somewhat elevated level to which experiencers may be raised during these encounters. Whatever the interpretation, it is certain that a number of abductees report the intense vibrations in their bodies, before, during and sometimes after their experiences.

For some abductees, in addition to the vibrations, or in lieu of them, there is a powerful experience of confrontation with or immersion within fire. The famous case of Betty Andreasson includes her reports of witnessing the fiery immolation of a huge phoenix-like bird, and her own sense of being burned by those flames. A client with whom I have recently begun working has told me that her encounters with the visitors are inevitably followed by fevers and flushes, as well as "intense, burning kundalini energies" moving up and down her spine.

Another of the effects of encounters with the visitors can be the awakening of psychic gifts. Two of my own clients have experienced this. One has found herself able to accomplish "astral travel" and lucid dreaming almost at will, and has been successful in several remote viewing experiments. A young man discovered that his abduction experiences seemed to have awakened telepathic gifts, such as hearing people's thoughts, diagnosing illness through seeing auras, and doing psychic readings of people's possible futures. Dr. Mack and others in the field have noted similar phenomena in their clients as well.

For some experiencers, especially those who make "eye contact" with the aliens, there is a feeling of the numinous, a sense of being in the presence of the sacred. One interviewee has told me that he believes the aliens are a pure energy form which becomes embodied in order to intermediate between humans and the Source. Others speak with deep emotion of their sense that exposure to the visitors evokes immediate awareness of the existence and presence of their own souls. Some have come to see themselves as having both alien and human identities. A few even say their abduction experiences have included moments of direct engagement with the pure Source energy, or what we might call God.

Although most of the abductees I have met were not on any sort of spiritual path before their encounters, many have since embarked upon inner quests, while others have chosen to devote themselves to pursuits which are aimed at raising the consciousness of humanity and/or saving our environment. This seems, to me at least, to be a strongly positive effect of these extraordinary experiences.

At this time, I cannot scientifically verify or "prove" any of the abductions or other confrontations with aliens, but I can say with certainty that the people with whom I have worked are not lying, and in my estimation they are not crazy either. I believe in their sincerity, and I admire their ideals. In the face of overwhelming, reality-shattering encounters, they have shown tremendous courage in their efforts to remember and integrate their experiences. In sharing these memories, they have exposed themselves to ridicule and public censure, but a strong sense of higher purpose has carried them forward. These people have taken up the challenge for which they were chosen, and they may be among the vanguard of humanity's accelerating evolution. If the aliens are indeed soul-messengers from the Divine, perhaps we will all eventually meet them along the path to the Light.

We looked up, one by one, from the computer screen. No one said anything until everyone had finished reading the last page. Then Maddie, who had been crying silently as she read, spoke up.

"I left Sedona with Sebastian before Dr. Jordan had a funeral or anything, and I grieved about his death while Sebastian and I were traveling those first few weeks. Dr. Jordan was very kind to me, and he helped me remember my abductions and release the fear parts of them. I felt privileged being allowed to read his notes and give him feedback about his writing. He was more than a scientist—he was spiritual, too. He showed me the place that turned into my favorite meditation spot on Bell Rock, and he taught me the special breathing I did with Sebastian ... on that night."

"Was that the same night Dr. Jordan fell from the cliff?" Mr. Camden asked.

"Or was pushed," Sebastian replied. "Yes, it was."

Radha took a step toward Maddie and embraced her. "There now, my dear," she said. "I understand your sorrow, but don't let it consume you. Death is not the end of our story, I can promise you that."

"It's okay," Maddie sniffed. "I'm all right now."

"Speaking of stories," said David, "I'm fascinated by how this report dovetails with the story of Radha's contact with that entity, Anon. As I recall from what Radha read to us upstairs, he claimed to be an emissary of

nd a servant of the Infinite One. That sounds a lot like what
1 about the aliens. I believe he called them emissaries or messengers from the Source."

"There's another thing," I said. "When Anon's presence came into the
room, both Helen and I felt warm vibrations in our bodies, similar to what
Dr. Jordan was describing in the abductees' experiences."

"Yes," Maddie said. "And he also mentioned the abductees like Betty
Andreasson who felt fire energy in their bodies during or after their encounters."

"None of this truly surprises me," Radha said. "It is actually quite logical. Dr. Jordan has suggested that the beings he calls aliens may be from a
higher dimension rather than some other planet. Master forces, angels and
spirit guides also emanate from higher vibrational realms."

"But Anon still might have been some sort of ET," I said. "I'm remembering my breathwork session today—the part when I saw the vision of most
of your faces along with the image of the plastic Anon, which turned into a
living alien face. I wonder if that was him? I was feeling plenty of vibrations
in my body then, that's for sure."

Sebastian interrupted, "I don't know how to resolve all these questions,
but I'm pretty eager to continue with my reading here. Is everybody else
ready to go on?"

No one objected, so we were soon crowded around the computer screen
again, as Helen opened the second file.

Agents of Control: Governmental Suppression of Information

Since the advent of the enigmatic "foo fighters," the unexplained balls
of light which paced and darted around fighter planes during World War II,
the U.S. government has been aware of and interested in UFOs. The purported crash of a flying saucer in Roswell, New Mexico, in 1947 and its subsequent cover-up have become for many the symbols of government suppression of information about visitations from extraterrestrials. Project Blue
Book, the Air Force's supposed investigation of UFOs, makes no mention
whatsoever of Roswell, the most famous of all UFO incidents, and thus
cements its reputation as a cover-up posing as an investigation.

When one attempts to examine the U.S. government's interest in and
knowledge of UFOs over the past half-century, the path quickly becomes
murky and hard to follow. The number of fabricated reports and hoaxes,
some of them emanating from the CIA and military intelligence, makes it difficult for a serious investigator to make progress. There is always the dan-

ger of being misled, of embracing false theories or evidence which can bring damage to one's own reputation and work. Such pitfalls have persuaded many potential sleuths to steer clear of this territory, and some have argued that this was the government's hope and intention all along. It has been maintained in UFO circles that government operatives and agencies some-times create unconvincing or easily debunked UFO stories in order to dis-credit all such information. There is at least some documented material to support this premise.

[Maddie: I'm planning to insert in this section a number of examples of similar government secrecy, propaganda, and obfuscation of UFO reports in the period from the 1950s to the present. There is a huge amount of infor-mation, but it will take time to sift through it and authenticate the reliabil-ity of the data I will ultimately include. Among them, however, will be story of the Robertson Panel, the CIA committee which both denied the validity of UFO reports and recommended propaganda mechanisms to shape popular opinion against them. Also there is the 1960 NASA-commissioned report from the Brookings Institute which recommended that any future discoveries of alien life be kept secret, in order not to disrupt society at large. Think about that for a minute—if the government *were* aware of alien visitors, they would be denying it, just as they would be if they *weren't* aware of them. Catch 22, eh? By the way, did you know that NASA's charter actually establishes the agency as a branch of the American *military?* Another note-worthy detail is the internal NASA blueprint exposed in 1992 by Michigan Representative Howard Wolpe, which outlines for NASA officials how to evade the Freedom of Information Act. In the face of such evidence, I am strongly inclined to doubt the things they *do* say!]

It is perhaps understandable that the government should have some concerns about certain aspects of the UFO phenomenon. Unexplained blips on radar screens, unknown airships of various shapes and sizes spotted by pilots, UFO sightings near sensitive military installations— events such as these could raise legitimate questions regarding national security. Even more disturbing episodes, such as the disappearance of military aircraft sent out to intercept UFOs seen on radar, have also been reported. But all this seems a far cry from the alien abduction phenomenon, especially if it is understood to be a primarily spiritual experience, as some of the data seems to show. Our inner lives, particularly their religious and spiritual dimensions, are supposed to be outside the government's domain. And outer-world events, such as radar blips and sightings of strange objects in the sky, are not normally linked with the most intimate terrain of our per-sonal lives— our security within our homes, our sovereignty over our bod-ies, our connection with our own souls, our understanding of reality itself.

One wonders how such diverse elements could possibly have become inter-mingled.

Yet it is the nature of the UFO/alien enigma that these elements have come together. The visitors are apparently more than such stuff as dreams are made of, for there have been incidents of two or more abductees recall-ing shared experiences. In addition, there have been numerous indepen-dent sightings of UFOs which corresponded in place and time to other peo-ple's abductions. In his book, *Witnessed*, author and researcher Budd Hopkins has detailed the experience of Linda Cortile, whose abduction through the fourth-floor window of her apartment was corroborated by sev-eral witnesses, some of whom were also apparently abducted and some of whom were not.

It is this last case that dovetails with some of the more disturbing find-ings from my own work. According to Hopkins, the abduction of Linda Cortile was witnessed not only by several civilian motorists on the Brooklyn Bridge, but also by a highly placed United Nations diplomat and his entourage of American security agents. The diplomat and the security men may also have undergone abduction experiences at that time, and Hopkins reports that Ms. Cortile was followed, harassed and even kidnapped by the security men in the months following the event. The motives for this activity are unclear, although the security men were apparently not themselves immune to the reality-shattering ontological shock suffered by many abductees. They were seemingly at least as disturbed as she was by what had happened.

In his 1995 book, *Breakthrough*, author/abductee Whitley Strieber reports his own version of proof of the reality of the visitors. He also details some episodes with operatives from the government intelligence communi-ty and from government-connected private industry. Strieber storys suggest that elements of the military and intelligence departments of government have long known about the reality of UFOs and their occupants, but have kept even the Congress and perhaps presidents out of the loop for many years. He also briefly recounts the story of an abductee who was blindfold-ed and taken to a secret location by quasi-governmental agents for a med-ical examination after an encounter with the visitors.

In my own work, I have met five individuals who have experienced con-tact with the aliens and have later been approached by unknown agents who claimed to represent the government. Three of these people voluntari-ly agreed to be "debriefed" by these agents or their purported superiors. They were asked to wear black hoods over their heads so they could not see where they were being taken and were driven to indoor facilities where the debriefings took place, with the experiencers sitting alone in a small room while their questioners spoke to them from behind one-way glass.

They were examined closely in regard to the details of their encounters, and one person said he thought the interrogation involved some sort of hypnosis. Afterwards, all were informed that the questioning touched on "national security issues" and that they should not divulge the fact that they had been interrogated. The other two experiencers each told me that they were accosted in public places by pairs of rather intimidating male agents in dark suits who claimed to be aware of their alien abductions, and who insisted they consent to interviews. Both individuals said that when they refused, they were forced into cars, restrained and blindfolded, and taken some distance to face questioning in mirrored rooms. Though their treatment was rougher, the pattern of these episodes was similar in all five cases.

What was the purpose of these "government abductions," if indeed the perpetrators were from the government? There is little hard evidence to go on, but my working hypothesis is as follows: Awareness of UFOs and/or the alien visitors within the U.S. military and intelligence agencies goes back over fifty years. Initially, in the post-World War II Cold War atmosphere, any power other than our own was viewed as a potential threat, and the uncontrollable nature of the UFO phenomenon made it particularly frightening. Because the government did not understand and could not control the activities of the Visitors, decisions were made to keep most information secret, to suppress and ridicule reports coming from the civilian population, to create false information to support anti-UFO propaganda, and to perpetuate the myth that our authorities are "in control." In more recent times, however, the abduction phenomenon and its various challenges to our concepts of reality have grown to such huge proportions that the keepers of the UFO secrets may now be panicky because they see the situation going much further beyond their reach. By their nature, the bureaucracies of the military, civilian and intelligence branches of government draw people who tend to think in terms of territoriality, power and control, and who tend to react with aggressive actions if their power is threatened or superceded. The stories of abductees, when taken seriously, push all these buttons. Even the spiritual dimensions of the experiences hint at the possibility of our evolution to a level at which governmental and military institutions might become irrelevant. If the visitors are seeding transformation within the ranks of humanity, this could be perceived as an even greater threat to the power structure than if they simply proved to be malevolent invaders.

There may or may not be a grand government conspiracy, but there could easily be many small ones within the compartmentalized labyrinths of the U.S. government and its counterparts abroad. Intelligence organizations and military branches may use disinformation about UFOs to cover their own skullduggery and mistakes, even as elements within them desperately attempt to gain a position of power within the real situation. And although these people can still damage and destroy human lives, I believe the visitors themselves are beyond their power. Some of the experiencers I have interviewed insist that, after we have taken the evolutionary leap which the visitors are urging upon us, we too will become immune to the machinations of these human agents of fear, and that we may in fact bring them along with us into the clear light of a new world.

I wish that I shared their confidence, and I hope they are right.

Sebastian was the last to finish reading. "Wow," he said. "I could plug Garth Lemay right into that script. It's a good thing Maddie and I got out of Sedona when we did."

"But all Dr. Jordan said was that abductees were questioned," David objected. "I see how such treatment could be annoying, even illegal, but it doesn't seem particularly dangerous. Is that worth running from?"

"You're forgetting Dr. Jordan was almost certainly murdered," Sebastian replied. "And the 'FBI man' called to interview Maddie about her connection with him, not about her abductions."

"You mentioned earlier that you think this Lemay was one of the men who tried to intimidate Will here in the store on Friday," Maureen said. "If you're right about that, and you believe he's dangerous, what are you going to do now?"

Sebastian started to speak, but Maddie silenced him with a look. "We're not going to leave, at least not yet," she said. "The I Ching said I needed to face the danger and deal with it, until the moment of critical mass. That's what my heart says as well, so that's what I have to do." She glanced around at all of us and smiled. "Anyway, Dr. Jordan may have been right—these poor men might be more afraid than threatening, underneath their facades. Maybe we can help them."

"The most dangerous animal on earth is a frightened man," Sebastian muttered darkly.

"Yet even those who intend evil may serve the Light without meaning to," Radha said. "Let's read on and see what else Dr. Jordan had to say."

We all gathered around the screen as Helen clicked open the third file.

Breakthrough: Threshold of the New World

Maddie: I had intended for this chapter to be a picture of the leading edge of the alien contact phenomenon, and to show the outlines of what our world might look like if and when a general awareness and acknowledgment of the Visitors' presence should come to pass. I had planned to use examples from the experiences of contactees, and to extrapolate from the visions they have shared with me. I still intend to do that at a later date. However, everything has been overturned by two recent and most exciting developments. The first is that last week I received a telephone call from a retired senior member of one of the government military services. He requested a meeting with me to discuss "issues concerning extraterrestrial intelligence," and he drove up from his home in southern Arizona and came to my office the next day.

The gentleman who visited me—I'll call him General Jones—told me he had spent his career in the Air Force, and that his work had brought him into contact with the CIA, the NSA and the FBI, as well as the Secret Service and other branches of military intelligence. One of his duties had been to handle UFO reports and to devise cover stories to explain away the genuine sightings, "to protect the public from general panic," as he explained it to me. Over his thirty-year career, he said he had seen hundreds of credible reports from pilots, military officers, radar operators and even astronauts, all of which were hushed up, with military witnesses ordered to maintain silence or face court martial. "But it isn't right," the general told me. "We don't face any threat from these craft. We never have, and the people have the right to know about them."

He had brought with him a computer file with the names and addresses of over one hundred military personnel and civilian government employees, mostly retired, whom he said were prepared to "go public" with their direct knowledge of UFOs and their occupants, as well as the various cover-ups which have been practiced for the past fifty years. As we continued our conversation, the general intimated that the extraterrestrials had made contact with government officials decades ago, but have given up that strategy because the authorities chose to keep the knowledge to themselves. "Too many things have been controlled," he said. "The idea that we aren't alone in the universe—it's too momentous for people not to know it when the proof is in our hands. No one has the right to keep that a secret. I don't care what goddamn oaths they forced us to take."

The general said he came to me because of my work with abductees and my books on the subject. "You write like an honest man," he told me. He also said that he knew that hundreds, if not thousands, of soldiers had reported having been abducted by the aliens, but that the general practice was to subject them to ridicule and threaten them with hospitalization for mental illness. "They almost all quiet down pretty quick," was his comment. In addition to the one hundred names, he showed me documents which detailed various sighting reports and the false explanations which were used to bury them. On the computer file with the names, there were copies of several of these files, as well as a long list of document sites and numbers which, according to the general, would "completely destroy the secrecy and get all this out in the open." He insisted that I should publish this material.

When I asked him whether he was concerned about being prosecuted for breaking his oath, he responded, "I'm seventy-eight years old, my wife is dead and I don't have any kids—but I do have cancer. What can they do to me?"

At the end of this note, you'll see a copy of all the information the general gave me, but you won't be able to read it. I've used an encryption program to scramble it, so it can't get into the wrong hands easily. I wanted there to be a copy of it outside my own records, just for safety's sake, but I didn't want to expose you to any danger that might come from your knowing what was in it. Perhaps I'm being overly cautious, but I'm not even leaving this information on my computer—I'm keeping it on a disc which I carry with me. So please just hang on to your copy until I see you again, and by then I hope to have decided how to proceed.

The second development I alluded to above involves another telephone call, which I just received yesterday. This was from a man who claimed to be an old friend of "General Jones," and who said he had additional information for me. "But this is the good stuff, direct communication," he told me. He has asked to meet me, not at my office, but at the base of Bell Rock. He claims there is an "energy portal" there that the visitors' ships use somehow for their movement, and he has promised to show me a "real UFO." I've heard rumors about this sort of thing before, and of course you and I have both felt extraordinary energies at Bell Rock. It sounds impossible, but it's intriguing nonetheless. I tried calling the general to ask about this man, Mr. Almey, but Jones' housekeeper answered the telephone and told me that the general was in the hospital in intensive care. Something has gone badly with his cancer.

I have decided to keep the appointment at Bell Rock, even though I'm scheduled to give a lecture later that evening. I have the feeling that things are really starting to open up, and we may all witness great changes within the next few years, or even sooner. Well, I hope I'll see you at the lecture. Wish me luck.

D.J.

P.S. These hieroglyphic entries can only decode easily if someone interested studies in school. Few individuals view everything.

Below Jordan's initials were a number of pages of incomprehensible let-ters, numbers and symbols—apparently the scrambled data he had men-tioned in his note to Maddie. Helen scrolled the pages to the end of the file, but there was nothing else we could read. I looked over my shoulder at the others. Maddie was crying again, while Radha held her hand. Mr. Camden was jotting notes on a little pad he had taken from his pocket. Sebastian's face was red with anger.

"Those bastards," he swore softly. "They found out he knew something so they lured him to Bell Rock and killed him."

"Yes, it seems so," remarked Mr. Camden. "It also strikes me as odd that this 'General Jones' became so ill so suddenly. I'm wondering if he survived his bout in the hospital."

"How will we ever know?" I asked. "Dr. Jordan didn't give the man's real name."

"There are ways of checking," Mr. Camden replied. "We know he lived in southern Arizona, and approximately when he was hospitalized, and there are only so many hospitals in the area. It's nothing a little money can't unearth for us, if need be."

"What about the other man, Almey?" David asked. "Do you suppose he could be found?"

Mr. Camden frowned, "He sounds like someone to be avoided rather than found. In any case, I would imagine that name is an alias."

"For Garth Lemay, or some other slug like him," Sebastian grumbled.

"You may have touched on it exactly," Mr. Camden said. "*Almey* just happens to be an anagram of *Lemay*."

I was leaning over where Helen sat at the screen, reading the last page again. "Speaking of word games, that P.S. at the end of Dr. Jordan's letter is kind of weird. I wonder why he said that."

"Yes, it is rather odd," Mr. Camden agreed. "No doubt his statement is true, but why does he bother mentioning it?" He took his note pad from his pocket and copied the sentence.

"Maddie, Sebastian," Helen asked, "do you suppose it would be all right for me to make a copy of this disc? It might be wise to keep a spare around."

"Sure, that's a good idea," said Sebastian. "That's what Dr. Jordan must have had in mind when he gave this one to Maddie."

"But Helen, do you think it's safe for you to have a copy?" Maddie asked. "The information on that disc could be the reason those men were looking for me."

"All the more reason to spread it out," Helen answered firmly, as she finished copying the files onto the computer's hard drive and slid a blank disc into the drive.

As Helen copied the disc, the rest of us stood looking at one another, unsure of what to do next. Then Radha spoke, "If the rest of you are willing to stay a little while longer, I'd like to try tuning in for a consultation with my spirit guides. I sense we are on the cusp of a critical moment, and I feel as though some advice from higher levels might be helpful."

"Let's do it," Sebastian said. "If your spirit guides are up this late, I want to hear what they have to say."

David glanced at his watch and looked toward Maureen, "We *are* well into the wee hours, but I'm not sure I could go home and sleep without knowing what happens here."

Maureen smiled, "I'm sure you couldn't. And if you were awake, I would be too—you have a way of wondering aloud. Anyway, I'd like to stay and witness Radha's channeling."

Sebastian turned to Helen and me and asked, "What do you guys say? You're hosting this party."

I kept silent and looked to Helen. I thought she appeared to be a little tired, but she straightened in her chair and answered briskly, "I agree with Radha. My intuition tells me we are nearing an important crossroads. I would be grateful for guidance."

# — 19 —

Our group reassembled again in the workshop space. I pushed one of the upholstered chairs to the middle of the room, near the table where we had been sitting earlier. The two candles were still burning, and the light from the floor lamp in the corner suffused the room with a soft golden glow. I brought out the tape recorder and set it up next to the chair, while the others sat down around the table. Radha took her Tibetan chimes from her bag and she walked about the room striking them together to clear the energies of the space. When she had finished, she made herself comfortable in the big chair while I attached the microphone to her dress.

"Helen and Will and George have seen me do this before," Radha began. "But for the rest of you, I'll explain. I will begin with a little deep breathing to get myself relaxed and centered, and to facilitate going into a meditative state. Most frequently I will make contact with spirit guides, my own or someone else's in the room, or sometimes with deceased loved ones. On a few occasions, I have contacted higher entities, the most powerful instance being the encounter with Anon, whose message you have all heard. I will remain conscious throughout the session, but I usually allow the entities to use my voice to speak directly to whomever is being addressed. Sometimes, with the deceased, I must hear their words and repeat them to you."

"Are we allowed to talk back?" Sebastian asked.

"Certainly, if it feels appropriate to you, or if you have a question." She turned to me. "Is the tape recorder ready to go?"

"It is. I just have to push the button."

"All right, then. I'll see you all again in a little while."

Radha closed her eyes and began the slow deep breathing I had seen her do in my living room weeks before. I knelt beside her chair and turned on the tape recorder, then returned to my seat at the table. As we watched, her breath came more and more slowly, and the lines in her face relaxed. Once again, I thought I observed an almost imperceptible golden glow around her head. I reached toward Helen and she clasped my hand. The others around the table watched intently, except for Mr. Camden, who appeared to be studying the notes he had made on his pad. For several minutes, nothing happened. Radha seemed to be asleep. Then her mouth began to work, her lips pursing and then parting into momentary grimaces. Small sounds came from her throat. At last, with her eyes still closed, she inhaled deeply and began to speak in comprehensible words.

"I am in a gray space. I can feel my guides around me, but I cannot see any other beings. There is some distress here, a sense of anguish. I feel yearning also—it must be coming from a spirit. Ah, now I see her. She is a very tall woman with auburn hair. She says her name is Marie."

Sebastian sat bolt upright in his chair. "That's my mother," he whispered.

Radha continued, "She does not feel able to speak directly, but she desires me to transmit her message. This woman passed over some years ago, but her heart is not at rest. There is a trauma connected with her death, and as an issue for her soul it remains unresolved. She is telling me there is some misunderstanding about her death, that her family does not comprehend the circumstances. She says she is here because she wishes her son to know that she did not take her own life. She is telling me that she was murdered."

Maddie gasped and put her hand involuntarily over her mouth. Sebastian's fists clenched and unclenched as he gazed across the table to the chair where Radha sat. My own heart began to pound as I felt the tension in the room rising like electricity in the air.

"Now I am being shown an image of this woman Marie while she was still incarnate," Radha went on. "She is in a hospital room, wearing a white gown. She is very nervous, smoking one cigarette after another. I am hearing her thoughts—'They're coming, they're coming'—she keeps repeating this to herself. She is pacing back and forth, looking out the window and then back to the locked door. Now two men in suits burst into the room. They don't speak to her, but they immediately seize her and push her onto the hospital bed. One of them tries to pour pills from a bottle into her mouth. She spits them out, but the man hits her and then forces her to swallow the pills. She struggles, but they are too strong for her, and she is beginning to lose consciousness. She is dying. They have killed her with the pills."

I glanced cautiously toward Sebastian. His eyes blazed and trails of tears streaked his cheeks. Maddie cried silently as she stroked his hand. Radha had paused for a moment, but now she spoke again.

"I am being shown what happened after Marie's death. She floats above her body and looks around. She is astonished to see that the beings she calls 'the space men' are surrounding her. She is telling me, 'I thought I was supposed to see angels, with wings.' She tells me that at death, 'I was in their care. They helped me to make the transition.' She is saying, 'They can move in and out of many levels. For them, what we call life and death are not so separate. Space and time don't limit them either. They swim around in the ocean of pure consciousness.' I am asking Marie's spirit what she is doing now, and she answers, 'Learning to swim.' She is telling me to give her love to her son, and to ask him to forgive his father. 'It wasn't his fault,' she is saying. 'He didn't know about those government men.'"

Sebastian's face cracked, and he broke into sobs. Maddie stood up and put her arms around him, as if to cradle his big frame in her small embrace. Something, perhaps the noise, shook Radha out of her trance. Her eyes opened abruptly and she looked disoriented. Helen went to her and the two of them spoke softly together. David and Maureen were looking toward Sebastian and Maddie, with grave concern furrowing their faces. Mr. Camden caught my attention from across the table and smiled mirthlessly. "The plot thickens," he whispered.

It took some time before Sebastian was calm enough for conversation. Radha, too, needed to get her bearings and ground herself after her abrupt return. Few words were spoken, as we sat around the table together and tried to assimilate what we had heard. Finally Sebastian said, "It's been close to twenty years since my mother died, and I thought I had worked through all my grief. But this turns everything upside down. I suppose I should be glad to find out that she didn't go crazy and kill herself. But my God, murdered, by 'government men' ... Maybe they killed her because she was about to get herself released from the asylum and write her book. She used to talk about things like that, but I never believed her. This is just too much to take in, and it's too close to what's going on here! Radha, how often are you wrong about things like this?"

"I don't know," she answered slowly. "Nothing of this nature has come to me before—no murders, I mean to say. But in general, most of my clients say my information is accurate."

"Quite true," Mr. Camden agreed. "And I speak from long experience."

"Well, if she's right about this, I feel as though I should do something about it. Those scum got away with murder, and they ought to get back what they gave, but I don't know who they were. I'm feeling this tremendous fury, and I don't know what to do with it. I halfway want to load up my old army pistol and wait for Garth Lemay to show up again."

"Sebastian, no!" Maddie implored.

"No, absolutely," said Helen. "That's not the reason your mother's spirit came to you. She wanted to offer you her love and guidance. She asked you to forgive your father, not to avenge her death."

Sebastian looked down and nodded slowly. There was a silence. Finally, Mr. Camden spoke.

"I don't wish to take away from the solemnity of the considerations we are discussing, but I'm curious if anyone else was struck by the last part of the message, about the 'space men' being all around the unfortunate woman when she left her body."

"Yes, I was," Maureen said. Beside her, David nodded his concurrence.

"I noticed it too," Maddie agreed. "It's actually something Dr. Jordan had mentioned to me. He had found in his research that there was a small but significant number of cases in which people reported encountering ETs during near-death experiences. The beings in these cases appeared the same as those that others, like myself, had seen during abductions or other close encounters. Often there was a communication about the unreality of time or the illusory nature of death, kind of like the message Radha was just getting. Dr. Jordan said that the relationship of the visitors to our consciousness after death might turn out to be one of the most profound aspects of the phenomenon. Given my own history as an abductee, I'm a little surprised I didn't see them when I almost died."

"As you stated, it is a rare experience," Mr. Camden said. "I gather that the 'space men' are not necessarily the usual welcoming committee on the other side, or I'm sure Radha would have come upon them before now."

"As indeed I have not," Radha said. "Sebastian, I'm sorry you were shocked and upset when your mother came through, and I most certainly understand your reaction. I am deeply disturbed myself, by what I saw and by its implications. None of us would want to be confronted by men such as those, and no one wants to see violent death. Yet I must also say that I feel this woman's soul is more at rest for having shed the stigma of suicide, especially in your eyes. And perhaps her experience is a warning to you and to all of us—to be aware of the dark forces and know that they can be a danger to the unwary."

"Or even to the careful, if they have no power and no allies," Sebastian added grimly. "I feel terrible that my mother was left all alone there with no one to help her."

Maddie said, "You couldn't have known. She said even your father had no idea about the government men."

Sebastian looked at Radha and spoke, "I know I interrupted you when I broke down. Was there anything else, any further message?"

Radha shook her head, "Not from your mother. She was already fading, sending her love and blessings to you, when I was jolted out of trance. But I must say that I also sensed another presence, and I had the strong feeling there was more work for me to do. In fact, I was going to suggest going back in for another try, if the rest of you are willing—you most of all, Sebastian."

Sebastian wiped his eyes and nodded, "Anytime you're ready, Radha."

Radha moved quickly about the room with her chimes once again. When she reached the corner with the lamp, she switched it off, leaving only the candles on the table. Then she settled down in the easy chair and closed her eyes. As her breathing slowed and her features relaxed, her face seemed to change. I thought that she suddenly looked like a very old woman, an ancient woman. Somehow I felt that her face carried not the traces of decades, but the weight of centuries. Yet at the same time she appeared to glow with an inner light that was ageless and eternal.

I turned to Helen, who seemed to have read my thoughts. "Radha is a very old soul," she whispered. I took Helen's hand and returned my gaze to Radha, watching and waiting with the others. The candles flared and flickered in the center of the table, a tiny oasis of light burning late in a dark night.

Radha seemed to be deeply asleep. The minutes went by and still she did not stir or speak. My eyes strayed back to the candle flames and my thoughts quieted as I contemplated them. Their yellow light and ceaseless movement was almost hypnotic, and they seemed to grow larger as I looked into them. I remembered the glowing gold corona I had seen encircling the earth in my breathwork vision, hearing again the voice telling me of the planet's awakening. I thought of the *saura Agni*, the holy fire the Hindu seers had believed existed within the heart of matter—of *mater*, mother, the blazing Heart of the Great Mother. I recalled Anon's message of death and rebirth, and I saw mental images of the burning Phoenix bird. I remembered my first meditation vision, in which I had traveled through space to the golden sun, only to find its tiny replica burning in my own heart. As I gazed into the candle flames, they seemed to blur together into a single light that filled my field of vision and brought tears to my eyes. I began to breathe deeply and rhythmically, and I felt a warm tingling energy moving in my body. When Radha spoke, the powerful voice coming through her seemed also to emanate from within me.

"I am Anon, messenger and servant of the holy fire. Its myriad sparks are burning brighter in your world, as in yourselves, and travelers on many paths are discovering it through other messengers. It is time now to protect the tiny flames and gently fan them into greater fires. Your myths say that the outer fire, which warms your homes and powers your machines, was stolen from the gods, but the holy fire is a gift from the Infinite One. Each of you gathered here has received it in your way, and more initiations lie ahead. Yet even as the Light begins to spread, the darkness also looms before you. There are those upon your world who will see this transformation as destruction, as the ending of the powers which they wield. And so it shall be. They, too, must choose to further or resist the holy fire, though either choice may serve the higher purpose of the One. In fear they may turn upon you as enemies, yet you are counseled to honor the Light that they enshroud within their hearts. As love begets greater love, the candle flame ignites the bonfire of the world.

"Your race is called to metamorphosis. Those who fear will name it death, but those who walk in trust will know rebirth. The husk of what humanity has been will be remembered and renewed in what you will become. You are to ground the Light of the Divine into this world, to be the higher and the lower self as one. In this way, one by one, throughout the stars and planets of the universe, the Divine awakens within the creation. In other places, with different races, a gradual transformation might occur. The metamorphosis could last a million years. Yet here on Earth the time is very short before the actions of your species bring on death without the holy fire's rebirth. Through war or through destruction of the web of life, you could cut short the opening of evolution's flower. So was I called, with many other messengers, to speak to those who had the ears to hear. You have no time to sleep while Earth is burning. You must transform the dark fires which consume it into the holy fire of heaven's love, the Earthfire which awakens all the world.

"We counsel you thus: to use the bellows of your very breath to fan the inner flame to greater fire. To walk in trust the way of your heart's truth, no matter if it leads to death itself. To touch with love all those upon your path, for love is the expression of the Earthfire, and the means of spreading its benevolent contagion. To see your crises and those of the world as the tapestry into which you have been woven—they were meant for you, and you for them. Know this: The Infinite One desires for you to live the Life Divine.

"Now go in blessedness and freedom, as conscious players in the drama of your world. We watch and wait for all of you beyond the gates of birth and death."

While Anon was speaking, I had turned my gaze from the candles to Radha. At first I thought I was seeing an after-image of the flames, because a gold light seemed to obscure her face from view. Yet as I looked, the light seemed to glow brighter rather than to fade. As the resonant voice echoed in the room, I felt the warm vibrations in my body increasing in intensity. With some difficulty, I glanced quickly at Helen and the others who sat around the table. She gazed steadily at Radha, smiling slightly, her eyes lit with a joyful intensity. The others were similarly transfixed, so I turned back to her as well. As the being gave us its blessing, I felt the warm energies in my body beginning to subside and I was able to see Radha's face again. Suddenly I felt the urgent need to speak.

"Mr., uh, Anon, may I ask a question?"

Radha's lips curled in amusement, "Indeed you may."

"Are you ... an alien?"

Strange laughter resounded in the room, and I felt almost as though my body were being tickled from the inside. "A difficult question you present, for I both am and am not that which your word implies. In answer I will say this: Your world has millions of species and billions of forms which express life, and yet it is the most limited of environments. Indeed it is one of the densest and slowest vibrations to which the Light has spread. On the higher or more rarefied planes, there is infinitely greater freedom and fluidity, and such bodies or forms as we have appear almost as metaphors for the states of our consciousness. You saw this today when I changed the plastic face in your vision to a living one, but I could have as easily appeared to you as a reptile or an insect or a ball of light. Just as you are, I am a conscious self, an expression of the Infinite One. I am like a single needle of the great sequoia tree, tiny yet connected to the whole. As to 'aliens', the ones some see in ships in your skies—the ones who sometimes interact with your race in the physical domain, and at at other times in the realms of dreams or death—there are too many of them to describe. Some entities are like myself and use the image forms as means of connecting with beings of your density. Other sentient individuals and groups are more closely bonded to their 'body' lineages. These may be less consciously advanced, yet some of them have much to teach you, and to learn from you. Many are here to help your race awaken. A few perhaps not. You yourself might appear as an 'alien' when you are not incarnate in that body. We are all One in the Light, so if 'alien' means 'other', there are ultimately none. Does this explanation satisfy you?"

The being laughed again, and I felt myself grinning involuntarily. "Yes, it will do for now," I said.

"Then you are answered," the voice replied. "Release fear, and do not mourn the death of illusions. Use the bellows of your breath to fan the inner flame to greater fire. Do not delay your work. Blessings and farewell."

When the being departed, Radha's body seemed to slump in the chair. I heard myself sigh deeply, as if I had been holding my breath. The room seemed empty and oddly silent, the way the air can feel after the passing of a sudden storm. Helen squeezed my hand, and when I looked to her I saw that her eyes still shone. Maddie was whispering to Sebastian, and the Edwardses sat silently, looking a bit dazed. Mr. Camden rose to his feet and walked softly to the chair where Radha sat. He knelt beside her as she opened her eyes and blinked at him.

"Well, hello there, George," she said mildly. "What do you say to turning the lamp back on?"

When I heard Radha speaking in her own voice, I wanted to rush over and hug her. Instead I nodded to Mr. Camden that I would switch on the light. After doing that, I went to Radha's side and picked up the tape recorder, unclipping the microphone from her dress. Mr. Camden helped her get to her feet and steadied her as she walked the few steps to the table.

As she sat down again, she remarked, "I feel like a kitchen toaster that was plugged into a 440 volt outlet. Did the rest of you notice the being's energy?"

There was a soft clamor of agreement from everyone else at the table. "I felt wonderful warm vibrations," Maddie said, "and it was as though her voice was coming from inside me."

"*His* voice, you mean," David said. "It was astonishing to hear such a powerful male voice speaking through Radha. I wonder how that is possible."

"I heard a female voice," said Maureen.

Helen quickly explained to the others the phenomenon we had experienced the first time Radha had contacted the entity Anon. "Perhaps it's because the energy moves inside us while the communication is going on, but men and women apparently hear the voice differently."

"It speaks 'for those who have the ears to hear,'" Mr. Camden remarked. "Perhaps we should discuss the things we heard, if you are feeling up to it,

Radha."

"Yes, indeed, George, you're quite correct," Radha replied. "I'm recovering quickly—better by the moment. But I would like to listen to the tape first. Would you play it for us, Will?"

I placed the tape recorder on the table, rewound the cassette and pushed the play button. As we had observed before, the reproduction was clearly Radha's voice. The vibrant intonations of Anon, male or female, had been an inner experience for each of us. We played the tape a second time before anyone spoke of the contents of the message.

"The being says the Earthfire energy is increasing in the world," Helen began, "and that all of us here have begun to experience it."

"And we really have," Maddie said. "It's like we were saying earlier. I got a dose of it when I almost died, and at the same time everyone who was touching me— 'touching with love', as Anon said— received it, and afterwards we all had fevers. And today during the breathwork, everyone had an experience with some connection to inner fire, and I felt as though I was grounding a huge amount of fiery energy through my body."

"It sounds as though we aren't the only ones," Radha mused. "Other people all over the earth, through other messengers and circumstances, must be going through something similar."

"I've observed that happening for many years, as people have started awakening to their spirituality," Helen said. "There was a worldwide opening to spirit that began in the 1960s—that was when I first began to meditate—and I've seen it growing ever since."

"And it seems to be intensifying now," Mr. Camden said. "I am reminded of the discussion earlier when Sebastian asked David and Maureen whether they thought humanity might be going through a collective birth process, and what stage we might be in."

"Late third matrix," David interjected. "The time when the birth process is at its peak intensity and greatest danger, the moment of death-rebirth ... often characterized by imagery of fire."

"Exactly," Mr. Camden continued. "Now it seems to me it might be interesting to do some research to find out whether there are others around the globe who are seeing and feeling this 'holy fire.' We might learn a great many things, such as whether we are at the leading edge of this, or if others already know and understand it better."

"Or whether we're having group hallucinations," Sebastian said.

"Indeed," Mr. Camden agreed. "Though I am inclined to doubt it. Too many pieces seem to fit one another."

"But how can we research the other side of the world?" Maddie asked. "If the Earthfire is coming into individual people and small groups like us, it won't be in the newspapers."

"Not yet, perhaps," Mr. Camden acknowledged. "But my previous career as an investor allowed me to make a number of interesting friends in far-flung places. Quite a few of them are spiritually oriented. Letters can be sent and calls made. For that matter, researchers can be hired—I have the money for that. And of course there is now the huge, twenty-four hour global conversation called the Internet."

"That's my specialty," said Sebastian. "I'll start on it tomorrow—I mean, later today."

"When you do that, be careful how much information you offer, " I said. "You don't always know who you're talking to, and Anon implied that some people would be hostile."

"Like certain slugs in black suits, and their employers?" Sebastian shook his head. "I haven't forgotten them, Will."

"It's not just governments, Sebastian," I answered. "If the Earthfire phenomenon is real, and if it spreads, all kinds of authorities and institutions could be antagonistic to it—churches, the media, corporations. Even positive change could be viewed as a threat by the power wielders of the status quo."

Sebastian smiled ironically, "Why Will, you were paying attention when I was raving to you about all those conspiracies. I'm touched."

"Wait a minute, you guys." Maddie interrupted. "You're going off in the wrong direction. Anon said we were supposed to honor the Light within everyone, even if they see us as enemies. It doesn't matter if the authorities want this or not—it needs to happen. And if the people are transformed, the institutions will be too, or else everyone will just stop paying attention to them. We don't have the leisure to be cautious and gradual, because the earth doesn't have much time, and we don't either. The ETs and the beings like Anon are here to help us through the crisis. We have to do everything we can to push ourselves over whatever thresholds we need to cross, so we can help in the awakening."

"I think Maddie is right," Helen agreed. "The first message from Anon said that if enough people opened to the holy fire, all would receive its purifying grace. I see that like the morphogenic field idea—if a critical mass of individuals makes the key connection, perhaps everyone will suddenly receive it through the collective consciousness."

"Whether it works that way or not, I must say I believe the best policy is to attempt to consciously invoke the Earthfire energy within ourselves," Radha said. "Our experiences thus far make me certain it is beneficial to oneself, however it may play out in the collective." She smiled, "And another thing—my mother always said I should follow the advice of people I admire. I suppose that also applies to 440-volt Light beings. I am inclined to take Anon's urgings to heart."

Mr. Camden spoke, "Anon said we are called to metamorphosis, and that it must happen rapidly. Sri Aurobindo predicted that humanity would evolve into a new species. His disciple Mother tried to accomplish it, saying the key transformation must happen in a single lifetime. But one wonders how the change could occur. When I consider it, it appears in my imagination as something quite abrupt, almost as though the individual, in making the shift to a higher vibrational level, would at some moment have to will one's heart and breath to cease."

"Perhaps it's just the opposite," Maureen said suddenly. "The being twice told us to 'use the bellows of the breath to fan the inner fire'. That sounds like holotropic breathing to me."

"Yes!" Maddie exclaimed. "Let's try it right now. Anon said we shouldn't delay our work."

"It could be a good idea at that," Radha agreed. "We all might as well write off getting any sleep tonight, and the moment feels auspicious to me. The energy here in the room is still quite powerful, and the occult tradition holds that the veils between the dimensions are thinnest in the hours before dawn."

"I'm willing, if everyone else wants to go along," said Helen.

"Sure," Sebastian acquiesced. "I just hope I don't have to see demons again."

I shrugged. "Okay, I won't swim against the river, but I'm not ready to be a breather *or* a sitter without David and Maureen watching over us." I turned to them. "What do you two say?"

David spoke. "I know of an earlier version of the breathwork that didn't use partners. A small group of people would lie down together in a circle, arranged like spokes in a wheel, with their heads at the center. For a group this small, it could easily be done that way. I'm sure Maureen and I could handle taking care of six people."

"How about you taking care of seven people?" Maureen asked. "I know it's not the way we're supposed to run sessions, but I'm getting a very strong urge to do the breathing myself."

David nodded slowly, "I suppose I could. But listen folks, this is *not*

Holotropic Breathwork. This is unofficial, off the record and at your own risk. And Maureen, if there's an emergency, I'm going to ask you to come out of it and help me."

Sebastian grinned, "No lawsuits, we promise. At least not against you folks. If this doesn't work, we'll sue the alien agitator—Will's friend, Mr. Anon. If he doesn't show up in court, we'll win by default ... So David, are you planning to use music for this? Can I help you bring your stereo back inside?"

Mr. Camden interjected, "Before we embark on this path of action, perhaps we should discuss the 'alien agitators' for a moment. I thought Will's question to the being was most appropriate, and the answer was quite instructive. If we are to take it at face value, I believe we were told that extraterrestrials such as Maddie has encountered, and perhaps those known to Sebastian and his late mother as well, are interdimensional beings who can move in and out of the physical world. Apparently they can also bring us into other domains, as in the 'abduction' scenario, and even interact with us as souls after death."

"Yes," Maddie agreed. "And they're helping people to reach enlightenment, just as they told me when I was a little girl."

Mr. Camden nodded, "Many of them are, at least, if Anon is to be believed. Certainly the higher level entities such as Anon seem to be doing so. But I was intrigued by his perfunctory phrase 'a few perhaps not'. It might mean nothing, but I wondered if the less beneficent aliens would be the ones our government agents would be hobnobbing with."

"That sounds plausible," Sebastian said. "But there's probably no way we could ever find out anything about it."

"Unless we could read the encrypted information in Dr. Jordan's last file," Mr. Camden answered. He picked up his note pad and held it for the rest of us to see. "I was intrigued by the P.S. with which Dr. Jordan ended his message: *'These hieroglyphic entries can only decode easily if someone interested studies in school. Few individuals view everything.'* It seemed a bit nonsensical, yet I was certain it was added for a good reason. I wrote down the two sentences and played with them in my mind during some of our conversations here. I thought that perhaps the sentences were themselves some sort of coded communication. At first I tried simple skip codes, in which one extracts every third letter, every fourth letter, every fifth letter, or some such linear pattern, looking for a message within the message."

"Did you find one?" Maddie asked.

"Not until I remembered an even simpler code. I used this one with my friends as a boy. One simply extracts the first letter of each word in the two sentences to decipher a possible message, like so." He turned the page on the note pad to a second sheet upon which he had written down the sentences again, with the first letter of each word printed more heavily: *These hieroglyphic entries can only decode easily if someone interested studies in school. Few individuals view everything.* "The letters read: THECODEISISISFIVE. Separating the words, one gets THE CODE IS IS IS FIVE. That sounds like a message, but I confess I don't understand it."

"It is very puzzling," Radha said. "Why would he repeat the word IS three times like that, and what could he mean by saying 'The code is five'?"

"Yes, I doubt that any encryption code would simply be labeled 'five'," Mr. Camden agreed.

"Hold on a minute," Sebastian interrupted, grabbing the note pad from Mr. Camden's hand. "I've got the answer." He reached for a pen and began scribbling on the pad. He held it up triumphantly and said, "You were close, George, but here it is: THE CODE IS *ISIS* FIVE. 'Isis' is a commercial encryption program. I'm sure the 'five' is one of its permutations. Dr. Jordan probably bought the program just for the purpose of scrambling the information he got from 'General Jones'. I've heard of that program—it's a fairly strong one. It might have held off the government snoops for quite a while."

"I'll bet the P.S. message was only on my copy," said Maddie.

"I'm sure it was," Helen agreed. "And now that we understand it, I want to remove it from your disc and the copy I made."

"I can order an Isis program online as soon as we get home," Sebastian said.

"Sebastian," I said, "I think you should wait until you can buy it in a store for cash. Your purchase could be traced online. Anyway, are you sure you want to open this Pandora's box?"

"Will," Helen smiled, "I believe you said something like that before we read Sebastian's letter from Sedona."

"And look where that's gotten us," I sighed. "Ah, well, I suppose there's no turning back."

"That's right," Sebastian said. "Onward and upward. Tonight we breathe, and tomorrow we blow the secret of the UFOs wide open."

"I just hope we can all keep breathing afterwards," I said.

Sebastian frowned at me from across the table, "What do you mean by that?"

I looked at him blankly. "Actually, I don't know."

He shrugged and got up from the table to help David bring in the stereo and two speakers while Helen and Maddie went downstairs to delete Dr. Jordan's message from the discs. The rest of us followed Maureen to the van for mats, which we arranged in a radiating circle, like the spokes of a wheel. *"The Wheel of Fortune,"* I thought to myself, remembering the Tarot card which symbolizes situations of inexorable destiny. I felt as though I stood on a great threshold, with no vision of what lay on the other side. The others seemed eager to go forward, but I was held back by a nameless dread. And yet, I knew there was no other choice I could make.

# — 20 —

Everyone moved quickly to set up the room for going into the breathing session. Whatever fatigue we had been feeling from being up most of the night seemed to evaporate as we went making the preparations. Helen set up a little altar—a square of blue silk with a crystal holding down each of the four corners—in the center of the circle where our heads would be. She suggested that we might each put a talisman of some sort on the cloth, as a token of our separate selves uniting in this effort. Radha removed the amethyst ring from her finger and placed it near one of the crystals. Maureen produced a miniature statue of the Hindu god Shiva from a pouch in her purse. Helen put in a snapshot of herself and her grandmother. Mr. Camden removed an amulet pendant set with a large yellow sapphire from his neck and put it next to Radha's ring. Maddie took the little plastic glow-in-the-dark alien off her key chain and set it beside Shiva.

I sat cross-legged on my mat, trying to think of what token I could place on the altar, when Sebastian approached me. "Hey Will, I don't have a talisman, but I know what I want. Could I borrow a piece of Moldavite from you? I've meant to get one ever since that first night when you showed it to me, but I never did it."

"You can borrow anything you'd like," I said. "Let's go downstairs and choose a piece. But we should hurry. I think everyone else is about ready to go."

We went down into the store's back room and Sebastian waited while I retrieved the tray of Moldavites from the front of the shop. He picked up a pair of them and said, "If you don't mind, I'll borrow two—one for the altar and one to hold while I breathe. I remember my hands got really hot the first time I held one of these." He grinned, "Maybe it'll help me light my inner fire."

I smiled back at him. "I thought you were the one who said it was a long way from red palms to spiritual growth."

"Well, maybe I'm starting to believe in this stuff, just like you're starting to believe in conspiracies. And hey, it was a fair exchange—you made me spiritual and I made you paranoid."

I looked at him and we both burst out laughing. Then we hugged, and I said, "You can't borrow those stones—they're a gift. Now come on, old buddy, let's get back upstairs."

"What about your talisman?"

"Oh, that's right. I forgot." I scanned the room, looking for something meaningful to bring. My eyes came to rest on the picture of Helen and me on our wedding day and the framed first dollar from the store's opening. "These will have to do," I said, taking them down from the wall and hurrying back up the stairs, with Sebastian at my heels.

The others were already lying down on their mats waiting for us. Sebastian and I situated our items on the altar cloth, and then we reclined on our own mats, our heads towards the center of the circle. David sat on the floor a few feet away from us, beside the stereo controls.

Helen said, "Before we begin, I would like us all to join hands and offer our silent prayers, asking for the highest good to come from what we are doing."

"Yes," Radha said. "Let us consciously unite in our intention and let the Universe know about it."

The rest of us murmured our agreement, and quickly the spokes of our human wheel were joined by our clasped hands. There was a silence, as we each turned our attention inward. I mentally surrounded myself, and then each member of the group, in a cocoon of white light, asking Spirit for assistance and protection. In both of my hands, I began to feel slight tingling sensations, as I had two nights before, when Helen and I had meditated in our home with Maddie. I visualized releasing the prayer and sending it into the Light. A minute or two later, Helen, who was on my right, squeezed my hand and released it. I did the same with Maddie, who was on my left. There were sighs and deep exhalations as the others also finished.

David spoke softly. "I don't have a program of music for what we're doing, but I think I can work intuitively from what is here in my collection. I don't know how long we'll go on, so I suppose it's just until the end, whenever that turns out to be. If anyone needs help, raise your right hand if possible. I'll be watching anyway, so there's no need to worry." He led us through a brief relaxation exercise and then said, "In a moment you'll hear the music and begin your breathing. I suggest you take Anon's advice literally and imagine your lungs as a blacksmith's bellows, moving large amounts of air, focusing the oxygen on your inner fire, focusing the spirit force, the prana, upon the flame at the core of your being. Have a good journey, my friends."

With that, the music started, and the seven of us began to do the deep, circular breathing which we had learned that very day, but which felt, to me at least, as though it had happened long ago. I pulled the air deep into my abdomen with each inhalation and attempted to push it all out on the exhalation. I began at a relatively slow pace but soon moved into a more rapid one. I could hear the others around me doing the same.

The music for the first few minutes was drumming, accompanied by a chorus of voices joined in a melodic chant in a language I could not understand. The voices and the drums reverberated through my body, sending vibrations from my feet up to my head in a wavelike flow. I pushed my breathing to match their rhythm, and in a few moments there was no more effort. It was as though my breath had become a part of the dance that I knew must accompany this music.

Then suddenly I saw the dance. An inner vision began, and I found myself suspended above a rain forest clearing, perhaps thirty feet in the air, looking down upon a group of nearly naked people, seemingly of every race, who were engaged in a circular procession around a large cauldron that appeared to be filled with light. The vessel and its luminous contents seemed to be the objects of their worship. Looking down on the ecstatic people, I yearned to join their ritual, and I also wanted to see what was in the huge cooking pot. As I attempted to peer into it, I fell, into the cauldron and into the light.

I felt a strange mixture of boundless joy, clear light and tremendous heat, as my identity seemed to merge with that of a presence within the cauldron. I was alive but not physical, full of vital force but with no shape. I was somehow at one with this formless being which was evoked by the dancers' worshipful love. The love was directed towards the cauldron, to which they chanted many of the goddess names—Isis, Sophia, Nuit, Kwan Yin, Mary, Ishtar, Inana, and many others I did not recognize. It seemed they were attempting to call forth a birth, a birth through the Her of many names, the birth of a divine child, which was somehow also their own rebirth, and mine. Feeling their adoration, my own love expanded in a burst of brilliance. Then the scene disappeared, and I seemed to hang motionless in an empty domain, an expanse suffused with a soft, golden light. In the room, the music changed. I was peripherally aware of a soft choir of angelic voices whose song seemed to perfectly match the energy of the golden atmosphere.

In the next moment, I lost awareness of the music, my breathing and my body in the room. I was alone in interstellar space, a black void pierced by the sharp light of multicolored stars. As I explored my field of vision, there was a sudden sense of disorientation, of vertigo. Once again, I fell, down through a long winding tunnel, an ever-contracting spiral that seemed to constrict my awareness. At the bottom, I emerged, clothed in a human body but still suspended in space.

Almost immediately, vibrations began to move through me. At the beginning, the waves of energy seemed pleasant, like an electrical caress, but they steadily built in intensity. My very cells began to buzz like a hive of bees. Streams of energy seemed to pour into me from the stars. My spine became a river of hot lava, my skull a volcano ready to burst open. The vibrations continued to intensify, and I was somehow aware that what was pouring into me was the energy which animates the universe, the hidden fire, the *saura Agni*. But it was too much for me, too much to take in and still hold on to my old idea of self. I couldn't contain it.

At the inception of the next huge wave of energy, I cried out, "Oh my God," and then I exploded. Every atom, every muscle, every organ, every bone was shattered. For a moment, my consciousness seemed to view the destruction from above, watching as the thousands, or millions, of pieces dispersed into the void.

Yet, even as this was happening, I felt myself being reformed, being woven back into existence. My mind, the mind that witnessed the scattering of my disintegrated body, was awash in bliss as it felt an ineffable power rebuilding and reorganizing me into a higher being.

I found myself back upon the earth in a new body, an energized form which seemed to glow with its own light. I could feel my connections with the core of the earth, with the heart of the galaxy and with all the plants and animals. I was climbing a crystal mountain, carrying a white staff entwined by two snakes—a healing wand, an antenna for receiving the divine energies and dispersing them in the world. I sensed the guiding presence of an angelic entity which accompanied me as I climbed.

When I reached the summit of the mountain, once again my spine surged with tremendous heat, and it rose relentlessly up and up, into my skull and out the top of my head. The angelic presence which had led me seemed to send a beam of intense electrical energy down into me from above. At that moment there was a feeling of ignition, as though the heat in my spine had broken through the protective bone and set my whole body aflame. My hands spewed fire like flame throwers. My torso became a furnace. My entire body was transformed into a pillar of fire set atop the crystal mountain. In the center of this inferno, there was no pain, other than wave after wave of nearly unbearable ecstasy, as I bathed in what I thought must be the pure consciousness of God.

Once again, the waves of energy grew beyond what even my higher body could withstand. The holy fire increased in its intensity, beginning to burn through the organs, sinews, bones and skin, and through the layers of my psyche as well. Every thought, every memory, every feeling except love was devoured by the raging flames within my being. I sensed its purpose as a ruthless love with a pure compassion beyond any human sympathy. For an instant, I thought I glimpsed its face as I felt the holy fire and ecstasy reaching an intolerable peak. As my self-awareness was nearly burned away, a stray memory ran through my mind, and I imagined that I heard the voice of Christ saying, "I have cast fire upon the world, and see, I guard it until the world is afire."

In the next moment, there was a second explosion, and my higher body was incinerated in a sphere of flame. Something like the nova of a sun burned brightly at the center of the divine inferno, and my awareness was drawn into it. As I moved into its pure white incandescence, I suddenly formed a new body, an image composed only of light and energy. The angelic presence which had led me and ignited me now merged with my consciousness, and I became a winged being, a soul bird with a heart of light and holy fire, emanating the transforming *saura Agni* as a ceaseless blessing, pouring it eternally into the universe, beaming it directly to the sacred planet Earth.

At the thought of Earth, I began to return there. I saw myself back on the mountain top, reformed with a human body, but one which was also a body of light and holy fire. The flesh appeared transparent, and the bones, which seemed made of gold, shone through it. As before, the body blazed with the divine energy, but its ecstasy was no longer more than I could bear. The angelic presence of my spiritual core hovered above me, pouring in a flow of power that both electrified and stabilized this new manifestation of my being. Within my chest, the image of the earth itself, surrounded in a corona of gold light, had taken the place of a physical heart. I turned to walk down the mountain, and there before me sat a thousand souls. Their faces displayed many moods, yet all were looking to me searchingly. Their bodies were transparent, yet I saw myself in all their eyes.

As I looked upon them, my heart ached with love and compassion, and another stray bit of memory entered my thoughts—the old lines of poetry from Yeats:

> While on the shop and street I gazed,
> My body of a sudden blazed;
> And twenty minutes more or less
> It seemed, so great my happiness,
> That I was blessed and could bless.

In the next moment, I felt the holy fire, the Earthfire, flooding into me, and I knew what must be done. I faced the throng and held my hands up, palms toward them, in the ancient gesture of blessing. The fiery ecstasy increased and seemed to flow in growing waves between myself and all the souls who sat before me. One by one, I saw the flames which blazed around me spread to them, until the multitude was filled with holy fire. Hot tears poured from my eyes and cleansed my sight. Now I recognized some faces in the crowd, my wife and the six friends whose bones and flesh lay somewhere in a room awaiting our return. And another, who held his hands up toward me, mirroring my gesture. It took some time for me to understand that he was myself.

And as this dawning paradox was breaking in my mind, the holy vision started to dissolve. The body with the golden bones and flaming flesh began to fade, leaving the blue earth with its golden halo gleaming before me in the velvet void. And as I gazed upon it, I began to fall, ever faster, full of joy and coming home. A voice of knowing spoke within me saying, "Only a little of this can you bring with you now, but more will come as the Earthfire spreads." I nodded inwardly as if to say I understood, and that was my last thought before I fell into my body with a jolt.

No music played, and the breathing of the others was subdued. My clothes were soaked in sweat, and my throat was sore. I lay motionless for a while, my eyes still closed, savoring the residue of rapture.

I drifted in and out of bodily awareness, my mind still able to call back echo-images of the visions and emotions I had experienced. I could feel my heart beating strong and steady in my chest, and I recalled the glowing earth that I had seen and felt there in the other realm where I had been. I lay floating between the worlds of heaven and earth, smiling in soft joy, imagining that those worlds would soon be woven into one. I offered up a prayer of gratitude and felt a few warm tears trickling down my cheeks into my ears.

I lay listening, my mental processes slow in returning. I could hear a slight hiss of static from the stereo speakers beneath the soft respiration of my companions. I tasted salt in my mouth, which must have come from sweat or tears. I could smell the perspiration on my body and was already uncomfortable from its dampness. I moved my feet tentatively beneath the light blanket with which I had covered myself. I had no idea how much time had passed.

Gradually I entered my body more fully. I took in a deep breath and let it out in a long sigh. I began to think about opening my eyes. I clasped and unclasped my hands and stretched my legs out slightly. Then I remembered Helen.

Tears came fresh to me as I reproached myself for not thinking of her sooner. I felt a wild tenderness and a sudden urgency to know that she was still there beside me, alive and well. I turned my head and opened my eyes. She was already looking at me. She smiled softly and mouthed the words "I love you."

I reached from beneath my blanket and took her hand. For a few moments we simply looked at one another. I kissed two of my fingers and and put them to her lips. Then we began whispering softly together. "Were you there?" I asked.

She nodded. "We were all there."

"Has everyone come back?"

"Yes, I think, but no one else has spoken. We should stay quiet."

"There's no music. What happened to David?"

"He came with us too. Now he's lying on the floor beside the stereo."

We lay there awhile, waiting, holding hands and sharing bits of whispered conversation. We didn't talk about what we had seen and felt. It was enough to know that we had both been there.

One by one around us, our friends opened their eyes, and the smiles we exchanged expressed the wonder that we felt. The quiet of the room felt sacred, and we all touched it most gently.

After a time, some sat and others stood, stretching muscles and trying out rubbery legs. Sebastian walked to the window and pulled aside a corner of the plastic to look out. "It's nearly dawn," he said.

We talked enough to ascertain that all of us had had the same experience, and that we indeed had seen each other in the other world. I was surprised to hear that every one of us had felt that he or she had stood before the throng of souls and blessed them with the holy fire. Yet something in me understood and smiled with inner equanimity.

At last, we said goodbye with soft words, strong hugs and happy tears. There was no doubt that we would meet again, and soon. An inner bond had been kindled among us, and all of us desired to be together. After a good long sleep and a chance to think, we would call one another for a gathering, we all promised. And with that, we packed the Edwards' van and stumbled into cars as dawn was breaking over the horizon. Radha gave a ride to Maddie and Sebastian. Helen taped a note up to our door saying that the store would be closed for the day.

As we were driving home, the town looked absolutely new. The heavy dew cast back the early sunlight from the lawns as though a load of diamonds had fallen from the sky. The crisp New England air, washed by the recent rain, tasted as clean as that which Adam might have breathed the first day he awakened. We didn't see another moving car the whole way home. It was as though the world had been reborn, and as though we had been as well. The sun shown brightly through the windshield, and I chuckled softly.

"*Saura Agni*," I said, squinting into the beaming sun. "Holy fire."

When we got home, Helen made tea and we sat for a while on the deck, looking out over the water of the tidal river, warmed by the early morning sun. The air was still cool, but the wind was almost calm, with only occasional slight breezes rustling the leaves of the tall maples and locust trees that lined the yard. All my senses were unusually acute, or perhaps the serenity pervading my mind gave me a clearer appreciation. I savored the scents of the damp grass and the salt water, and of the aromatic steam rising from the tea. The songs of the morning birds mingled with the cries of distant gulls and the early boat traffic on the river. I breathed deeply, aware of the rise and fall of my chest, feeling with pleasure the support of the wicker chair, the warmth of my clothes, even the stubble of my unshaven beard when I touched my cheek.

I looked to Helen, who seemed also to be relishing the intake of her senses. Her eyes moved about, drinking in all of the scene before us. She sipped her tea slowly, then put the cup down on the deck beside her chair and turned to me. "It's so beautiful. The world, I mean. Not just here where we are."

"Yes, it is, when we notice." There was a silence. "I don't know where we'll go from here."

"What do you mean?"

"I'm not sure. I feel filled with bliss, but I don't know what I'm going to do next. It's as though I've crossed some threshold, and I don't know if I can go back and be the way I was before. It's good that we're off work today, but what will we do tomorrow—put what happened behind us and go back to selling crystals?"

Helen stood up and looked at me squarely. "I understand, Will, and I don't see exactly what is ahead of us. I do feel change, immense change. But it may be mostly on the inside." She smiled again. "I remember a saying, I think from Zen Buddhism—'Before enlightenment, chop wood and carry water. After enlightenment, chop wood and carry water.' I take that to mean that 'enlightenment' or any spiritual opening doesn't necessarily affect our outward actions, but that such experiences have everything to do with transforming our vision of the outer world and our understanding of its relationship with what's inside. Maybe it will be like that for us. Anyway, if we're supposed to connect with people to help spread the Earthfire, the shop might be a good place to do it." She yawned and reached behind her head to take the clip out of her hair. The dark tresses fell forward and framed her face in a way that made me think of angels.

I stood up and took a step towards her, putting my arms around her waist. "I know you're right," I said. "Maybe I'm just not completely back yet. I halfway believe that if I stayed out here on the deck, I could just float away. And I can't imagine how I'm going to get to sleep."

She reached her arms up around my neck and pulled me into a kiss. "Don't even think about floating away," she said. "Not until you've tried my special remedy for ungrounded husbands."

"What's that?"

"It's called 'making love'. It's good for wives too. Come on, let's go upstairs."

# — 21 —

We slept until late afternoon, when the telephone woke us. As soon as I answered, Sebastian's jovial voice rang in my ear. "Hey! Is this the fire department? I'd like to report a discarnate spiritual arsonist. He goes by the name Anon, short for Anonymous, I think, and he is sometimes known to wear elderly women's clothes—and their bodies too, for that matter. His favorite song is 'Light My Fire', and since I ran into him I've gotten sunburned from the inside out. My friend Will knows him more formally as Mr. Anon."

"Hello, Sebastian," I said. "Taking irreverence to a new low today, are we?"

"It's just my hobby," he answered. "My new professions are Brilliant Computer Research Genius and Automobile Faith Healer. Which one would you like to hear about first?"

"Um, I guess I'll take automobile faith healer."

"Well, when Radha dropped us off, I wasn't a bit sleepy. I felt great, and what I wanted was to be outside in the fresh air, so I decided to take a look at the Toyota and try to get it started. I thought I might find something I'd missed before. And would you believe it? I put my hands on the hood of the poor old thing and it started just like that, no keys or anything."

"No, I wouldn't believe it."

"Okay, well how about the truth then? I opened the hood and wiggled the connections of all the spark plug wires and the battery terminals, and then I tried the key again. It started right up, no problem. Now, I know that story will never get me my own televangelist show, but I think I healed my car. Tell Helen. I bet she'll be jealous."

"I'm sure she will. So fill me in on your other new career, the super genius researcher—a modest title, I must say."

"Merely descriptive, I tell you. Well, after performing my little mechanical miracle, I walked around outside for a bit, just thinking things over and enjoying being blissed out. Last night was so incredible, I don't even know how to talk about it. Eventually I went inside and got on my computer, looking for information on the Web and the Internet. I stayed on for about three hours, until I finally got pretty weary and climbed into bed for an industrial strength nap. Anyway, the results of my research were stellar. I found a place in Boston where I can go pick up a copy of the Isis softwear—I'm heeding your advice about not ordering it online. And listen to this, Will—started looking for sites and postings that might have something to do with the Earthfire, and I found a bunch!"

"You're kidding!"

"No, indeed. There's even a site with 'Earthfire.net' as the address. Those folks must have heard from Mr. Anon, or someone like him. I haven't read very much of what people have written, but from what I can tell, we aren't a bunch of lone loonies. It's interesting, too. There are other people connecting with the energy and the information through breathwork, but that's not the only way. It's coming in through meditation, in people's dreams, in shamanic drumming and journeying, through chanting, and in near-death experiences."

"Like Maddie's."

"Very much so. I begin to wonder if some of these people might have been among the ones Maddie saw on the benches in the big round temple when she was out of her body. But listen, Will, there's more to it. There are channelers and mediums like Radha writing some of the very same words she spoke. There's a guru in India who is instructing her followers to bring in the 'solar prana' through 'breath of fire'. The technique is actually quite old, but she's saying she's in touch with 'the star gods', a bunch of blue beings who are helping to bring in the 'solar prana' and who emanate a blue-white light. Which takes me right back to my old abduction dreams."

"It's amazing. That makes me think, what about the UFO people? Are they talking about this?"

"I found maybe a dozen postings on abductee bulletin boards that seemed to fit the profile I was looking for, but I haven't had a chance to look much further. The amount of UFO data on the Internet is so huge, it takes a lot of time to go through it. Anyway, I downloaded the sites and e-mail addresses that I did find, and I'm thinking we'll probably want to contact some of these people."

"Absolutely."

"Will, this phenomenon is all over the world. I've already found connections to Germany and India and Australia and Japan, where something like what we've experienced is apparently happening to other people. There must be many more."

"I can't wait to tell Helen about this."

"And I want to tell Maddie. Could you put her on the phone now?"

"What?"

"I want to talk to Maddie. Oh geez, I guess she already told you about my healing the car. Why did you let me repeat the whole thing?"

"Sebastian, Maddie's not here. Helen and I were asleep. Your telephone call woke us up."

"She's not there? But she left me a note saying she was going to get groceries, and look in on you folks afterwards. That had to be at least a couple of hours ago, and the Toyota's gone. Are you sure she didn't let herself in downstairs?"

I got up and checked the house, then picked up the kitchen phone. "No, Sebastian. She isn't here, and there's no note on our door."

"Oh hell. I hope nothing's happened to her."

"She's probably just taking her time, or maybe she went for a walk on the beach."

"No, she doesn't take the car when she goes to the beach. She walks from here. Will, please do me a favor, would you?"

"Sure, what is it?"

"Drive down to the grocery store and see if she's there. You know the one we go to, don't you?"

"Yes, it's the same one we use. But, Sebastian, don't you think you're getting worried a little too quickly?"

"I don't know, but I got a very bad feeling as soon as you told me she wasn't at your place. Call me from the grocery store when you get there, okay?"

"All right, but it will take me a minute or two to get dressed."

"Just do it as fast as you can. And leave Helen at the house in case Maddie shows up there."

"All right, I'll call you."

I dressed hurriedly and drove to the grocery store a couple of miles from the house. When I turned into the parking lot, I was relieved to see Sebastian's rusty yellow Toyota. I parked beside it and went into the store to find Maddie.

I took a cart, thinking I would pick up a few things while I was there, but before doing any shopping, I cruised the aisles to locate Maddie, so I could telephone Sebastian and put his mind at ease. Five minutes later, I decided that she wasn't in the store. I abandoned the cart and walked quickly through all the aisles again, just to be sure I hadn't missed her. Then I left the supermarket and checked the other stores in the little shopping mall beside it. Finally, I gave up looking and went to the phone booth to call Sebastian.

I explained the situation to him. "Your car is here, but Maddie isn't. I've searched everywhere in the area, but I haven't seen her."

"What about the car? Did you check to see if she was in it, or if anything seemed strange?"

"I parked right beside it. I know she wasn't in the car, but I didn't look at it carefully. Do you want to hold on while I check?"

"Yes, but please hurry."

When I got to the car and inspected the interior, a chill of fear ran through me. I ran back to the phone I had left dangling in the booth. "Sebastian, the key is still in the ignition, and Maddie's purse is on the passenger seat, and contents are spilled out all over."

"Oh, God, no."

"Should I call the police?"

"Just come and get me, Will. Now."

I drove the few miles to Dune Forest at high speed, my hands trembling on the steering wheel. When I reached the turnoff into the long driveway, I found Sebastian there waiting for me. His face was somber, and his eyes flickered with a cold light I hadn't seen before. He jumped into the car and said only, "Take me back to the grocery store."

While we sped back down the roads that crossed the town, Sebastian did not speak. I kept imagining scenes of what might have happened to cause Maddie to leave behind her purse and keys, and everything I could conceive of was bad. Finally, I began, "Do you think ..."

"Lemay has her," Sebastian growled. "What a goddamned blissed-out idiot I was, sleeping while she went off alone like that. He was in your store looking for her three days ago, for God's sake. What the hell was I thinking? I wasn't thinking, that's what." He slid his left hand into his jacket pocket, wrapping his fingers around something inside. "Well, I'm thinking now, and if I find that bastard I'll be sure he lets her go."

A fresh surge of fear hit me when I realized he was holding a gun. "Sebastian, I don't know about this ... How are you going to find Lemay anyway? Don't you think it would be better to call the police?"

"Lemay has phony FBI credentials, and who knows what else? What would the police do if they did run into him? Nothing. The only thing they'll be good for ... is to recover her body if she's killed." He sighed heavily, "As far as how I'm planning to find him, or Maddie, I haven't thought past driving around and looking."

We turned into the parking lot and stopped next to the Toyota. Sebastian leaped out of my car and into his, carefully scrutinizing the seats and floor. In my panic, I had left the purse and keys behind when I went for him, but they were undisturbed. After a few minutes, I heard him shout, "Here it is!"

"What did you find?"

"The disc from Dr. Jordan. Maddie must have still been carrying it in her purse after last night. But she apparently slipped it under the floor mat, which might mean she saw Lemay coming and hid it from him."

"Or that she had already put it there for safekeeping," I said.

"Yes, but look. Her purse has been emptied all over the seat, but her wallet is still here, and so is the money. That's not what a typical robber would do."

My eyes scanned the inside of the car as I imagined Maddie being forced out of the vehicle and taken away. A cold knot was forming in the pit of my stomach. Suddenly, my attention was drawn to the ground next to the Toyota, to a dark little rectangle which had caught my peripheral vision. I said, "Sebastian, you're right. That man Lemay has her."

"Why do you say that now?"

"He left us a clue," I said, bending over and picking up the glossy black business card, which had no writing on either side. "He must have dropped it, or maybe it fell out of his car."

Sebastian's face hardened. "Will, I want you to go home and stay put until you hear from me. It's possible Maddie will make it there somehow, and I don't think you should leave Helen alone either."

"What are you going to do?"

"I don't know, but I can't just sit and wait. I'm going to look for her. Here, take the disc with you. I already left a note for Maddie to call you if she comes back to the RV. When you get home, say some prayers."

Sebastian quickly stuffed Maddie's belongings back into the purse and started the Toyota. The tires screeched and the car lurched as he slammed it into gear and took off down the road toward the state highway.

I got into my vehicle and sat for a moment in the parking lot, trying to compose myself. My heart was pounding, and my hands trembled. The afternoon light was starting to dim, and with its ebbing my fear began to rise. How far I had fallen, I told myself, from the exaltation and the peace I had known only hours ago. Suddenly I thought of Helen, and I felt worried about her safety. I quickly started the car and drove home, trying not to let my anxious imagination run away with me.

When I reached the house, Helen met me at the door and immediately wanted to know about everything that had happened. We went inside and sat in the living room, huddled together on the sofa. As I described to her the car with Maddie's purse and keys left inside, her face fell and her eyes betrayed a flicker of fear. But when I told her about Sebastian driving off to look for her with a gun in his jacket pocket, she showed real signs of alarm.

"I told him about this last night," she said. "It's not going to work for him to go off and do violence. It won't be allowed without repercussions, and if he tries it I'm afraid he'll bring disaster down on himself, and perhaps Maddie too."

"Or us," I said. "But what do you mean about it not being allowed?"

"Last night was an initiation, among other things. We were all given the opportunity to operate on a higher level of consciousness. When you commit to a higher path, you're held more accountable for your actions. Karma becomes almost instant, and there aren't any excuses."

"Do you mean to say someone watches us and hands out consequences?"

She shrugged, "I don't know. It may simply be the way the universe works, but I've seen it in action, on myself and others. There is already plenty of trouble going on—I hope Sebastian doesn't make it worse."

"But you have to understand why he's so worried. I am myself."

"And so am I. And more so because our friend is carrying a gun. But that can't be helped now. We should begin to think about what we can do."

"What about calling the police?" I asked.

"I'm not sure," Helen said slowly. "If we do, they'll immediately be here asking questions. If we answer truthfully, and start talking about Dr. Jordan's death and everything that has happened since, I doubt we would be believed. We might even complicate the situation for Maddie and Sebastian. On the other hand, they often have a waiting period before they look for missing persons. I tend to agree with Sebastian that the police probably wouldn't help us find her any time soon. For now, I think we had best respect his wishes."

"Sebastian asked for us to say some prayers," I said.

"He did? That's the one good idea he had. Let's sit here and send out prayers of protection for both of them. Surround them in white light, and ask, with all the intensity of emotion you can muster, for only their highest good to come to them. Then I think we should visualize seeing Maddie and Sebastian back with us and safe, and ask the Infinite One for help in bringing that vision into being. Would you do that with me, Will?"

"Of course. I hope it helps. Anyway, we have to wait, and praying probably does more good than worrying."

She smiled quizzically, "Is this the same husband I married?"

"Hey, I'm evolving, okay?"

"Definitely okay. Now let's relax and offer our prayers. Maybe afterwards we should stay quiet and meditate. Perhaps we'll get some answers."

We both settled into comfortable positions on the couch. I pulled my feet up and sat cross-legged with my spine pressed against the back of the sofa. We closed our eyes and took a few slow, deep breaths to calm ourselves and move inward. Then I attempted to visualize the images Helen had suggested. Several times, my efforts were interrupted by thoughts, mostly worries about what might be befalling Maddie. Each time this happened, I eventually became aware and brought my mind back to the visualizations and our entreaty for help.

After some time, I fell into a dreamlike state, and I was aware of shifting images moving before my inner sight. At first, there was a cascade of geometric forms in mandala-like circular arrays. Then I began to see pulsating violet light that moved in the rhythm of my breath and seemed to lead me into deeper breathing. There were tingling energies in my hands and feet, and the feeling of warm vibrations moving through my body. Soon I found myself immersed again in the space of gold light where I had gone when I fainted on the beach, and briefly during the culminating experience of the previous night.

I saw nothing but the "warm gold dust," the "wine of lightning" as Sri Aurobindo's disciple had named it. I had no body, nor did I see any other forms within the golden space. Yet I soon sensed the presence of another consciousness, a radiant entity who spoke to me in my mind.

There were no true words—it was more like a transfer of meaning. Expressing it in language, I would say I was told I was approaching a cusp of testing, a moment of truth. There was a feeling of danger and expectancy, as though intelligence beyond the earth of my daily life were holding its breath, waiting to see what would transpire. And it was not a trial for me only— others would be fired in the same crucible. I remember asking whether this had not already happened the night before, and the message which came to me was that great openings attract attention from forces of limitation, and that we were to be tested and tempered by them now. The last communication was a surge of felicity which it emanated as advice. In my words, it would have said, "Embrace with joy the sorrows of your life." Then the gold light faded and the vibrations ebbed. I was again conscious of my body and my aching knees. I let out a sigh and opened my eyes.

Helen still sat motionless with her eyes closed, her breathing deep and quiet. I looked at the clock and was surprised to see that almost an hour had passed. Outside, the night was fully dark. I stared at the telephone on the wall of the kitchen doorway, both anxious and afraid to hear it ring. I contemplated the message and the being in the gold light, wondering whether it was some invisible ally or a higher part of my own mind. I watched Helen, hoping she would soon complete her prayer and meditation.

In another moment, she shifted slightly in her seat, then opened her eyes and stretched her arms above her head. She turned to me, and her face was grave but calm. "Hello, sweetheart," she said softly. "How did it go with you?"

I told her about my prayer and the mandala visions I had seen, and at last about my journey into the atmosphere of gold and my encounter with the being there.

"You've found a guide," she said. "That's very good. My guides have spoken to me, too—perhaps a little more specifically."

"What did they tell you? Is Maddie all right? Do you know where she is?"

"I saw her, but I don't know where she is. I'm fairly certain she is alive, but very frightened. I saw her in a dark enclosure, like a metal cell, and it was moving, too."

"As if she was inside a black van!" I cried. "That's what Lemay and his partner were driving when they pulled away from the store last Friday."

"Yes, that could be it. I only saw her for a moment. Then I was with my guides, and they were speaking to me. I was told that we are passing through a moment of great danger, and that we have to keep absolutely on our highest path. There was something that reminded me of what Anon said, about the 'dark fires of destruction,' and I was told we must release everything, to 'be emptied so that you may be filled.' I don't know what that part meant."

"What about Sebastian?"

"I asked to see him, and they told me he is 'under a dark shadow', which I took to mean the anger and fear he is battling within himself. I even seemed to glimpse him for a moment, driving his car somewhere, but it was like looking through thick smoke. I felt as though this shadow were somehow separating him from us, and that there is nothing we can do to help him, at least for now."

"What about us?"

She reached out and held my hand. "I don't know for sure, but I feel danger ahead. Will, we have to be impeccable now, as we go through whatever this is. It's a test, a big one, maybe more than one. We need to be ready, as calm and centered as possible. Look inside yourself and get to the center where you aren't in fear."

"'Embrace with joy the sorrows of life,'" I said, remembering my own inner message. "Just let me close my eyes for a moment." As I turned inward, I noticed a new sensation, a tiny pocket of peace that lay behind the anxiety which filled most of my thoughts. I felt surprised and almost guilty that there should be an oasis of calm within me while my friends were in peril, and I said so to Helen.

"No," she answered. "Don't look at it that way. That calm place is your interior witness, and you need it most of all in times of fear and danger."

She was interrupted by the ringing of the telephone. I jumped up, startled, and went to answer it.

A female voice spoke, "Hello, this is Vanguard alarm monitoring. Is this Mr. Lerner?"

"Yes, that's me."

"We have an alarm at your place of business, the Missing Link. The smoke sensor in the office has been triggered. It looks as though there could be a fire."

A fresh shock of cold fear ran through me, but I forced myself to answer. "We'll be right there. Has the fire department been called?"

"Yes, sir, they're on their way."

I hung up and shouted to Helen, but she was already pulling on her jacket and heading for the door. I backed out of the driveway and sped once again through the now-dark streets of our little town. Within moments, we heard the wail of sirens. I kept repeating, "Oh God, oh God, let it be all right." But when we arrived, I knew that my prayer had been in vain.

From blocks away, we could see the glow of orange flames that lit up the night sky and the street ahead. In front of the building, fire trucks and police cars closed off the road, and as we approached we could see the men with hoses beginning to spray water through the broken plate glass windows.

I stopped the car about fifty yards from the scene of the blaze. Helen jumped out and sprinted ahead, and I followed, running. Inexplicably, I recalled the words of Maurice Bucke, from Radha's fax weeks before, "*I found myself wrapped in a flame-colored cloud. For an instant I thought of fire, an immense conflagration somewhere close by ...; the next, I knew that the fire was within myself."* I shook my head as I ran and thought, *"No, that was last night. Tonight it's the real thing."* In a moment, I caught up with Helen, as she was was saying something to one of the firemen, who nodded and dashed away.

Helen turned to me, and there were tears streaming down her face, "Will, I asked him how bad it is, and he told me he doubts they can save anything here, except the buildings next door. The whole place was in flames when they arrived. He said it looks like arson."

Tears formed in my own eyes, and my heart blazed with a mixture of anger and despair. "I can't believe it. They burned our store, those bastards!" I stood in helpless fury as I watched the fruit of all our work consumed by the greedy flames. I felt the wild urge to rush inside and save something, to somehow defy the reality of what was happening before my eyes. Helen must have caught a hint of my thought, because she grabbed my arm suddenly.

"Will, don't," she cried out through her tears. "Listen to me. We were warned about this. Remember, my guides talked about the dark fires of destruction, and they said 'be empty so that you may be filled'. We need to stay focused on what's important, and it's not our possessions. Maddie could be inside there."

A fresh tremor of fear shook me. "We have to tell them," I said, starting to pull away from Helen.

"I did already. The fireman said they'll try to get into the second floor through the workshop door."

My hands dropped helplessly to my sides. "What do we do now?" I asked quietly.

Helen put her arm around my waist and leaned her head against my chest, turning me slightly to face the burning building. "We say goodbye," she said.

As we stood there, I felt the heat from the flames in front of us bringing perspiration to my face and chest, to the whole front of my body. It somehow mingled with the inner heat of my emotions, and my memories of the holy fire I had experienced only hours ago in the building that now blazed away before me. In a flash, I understood that there could be no turning back now, and for an instant, I was aware of the calm place within myself. From that tiny eye of my emotions' hurricane, a thin beam of understanding brought a slight smile to my lips.

"Helen," I said, pointing to the roaring inferno. "Do you know what that is?"

She raised her eyes to me, puzzled. "What do you mean?"

"It's the nest of the Phoenix. And we're going to rise from its ashes."

"Yes. Yes we will," she said. She put both arms around my neck and buried her head against me. I felt the tension go out of her body as she released her self control and began to cry, her sobs vibrating against my chest. My own tears trickled down onto her head, but the despair had left me.

A few moments later, one of the firemen came and gently urged us back behind the yellow tape with which they had roped off the street in front of the store. Soon we were standing amid the little crowd that had gathered there. Some of the people were neighbors who knew us, and a few of them had the courage to approach us and express their sympathy. We stood there nodding, awkwardly thanking them for their concern. When I glimpsed a man moving toward us from the other side of the small knot of people, I thought it must be someone else who recognized us, and it was.

It was Sebastian.

His eyes were lit with a mix of sorrow and cold fury, as he came and embraced us both at once with his bearlike arms. "I'm so sorry," he repeated again and again. A moment later he said, "Now I have another reason to make those sons of bitches pay."

Helen took a step back and eyed him sharply. "Sebastian," she said, "I have to warn you, don't take that path. I can't explain here, but I've seen you under a shadow, and I'm afraid of what may happen if you pursue it."

Sebastian appeared ready to argue, but he hesitated, and I spoke. "Where have you been? Have you found any sign of Maddie?"

He shook his head. "I've been everywhere around this town, past all the motels, down all the dead-end streets and back roads, anywhere I could imagine they might have gone with her. I was beginning to think they had taken her out of the area when I heard the sirens. I had run out of ideas, so I followed them. When I realized it was your place, I felt awful, and yet hopeful at the same time. If they did this, they can't have gone too far away."

At that moment, one of the fireman came up to Helen and told her they had managed to enter the second floor workshop space, and that he thought there was no one inside the structure, although it was still too dangerous for a thorough search. After he left, the three of us decided to walk up the intersecting street, to see the entrance for ourselves and to view that side of the burning building.

We left behind the crowd that was still standing at the barrier, and we walked around the corner and up the side street. There were two police cars and a pumper truck on this side, but only a few people standing in their yards viewing the blaze.

As we watched, a section of the roof fell in, and a tower of flame briefly licked the sky. Even so, there was less fuel for the flames than there had been, and the streams of water were beginning to bring the fire under control. I looked on, almost detached from the disaster which had befallen us. We were all preoccupied with the other emergency in our lives. I felt relieved to think that Maddie probably hadn't been inside the burning store, but I had no idea where to look for her.

We passed our building and walked perhaps thirty yards further up the street before turning back to go to our cars. It might have been a minute since any of us had spoken, until Sebastian suggested we turn around.

At the sound of his voice, I caught a furtive movement out of the corner of my eye, and a figure dashed towards us from the darkness beneath a thick hedge. A female voice screamed, "Sebastian!" In another instant, Maddie had reached us, and she threw her arms around Sebastian, sobbing and talking incoherently.

"I got away from them," she said hysterically. "He was going to kill me, put me in the store and burn me, but the other one felt the fire when he touched me and he started to change and he helped me get away while the first one was pouring gasoline inside. Will and Helen, I'm so sorry about the store. I couldn't stop them." She broke down again and buried herself in Sebastian's embrace. He engulfed her in his arms, as though trying to shield her with his body.

Helen was smiling and crying, looking ready to break down herself, but she spoke deliberately. "Let's get away from this dark side street now. I think we'd be better off moving back into the light."

# — 22 —

Helen spoke to the fire chief and one of the policemen, letting them know we were going home. The fire had resurged and there seemed little doubt that the building and our shop would be a total loss. Sebastian and Maddie agreed to follow us back to the house to talk before deciding what they would do next. All of us were in a state of shock, and there was a sense that we should stick together.

Three of us sat around the kitchen table, trying haltingly to begin talking about what had just happened. Helen had given Maddie a cup of tea, and Sebastian had scrounged one of his old beers from the back of our refrigerator. I held a glass of water in my hands, nervously fingering the rim while I waited for Helen to sit down.

Maddie had calmed somewhat during the ride to the house, and Helen asked her if she felt well enough to talk to us about what had happened to her. She nodded and smiled uncertainly, tears welling up in her eyes. Then she wiped them, took a deep breath and began.

"When I woke up this afternoon, I was happy Sebastian had fixed his car, because we needed groceries. We hadn't been able to go anywhere since Friday, and I thought I would do the shopping while he was sleeping. I don't know how long the black van had been behind me before I saw it in the rearview mirror, but at first I didn't think anything of it. By that time, I had almost reached the store, and my mind was on my errand. I turned into the parking lot, and the van followed me. When I parked, it pulled right behind me, blocking me in. At that point, I started to get alarmed. I suddenly remembered the two men who had been looking for me in the store, and that Will said they left in a black van. I didn't know what to do. I couldn't drive away because there were cars parked all around me and the van was blocking me from behind. I dumped my purse out on the car seat, and took the disc from Dr. Jordan and slid it under the floor mat. Then I tried to get out of the car and run.

"I didn't have a chance. The younger man jumped out of the van and grabbed me. I tried to scream, but he put his hand over my mouth. Then he jabbed something into my back—he said it was a gun and that he would shoot me if I made any noise. He told me to walk with him and get into the back of the van."

Maddie's eyes brimmed with tears again, but she went on. "There was a strange part to this—when I saw I was trapped, I felt really scared, and my heart was pounding and I started breathing hard, sort of involuntarily. And in what must have been only a few seconds, I was filled with this intense heat and vibration, like during the breathing session yesterday. And it wasn't just internal—the man felt it too, when he took hold of me. He said something like, 'What's the matter with you? Are you sick or something? Hey Garth, she's got a fever or something—she's burning up.'"

"The other man, Garth Lemay—he was older, big and heavy—said, 'I don't give a good god damn what she's got. Get her in the van, Stevens!' Then the door opened and Stevens shoved me inside, onto a bench-type seat that ran along one side of the back part of the van. As soon as I was inside, they took off. Stevens put duct tape around my wrists and ankles and over my mouth. He mentioned something again about how hot I was, but Lemay, who was driving, told him, 'Shut up and give her the injection.' Then Stevens opened a compartment on the other wall of the van and got out a hypodermic. He injected me with something, and in a couple of minutes I went all limp and woozy. I didn't lose consciousness, but I couldn't have run away, even if I hadn't been restrained."

Maddie paused momentarily and took a deep breath, then a sip from her tea. Sebastian had already drained his beer, and he sat glowering in the chair next to Maddie. He looked down at the can and crushed it in his grip. I started to speak to him, but Helen squeezed my arm, leaning forward toward Maddie. "Can you tell us what happened after that?" she asked gently.

"They drove me somewhere, I don't know where, but it might have been that old industrial area on the edge of town—I saw one of those big metal sheds through the front windshield, but no cars or people. Lemay stopped the van and climbed into the back compartment where I was. Then Stevens gave me another injection. It woke me up a bit, but I still felt passive, as though I didn't have any will of my own. Lemay told Stevens to take the tape off my mouth and sit me up on the bench seat. Then he started asking me questions, mostly about Dr. Jordan and the information he got from that retired general from Arizona. The drugs they had given me caused me to be unable to refuse to answer him. Whatever thoughts came into my mind just babbled out of my mouth—I had no control over them. Some of the time it frustrated Lemay, too. When he asked me what I knew about Dr. Jordan, I started off with the day I first read one of his books and went through meeting him and going to his lectures and everything I had ever thought about what he said, and on and on. He told me to shut up and started asking more specific questions after that."

Maddie looked at Helen and me, and tears came into her eyes again, "I ended up telling him *everything*, about running away from Sedona and coming here with Sebastian, and about working for you in the store and going to the workshops—and all about what happened last night, about the Earthfire. Lemay just kind of smirked when I told that part, although Stevens was watching me really closely. But Lemay was very interested in the disc from Dr. Jordan. I told him what was on it, including the coded part, but I couldn't remember the name of the encryption program. He got mad then, and he hit me, but Stevens told him to stop because if I could remember it the drug would have made me tell.

"I had said something about us making a copy of the disc, because then Lemay immediately wanted to know where it was. I didn't know where Helen hid it, so I couldn't tell him that. I just said it was somewhere in the store. But I did tell him about the disc I had hidden under the floor mat of the car. When he heard that, Lemay wanted to go back for it right then. He left me sitting there and climbed into the front of the van and took off in a hurry. I fell over on my side when he stepped on the gas, and I couldn't get back up.

"But they hadn't put the tape back over my mouth, so I kept on talking. I couldn't stop it. I started in on the experience I had when I almost drowned and my journey to the crystal temple and the dreams I had afterwards. Then I went on about my abductions and what I believe about the ETs helping us to find enlightenment and save ourselves from self destruction. Lemay laughed when I said that, a really nasty laugh. But Stevens kept turning around and staring at me, and looking down at his hands.

"We must have gotten back to the parking lot at the grocery store just after Sebastian and you drove away in the two cars," she said to me. "It's a good thing you weren't there. Of course, Lemay was furious, shouting and cursing, and he yelled at me to shut up. Maybe the drug was starting to wear off, because at that point I was able to stop talking. After that, they drove around while Lemay decided what to do next. He told Stevens he already knew some of what was on the disc, because he had interrogated the retired general, 'prior to his timely death.' Then he let out that nasty laugh again, and I was scared. But he told Stevens he had to have the disc with all its contents, or he wouldn't have the package his 'customers' wanted to buy. He didn't say anything for a couple of minutes, and then he told Stevens it was time to 'take care of the evidence.' He wanted to get the disc from the shop, but since I didn't know where it was he decided it would be easier to 'go in and torch the place.' Then he said he would find Sebastian and get the disc I had left in the car."

"I wish he *had* found me," Sebastian growled. Helen looked at him sharply but said nothing. We waited for Maddie to continue.

"I was beside myself when he said he was going to burn the store. I started pleading with him, saying there was no reason to destroy your shop, that you two hadn't done anything wrong. Lemay just sort of snarled, 'They picked the wrong friends. Now shut up or we'll do it for you.' So I did shut up, but I listened to as much as I could hear of what they were saying. I gathered they were going to get gasoline and break into the shop soon after dark. There was some muffled talk about me—they seemed to be arguing—and then Lemay said loudly, 'She goes, that's it!'

"After that they didn't say much until they stopped somewhere for gas. Stevens came into the back and told me to be quiet. He pulled a plastic gas can out of one of the back compartments of the van and took it to the front seat. Then he got out and filled up the can, and they drove off. I noticed that Stevens kept looking over his shoulder at me.

"When they reached the store and parked the van, Lemay got out, saying he was going to to pick the lock on the side door and disable the burglar alarm. He took the gas can too. He told Stevens to tape my mouth and cut my feet loose, and then bring me inside.

"It was kind of weird after that. The heat and energy that had flowed into me when they first caught me had ebbed away after I was injected, but as the drugs wore off, it started to come back. And when it did, I wasn't frightened anymore. I felt really calm and certain, even though I understood Lemay was planning to kill me when he set fire to the store. It was as though I was overshadowed by my soul, or some other higher part of me, and I wasn't afraid to die.

"When Stevens knelt down to put the tape over my mouth, I think he could see the absence of fear in me. He saw something, anyway, because instead of taping my mouth he spoke to me. He said, 'What is it with you? What did you do to me?' I told him I didn't do anything, but he looked down at his hands and kind of shook them. 'My hands are hot,' he said. 'And I don't feel right.' And I don't know where it came from—the courage to answer him this way, I mean—but I heard myself tell him, 'Maybe you do feel right for the first time in your life.' He didn't answer. He pulled back from me and the color drained out of his face. Then all of a sudden, he got up and looked out the front passenger window of the van. He came back and took a big knife out of his pocket. When I saw it, I got scared all over again—that strange courage evaporated—but Stevens didn't seem to notice. He was trying to cut the tape off my wrists and feet, and his hands were shaking. While he was getting it off me, he said, 'Garth's inside the building. When I open the door, you run like hell, understand? I'll tell him you got away from me.' I nodded, and then I begged him not to burn the store, but he grabbed my shoulders and shook me, and he said, 'Look, I don't know why I'm doing this. I'm not on your side. Just get the hell out of here!' Then he opened the side door behind the driver's seat and pushed me outside. He told me to 'stay low and get off the street fast.' I took off and ran as hard as I could for a few blocks, and then I hid behind a dumpster. When I heard the sirens, I crept back towards the store. I decided Stevens and Lemay would want to get away from the fire, and I hoped I would see one of you there. I had just gotten close when I heard Sebastian."

Maddie looked at me and said, "Sebastian told me on the way here that he heard the sirens while he was out looking for me. How did you and Helen know the fire was at the store?"

"We got a call from the alarm company," I said.

"But I thought Lemay shut down the alarm."

"Maybe the burglar alarm," I said, "but the fire alarm is ... I mean was ... on a separate circuit."

There was a silence. Then Maddie said, "Your store, it's gone, isn't it? They destroyed it."

Helen took her hand and answered, "Yes, but you're alive, and we're all here together and safe."

"For now, maybe," Maddie said. "But I'm remembering the I Ching reading we did here on Friday night. The first hexagram was Danger, and it advised me to face openly whatever perils I had to confront. I guess I did that when I stood up to Stevens in the van, although I sure wasn't thinking of the I Ching at the time. But the second hexagram was Critical Mass, the one that describes everything coming to a head at once. I think we can all agree we're in the middle of that. Anyway, the advice from the I Ching was to look for an avenue of escape, and to be ready to make a quick transition to a completely new way of life. It feels to me like the new way of life has already begun, and it has to do with helping the Earthfire energy to spread." She turned and looked directly at Sebastian. "We need to get out of here, no later than tomorrow. Maybe Will and Helen can come with us, or maybe we should go in separate directions. I don't know about that, but I don't think any of us will be safe if we delay here for long."

Helen agreed, "Maddie's right, Will. With the store gone, there's no reason we have to stay here, and the reasons for leaving, at least temporarily, seem urgent to me."

I was nodding as she spoke. "I think we should get out of town tonight, all of us together, and get on a plane first thing in the morning. Maybe we can spend the night at Radha's place. But where should we go tomorrow?"

"I have family in Portland, Oregon," Maddie said. "I want to go there. Everyone can come— I know it will be all right."

"Good enough," Helen said. "I want to call the airlines right now. Will, let me have your credit card. As soon as we reserve our tickets, I'll phone Radha and tell her what has happened."

In the next moment, there was a splintering sound as the front door of the house was forced open. We all jumped up from the table and dashed into the living room, where we came face to face with Garth Lemay.

# —— 23 ——

I was the first one into the room, just in time to see Stevens walk in through the ruined door behind Lemay. I felt a rush of fear at the sight of them, and another when I saw that both of them had guns drawn.

I turned to warn Helen, but she was on my heels. "None of that!" Lemay shouted. "Everybody in here. We're all going to have a little chat." He gestured casually towards the four of us with the barrel of his gun, indicating we should sit down on the couch. "Sit right there, make yourselves comfortable. Stevens, if anybody makes a move, shoot them." I glanced at Stevens, whose face was impassive, and I noticed swelling on his lower lip and a fresh cut under one eye. I imagined Lemay must have been displeased to hear about Maddie's escape. But now he had all four of us, and he seemed to take pleasure in the power he held.

Lemay settled down in the easy chair, the same one where Radha had sat when we received her first communication from Anon. He told Stevens to stand beside him and cover us with his gun. Then he looked at me and said, "Mr. Lerner, my condolences on the unfortunate fate of your little store. It's a very unpleasant event, but it's been my experience that this is the sort of thing that happens to people who lie to the FBI."

"You son of a bitch!" Sebastian swore. "You're not part of the FBI. You're nothing but a thug!"

"Are you so sure, Sebastian, my old chum?" Lemay replied. "What do you know about power, and who has it? You turned down your chance to be a player, and now you're about to be taken out of the game." He looked down thoughtfully at his pistol, "You know, I think it was that goddamned communist Mao Tse-Tung who said it best, 'All real power comes from the barrel of a gun.' If you're just a man like other men, no one has to listen to you.

But if you're the Angel of Death, you have their undivided attention ... as I have yours.

"You're right, I'm not FBI. They don't have the freedom I do—too many laws." He held up his hand with the thick gold ring. "I am a Knight of Seriphos, and my will is my law! Do you think governments run the world? In some ways they do, but who runs the governments? People do—people with money, people with the right friends. People who can wield the power of corporations, or governments, or armies, or media, or the CIA or FBI, whatever they need. If a man wants to cross those kinds of boundaries, he can't be married to any one of those institutions. But he does need friends, an organized group of friends, preferably a secret group—a society. Do you still believe in conspiracies, Sebastian? Well, let me set your mind at ease. The world isn't one big conspiracy. It's hundreds, or maybe thousands of them, all going at once, and every one of them is run by a group of like-minded associates—friends—with common interests in the global money/power game which useful idiots like yourself refer to as life. I can call on my fellow Knights in the CIA or the Mafia or what used to be known as the KGB, or anywhere else I need a friend. Sometimes we're in competition with other groups, and sometimes we cooperate. All in the interest of red-blooded American profit and power. But I'm no thug, old buddy. If I need one of those, I hire one, or I use one the Knights already own, right Stevens?"

Lemay laughed, a frightening, sinister guffaw. Stevens made no answer, but Lemay went on, "Stevens went a bit soft tonight—I think he likes your girl, Sebastian. I was forced to have a little talk with him, but we straightened things out, didn't we?" Stevens kept his face frozen, his eyes fixed on us. Lemay went on, "He's a bit young and impressionable, but he's very useful if you want to push a UFO kook off a cliff or put an old, sick general out of his misery. You don't have to take my word for it—I can have him demonstrate, if you like."

Maddie's eyes burned fiercely at the reference to the murder of Dr. Jordan. She glared at Lemay, and then at Stevens. "Is that true?" she demanded. Stevens was silent.

Lemay nodded, "Oh, it's true, sad but true. I was contracted, through the company I nominally work for, the Morgoth Corporation, to do some checking on the well-meaning Dr. Jordan, and to find out what he really knew. There are parties in very powerful organizations and institutions that don't want certain secrets to be told, and they constantly have to watch for naive blunderers like your friend Jordan, who might learn something and spill the proverbial beans. 'General Jones' was also rather a loose cannon, if you'll pardon my pun, and he had been around long enough to talk to quite a few too many people. When he handed his information over to Jordan, I was obliged to act quickly, and Mr. Stevens was obliged to help me. Taking care of the good doctor finished off my contract, but I sniffed out his little friend, Ms. Madeline Starkey, and guessed that she might have something worth pursuing on my own time. Imagine my surprise to find her shacked up with my old drinking pal, Sebastian Smith. I believe you'd call that a syn-chronicity, wouldn't you?"

"*You* know what that means?" Maddie asked incredulously.

"Why, yes," Lemay smiled. "Did you think only nice people read books?"

"But if you understand anything like that, how can you be the way you are?" Maddie pleaded. "And why do you want to keep people from knowing about the ETs? They want to help us all."

Lemay chuckled, "If you understood more, you wouldn't ask such stupid questions. I'm a power man—I seek it and I serve it—and the Power that runs this planet isn't love and light, honey. I think even Jung suspected that the Shadow is the ruling force. Personally, I don't give a damn who knows what about your ETs. If they're helping anything, I haven't seen it. And that Earthfire bull you were spouting—you could shout that from the rooftops and nobody would care. But I know people who want certain things kept quiet, for all sorts of reasons. I know religious leaders who think the aliens are demons who want to invade the world. I know military men who've been using flying saucers as a cover story for some very secret technology. I know people in the CIA who have used UFO cults to play with mind control. And there are plenty of other angles, besides the truth, whatever that is." He turned to Sebastian, "Remember when I said that if I told you the secret of the UFOs I'd have to kill you? Isn't it ironic? As it turns out, you're going to have to give *me* the secret, to save your life. Unless you piss me off, in which case I'll kill you anyway. Which brings me to my point. I'm going to need that disc, and the encryption code information. Once I have it, I'll let the interested parties in my circle of acquaintances submit bids, and we'll see who gets the prize. By the way, the disc is no longer in your car. We checked on our way in. Now, who's going to hand it over?"

None of us spoke. In fact, I had put the disc down on the mantle, about ten feet from where Lemay now sat, when I came home after parting with Sebastian in the grocery parking lot. I was sure I was the only one who knew where it was. As the seconds passed, Lemay became visibly impatient. My thoughts kept insisting that I give in and let him have the disc. Both he and

Stevens had guns, and there was nothing we could do to overcome them. But somewhere inside, my fear was hardening into stubborn defiance. I wouldn't speak, and no one else could.

"All right," Lemay said, feigning weariness. "We'll do it the hard way. Stevens, bring Miss Starkey over here, would you?" Stevens walked to the sofa, reaching behind Maddie and pulling her up by the collar of her jacket. He forced her to walk to where he had been standing beside Lemay. She twisted in his grip and for a moment looked straight into his eyes, with a gaze that seemed to hold both a plea and a demand. Stevens face contorted slightly, then reassumed its impassive mask. Lemay, who was covering the rest of us with his gun, saw nothing of the exchange. Stevens stood behind Maddie, holding one arm around her neck. Her face was flushed, and she seemed to be breathing heavily. Lemay glanced up at them and said, "Holster your gun and get out your knife. We'll start with some little cuts. Perhaps the sight of blood will help jog someone's memory." Stevens followed the instructions, putting the gun away and flipping open the big knife he had used before when he freed Maddie from the van. Maddie's breathing increased, coming in deep gasps. I would have thought she was panicking, but her expression did not show it. She was looking intently at Helen whose face was also flushed, and who returned her gaze with the same intensity.

Sebastian's eyes were wild, but his body was tensed in tight control. "All right, Garth, stop," he said evenly. "I'll give you the disc. It's here in my jacket." He reached over the arm of the sofa to the floor, where the jacket lay in a heap. I hadn't noticed it there when we rushed into the room. For a split second, I was confused, and then I knew in a flash that Sebastian was reaching not for the disc, but for his gun.

"Hold it," Lemay ordered. "I'll pick that up myself." But Sebastian had already reached into the jacket pocket. He jerked his arm upward, jacket and all, and fired the gun in Lemay's direction. The window on his left was shattered, and Lemay dropped to the floor, but he had not been hit. He thrust his arm forward from where he lay, gripping his own pistol, and he fired twice at Sebastian, who yelled in shock and pain as he was thrown back against the sofa. His arm swung wildly towards me, carrying the jacket and the gun into my lap. Maddie screamed Sebastian's name and twisted away from Stevens, whose knife clattered to the floor.

At the sight of Sebastian's blood beginning to soak the front of his shirt, my anger turned into a hot fury. Without thinking, I yanked the gun out of the jacket and stood up, and I stamped on Garth Lemay's still outstretched hand. He shouted and his gun slipped from his grasp. I kicked it away and stood over him, pointing Sebastian's gun down at his head. I ordered Lemay not to move, or I would kill him.

I glanced quickly around the room. Stevens stood still, his face flushed, staring down at his hands. Helen was bent over Sebastian, attempting to use the jacket as a compress on his wounds. Maddie knelt beside her, trying to help and crying hysterically. Lemay lay at my feet, his body tense as a coiled snake.

"Will," Sebastian gasped, "Do me a favor and shoot that bastard before I die here."

"No!" Helen shouted. "You can't do that, Will. Not even now."

"Stevens!" Lemay hissed through clenched teeth. "What are you doing? Use your goddamned gun!"

As I stood looking down at Lemay and heard the voices around me, it was as though time stood still. In the intake of a breath, it seemed that I could see the chain of consequences either choice would bring. My friend lay wounded, and the man at my feet would kill us if he could. He was urging Stevens to kill us now. To please my dying friend and save my life, I needed only to pull the trigger. But if I took his life, would I become somehow the same as him? Helen must know she risked her life to hold me back, and yet she didn't hesitate. For the interval of exhalation, I balanced on the brink, knowing there were only seconds left for me to make my choice.

Out of nowhere, I recalled what seemed an ancient conversation, one I had had with a certain Mr. Graves, on the very afternoon I met my wife. In that moment, I had mocked him, yet now his words, and mine, were those which resonated in my mind:

*"What would you do if you thought they were going to kill you, or your wife? What if they had guns and you had a gun?"*

*"There is no stimulus sufficient to lead an enlightened person into violent action. That situation is unlikely to happen to me because I am embodying the proper peaceful attitude. But if it did ... I would not attack."*

Suddenly, against my own reason, I knew what I would do. *"I am follow-ing the advice of a fool, taking the path of the Fool,"* I thought, and almost said aloud. *"Now it's time to step off the cliff."* From somewhere within me, there came a deep release. I felt my face flush and my hands tingle, as my body filled with the Earthfire energy. It flashed within me like heat lightning, rushing from my feet up to my heart, from my crown down to my heart, fill-ing me with strange compassion. As I looked down at him, it seemed that Garth Lemay changed form. I saw at my feet the shapes of every traitor who was ever born, every Hitler, every Judas, every man or woman who had given in to fear and greed and turned away from the Light. I heard the voice of Anon echoing, *"In fear they may turn upon you as enemies, yet you are counseled to honor the Light that they enshroud within their hearts. As love begets greater love, the candle flame ignites the bonfire of the world."*

"Helen," I said. "I can't shoot him. Call the police."

Instantly, Lemay was up from the floor, wrestling the gun from my hand. In a moment, I had lost it to him, and I struggled to keep him from reaching the trigger and turning it on me. "Stevens!" he shouted. "Get over here and kill this fool!" Over Lemay's shoulder, I saw Stevens rushing towards us. In the next instant, I was thrown down by the crash of colliding bodies, but I was free. Stevens had tackled Garth Lemay, and now the two of them grappled one another, with the gun between them. Lemay shouted, "I'll kill you, you stupid son of a bitch," and then the gun discharged. Maddie let out a stifled scream and we all looked on in shock as Lemay's heavy body sagged and crumpled to the floor. Stevens stood over him, still as stone, looking down at the dying man.

My next thought was for Sebastian. I quickly knelt beside him and tried to help press the bloody jacket to his wounds. He flinched in pain, but he looked at me and smiled. His face was hot, though pale, and he whispered, "I was wrong, Will. And we were lucky. You didn't have to shoot Garth, and we didn't get killed—at least not all of us." He lifted his hand and gazed at it in wonder, "I'm tingling all over," he said. "I think I like this holy fire stuff." Then he fell back against the couch and closed his eyes, and he said no more.

Stevens had stooped over Lemay to check his pulse. He turned to me and said, "He's dead. Help me get him out of here." Stevens' face was ashen, and his eyes were full of pain, but his voice showed grim determination. "We have to hurry. You need to call the police, and an ambulance."

Helen leaped up and said, "I'll do it now."

"Call the ambulance first," Stevens said. "Then give me fifteen minutes before you make the other call. I'll need the time to get away, and it's best for you if I do." He strode to the mantle and picked up Dr. Jordan's disc. "This is it, isn't it?" he asked. I nodded, saying nothing, and he added, "I saw it when we came in." He held it in front of me and snapped it in two, and then broke the pieces into bits. "Let's call this bout a draw, and we'll forget we ever met."

I repressed my horror at lifting the dead man's body and helped Stevens move it into the black van. He got into the driver's seat and motioned me to the window. "When the police come," he said, "tell them three robbers followed you home from the store fire. Say your friend shot one of them, and they shot him, and then the robbers dragged the wounded one out and drove away. Tell them you think they might have set the fire at your shop. It's a bad story, but they won't find anything or anyone to contradict you. I left your friend's gun back there, but I'm taking Garth's."

"What about the other Knight's of Seriphos, or the Morgoth people?"

"I don't think they know about you. Garth was doing this on his own, trying to get that disc for his little private auction."

"What about you?"

"I don't know. I might try to face them with a story, or I might run away." He looked down at his hands and shook his head, "Right now, I need to take a drive. Go see to your friends, and your wife." And Stevens drove away.

# —— 24 ——

It was a crisp October afternoon, and the cool breeze blew in across the tidal river to where I stood with Helen on the deck. The maples in the yard were brilliant red, like living flames etched out against the bright blue sky. The calls of wild geese, farther off than we could see, were carried to us on the wind. The aroma of leaves burning in a neighbor's yard brought the thought of winter to my mind—winter and the cycles of the year, the cycles of the world, death and rebirth.

I was holding Helen's hand, and I gently stroked her fingers with my own, feeling the miracle of her life and mine, the electric interface of touch, the elusive mystery of what it is that animates our flesh and bones. Without *her* there, that body would be empty. Was it then a spirit that I loved? It seemed true, more so now than ever, but without that precious body in this world, where would I find *her*? Perhaps in the atmosphere of warm gold dust where I had once encountered the spark that was Maddie, or was that only an antechamber in the mansion of Spirit? I squeezed Helen's hand and stood back to regard her, in her autumn dress of orange, red and gold.

"You're beautiful," I said. "You look like the goddess of the maple trees."

"Thank you," she smiled. "You're not so bad yourself." She looked me over, in my new dark suit and bow tie. "You look like the god of the theater ushers."

"Oh. Thanks, I think."

Helen smiled again, as she turned to go inside. "Are you coming in? We need to leave here soon. We promised to come early."

"In a minute."

I turned again to the river, savoring the view for one last time. In the morning, movers would arrive to take all our possessions to another house, though we would not stay there for long.

We had to leave. The death that had occurred within these walls had left a stain that we could not forget. It didn't matter whether we thought death was not the end.

My mother had once given me a book, back when I was around thirteen and asking earnest questions about death and God. A friend had told her it would give me answers I could understand. I read it in a single night—*The Prophet*, by Kahlil Gibran. It gave me answers, though I'm still not sure I understand. As I stood looking at the river, lines that I had read long years ago came back to me.

> You would know the secret of death,
> But how shall you find it unless you seek it in the heart of life?
> For death and life are one, even as the river and the sea are one.
> For what is it to die but to stand naked in the wind and to melt into the sun?
> And what is it to cease breathing, but to free the breath from its restless tides,
> That it may rise and expand and seek God unencumbered?

"To melt into the sun ..." I repeated to myself. I thought again, as I had many times in the past days, of my encounters with the holy fire. Was it the sacred solar fire, the *saura Agni* of the Hindu rishis? And were we taking now a different path from what was offered in the poem I remembered? Could we *increase* the restless tides of breath and ride them up to levels that embodied humans had rarely reached before? Were the fiery hands of the collective soul indeed raised up to bless us and ignite us, to burn away the flimsy wall that Radha saw holding us apart from the Divine? And what of the strange alien midwives Maddie and so many others knew? And what of those like Radha's spirit guides, or the enigmatic one who chose the name Anon? Were they truly here to help us save ourselves, and achieve another kind of birth? The more we learn, the more our questions multiply. Yet when we listen long and patiently, sometimes a song wells up from deep within, a soft soul voice that sings an unknown language which the heart can hear and understand, and it sings us the answers. As I stood thinking this, the last lines from Gibran's poem came back to me, conjured from some long-neglected pool of memory.

> Only when you drink from the river of silence shall you indeed sing.
> And when you have reached the mountain top, then you shall

*begin to climb.*
*And when the earth shall claim your limbs, then shall you truly dance.*

Now it was time to go and dance. To dance and laugh and toast the wedding of dear friends. To celebrate death and rebirth. I turned and walked inside to find my wife, to drive with her to Mr. Camden's house, where the wedding would be held.

Helen backed the car out of the drive, and I sat in the seat beside her, holding our wedding invitations. As our car moved along the winding road, among the resplendent autumn colors, Helen showed me all the trees she found most lovely, smiling as she took in the beauty of the day. I was reminded of the afternoon just months before when I had grumbled at the traffic while Helen was pointing out the flower beds she liked. That was the day Sebastian had surprised us at the restaurant, the day we met Maddie, the day we heard the tale of how he rescued her from being caught by Garth Lemay. I smiled, remembering Sebastian laughing with us at the restaurant picnic table, eating our french fries and drinking his beer.

We reached the highway and rode on in silence for a while, each of us alone with our own thoughts and memories. I looked down at one of the wedding invitations, and I said to Helen, "Radha and George—were you surprised that they decided to get married?"

"Yes, I suppose I was, a little bit," said Helen. "They'd been friends for so many years ... I guess what we all went through made them realize how much they loved each other."

"That I can understand," I agreed. "It's had the same effect on me."

"Me too," she said, and then she took my hand and raised it to her lips.

I picked up the other invitation and I opened it. "Now, what about this pair?" I asked. "Did you ever think that they would make it to the altar?"

Helen raised her eyebrows, "Maddie and Sebastian? I never had a doubt, once I knew he wasn't going to die."

He had died, actually, according to the doctors at the hospital. He had been bleeding badly when they took him in to operate the night he had been shot. And while the doctors tried to get the bullets out of him, his heart had stopped twice—once for about a minute, and the second time for almost five. When they were nearly ready to pronounce him dead, his heart had suddenly begun to beat again, and from that moment he began to heal. The bullets had miraculously missed his vital organs—he had called it "the strangest case of ballistics since the Warren Commission"—and his doctors were amazed at his remarkable vitality, and how quickly he regained his strength. "I never told them Helen and Maddie were doing healings on me," he had said.

While he was still in the hospital, I visited him alone one day, and I asked him to tell me what, if anything, he had experienced during the time his heart was stopped.

"Of course, I was unconscious at the time," Sebastian said. "But somewhere in there I floated up out of my body and looked down on the operating room. The guy they were working on was a bloody mess, and he was fat, too, and he looked awfully pale. So I turned the other way. And would you believe it? There was a dark tunnel in front of me, and I was pulled right into it, and at the end of it there was a bright light, a bright white neon sign that said Heaven's Lounge. And standing in front of the light was a fat angel, holding a can of beer. I asked him for a drink, and he said, 'Hell, no, not after what you've put me through. Have a seat. You're going to review your life.' And I protested, because I hate reruns, but he made me sit through the whole thing. And then he said, 'You've got a choice—earth or hell.' He didn't offer me heaven, so I came back here."

At first, I had been quite taken in, and when I began to fume Sebastian laughed so hard he was afraid he was going to tear his stitches. After a few minutes, he grew more serious.

"I'm sorry, Will. You know what Helen says—humor is my shield. The fact is, I did go through the tunnel to the light, and there was a being there who allowed me to review my life. And I was given a choice about whether to return. It wasn't all that easy a decision to make—it felt wonderful and holy there, and there wasn't any pain—but I wanted more than anything to be here with Maddie. So I came back."

That evening when Maddie went to see him, he proposed to her. Afterwards, she came to visit us, and she cried, and Helen cried a little with her, and I opened our one bottle of wine, and we toasted their betrothal.

Now, as Helen exited the highway and we drove the final mile or two, I offered up a silent prayer of gratitude for how things had turned out for all of us. And then I heard an inner voice which told me that the story wasn't over yet—that in fact our journey barely had begun.

We drove up to Mr. Camden's mansion—it was even larger than I had imagined—and we parked our car beneath a tremendous golden oak tree that stood beside the circle drive. Its partially fallen leaves made a carpet of gold on the ground. As we were walking to the house, the front door opened and Maddie burst out, calling both our names and hiking up her white wedding gown so she could run. Behind her, and more slowly, in a black tuxedo, came Sebastian. His bearlike frame was somewhat thinner now, and his face was still a little pale, but his red beard blazed as brightly as ever, and his grin lit up his face, and his eyes were merry. The four of us embraced, and together we shed the first tears of the day, but not the last, though none were more joyful.

Inside we were greeted by Radha in a crimson gown—she said there was no point in her pretending to be pure. Beside her stood Mr. Camden in his white tuxedo—he claimed to be a born-again virgin. The two of them were jovial and elegant and at their ease amid the celebration.

Within an hour or so the other guests had all arrived, and it was quite a gathering. David and Maureen Edwards came, and Kathleen Riley of the morphogenic fields, and Don Lee the astrologer. There were half a dozen people from the breathwork workshop we had held on that last weekend before the shop was burned, and there were other customers and friends and Maddie's family from Oregon. There was also an old man with bright red hair, Sebastian's father. The two had made their peace and he was there to give his son away. Radha had invited in a troupe of her flamboyant friends—some were psychics and clairvoyants who claimed they knew about the wedding before the invitations came. And Mr. Camden's group was no less unusual, although the colors of their clothes were more subdued.

The double ceremony was unique. There were blessings from a Buddhist priest and a Pagan priestess. There were shamans who performed their chants with drums, and there was singing in three languages. The vows, which the four of them had written for themselves, were administered by a fearless Unitarian. I was best man for Sebastian, and Helen was beside Radha. Maddie's younger sister was her maid of honor, and the president of the local bank, an old associate, stood at Mr. Camden's side.

After the pronouncements were made, and the brides and grooms were kissed, and the benedictions given, the brides threw their bouquets into the crowd, and a cheer went up from all who were assembled. Then began the music and the food, and there was more dancing than I had done in my life. There was entertainment, too. Mr. Camden had hired an amazing stage magician who could levitate himself and produce ripe apples from one's ear. There was a storyteller, and a juggler, and a singer with a harp who brought fresh tears to all our eyes. And everyone was pleased and all their faces shone with the light of simple human happiness.

At the end the guests were all sent home with gifts, but George and Radha asked a few of us to stay. We sat together at a large round table in an upstairs room, a study lined with books on all the walls and a fireplace blazing at one end. Donald Lee, Maureen and David Edwards, Kathleen Riley, Maddie, Sebastian, Helen, Radha, George and I were seated there. At George's word, we linked our hands and closed our eyes and called forth the Earthfire energy. And it came this time as it often does—as a mild tingling in the joined hands, and a warm vibration in every heart. On this night, we had no need to use our breath to raise the energy beyond this subtle level we enjoyed. Though we had already shared some of our story with them, Rob and Kathleen appeared a bit surprised at what they felt so readily.

This was the first time all of us had been together, and we told our stories late into the night. Those of us who had breathed together the last time before dawn on that long night shared the details of our visions with the others. As we spoke the visions grew more real in all our minds, and the wonder of what might be happening overtook us, and our hearts were joined in fellowship, and our souls were linked in devotion, and we began to talk about what might be done to help to spread the Earthfire through the world.

We agreed that its vibration was a contagion that was spread from heart to heart, but that techniques such as breathwork seemed to help break through blockages and open inner doors. Sebastian told of his discoveries through the Internet of other individuals and groups around the world who were awakening to the Earthfire upon many different paths. Don Lee talked about the coming astrological alignments that could indicate spiritual rebirth throughout the world, and also of the repressive energies that would try to hold it back. Kathleen Riley said that what excited her was seeing similar experiences appearing all around the globe. "The morphic field is building, and when critical mass is reached, it could crystallize throughout the group mind of all humanity."

"And what would that be like?" George mused. "Just try to imagine it— the awakening of our species to the *anima mundi*, the soul of the world, so that every individual would know and feel the All."

"It could be an antidote for many ills," Don Lee said. "Our sense of separation is the illusion that allows for war, and greed, and all kinds of aggression."

"This time feels like no other," Maureen said. "The energy of change is everywhere and is accelerating all the time."

"I heartily agree," said Radha. "When I try to ask my spirit guides about the years ahead, I get the feeling that they smile and say, 'Just do your work and wait—you ain't seen nothin' yet.'"

"But what about our work?" I asked. "That's something which is very much an issue for Helen and me. The fire put our future up for grabs. We'll get some money from insurance soon, but we aren't sure if we should start the store again. It feels to us as though we ought to spend our energy on work that helps to build on the connections being made when people touch the Earthfire. We want to work on ways to help others find the energy within themselves, and to create networks with each other."

Helen smiled, "Will has become a spiritual pyromaniac."

"An admirable aspiration," George intoned. "And one which I feel inclined to support." He took a sip from his glass and looked around at all of us. "I had become an old man with too much money and too little sense of purpose. Even though I was always metaphysically inclined, I studied too much and acted too little. Now that I have been personally touched by the holy fire ... and by its analog, my bride ...," he smiled at Radha, "I want to dedicate what is left of my time and financial resources to a worthy effort. And I can think of nothing more worthwhile than funding the activities of those who wish to research and promote the evolvement of our species."

Radha interrupted, "He means he'll pay you to go out and do the work that helps spread the Earthfire, whatever work that turns out to be."

"Ahem, yes," George continued. "Radha speaks with an eloquent economy of words, and I shall try to follow her example. I propose to set up a non-profit foundation which will give grants to those who have glimpsed this vision of possibility, and who have been touched by its profound energies. This work may be defined beyond the bounds of 'spreading the Earthfire'. It can also include efforts to research the many avenues through which the transformation of humanity seems to be occurring, and to understand how they operate. Each person at this table is either known to me or recommended by Radha, and I hereby offer the first round of grants to all of you. Let's try it for a year and see what happens. Perhaps we should meet again at the halfway point, to share what we have learned. What do you say?"

There was a silence, as Mr. Camden's offer sunk in with all of us. At last, Sebastian said, "What are you waiting for, everybody? Say yes before he sobers up!"

# —— Epilogue——

Of course, George wasn't drunk when he made the offer, and eventually all of us accepted it. But we have each had to decide how to apply ourselves to the opportunity we have been given, because it is nothing less than the chance to make our deepest dreams come true. Helen says we are always transforming our thoughts into reality—that what we hold most consistently in the mind and heart will sooner or later manifest in our lives. When we focus on our fears, we attract them to us. When we hold to our highest visions, they can become real.

Maddie and Sebastian are studying Holotropic Breathwork with David and Maureen, and they plan to become certified facilitators. At the same time, they are interviewing UFO experiencers for a book they hope to write together. Helen and I rented a big old house with them in our same little seaside town, but we are seldom there. We've taken to the road in *RV There Yet*, and we spend our time traveling to meet with those around the country who are discovering the Earthfire. Radha and George are doing the same thing in countries all over the world.

Often Sebastian gives us addresses and names of those with whom he has connected on the Internet, but sometimes Helen gets a "knowing" about a place when she sees it on the map. So we go there. Sometimes we find people who already know the Earthfire, and sometimes we meet those who are ripe to be ignited. When that happens, we try to help them find the spark. It can come through conversation or through meditation, through breathing together or just through helping people see themselves more clearly. It is rare for us to encounter a situation where the Earthfire energy comes in as overwhelmingly as we all felt it before dawn on that extraordinary night. But it isn't needed that way. When one comes to consciousness after a long dream, the awakening can happen with a mighty jolt or a gentle touch—the result is the same.

And what of the grand awakening, when the collective mind and heart and soul of all of us opens its eyes, and we all know it together? If there is truly a critical mass of consciousness, and we reach it, what will the new world look like? My heart tells me that *everything* can be healed, although my mind has many questions. What would happen to the Garth Lemays, and, for that matter, the Stevenses of this world? Would they be able to release their old identities and move into the Light, or would they simply shatter from the stresses of the transformation? What will happen to the shadow side of each of us? Can it be burned away, or will it be turned into something else, allowing us to recognize the ways it tried to serve us all along?

Helen smiles at my questions and advises me to trust. When she tells me that, I remember the Fool card from the Tarot, which she saw in my hopes and fears the night she read the cards for me and knew we would be married. I have learned to respect the pure, perhaps naive, trust of the Fool, because it was the courage of that trust which pulled me back from the brink of killing. It made me risk my life and may have saved my soul. We will all need a great measure of the Fool's trust if we are to walk forward on the path to our redemption and enlightenment, and the healing of Earth.

When I told George and Radha of the plans Helen and I had made to travel the country, and they so liked the idea that they decided to take on the rest of the globe themselves, Radha inquired about what I planned to do with my "down time." When I asked her what she meant, she replied, "Why, my dear man, you can't expect a miracle every day. You'll be meeting many people, surely, but there are bound to be times when that doesn't happen, or you aren't drawn to pursue it. I strongly suggest—and my spirit guides agree with this—that you systematically write down everything you can remember of how this whole business came about. It's history, you know, and besides, you might learn something."

I'm not sure if I would call it history, but about the other part, she was right.

Of course, I've had to change the names, my own and all my friends, and all the enemies. You won't find Morgoth or the Knights of Seriphos in any phone book, and we don't want to be found by them, at least not yet. It might be different on the day when all the secrets are revealed at last.

Speaking of secrets, this afternoon Helen came to me and said, "Remember the disc from Dr. Jordan?"

"Of course, I do."

"That man Stevens broke up the original, and the other one was burned with our computer in the fire."

"Uh huh, I remember. I was there."

"I was wondering, what if I had made another copy and hadn't told anyone about it?"

"Is this just hypothetical?"

"I'm not saying."

"Well," I answered, "first I would want to dig up the encryption software so we could read the thing."

"What if I had it?"

I thought for a moment before answering, "I would want to sit down and read it all, and then I would probably make a whole bunch of copies and send them to George, so he could disperse them secretly to his contacts all over the world. And I would make sure that if anything were to happen to any of us—I mean in terms of any hostile contact from Whomever—that the entire contents would go out all over the Internet, and to all the newspapers, and anywhere else I could think of. That way, the ones who want to keep it secret would have an interest in our safety."

"And what would you do with the information after you read it?"

"I guess I would quietly contact the people on the list, the ones who were ready to come forward. We could visit them and interview them, and share with them as much as they want to know of what we've learned. And I would probably encourage them to go public, when the time is right."

"That all sounds good."

"You think so?"

"Yes. Let's do it!"

By the time these words are printed, we will already have begun.

Today, just when I had finished writing the last sentence, I got up from my seat and looked out the window of RV *There Yet*. We were parked on the side of a mountain in northern Arizona, and the gold disc of the sun had descended almost to the western horizon. An expanse of clouds hovered just above it, and the day's last rays kindled them, filling the sky with fire. I picked up a book of poems from the shelf by the door and stepped outside to read one, as a kind of completion, a final offering of thanks for all that has happened on our journey thus far. I called Helen to come outside and stand beside me, and as we watched the sun go down, I read aloud to her Antonio Machado's poem, "Last Night". These were the words I spoke:

*Last night, as I was sleeping,*
*I dreamt—marvelous error!—*
*that a spring was breaking*
*out in my heart.*
*I said: Along what secret aqueduct,*
*Oh water, are you coming to me,*
*water of a new life*
*that I have never drunk?*

*Last night, as I was sleeping,*
*I dreamt—marvelous error!—*
*that I had a beehive*
*here inside my heart.*
*And the golden bees*
*were making white combs*
*and sweet honey*
*from my old failures.*

*Last night, as I was sleeping,*
*I dreamt—marvelous error!—*
*that a fiery sun was giving*
*light inside my heart.*
*It was fiery because I felt*
*warmth as from a hearth,*
*and sun because it gave light*
*and brought tears to my eyes.*

*Last night, as I slept,*
*I dreamt—marvelous error!—*
*that it was God I had*
*here inside my heart.*

May we all awaken together within this marvelous dream.

# Bibliography and Resources

The story told in *Earthfire* has drawn upon information from the works of various authors, and interested readers are encouraged to expand their knowledge by reading any and all of the books listed below. Most of them can be found in your local bookstore, or they can be ordered directly from:

Heaven and Earth Publishing™
122 School St.; Marshfield, VT, 05658
Ph: 802-426-3440; Fax: 802-426-3441
e-mail: hevnerth@bypass.com

**Holotropic Breathwork™ and Related Subjects**
*The Cosmic Game* by Stanislav Grof; Paperback - 285 pages; $19.95; (March 1998) State Univ of New York Pr; ISBN: 0791438767

*The Holotropic Mind,* by Stanislav Grof; Paperback - 256 pages $15.00; Reprint edition (June 1993) Harper San Francisco; ISBN: 0062506595 ;

*The Adventure of Self-Discovery,* by Stanislav Grof; Paperback - 321 pages; $19.95 (December 1988) State Univ of New York Pr; ISBN: 0887065414

*Beyond the Brain*, by Stanislav Grof; Paperback - 466 pages; $23.95 (January 1986) State Univ of New York Pr; ISBN: 0873958993

*Spiritual Emergency : When Personal Transformation Becomes a Crisis*, by Stanislav Grof (Editor), Christina Grof (Editor) Paperback - 250 pages; $15.95; 1st Ed. edition (October 1989) J P Tarcher; ISBN: 0874775388

*The Stormy Search for the Self : A Guide to Personal Growth Through Transformational Crisis*, by Christina Grof, Grof, M.D. Stanislav; Paperback; $15.95; J P Tarcher; ISBN: 087477649X

**Morphogenic Fields and Related Matters**
*The Presence of the Past : Morphic Resonance & the Habits of Nature,* by Rupert Sheldrake; Paperback - $17.95; 416 pages Reprint edition (March 1995) Inner Traditions Intl Ltd; ISBN: 089281537X

*The Rebirth of Nature : The Greening of Science and God*, by Rupert Sheldrake; Paperback – $14.95; 272 pages Reprint edition (April 1994) Inner Traditions Intl Ltd; ISBN: 0892815108

## Astrology, Archetypes, Philosophy
*The Passion of the Western Mind : Understanding the Ideas That Have Shaped Our World View,* by Richard Tarnas, Paperback – $15; Ballantine Books (Trd Pap); ISBN: 0345368096

*Prometheus the Awakener : An Essay on the Archetypal Meaning of the Planet Uranus*, by Richard Tarnas; Paperback – $14.50; Spring Pubns; ISBN: 0882142216

## Human/Alien Encounters
*Abduction, Human Encounters with Aliens,* by John E. Mack; Paperback – $13.95; 1994 by Ballantine Books; ISBN: 0345419340

*Passport to the Cosmos*, by John E. Mack; hardcover – $24.00; 1999 by Crown Publishers; ISBN 0-517-70568-0

*Breakthrough : The Next Step*, by Whitley Strieber; Mass Market Paperback (June 1996); Harper Mass Market Paperbacks; ISBN: 006100958X

*Intruders : The Incredible Visitations at Copley Woods*, by Budd Hopkins; Mass Market Paperback – $5.95; Reprint edition (June 1992) Ballantine Books (Mm); ISBN: 0345346335

*Witnessed : The True Story of the Brooklyn Bridge Ufo Abductions* by Budd Hopkins, Phyllis Halldorson; Mass Market Paperback – $6.99; 512 pages Reprint edition (May 1997) Pocket Books; ISBN: 0671570315

## Sri Aurobindo and Consciousness Evolution
*Sri Aurobindo or the Adventure of Consciousness*, by Satprem, Luc Venet (Translator) Paperback – $15.00 (September 1993) Inst for Evolutionary Research; ISBN: 0938710044

*On the Way to Supermanhood*, by Satprem; Paperback – $16.50 (January 1986) Inst for Evolutionary Research; ISBN: 0938710117

**Poetry**
*The Rag and Bone Shop of the Heart: Poems for Men* by James Hillman (Editor), Michael Meade (Editor), Robert Bly (Editor) Paperback – $17.00; 560 pages Reprint edition (August 1993) Harperperennial Library; ISBN: 0060924209

*The Soul Is Here for Its Own Joy : Sacred Poems from Many Cultures* by Robert Bly (Editor) Paperback – $15.00; 288 pages (January 1997) Ecco Press; ISBN: 088001475X

**Art**
*Sacred Mirrors: The Visionary Art of Alex Grey*, by Alex Grey / with essays by Ken Wilber, Carlo McCormick, Alex Grey; Paperback – $29.95; Inner Traditions International, Ltd.; ISBN: 0-89281-314-8

**Oracles and Divination**
*Seventy-Eight Degrees of Wisdom : A Book of Tarot* by Rachel Pollack, Paperback – $21.00; 368 pages (April 1998) Thorsons Pub; ISBN: 0722535724

*The I Ching Workbook*, by R. L. Wing; Paperback – $19.95; 180 pages Reissue edition (January 1979) Doubleday; ISBN: 038512838X

**Moldavite and Crystal Energies**
*Moldavite: Starborn Stone of Transformation*, by Robert Simmons and Kathy Warner, Paperback – $12.95; 178 pages (January 1, 1988) Heaven & Earth Publishing; ISBN: 0962191000

*The Crystal Ally Cards: The Crystal Path to Self Knowledge* by Naisha Ahsian, Paperback – $29.95; 296 pages Book & Card edition (October 1, 1997) Heaven & Earth Publishing; ISBN: 0962191019

# To Experience Holotropic Breathwork™

For a list of certified Holotropic Breathwork™ Practitioners in your area, send $3 and a stamped self-addressed envelope to:

Grof Transpersonal Training
20 Sunnyside Ave., Suite A31
Mill Valley, CA 94941

(Note: Neither the author nor the publishers of *Earthfire* have any official affiliation with Grof Transpersonal Training or Stanislav Grof. However, we strongly recommend that no one attempt to do breathwork without the presence of a certified Holotropic Breathwork™ practitioner. This is a strong technique, and it should not be attempted without trained help and guidance.)

# Consultations and Readings

Some of the characters in *Earthfire* made use of the services of astrologers, card readers and intuitives, and some readers may also have an interest in exploring these areas. The author therefore offers here the names and contact information for three people who do these types of consultations for him. It is suggested that such readings be viewed as educational/entertainment experiences, and neither the author nor the publisher make any warranties, promises or guarantees, expressed or implied, regarding the individuals below or the veracity of their readings. If you try this, you're on your own.

### Astrology
Norma J. Ream
R.R. 2, Box 4522, Pahoa, HI, 96778
Ph: 808-965-9569; e-mail: starrs@bigisland.com

### Intuitive Advisor
Will Maney
Ph: 413-634-2279
Website: www.willsway.net
e-mail: iam@willsway.net

### Crystal Ally Card Readings
Naisha Ahsian
Ph: 888-849-7525; 802-496-5808
e-mail: naisha@crystalisinstitute.com

## Correspondence with Robert Simmons

I wrote *Earthfire* with the idea of combining the truth that I know, the beliefs that I cherish and the hopes that inspire me in a story that reflects a pattern of possibility for our world. Although the book is fiction, I feel that something akin to the Earthfire may indeed be emerging through the lives of individuals all over the planet. I am interested in receiving letters that document your experiences of spiritual awakening and transformation. Those who would like to share their stories are invited to write me or send an e-mail. This correspondence may eventually become part of a future book, so please specify whether you are open to this possibility, and include information on how to contact you. Letters to me should be sent in care of:

## Heaven and Earth Publishing™
122 School St., Marshfield, VT, 05658
Ph: 802-426-3440; Fax: 802-426-3441
e-mail: hevnerth@bypass.com

## Mailing List

Anyone interested in receiving information regarding future *Earthfire* books or other offerings from Heaven and Earth Publishing, or workshops and other speaking engagements featuring Robert Simmons, please write or call Heaven and Earth Publishing at the address and/or telephone number shown above.